John H King

Man an Organic Community

Vol. 1

John H King

Man an Organic Community
Vol. 1

ISBN/EAN: 9783337365547

Printed in Europe, USA, Canada, Australia, Japan

Cover: Foto ©Andreas Hilbeck / pixelio.de

More available books at **www.hansebooks.com**

MAN AN ORGANIC COMMUNITY

BEING AN EXPOSITION OF THE LAW THAT THE
HUMAN PERSONALITY IN ALL ITS PHASES IN EVO-
LUTION, BOTH CO-ORDINATE AND DISCORDINATE, IS
THE MULTIPLE OF MANY SUB-PERSONALITIES.

BY

JOHN H. KING,

AUTHOR OF "THE SUPERNATURAL, ITS ORIGIN, NATURE, AND EVOLUTION."

IN TWO VOLUMES.
VOL. I.

WILLIAMS AND NORGATE,
14, HENRIETTA STREET, COVENT GARDEN, LONDON; AND
20, SOUTH FREDERICK STREET, EDINBURGH.
NEW YORK: G. P. PUTNAM'S SONS.
1893.

CONTENTS OF VOLUME I.

MAN AN ORGANIC COMMUNITY.

INTRODUCTION.

THAT the apparent conditions in things do not express their real relations, is a familiar doctrine and has been accepted regarding many presentations in the natural world; but that vital beings, whether men or animals, represented distinct individual organic unities, would appear to have been in all times and among all peoples a fundamental affirmation, and most men still entertain the doctrine of their own absolute individuality. The first break in this doctrine of personality being homogeneous, was when men differentiated the soul from the body, and conceived that it expressed a distinct personality in principle diverse from the organic constitution, and that these special personalities, the spirit and the organism, had primary natural differences; the one was constructed of atoms, the other, if material in its nature, was of a highly refined character—the life of the one the aggregate of its chemical elements; that of the other outside the ordinary relations of matter to whose laws it was not amenable. Nor were the ties linking these diverse entities persistent. The soul, it has been generally affirmed, may exist and manifest itself outside the body, it may enter into and act through the members of another body—it may be persistent, unchangeable, immortal. All these attributes are conceived to express the distinct natures of the mental and organic principles constituting the two generally united entities.

For many years the necessary unity of the organic corporeal and of the incorporeal elements has in many cases been doubted, and the mental changes and the structural workings betimes were recognized as expressing diverse potencies, diverse wills. Part of the organism of one man might be attached to another man and become associate in the new status as if an integral part of the receptive organism, and responding to the conscious will of its ego. So growth influences were noted as adding new faculties and powers, and these in various ways might pass away, and the compound double nature of the entity be thus changed. It was also observed that various organs and faculties would cease to be normal, disintegrate, may be pass away, and yet not affect otherwise than in their special loss the unity of the being. So in like manner any mental attribute, any moral affinity, might be lost or changed, and as so commonly occurs in many forms of insanity, the original character of the individual is lost, and a new distinct, mental, moral, and personal character has supervened. Such changes in a lesser degree accompany every great growth output in the human organism, whether it is an advance to maturity or a secedence to senility. More especially may be noted this loss of the primary attributes in a woman's nature that often ensues under the influence of her after-maturity organic changes; at that period in a woman's life there is not an attribute of her mental or moral character but may fall into abeyance, degenerate, or be altered in its co-ordinate aspect. This mental change betimes is accompanied with a corresponding organic change; the softness and sweetness of the voice is lost, the refined features may become coarse, and the expression and movements sympathetically respond to the new mental influences. There is not a medical man who has not noted instances of both moral and physical deterioration with such lady-patients. In other cases, the change takes a re-integrating course, and the once gay and volatile exponent of fashion becomes staid and devoutly inclined. In the various normal states the psychical faculties, as well as the organic members, were under the guidance of the then definite co-ordination; but under the changing influences we have referred to, there occurs derangement of parts, special antagonisms leading occasionally to the expression of two or more distinct and discordant personations by the one physical entity.

There are some who are unable to associate these diverse forms of expression with an ever singleness of purpose, singleness of conformation in the one human personality, and who conceive that the individual personality in each diverse presentation represents distinct combinations of its many faculties and powers, each group representing the activities of a state, not of a self-contained individual, each part of which has its own individual duties, its special range of relations, and special forms of combination. Thus in each organic co-ordination there are not only the ruling and working sub-personalities of an individual character, there are the associate actions of combined and representative personalities, the same as in a state; and as in a state one personality may be attached to another personality as a check, so diverse organic attributes check other organic attributes, and regulate the general state equipoise by their varied interactions. As with the organic so with the mental attributes. These work collectively, they work individually, they work as committees in sets, and the associate relations are ever changing. The co-ordinate individual is built up of a distinct combination of its many forces, any one or more of which may pass out of co-ordination, and the faculty thus expressed may be lost, reverted, or rendered dormant, as if encysted, the human personality continuing to present all those attributes that at the time are in active co-ordination.

Hence we start with the assumption that the human personality is a co-ordination or growth combination of many differentiated distinct sub-personalities, and that these sub-personalities in like manner consist of aggregates of lower class differentiations, until we arrive at the primary constituents of organisms, the free-moving granules of plasma.

The common principle of growth characterizes the life of all organisms from the monad to the man, and every stage in the differentiation of a faculty or member is common to all—they are all built up of like units. In organic co-ordinations, while life exists, cells may blend or separate, tissues may advance or degenerate, parts work in unison or be severally repellant. The associative principle which began in the individual's first differentiation is never wholly lost, it never foregoes its earlier associative relations: each cell, each tissue, each aggregate in unity, each organ or member, whatever its complexity, ever retains all and each of the several powers that, by new and enlarged differentiations, has been attached to it. No organic evolution is ever lost.

The associative principle present in the various stages of the personality represents the mere impact of solvent granules, which may mutually act and re-act on each other, may be blending or separating as processes of vital growth, or by accidental physical change altered or re-arranged. The first stage in fixed aggregation ensues when free cells, which have evolved integumental walls when impact through their own volitions or the force of outer conditioning, fuse together, and thereby induce internal processes of growth and reproduction. The introduction of this faculty of organic blending, and that of the constriction of the cell wall as the necessary result of super cell growth, express the general law by which multiple cell segmentation induces multiple aggregations, cell fusions, and all graft cohesions. As these distinct powers are continually at work in all sub-personalities, their higher relations ensue from the parts anastomosing or separating, and under the co-ordinate pressure severally modifying or accommodating their relations to the local conditions.

This faculty of inducing associative results through growth developments, designates neither a personal or impersonal entity, even the present consciousness in higher forms only represents the co-ordinate principle present for the time it varies, as the aggregate mental co-ordination varies, and at the time when it seems mostly to represent the associate individual, there is going on in the organism the whole series of subordinate workings that mark the self relations of every faculty, every part.

The law of co-ordination, like that of chemical affinity, attaches and governs the resultants of elements in affinity, and there is no greater sympathy expressed in cell attaching to cell, than in the atoms of crystals self-cohering in definite lines of affinity. Of the origin and nature thereof, and the laws that govern the affinities of atoms, whether organic or chemical, we can have no concepts; they are outside our powers of investigation, we can only conceive that they represent the first principle of associative relations, but how they come or what they are, are as inconceivable by us as the nature of objects by the blind.

When we speak of the laws of electricity, of crystallization, and of chemical combinations, we only announce that we have reached the ultimate base in this direction of the mental enquiry, and that we can carry our investigations no further. These, then, become first principles, and we have to accept them, the same as we accept the phenomena of our own existence and the existence of externals. What we have to do, and which we may always do, is to trace out the necessary results of the special aggregations in organic co-ordinations and mark down the unassociative characteristics, the modes and processes which occur in blending, and the higher states induced by each successive series of differentiations. Such enquiries will not only enable us to note down the immediate results in the present, but to postulate what must ensue by other like changes in organic relations.

There are no sovereignities in the natural world, no autocratic ruling and presiding entities; the volcano, the earthquake, the heaven-aspiring mountain, represent only the combined energies of their many special atoms; even the great ocean itself is constituted of minute atoms, each of which bears its part in the great tidal wave that encompasseth the earth. So it is with all organisms, even man. The humble leucocytes in the blood, the innumerable cells that give substance to muscle and bone and sinew, are of the same co-ordinate energy and origin by differentiation, as are the cortical atoms and the nerve elements, the oneness of the organization is due to the common affinities in all the parts. It is not the ego that builds up the man, but the self-contained omnipotence of growth that pervades every vital atom.

As the chemist records the phenomena resulting from the relations of the chemical atoms, so have we to illustrate the phenomena due to the organic changes in growth, and we follow them through all the advancing series of differentiations from the interaction of plasma on plasma under the influence of light, heat, and moisture, to the multiple personalities presented by the life-history of man, and that, too, not only as an aggregate of all its parts and members, but in the infinite series of sub-personalities from the relations of functions and members to those of contingent cells.

We propose to first take into our consideration the nature of the elementary parts which constitute in their aggregations the personality of man, then the phylogenic stages they pass through as forms of growth, the sexual differentiations that they present, and the principles of co-ordination they conjointly manifest.

We will then define the normal, active, and quiescent forms in which the living human personality is ever present to us, then the series of variations in which the co-ordinate affinity continues manifest, but alternated by the successive

.

prominent activities of some of the faculties, and also those special variations that are due to the transfer of energy and the successive forms of growth.

Of the abnormal discordinate states we first take into consideration those physical only, then those expressing both mental and organic discordinations, and those mental only under the forms of depression, excitation and exaltation. Another large class of abnormal personalities represent various forms of reversion, as physical reversions to lower animal forms, reversions to lower civilized forms, then to semi-civilized states, to barbaric states, and to the condition of the rudest savages, even in some cases to forms of animal consciousness.

We then carry our enquiry into the nature of the principles through which the human co-ordinations are self-governed, the inter-relations of the parts, their association with the central personality, the varying and multiple personalities that betimes ensue, and their assumed supernal relations. Lastly we treat on the general and special powers of suggestion that the various inter-workings express, and the influence of other personalities, both general and special, on the co-ordination, concluding with a general summary of the laws affecting the evolution of the multiple human personality.

BOOK I.

THE ELEMENTS CONSTITUTING THE HUMAN PERSONALITY.

CHAPTER I.

The Origin and Nature of the Human Personality.

THE world-wide concept of the human personality was that of a conscious ego, a ghost, a something scarcely definable, dwelling in and presiding over the organic faculties constituting the individual. These were affirmatively known to have grown up in and about this consciousness; they were derived as offshoots from the parent organism, gradually evolving to their full standard, and subsequently declining, until general decay or local discordination caused the change known as death.

This simple individual identity was thus constituted of a thinking volitional ghost and its material faculties or parts; all their powers and energies were considered as arising out of their association with the spirit within. Of themselves they were nothing but subordinate faculties, and members without personality, and only manifesting will in organic response to the presiding spirit.

Not so the nature of the indwelling ego, the ghost-spirit. It was in no way absolutely attached to the organism, but had a life of its own, independent of its attachments; they had grown up around it as supplementary faculties, and it had the power of separating itself, if it so willed, from the entire organism. In this ghost state it retained all the mental powers and emotions that were manifested by it in its organic affinities. More from dream and other phenomena, which we need not now particularize, it was generally affirmed that it could not only go forth from its own organic entity, but that, in a similar manner, it could enter another organism not necessarily human, and exercise on all its faculties and members the same volitions that it had manifested through its own parts; in like manner any other ghost-spirit could occupy its proper organic body, such new association might take place either with or without the presence of the rightful ghost. So general and universal have been the affirmations of these co-ordinate relations, and of the possibility of the spirit being a distinct entity, only using the organism for vital volitions, that the ghost nature has been esteemed to have a life of its own, continuing to exist after the body has returned to its element, and even affirmed to have previously existed before the period of its organic birth. Thus, the general theory of the human personality ever was that of a ghost-spirit attached during life to its organic parts, they merely its vital appendages.

This simple and common affirmation came in time, among many enquirers into the true nature of human and other personalities, to be disputed, and only those explanations were retained by them that harmonized with the accepted physical laws; they affirmed that all the ghost appearances were delusions, that nothing existed but matter, of which thought, emotion, and volition, were but modes. Hence, they asserted the absolute associate unity of all the phenomena manifested by vital organisms, that each one was a distinct personality, the source of all the mental and physical volitions—the common energy.

That the nature of the ego and its relations to its organism have been matters of dispute and enquiry among the more advanced men in all countries is too well known to need any illustration; and while in one direction mind as a distinct entity was denied, in the other matter was affirmed to be but a form of thought. With these speculations, which never became popular sentiments, we have nothing to do; at best they became but transcendental idealisms, tests rather of the vagaries of the human imagination than of its rational realisms.

Intrinsically we had only the assumption of the separate soul and the organic associate personality to consider, until Dr. Wigan, in his studies of the forms of insanity, propounded the theory of the dual personality of the consciousness. He found phenomena in the discordinate phases of the human entity that led him to infer that the thinking and emotional ego was not one but two. Dr. Holland, before him, had observed that each cerebrum was a distinct organ, capable of a separate volition, and that if one is diseased the other can control it; and that when this fails there are two lines of thought, with irregular alternate utterances, the one of which may be rational, the other irrational. Before Dr. Holland, Dr. Gall had distinctly noted not only the double nature of the parts of the brain, but that each presumed function was dually presented. Even long before, many physiologists and naturalists had observed the dual bilateral system, not only in man and the higher animals, but in the nervous and associate organic parts of insects and many of the lower classes of organisms.

Of the human brain itself as a conscious power, Dr. Draper, in his *Human Physiology*, says:—"That the two hemispheres act severally and separately is clear, from what sometimes ensues in diseased conditions of one of them, or when, perhaps, there is a want of symmetry between them, those remarkable forms of mental derangement sometimes known under the designation of duality of mind then ensuing" (p. 325). More, he writes:—"There can be no doubt that each hemisphere is a distinct organ, having the power of carrying on its functions independently of its fellow; that each can act separately, both can act simultaneously, and it would seem that we are justified in inferring that the

common action of the two hemispheres is not for the
purpose of heightening the effect, but only for greater
precision. Of the independent and yet complete action of
each of the cerebral hemispheres we have abundant proof.
Mental operations are carried on in a profoundly diseased
state of one of the organs, even when the lesion has gone
on so far as to amount to an absolute and entire disorganization of one of the hemispheres, as in a continued
mental occupation we are troubled with suggestions of a
different kind; thus a strain of music may be perpetually
protruding" (p. 329).

Dr. Wigan looks upon the mental duality as a sort of
partnership association in which one becomes the general
acting agent, and the volition of one consciousness alone
is present to external personalities. But, as in trading
partnerships, antagonistic feelings are apt to arise, and discordant, even opposing volitions, ensue. As Wigan writes:—
"There are two lines of thought with irregular alternate
utterances, and of these one may be rational and the other
irrational," and like as with disputing partners, "One man
is capable of watching the vagaries of his other self, and
even finds amusement in the process, another is distressed
and alarmed at the contemplation."

With Drs. Gall and Spurzheim, the full active consciousness was not simply a partnership affair between two
active consciousnesses which alternately used the common
vocal organs for their special utterances, but a federation of
powers each fulfilling its own distinct duties speaking
through the common tubes, working co-ordinately with the
same nerves, and receiving their supply of nutriment
through the same common circulation. Ever when
necessary they acted in co-ordinate unity, and as in all com-
mercial federations, naturally the most energetic came to
the fore. Hence the expression of the consciousness and
the emotions varied, sometimes one set of feelings pre-
dominated, or distinct lines of thought implied the prevailing

influence of certain mental faculties. The ego for the time denoted the special faculties in ascendency, and the general subserviency of the perceptive powers and the memory, implied that at any instant those resources were available for the service of the leading faculties.

Dr. Gall ascribed a limited individuality to each locality of the brain, and a limited individuality is implied in the modern localisation of the brain centres and their special control over the volitions, the senses, and the intellect. But according to Haeckel the human individualities are as numerous as the cells constituting the entire organism. He writes :—" In the earliest period of individual existence the organism is a simple cell, it afterwards forms a cell society, or more correctly, an organized cell state. The human body is not in reality a simple life unit, it is rather an extremely complex social community of innumerable microscopic organisms, a colony or state consisting of countless independent life units of different kinds of cells." (*The Evolution of Man*, I. p. 123.) He further shows that though these cells differentiate, they still continue as individual cells, thereby having higher special powers accompanied with corresponding loss of the general powers of the egg cell. Thus the nerve cell of the brain cannot, like the egg cell, develop from itself numerous generations of cells. (*Ibid.* I. p. 129.) It seems to us a certain fact that each and every one of these deductions as to the association of the human faculties, and the human organic elements, and their manifestations, consciously and unconsciously, are founded on deductions derived from a very limited consideration of the many phases of association that are presented by the same human co-ordination. These may not only exhibit all the ontogenic ranges of power, all the varieties in the manifestation of normal faculties, all forms of change, whether by exaltation, degradation, or reversion ; but every discordinate manifestation by any one or more faculties or powers, organic or mental.

When we consider the vast advances that have been made in late years in all the directions of thought we have indicated, and the accumulation of facts that have thereby ensued, it seems that the time has arrived for classifying under their due divisions each series of special presentations, and from a full consideration of their many conjoint relations, deduce the true typical characters that constitute the mental expression of the human co-ordination. We thus become conscious that not only is Haeckel correct in his affirmation, that each organic cell is a self-governed organism; but Gall and the modern physiologists are right in the perception of compound centralized organs. Even with Wigan there may be two fused or two alternate consciousnesses.

Normal man constitutes both in his conscious and in his unconscious parts, one individuality, an active and passive personality. Abnormal man may present many forms of discoordination, many phases of personality. We may not only perceive several distinct states of consciousness, each having many associate parts, but we may note the total loss, divergence, or derangement of any one or more faculty or power, mental or organic.

These facts imply that any faculty or power, physical or mental, capable of withdrawing from the co-ordination must express a moral unity, and be at least a corporate personality. But this sub-personality itself expresses the association of a lower series of personalities; and into how many stages of cumulative personalities we have to descend before we arrive at the undissoluble unit, the simple cell, depends upon the nature of the faculty we are considering, and the differentiations through which it has passed. Now all these associative groups have been stages in the human evolution, both phylogenic and ontogenic, and they all either continue to exist in the organism of the human personality or manifest their presence by reversion or rudimentary parts, may be all, according to their differentiated capacities, exhibiting their modes of inter-relation.

We thus become conscious that the lowest elements in the organism are the plasma and the cell, and that as independent organisms each cell, according to its nature, guides and controls its own internal and external relations. Secondly, that when these cells become associate groups there are manifested not only the status of each individual's vitality, but that a common principle of personality gives a unity to the group, they act in concert, and that this united action is not the result of special inheritance and a common factor in the personality may be noted by several organic results that accrue in skin grafting. Thus the loss of a local group or groups of associate cells, acting as a sub-personality in the individual organism, may be replaced by the associate grafting of foreign skin from any other animal or man, or from any other part of the same organism. No matter what may have been the original nature of the skin thus transplanted when it is made part of the new organism, like an emigrant alien in the new community to which it has become attached, it has to forego all the local rights and responsibilities of its first association, and becomes amenable to and abides under the organic laws of its new condition. Thus, a boy lost the whole of the skin of his leg, from the knee to the instep, by accidentally slipping his leg into a cauldron of boiling fluid. To reintegrate the limb with cuticle it was found necessary to graft over the extended surface pieces of skin from various sources ; some small portions were pieces of skin from other human beings, others, to fill up small gaps, were constituted of skin from a frog, but the greater part was made up of long strips and small squares of the skin of a puppy killed for the purpose, the whole of the hair having been first of all shaven off. The greater portion of these grafts took, and, with a few supplementary grafts, the leg was restored as before. It was then found that no matter, from whatever

source the graft had been obtained, only one co-ordinating
series of influences were now manifest; the once hairy skin
of the dog ceased to produce hair, the moist coloured skin
from the frog ceased to exhibit those characters, the colour
of the whole skin had become similar to the normal skin
of the boy; there was no development of hair or special
cutaneous secretions, ordinary sensation had ensued, and
the temperature of both legs were alike. (*Lancet*, 1890,
I. p. 594.) It is evident in this case that the local governing
principle that presided over the cuticle in the boy, whether
limited to the special parts or general over the organism,
had the power of absorbing into its substance, as living
organisms, the foreign cuticle cells, and reducing them to
the same homogenous state as its own native born cells.

It is the same, as we shall show, with other forms and
modes of grafting, whether bone, muscle, tendon, or nerve,
in all cases the native character of the newly added structure
is cast off, and it becomes an integral part of the organism
to which it has become attached, obeying the local
regulations of the part, and receiving all the organic
attributes of the original cells.

Grafting may take place under new conditions, and the
organic powers that the part originally manifested may
thereby be enabled to attain a status it never could have
presented normally. Thus, as John Hunter demonstrated,
the spur of a cock grafted on the comb evolved to an
extraordinary extent.

Other evidences of foreign groups of cells taking the
local character of the parts to which they are attached, are
noted in the grafting of muscles, bones, and nerves, in all
cases not only does plasmic granulation ensue, but the cells
become conjugate, the capillaries become local in character,
and the nerves accept their new situation, not only
responding to the neighbouring ganglion, but acting in
harmony with the general nervous system.

In the principle of transference, so common in the

personality, we have evidence not only that the local parts have their local centres of action, but that any discordination of the common energy may be transferred from one member or faculty to another, the same local centralization and general co-ordination is also evinced in the sympathetic unity often manifested by widely divergent parts. The evidence of these facts which ·we shall present, go far to intimate the truth of our assumption, that the human personality has not only a co-ordinate unity, but that it is constituted of sub-personalities, having their special associative and responsive rules in a varying administrative series of groups until we descend to the ultimate integer, the self-contained, self-governed primary cell.

Before we specialize the many distinct attributes of the individual man, it is judicious to take note of his relations to other forms of vitality. No man exists by and for himself, he is associated with his family by definite hereditary characteristics, he is linked to all men by common faculties, to all organic beings by the possession of like structural functions, and like vital principles. So clear, so determinate is the fact of these bonds of unity linking all living beings, that every enquirer now admits the co-ordinate unity of all organisms as expressed by the common line of evolution, both in the history of the race and the development of the individual. Hence every individual organism represents a special phylogenic advance, as well as the individual ontogenetic stages of growth. These two scales are in fact but one, the individual but represents in rapid transition the leading structural types through which the race had progressed.

Primarily the germ plasma, whether of all races or of any individual, was homogeneous and undifferentiated, it in its unity possessed all the general faculties and powers that in successional development have become more and more defined and distinct, whether as structural acting parts or as functions. Hence we have first to consider the true relations of these attributes to the organism.   Can we affirm that every single cell, every distinct particle of protoplasm is simply an individual, whose several powers are the reflex activities of an individual entity, be it expressed as a mental power or the power of growth?   Or are we to consider that even the minutest germ out of which a cell may be evolved, which cell may ultimately express several distinct functions and powers, is in fact an associate entity consisting of blended functions and faculties, which ultimately more fully express their individual activities?

From the nature of the relations of the parts and functions of our own organization to the ego, we have acquired the habit of describing all the interactions as well as all outward manifestations made by the organism, as being the responds of the ego.   We take no account of the great series of organic activities ever at work in us which the ego in no respects influences, and which go on without its volition or even without its consciousness that such processes are in continuous operation.   We have been so apt to ignore all functions not appealing to the ego, many of which never intimate their existence until some abnormal conditions project them into perceptive or conceptive presentations, that we are by no means surprised that we are apt to ascribe a special individuality to every organism, and to conceive it necessary for every association of individuals in society to act under the influence of a special head.

If it is so in organisms in which the conscious ego has become the presiding power, we may judge how much more difficult it is to distinguish the individual action of parts in a seemingly homogeneous organism. We assume its oneness. Of such an organism Dr. Foster says, if we divided it into small pieces, each piece would be like all the others.   Tremblay, many years ago, showed the same simple unity in every fragment of the fresh-water polype.   The implication in these cases is that every possible atom of the amœba and the polype possesses all the elements that constitute the complete animal, that in it nothing is differentiated.

But in this initial stage of our enquiry we must feel sure of every step we take. With Dr. Foster, we note that "the great characteristic of the typical amœba (leaving out the nucleus) is that, as far as we can ascertain, all the physiological units are alike, they all do the same things. Each and every part of the body receives food more or less raw, and builds it up in its own living substance, each and every part of the body may be at one time quiescent and at another in motion. Each and every part is sensitive, and responds by movements or otherwise to various changes in the surroundings." (*Text Book Phy.* p. 6.) Accepting this undifferentiated unity of the substance of the plasma, our first enquiry is limited to the nature of the nucleus, as it is evident that it is the key of the solution. An amœba, then, consists of a nucleus and a certain amount of homogeneous substance, the two constituting the individual. Of the relative importance of these two parts we know that duplication can only take place by the division of the nucleus, and if in treating amœbic matter the nucleus is separated from the plasm it will continue to live and, under favourable conditions, gain new plasma, but the plasm without a nucleus perishes.

Hence it is evident that the principle of retaining the power of continuous life is not the attribute of the plasm, but of the nucleus. It is the nucleus that begins the work of building up the developing organism, and the plasm is the vitalized substance that serves for that purpose. The primary individualism is in the nucleus, and it is at first single, though capable by fission to become divided into two organisms, each having its own secondary plasma.

That the simple cell is a co-ordinate organism in which the various parts are in mutual relation we infer, but the separation of functions have already had their commencement, reproduction, and, may we say, mental control, though only representing growth impulse, are the special attributes of the nucleus, and to the plasma is attached the nutritive, secretive, sensitive, and volitional powers. As yet we know very little of the phylogenic history of the nucleus. It has been followed in the case of the *Asterias glacialis* in a series of metamorphoses, and a corresponding conversion of the germinal vesicle in the human ovum has been presented ; but the powers expressed by the nucleus may be blended in the plasma-soma of the organism in various ways. Thus it pervades the whole body-substance in hydra, and every part has in it all the general attributes of a living organism. There are other classes of organism in which the individualizing, reproductive, and co-ordinating powers exist in separate body-segments. In the star-fish they are located in the edge of the disc. These several divergent modes in which the interactions of the nucleus and soma take place, imply divergent lines of individualizing.

To return to the earliest type of an individual, we are not only assured that the nucleus responds to its internal and external relations, but the plasma also does the same in the range of its powers. Mr. Montgomery describes the current of hyaline material issuing from globules of most primitive living substance. "Persistently it forced its way into space, conquering at first the manifold resistances opposed to it by its watery medium. Gradually, however, its energies became exhausted, till, at last, completely overwhelmed, it stopped: an immovable projection, stagnated to death-like rigidity. Thus for hours, perhaps, it remained stationary. By degrees, then, or sometimes quite suddenly, help would come to it from foreign but congruous sources. It could be seen to combine with outside complemental material drifted to it at random. Slowly it would thereby regain its vital mobility, shrinking at first, but gradually and completely restored and reincorporated into the outward tide of life. I watched, also, the brisk current of more highly elaborated, but still homogeneous protoplasm, proceeding in unbroken continuity and direct line, never fully overcome by normal surroundings, but always replacing its foremost substance as quickly as it became shattered against the powers of the medium, the whole molecularly mobile being constituting a continuous flow of ever renewed life, forward pressing, and triumphing over the dis-equilibrating forces by dint of prompt but adequate reintegration." (*Mind,* V. p. 465.)

The nucleus, as Gegenbaur writes, "in the *Protozoa,* appears to be of great importance in all their modes of multiplication. It is a firm structure. Sometimes provided with an envelop very various in form. It lies in the cortical substance of the body, or is surrounded by a continuation of this substance. It is sometimes oval or round, or is flattened and curved, or elongated and regularly constricted." (*Elem. of Comp. Anat.* p. 88.) It has been assumed that sometimes the molecules take the function of a sperm-forming organ and the nucleus of an ovary. In all the early processes of reproduction, the nucleus either divides, as in cases of fission and multiplied fission, or a small bud or buds evolve from it, or, as in the cyst, it breaks up into proliferous buds.

Seemingly, by the analogy of the histological development of the other organic attributes of the cell, we should be apt to infer that the germinating power of the nucleus was at first distributed, the same as the nutritive and volitional activities, throughout the substance of the plasma, and that after it, as well as the other functional attributes, were specialized in distinct parts, centralized in single organs, or diffused through the whole substance of the organism, which, specially in its parts at diverse times, manifested any one of the common attributes.

We observe that the power of reproduction at first contained only in the nucleus becomes diffused in the whole substance of the polype, and in the segments in vermes and other types of animals. With more advanced animal structures it is located in the epithelium of separate cells, as in some worms, rotifers, arthropods, &c., and in the highest forms in a special epithelium in the body cavity, as in chætopods and vertebrata, or between two generally contiguous primitive, germinal layers, as with cœlenterata. In the vertebrata, the highest organic type, the germinal cell enlarges, and a mass of cells with nuclei ensues, which are gradually associated in groups, assume stellate forms, and become reticulated in the process. Some of these nuclei atrophy, others are absorbed as food by the more energetic nuclei, and gradually a constriction of the protoplasm separates these into individual ova." (*Balfour, Embr.* I. p. 46.)

As the nucleus is not present in all cells at all times, it seems to follow that the primary cell was absolutely homogenous, and that the common property of reproduction resided in the soma, as well as every other of the after-developed attributes. Hence we begin with a primordial cell or aggregation of plasma granules having no developed powers in its incipient vitality. Any part could move of itself, atom by atom, the volition being general, and in accord with the attractions of growth; any part could assimilate an immolated germ; any part could separate and become an independent being. Devoid of memory, desire, or special volition, the organizing mass had no associative co-ordination, no habits or instincts, it aggregated and segregated as the accidental circumstances affected its environment; induced mechanical forces, built up each integration, until it fell to pieces by its own failure of cohesion. Such appears to have been the primary vital state. The organic atoms had no individuality, they had no parts, no special functions, no personality; the accident of chance anticipated desire and will, and these severally in their varied manifestations became first a tendency, then a habit, then an impulse, and lastly, an instinct.

We cannot conceive that the homogeneous granule of plasma, any more than the homogeneous atom of air or water, constitutes an individual. The attribute of a mere substance is the capacity of unlimited aggregation of like particles with like; that of an individual the combination, in its lowest manifestation, of like particles in definite formative aggregations associated by growth limitations, in the higher forms expressed by the power of self differentiation according to their special standards in evolution.

In undifferentiated plasma we have vital stuff only, but in the cell without a nucleus we have the incipient stage of individualism, and in the cell having a nucleus is presented the first individual, a co-ordinate being whose plasma has the general vital attributes, the nucleus the first specialized power. Such a being is the lowest form of co-ordination with which we are acquainted. Mental will and mental thought are expressed by growth and reproductive impulses of an unconscious but structural origin. The subsidiary functions are common, and, with all vital constituents, the individual grades through the series of stages denoting evolvement, maturation, reproduction and decay.

In this view of the origin of an individual we are assured that it is not a combination of several organic elements, but the attributes the parts are differentiations from the one entity, capable, if separated, of becoming distinct individuals; but, while associated, more appropriately distinguished as individualisms, a term intended to express their self-possessed special powers in connection with the individual co-ordination.

In animal organisms there are two absolutely distinct classes, the one unicellular organisms, the other multicellular organisms. Unicellular organisms may aggregate in masses, these never constitute an individual, but all multicellular organisms are co-ordinate aggregations of cells evolved from the same parent cell, and held in affinity under the laws of their differentiation.

The distinction of unicellular and multicellular is due to

the process by which reproduction ensued, the unnucleated cell simply multiplied by division or constriction. In the case of the nucleated, it was necessary for the constriction to take place through the nucleus, but all multicellular organisms required the combination of the reproductive elements of the sexes.

The unicellular organism in growth differentiates by modifications of parts of the individual cell, its individualisms are supplementary extensions of its own body substance, and are never converted into cells, hence its form is limited, and its power is limited. Not so the multicellular germ; it arises from the same unicellular element, but instead of a single duplication by constriction through the effect of the sexual fusion, it has the power of multiplying by colonies, and the new germs of organisms so produced have the power of integral attachment to the parent or evolving into separate individuals, those attached retaining the same cell-generating power as when distinct individuals. Hence in multicellular organisms the powers of change of growth of differentiation are unlimited. In all cases the multicellular organism begins its life series as a single cell, progressing through a series of evolutions to a multicellular organism according to its hereditary status.

From these observations it follows that the unicellular individual expresses only self modifications, but the parts and functions of a multicellular individual are distinct differentiations, each cell in which is of the morphological value of the whole unicellular organism. Hence there is a wide distinction in the powers of each form of individuality and the sub-personalities they represent.

Monera are unicellular organisms possessing neither nucleus nor investing membrane, and which have independent being. In these beings organs only appear at any part of the body the moment they are needed, they are not developed beforehand, and have no definite shape. By means of these pseudopodia the body crawls about, and when the cell returns to a condition of rest, these flow back and disappear in the common substance of the body. (*Eimer, Organic Evolution*, p. 316.) In the amœba, the cell nucleus has become a permanent **organ**, representing the differentiation of a distinct function, special reproduction. In the next stage a membrane appears as a permanent organ, cilia succeed pseudopodia, and a mouth for **food, further on an anus for the secretions** to be expelled from. Other **changes ensue in some, the body** becomes capable of **certain differentiations, the** outer layer becomes striated **or** fibrillar. That the same line of development ensues in unicellular as multicellular organisms, allowing for the great distinction that multiple cells have in differentiation over unicellular organisms, may be noted. Thus, **in the** stalk of the vorticella, the fibre to which **the power of** contraction is due, is described by Eimer to **have the same** physiological properties as the muscular **substance of** multicellular animals. (*Ibid.* p. 317.) **Necessarily the process** of development, even for the power of **movement, differs in the unicellular** and the multicellular **organism. We have seen in** the lower form, the process was first a **simple** projection of the whole body substance to the growth-attracting media, this was followed by portions of the plasma indiscriminately undertaking the duty, and these **subsequently became** converted into **rays, filaments, or cilia, in all cases** mere extensions of the body surface. **Of** the extent to which this limited process of differentiation may proceed, Eimer refers to the case of the ciliated infusoria, *Euploles Charon*, that at one moment shoots through the water with the cilia in rapid motion, at another it **runs** about on algæ at the bottom, using the cilia as legs, and moving like isopods. (*Ibid.* p. 319.)

That the limits of unicellular evolution are naturally restricted **by the** nature of the organization, we infer from the apparent impossibility of **their** progressive advancement. **Rather than presenting a continuously** advancing series, we have to consider them as representing the preliminary state that was to give origin to multicellular organisms; which, as far as we can judge, possess unlimited powers of progressive evolution, and in the geological period have progressed through ever ascending types from the primary sexually distinct organism to man. Hence, the human personality, which we have now to consider, is the complement of all forms of vitality, and it represents all unicellular as well as cellular life, each individual organism having in its own personality to repeat all the fundamental principles presented in the series of organic beings, from the unnucleated germ plasma till it becomes a human personality.

That the human personality, in common with all other organic personalities, has to pass through the whole of the elementary stages to its special mature standard, has been long affirmed in the law of ontogenetic development, being in accord with the phylogenesis of the race. But not only does the organism pass through the typical stages of the racial evolution, every one of those stages is continuously retained, subjectively dormant or actively present, in some part of the organization constituting the human personality. Thus every mental phase of every ancestral organism may be restored to active expression by reversion, every function may assume an earlier type, and the general consciousness not only revert to the state of an invertebrate but even to that of the undifferentiated plasma.

More, we have the still more startling fact to express, that not only does the human personality hold all the past racial attributes, but the principles they express of individuality constitute parts in every human organism. In other words, man, at first, is only organic plasma, then he is constituted of plasma *plus* cell organization, then of plasma unicellular and multicellular parts. Some of these continue to differentiate to the staple stages of structural organization until the perfect man standard is attained; but ever the broad distinct individualities defined in each

stage continue their individualities through every subsequent stage, and the complete mental and organic man is
a co-ordinate compound combination of the mental and
structural fundamental individualities through which his
organism has progressed.

Thus we have confluent plasma, undifferentiated individualities gliding through our veins and lymphatics
attaching themselves to all growing or disorganizing parts,
and in due course, the same as external independent
organisms, becoming transformed into nucleated cells. In
like manner, the nucleated cells as leucocytes represent the
free individual cells; more, the higher forms of unicellular individualities, which in the external world are
represented by polypodiums, each member having its own
self-evolved cilia, in the human organism, have the same
sub-individualities in the ciliated cells that in like groups
line the mucous membrane. Like sub-individualities of
higher types constitute muscular fibrils, then muscles—
nerve cell connections, then nerves rising to ganglions,
and, lastly, forming individual cortical centralizations. At
every stage in nutritive differentiation the parts become
individualisms, and the individualisms of these and other
functions if superseded do not wholly perish; they become
dormant, exist as rudimentary organs, or only manifest
their continuous presence for a period in the ontogenous
evolvement of the individual.

Our purpose is not only to show the many relations of
the unicellular distinct individualities in the human organism
and the associate multicellular sub-individualities, but to
trace the many forms both of integration and disintegration
they present, both mental and structural.

At all stages of evolution the human personality may
express co-ordination or discordination. In the one, it
comes before us as a distinct personality however numerous
may be its parts, however numerous the lower class of
individualities within it, in the discordinate state the

deranged association may have its origin in the antagonism of the ordinary plasma and cell inhabitants in the organism, or by the introduction of other unicellular organisms not in harmonious relation with the co-ordinate organism; or any one or more associate member, function, or organ, dissatisfied by the nature of the energy transmitted to it, may thus exhibit its individual dissent from the prevailing status.

As the human personality in its ontogeny is representative of all animal types, it is requisite that where necessary we should recapitulate all the associative illustrative presentations of modes of development, mental and other phases, in animals that aid in explaining the developing or retrograde peculiarities of the individual man.

The human personality is no mere ghost-spirit, soul, or other simple nameless entity, unique in its individuality and manifesting through its single will the various attributes as qualities that characterize its nature, according to all embryonic observation, it only passes from the unicellular stage by becoming a co-ordinate combination of two or more cells through which it obtains the power of multiplying and aggregating parts, which parts have equal power to attach themselves to the two or more primary elements, each manifesting its own special differentiation through the co-ordination of which it constitutes a part. Every multicellular organism is a social organism made up of as many distinct parts as its status in evolution expresses. There is no central sovereignty, no committee of public safety, no representative board. When the co-ordination is harmonious, each member self-impelled, as in a community of ants, fulfills its special duties, which are implied, as in the distinct forms of ants in a common community, by its structural character and its mental qualities.

Not only is the human personality a co-ordination of many sub-personalities, it is a varying compound, and the general expression differs according to the constituent elements present at any time in the co-ordination. We have said that each individual progresses through a series of stages, and these stages are represented by the additions to or withdrawals of some elements from the combination. It never is a unity, and never continues to represent like co-ordinate elements. From the instant the sexual blending starts the *rôle* of its living manifestations, until the disintegration of the last cohesive elements of the organism resolve all to the devitalized state, new faculties, functions, parts and powers are arising as inseparable members to the binary elements constituting the primary multicellular germ. Some of these are mental, some of these are structural, but each as evolved takes its due status in the co-ordination, and the co-ordination for the time expresses their special manifestations. The full co-ordinate individuality is the sum total of these aggregations. In like manner, as thus new attributes were added to the co-ordination, so any withdrawal, either by decay, using up, disease, or loss of parts or powers, is followed by the cessation of the special attributes such parts induced. Hence, each human personality is a varying aggregate, whose sum total of capabilities are the parts and powers for the time being constituting the co-ordination.

Necessarily, according to the extent of its differentiation, each faculty or power takes a more or less important status in the compound organism. There was a time when the co-ordination existed without its special manifestation; it might be in it in a comatose state, or it might be yet an undeveloped structural memory, an unfructified instinct; so a time will come when the co-ordination, which continues, has to do without it. We may well illustrate the varying phases of the history of any single sub-personality; and as the reproductive is not only one of the most important, but the first to be distinguished as a sub-individuality we will refer to its vital phases. Even in the unicellular stage we have seen that the nucleus represents as a reproductive power an advanced stage in unicellular

life, so in all forms of multicellular organisms the co-
ordinate individuality passes through many continuous
stages before it manifests reproductive impulses and
powers.

These parts may and do exist in an incipient stage for
many years in the developing personality of man, then
when mature they often advance to be the most persistent,
most dominant force, in the personality. As a power it is
present only in a small part of the organism, and if this
part is either lost by disease or removed, the impulses and
power it represented are absolutely lost—the co-ordination
minus that faculty may go on as before its evolvement.
More, the tension of its domination when present is not
only manifest in its control of the emotions, the will, and
the thoughts, but in the many influences it exercises
sympathetically on other structural attributes, both in the
male and female, in every vital personality, animal and
human, as in the growth of horns, beards, feathers, the
breasts, and so forth in the female, and the general structure in all.

More, though so influential a faculty in the mature organism,
this sub-personality has but a limited period of manifestation. It may be a seasonal capacity, or its duration may be
restricted and the capacity wholly pass away, even become
repulsive, at best it lingers more as a memory of the past—
a wish rather than a will. Now if we take note of the
complement of the personality in these widely divergent
states, they present us with essentially distinct individualities.
All the other faculties and powers may urge their special
influences through the co-ordination as before; but those
constituting the reproductive powers and impulses at one
period had no existence, at another they dominated more or
less over the personality, and in a third stage they became
generally quiescent. There are few but know instances of
these marked distinctions. Have they not known the
genial and studious lad withdraw from all his intellectual

studies, his industrious or professional pursuits, or perforce
of circumstances perform them perfunctionally ; mind and
body wholly engrossed on gross sexual concepts, the mature
man wasting body and soul on the one dominant passion
that over-rides its co-ordinate personality ? So the modest
self-retiring girl, under like influences, has ceased to possess
the delicacy and refinement of her sex and has allowed her
animal nature to destroy or over-power every pure instinct
in her being.

Even when the mature sexual relations held in bounds
have conduced not only to bless the personality itself, but
all other personalities in which it has been brought into
relations, yet often then there ensues a time, more especially
in the female, when the power, the impulse, the capacity
ceases, and the co-ordination, unhinged from its precedent
harmony with its own individuality and other individualities,
becomes selfish, morose, antagonistic, may be repulsive and
spiteful to all other personalities—only the shadow of its
once genial self.

In these varying phases we have only taken into consideration the changes induced in the personality by the
respective influence of the varying stages of the reproductive power. We might follow the like varying differentiations
of the personality induced by the corresponding changes
in the associative aspects of every other attribute in the
developing personality. Thus, if we take note of the
nutritive supplying impulse, we find it an attribute in the
primary plasma. Any substance that its chemico-vital
functions can render solvent become to it as food. So the
boy to supply this want will consume with but little discrimination the most varied materials ; no nut is too hard
for his teeth, no fruit too astringent for his palate ; he will
chew herbaceous stems for their juices, and test the merits
of every edible. Eating is a purpose in but not *the* purpose of his life. But let this become the precedent dominant
impulse in the co-ordination it will command its forms of

expression; what he shall eat and drink, and when and where, become the predominant forms of thought. The man lives to eat, and ere one meal is ended he is calculating on the nature and quality of the next, who will be present, and the witticisms that will conduce to stimulate the jaded and dubious appetite. The boy ate to satisfy, even though in excess, the craving of his instinct, but the man lives to eat; the boy's volitions might be the most varied, but the man's, as a *bon vivant*, are all directed to the means to supply and the power to gratify the dominant sub-personality. As in excess of all kinds, there ensues failure by loss and failure by reaction, so is it when this attribute has become dominant and the epicure, the man who lived to eat, becomes a changed personality, gout and indigestion, decay of taste and dyspepsia have altered the expression of the co-ordination; and the omnivorus boy, the epicure, and the digestive invalid, represent very distinct characters, very diverse forms of personality, and they, in their varied aggregations, constitute the assumed ego.

Such are the ordinary normal growth variations only of the human personality representing the prevailing influence of the sub-personalities in their successional developments; but the co-ordination, by the deranged action of any one or more of the sub-personalities, may become discordinate, the discordination taking every possible form that the abnormal influence of any one or more of the sub-personalities may present. Whatever the loss by disease or otherwise, whatever the co-ordinate derangement by disease, failure of conditions, or external influence, the co-ordination over endeavours to sustain its complex personality; one structural part endeavours to supply the place of another lost or deranged, one controlling power essays to fill up the gap caused by the failure of another power, and even to sustain the general co-ordination by recouping the loss of energy, all the active parts revert for a time to a more primary state of co-ordination.

All these varying phases of the human personality are possible to any one co-ordination, and they all alike imply that the status, the character, the personality of the individual is no self-contained and definite unity, but that it is the aggregate influence for the time of the immediately present and influencing sub-personalities.

To arrive at a full and mature concept of the true nature of the human personality, we purpose enquiring into all the co-ordinate and discordinate states it presents and through them distinguish the various powers it is capable of presenting.

CHAPTER II.

The Phylogenic stages in the evolution of the Human Personality.

It has been usual to commence the individual vital history with that of conception, but modern embryology has determined that the personality has a far earlier origin, and that at that period the germs which coalesce to form the duplex unity have each passed through many compound conditions, and represent as yet many undetermined elements of personality and many transition phases. We in all cases select our statements from the latest authorities, and present as full and complete a record of the differentiation of the human personality as modern science expresses.

Section 1. *The Protoplasmic Stage.*—Protoplasm, the lowest as yet determinate basis of life, exists in the form of granules or masses of many granules. It is homogeneous, each and every part unconsciously fulfilling every function necessary to continue and support the individual vitality. It may exist isolated or in groups in any medium containing the necessary food to sustain its vitality. It also exists under like conditions in all complex animal forms, pervading their tissues as long as suitable conditions prevail. All animal forms begin life as minute particles of plasma, and all the special parts, all differentiated structure, all the mechanism observed in the bodies of animals and men, result from changes that ensue in this primary material. Nor is it only growth and development that result from its special manifestations, it is equally the basis and source of all morbidly destructive germs that prey on the general vital substance.

The amœba is typical plasma. As Dr. Foster writes: " It renews its substance, replenishes its store of energy, now in one form, now in another, and yet the amœba may be said to have no tissues and no organs ; at all events this is true of closely allied, but not so well known, simple beings. Its body is homogeneous, that is to say, if we divided it into small pieces, each piece would be like all the others. In another sense it is not homogeneous, for we know that the amœba receives into its substance material as food, and that this food, or part of it, remains lodged in the body until it is made use of and built up into the living substance of the body, and that each piece of the living substance of the body must have in or near it some of the material which it is about to build up into itself. Further, the amœba gives out waste matters, and each piece of the amœba must contain waste matter. Therefore each piece of the amœba will contain three things : the actual living substance, the food to become living substance, and the waste of living substance." (*Text Book of Physiol. 5th Edit.* I. p. 3.)

Its elementary form is evidently a protoplasmic granule, unassociated or associating purposeless in irregular groups. These may be found externally in water and damp places, internally in the tissues of every animal form. If they cohere they do not loose their individuality, nor if they break up. Their unconscious mental status, their common possession of all the vital functions, precludes the idea of any united volition, any associative activity, in fact they represent the stage of undifferentiated substance, unspecialized vital power, inert mental force. Their move-

ments are rather the flow of a plastic glare, induced by
atmospheric pressure or the force of gravitation, than a
voluntary consensus. The movement thus originating
in an unbalanced granule becomes a pseudopodia by
coherence as in the flow of water. If in its course it comes
in contact with a particle suitable for food, the common
digestive granules in contact commence their chemical
vital process of assimilation, if unnutritive they merely flow
round or over it. At the same time, equally unconsciously,
within the granules respiratory functions are performed,
oxygen being absorbed and carbonic acid being eliminated.

Yet in some amœba masses we seem to be in the
presence of the primary structural differentiation if the
effect described is not rather the shadow markings of the
irregular granules constituting the mass, and not a true
primary dermal formation. In the article " Physiology " in
the last edition of the *Encyclopædia Britannica*, " In the
amœba," we read, "in the body of such a creature the
highest available powers of the microscope reveal nothing
more than a fairly uniform network of material, a network
sometimes compressed with narrow meshes, sometimes
more open with wider meshes ; and the intervals of the
meshwork being filled now with a fluid, now with a more
solid substance, now with a fine and more delicate network
and minute particles or granules of variable size being
sometimes lodged in the open meshes, sometimes deposited
in the strands of the network. Sometimes, however, the
network is so close, or the meshes filled up with material so
identical in refractive power with the bars or films of the
network, and at the same time so free from granules, that
the whole substance appears absolutely homogeneous, glossy,
or hyaline. Analysis with various staining leads to the
conclusion that the substance of the network is of a different
character from the substance filling up the meshes. Similar
analysis shows that at times the bars or films of the network are not homogeneous, but composed of different kinds

of stuff, yet even in these cases it is difficult, if not impossible, to recognize any definite relation of the components to each other as might deserve the name of structure " (XIX. p. 12).

The nature of the individuality expressed by the amœba, whether an independent substance inhabiting the water or located in any animal tissue, is that it "has all the phenomena characteristic of a living being, chemical transformation, the same rise and fall in chemical dignity,—the change of dead food into living substance, the fall of living substance into waste products,—active movement, movement of one part of the body on another, inducing change of form and resulting in change of plan, the mass rearranges itself in various directions, without change of substance." (*Ibid.*) Dr. Laycock says, "the body of the amœba, a jelly-like mass of cells, is at once an organ of prehension and inter-susception, of digestion, absorption, circulation, nutrition, reproduction, and co-ordination. It is a community of cells, with similar endowments, co-operating for the common ends of their existence, their maintenance, and continuance in time and space." (*Mind and Brain,* II. p. 246.)

It is evident that the various writers, in treating of the amœba, are not all describing the same vital substance. We seem advancing from mere nutritive fluid to jelly, streaming from atomic granules to proteid cells, indifferentiated in some cases, in others granulating into tissue. What are we to say regarding the movements indicated? Can there be any consciousness in the granules; are the impulses mere vital attractions, not purposive, a mere quality of vital matter, ranging, may be, no higher than electric attraction, chemical cohesion? We may term it reflex, not muscular but granular. All we can assert is that it is a property of vital substance.

We can scarce speak of co-ordination where the vital elements are of so low a nature; but even in the lowest

amœbic group there must be some associative integer, the unity even in each granule must be sustained by a common vital energy, substantial, though not personal. To express the co-ordinating principles constituting the amœba, we have seen that they represent all the nutritive and self-continuing vital powers, and to these is superadded the primary mind force or impulse of volition. We cannot express it as containing consciousness or memory. We speak of reflex actions as being responses to stimuli; but whatever may be the nature of the movements in the amœba, they serve as exhibiting the potency of individuality. Of the nature of these movements Dr. Beale says :—
" I have been able to watch the movements of small amœba under a magnifying power of 5000 diameters. Several were less than the 100,000th of an inch; the alterations in form were very rapid, and the different tints, resulting from alterations in thickness, were not distinctly observed. A portion which was at one moment at the lowest point of the mass might in an instant pass to the highest part. In these movements one part seemed, as it were, to pass through other parts, while the whole mass moved now in one now in another direction, and movements in different parts of the mass occurred in directions different from that in which the whole mass was moving." (*Protoplasm*, p. 203.) " Whether bioplasm moves in its entirety or, advancing from a fixed point, forms a filament, a tube, or other structure, which accumulates behind it, or remaining stationary itself, the products of formation are forced onwards in one direction as they accumulate or outwards; in all the nature of the force exerted is the same, and due to the marvellous power which one part of a living mass possesses of moving in advance of another portion of the same, as may be actually seen to occur in the humble amœba in the simple mucous corpuscle, or in the white blood corpuscle and the pus corpuscle." (*Ibid.* p. 201.)

From these observations of Dr. Beale it is evident that

the movements in the plasma have no relation to mental impulses, and are induced, the same as all the unconscious movements in every animal organism, by the impulse of growth—that form of energy which traverses every part of every organism, and is the co-ordinating power alike in every animal, every human form. It is the primary sustaining power in the plasma, and even in man it guides and controls all the animal functions, whether the conscious ego is present, or whether it reposes, or is in a cataleptic state.

It is due to the interactions of this vital force that the plasma itself is capable of differentiation, and that from its simple elementary constitution have been evolved the numerous forms of animal organisms, with their many powers and functions. More, we only know of the existence of mind in connection with this plastic energy.

The first specialization of the plasma by the influence of this co-ordinating force is to convert it into the undifferentiated cell—that is, the lowest defined organic entity, which contains a limited substance, individualized by its retaining integument. The primary differentiation of the enclosed plasma is its developing out of its constituent elements a nucleus and nucleolus, the first germs of growth.

We have spoken of the nucleus as representing the first differentiation of the integration, the first specialization of a function, is that of reproduction.

Section 2. Undifferentiated Cells.—As in free nature, the amœboid substance passes from the unformed granular to the more definitely differentiated amœbic groups; so in the human, as in all animal organisms, we may trace like intermediate forms. While in the bulk the human organism is made up of highly differentiated cells, there also exist certain elements which show no differentiation whatever. "These amœba-like cells retain even

that power of movement from place to place which a cell
first forfeits as the penalty of specialization. They have a
wider anatomical distribution than any other cells, either
aggregated in masses of lymphoid tissue or forming the
corpuscular elements of circulating fluids, or as errant
leucocytes constituting essential though inconspicuous
features in the anatomy of all tissues. In the blood they
are called white blood corpuscles, in the lymph channels
lymph corpuscles, elsewhere leucocytes. The amœboid
elements are as distinctive (in contrast with the specialized
elements which make up the bulk of the body), as the
elements of any tissue. Within the organism is being
epitomized the whole course of cell evolution through the
various stages of cell differentiation. Leucocytes are the
representatives of the primary indifferentiated stage of cell
evolution ; among the elements of every other tissue isolated
cells of this type are always found wandering." (*Lancet*,
1889, II. p. 585.)

The great work of these free cells thus coursing with the
nutrient fluid through all the channels in the body is two-
fold ; first, they act as new tissue, becoming grafted, as it were,
in every extension of substance, and through their ministry
" the tissues of the body are all built up of various materials
supplied from the blood, and which are deposited here in the
skin, lime there in the bones, phosphorus throughout the
brain, carbon in the pigment tissues, albein or protein compounds everywhere in their proper proportions." (*Laycock,
Mind and Brain*, II. p. 265.) Secondly, they are the scavengers
of the body ; like the half-wild dogs in eastern cities, they
traverse through the highways and byeways of the body
and frequent the water-courses therein, and feed on the
excrementory matter that would otherwise clog and pollute
the vital forces. Externally the worn-out and cast-off cells
are removed as waste scurf, internally this is presumed to
be effected in the vascular tissues by the old or effete
matter being reduced to a liquid state, in which it finds its

way into the blood vessels of the lymphatics along with the residual plasma, and is by them carried off. In inflammation the leucocytes line the blood vessels, then little processes appear on the outside of the vessels which grow while the leucocytes, to which they belong, diminish till there is complete disappearance from within and reappearance without, and then their connection with the vessels is severed and they are at large. To do this the leucocytes insinuate pseudopodia, and then flow along the narrow channel so formed. (*Lancet*, 1889, II. pp. 635-636.) C. H. Fagge says :—
"It seems to me, when a part is injured the removal of damaged tissue elements is an essential preliminary to the work of reconstruction and repair. I have, for years past, ventured to teach that the emigration of leucocytes in inflammation serves this special purpose of clearing away of such portions of injured structure as are no longer fit to remain. Leucocytes have been seen to take up granules of vermilion, milk globules, and particles of myelin, when these substances have been placed in their way."
(*Principles and Practice of Medicine*, I. p. 55.) That they not only can but do effect such removal is proved by the fact that the separation of sloughs is effected by their agency, or that of their more immediate products, which eat through the sloughs attachments and substitute themselves instead. Leucocytes seize upon all material that submits itself, carrying them off and subjecting them to a process of intracellular digestion, or depositing them in a new situation. (*Lancet*, II. p. 586.)

Section 3. Differentiated and Associated Cells.—We have seen that the differentiated cell consists of the enclosing envelop, the fluid mass, and the nucleus and nucleolus. In this state they may live as single cells. But " under certain conditions, the nucleus may increase and exhibit all the phenomena of bioplasm, new nuclei may be developed within it, new nucleoli within them, so

that ordinary bioplasm may become formed material, its
nucleus, growing larger and taking its place. The whole
process consists of evolution from centres and the production
of new centres within pre-existing centres." (*Beale, Protoplasm*, p. 212.)

This change by the growth and division of the cell may exist
and be presented by any single-celled organism, or may be
the first stage in the evolution of each and every tissue in
complex animal organisms. In the isolated cell it may
never advance from the primary division of a cell into halves,
the same halving constituting its highest organic power;
or the halves of a cell may continue together as associate
cells, and at every division agglomerate into special masses
of cells. The growth of the mass, influenced by a power
within, may take certain definite directions, and simple multicellular organisms be evolved or differentiation of power
may accrue in the group of cells; they may grow in special
directions, or they may select or be appointed to special
limited functions, their substance modifying into distinct
tissues and fulfilling diverse duties.

The result of these various forms of cellular aggregation
is to constitute more complex isolated organisms than those
we previously described, having distinct cellular-shaped
structures growing in definite directions, the parts having
diverse and special secretory powers, as in many of the
lower protozoa, which form chitin and lime envelops for
protective purposes. In the same category are ranked all the
elementary tissues of higher organisms. The first specialization of cell function is simple not multiple. There may
be low general functional power, but not selective complex.

The lowest form of cell aggregation multiplying by
simple division, and forming irregular groups, may be
seen in the yeast plant. In each individual cell may be seen,
by colouring with ammoniacal solution of carmine, the
germinal or living matter tinted red, while the formed skin
or envelop is colourless. In these may be seen the whole

process of simple growth in the cell, the process of cell
division, the attachment of two or more cells into a group
in every direction, no integration existing in definite lines
or contours. Then the next stage in the formative process
is to deposit the new cells in the line of a single axis, as in
most bacteria growths, like lowly developed, formed, or
secreted matter in one direction as may be seen in the horny
tissues, in teeth ; and as associate layers in one direction, as
in the shells of molluscous animals. The epidermis itself is
only an extended aggregation of such cells, each forming
the new cell in the same line of growth as with the cuticle,
in some cases this cell growth is partly modified, and takes
definite forms, as in nails, claws, hoofs, and shells. In the
state of formed matter these pass from growth to a dormant
unchangeable state and become protective. The envelop
of the simple cell is the first differentiation of formed
matter, and as in that, in all other forms of aggregation
on a single axis they represent the lowest stage of form
differentiation.

Roughly the evolution of these passive-formed members
may be followed in the growth of the human nail, through
simple cells at the base it is in connection with the nerves
which are keenly sensitive at the quick ; further up the
parts are soft, and at the summit hard and merely dead
matter. If a mark be impressed on the lower soft surface
of a nail, it will be gradually observed to travel to the top
of the finger until it is cut off or worn away. The life of
such a cell only dates for a certain number of weeks. So
it is with the external skin, the cuticle only lasts as organic
matter for a certain time, and is then cast off as scurf, the
middle layer then takes its place, and the rete mucosum
moves outwardly, its place being taken by the new cells
ever deposited on the inner plane.

The specialization of growth in one direction is very
definite in the growth of hairs, these develop by the
addition of new matter at the root or point of attachment,

horny matter is secreted at the top only of the bulb, and the lower layer ever pushes up all antecedent growths, even when single hair measures several feet in length. The frontal horns of ruminating animals are formed by like secretions of successive layers of horny substance in one direction, these are secreted like the hairs, one below the other on the internal matrix.

In the case of shells, and that of horns and teeth, we have growth from groups of primary cells in one direction only. The horn of the rhinoceros consists thus of numerous formed fibres agglutinated together, rising in like manner into definite forms. We may follow the same process of longitudinal growth in the clusters that form the specialized growths of the grinders and incisor teeth in most animals, more especially with ruminants and the rodentia. Among these the teeth continue to grow, like hairs, from the roots as the top surface is worn away in the process of eating. Even where this continuous destruction does not take place, as in the tusks of the elephant, they continue to grow by the successive deposition of new matter on the inner surface by the conical pulp which fills the cavity.

We have in this spoken of the differentiated cell in its relation to a complex organism, but the differentiated cell exists as a perfect organism in its own right. It has growth, individuality, it divides by fission, and thus multiplies and continues its race. These unicellular organisms, so minute in size as to be unseen by the keenest eye, exist in countless myriads wherever the conditions are favourable to their manifestations. A drop of water may contain hundreds, they find fields to pasture in on every damp wall, and wherever the least moisture retains nutriment for their support. Even in our own bodies they course in myriads with the blood and lymph, and permeate all animal substance. It is well we cannot see them, for they live also as parasites in our bodies and the bodies of all animals, preying on not only the fluids in the digestive parts, but they penetrate muscle and bone and ligament, even holding their high carnival in our brains. In the *Annals of Natural History* we read of a parasitic amœba, an active nucleated organic corpuscle without a cell wall, found associated with other low forms of life, as *Nyctotherus ovalis*, a ciliated infusorian, and various other unicellular organisms, even an algoid plant in the intestine of a cockroach. (*5th Series*, V. p 193.) Still more expressive of the enormous distribution of unicellular organisms in the same publication we are told that the "intestines of the batrachians harbour a whole world of parasites, which live in them and multiply with a truly surprising abundance. Micrographers especially may get from them the finest harvests of infusoria and bacterians. Swarming among the large ciliated infusoria were myriads of bodos, monads, amœbas, bacillio, vibrios, and bacteria." (*Ibid.* IV. p. 97.)

The diffusion of parasitic bacillio in the human as well as in animal organisms has been confirmed in the researches to determine the phenomena of disease germs. So amply has their presence been confirmed, that we need but refer to it. In general, like the trichina, the unicellular organisms are found in the intestines and muscles, and sometimes in the brain stuff, but some evidence demonstrates they may live in other parts, even in the blood. A ciliated infusorian, *Anopbophrya branchiarum*, was found in the branchial lamellæ of *Gammarus pulex*. Another of the same family in the blood of *Asellus aquaticus*, it travelled with the blood corpuscles through the system. Another ciliate infusorian was found in quantities in the blood of *Carcinas maenas*, a crustacean, it travelled with the amœbid cells through the animal. (*Annals Nat. Hist.*, 6th Series, II. p. 426.) We may also refer to the microbe germs denoting various special diseases as being present in human blood, and traversing the mucous membranes of men.

Section 4. *Specialization of Parts.*—This is primarily
seen in the hardening of the cuticle or integument of a
cell, and in the differentiation of the nucleus and the
nucleoli.   This is the primary form of exaltation, and these
specialized members, even in the simple cell, appear to
take up the protective, sustaining and multiplying powers
of the organism.   Wherever there is special exaltation,
whether of mental or physical function, it is always
attained by the withdrawal of energy from other portions of the co-ordination.   It is so with the cell, the
layer of plasma constituting the envelop has lost the
motile power that characterizes the protoplasmic whole,
and the nucleolus ceases to exercise the function of
assimilation to any extent, it is mainly set apart to commence the generative process.

When the cells in connection with the free plasma become
specialized into tissues, the work of mutual aggregation
induces to a much fuller extent the division of labour, and
each cell and granule of plasma, or more specialized form of
vital substance in the process of co-ordination, resign some
of the constituent powers that we observed formed the
homogeneous protoplasma, and more directly devote themselves, or are by the common aggregate vital energy
devoted to the duty of forming special tissues, and sustaining their working capacities.   That the nature of this
association necessitates the suppression of some forces, and
the exaltation of others, Dr. Foster asserts in his *Text
Book of Physiology*.   He says:—"Groups of cells distinguished from each other at once by the differentiation of
structure and exclusiveness of functions are named tissues.
The units of one class are characterized by the exaltation
of the contractility of the protoplasm, their automatism,
metabolism, and reproduction being kept in marked
abeyance, these constitute the muscular tissue.   Of another,
the nervous, the marked features, are irritability and
automatism, with almost complete absence of contractility,

and a great restriction of other qualities. In a third group
of the units the activity of the protoplasm is largely confined
to the chemical changes of secretion, such tissues, consisting
of epithelium cells, forms the basis of the mucous membrane
of the alimentary canal. The renal tissue may be considered as excretory. In the epithelium cells of the lungs
the protoplasm plays an altogether subordinate part in the
assumption of oxygen and the excretion of carbonic acid—
it is the respiratory tissue. In addition, there are the fat
cells in the adipose tissue, the hepatic cells of the liver,
and probably others." (*4th Edit.* p. 4.) That this specialization of function necessarily alters the organic character
of the cells and tissue is seen in the fact that "each of the
units retains the power of reproducing itself in kind, but
neither units nor tissues can reproduce other parts than
themselves—to reproduce the entire organism certain units
are set apart." (*Ibid.* p. 4.) So other units constitute bone
and cartilage, connective tissue and the cuticle.

The process of specialization in the primary differentiations is limited. As Dr. Foster says:—" We may therefore
consider the complex body of a higher animal as a compound of many tissues, each tissue corresponding to one of
the fundamental qualities of protoplasm, to the development of which it is specially devoted by the division of
labour. In each and every tissue, in addition to its leading
quality, there are more or less pronounced remnants, or at
least some traces of all the other protoplasmic qualities.
Thus, though we may call one tissue *par excellence* metabolic, all the tissues are to a greater or less extent metabolic. The energy of each, whatever be its particular
mode, has its source in the breaking up of the protoplasm.
Chemical changes—including the assumption of oxygen and
the production, complete or partial, of carbonic acid, and
therefore also entailing a certain amount of secretive and
excretive—must take place in each and every tissue. And
so on with all the other fundamental properties of proto-

plasm; even contractility, which, for obvious mechanical reasons, is soonest reduced where not wanted, is present in many other tissues besides muscle. And it need hardly be said that each tissue retains the power of assimilation. However thoroughly the material of food be prepared by digestion and subsequent metabolic action, the last stages of its conversion into living protoplasm are effected directly and alone by the tissue, of which it is about to form a part. (*Ibid.* p. 5.)

Of the origin of the various tissues Beale says (*Bioplasm*, p. 13):—"A mass of bioplasm exposed to certain special conditions, which differ as regards heat, moisture, pabulum, and which vary with every kind of bioplasm, grows, divides, and sub-divides into multitudes of masses. By these apparently similar masses of bioplasm, different tissues, organs, and members are formed. Some give rise to tubes which carry the nutrient fluid to all parts of the body. Some are concerned in taking oxygen from the atmosphere and giving up carbonic acid to it. Others separate materials resulting from decay, and convert them into substances which can be easily removed altogether from the body. Other collections of bioplasm give rise to bone, to nerve, to muscle, and other tissues, which form other organs so delicate as the eye and the ear, proceed by gradual process of development."

On the formation of structure the same writer says :— "In the process of healing of a wound lymph is poured out, in which may be found bioplasts, which have descended from white corpuscles. Of these, some produce epithelium, others fibrous connective tissue. Their structureless expansions may be produced directly by bioplasm, or fibrous-like membranes may be formed. The fibres may run parallel, or they may cross at various angles, giving rise at last to a tissue of such extraordinary complexity that it seems almost hopeless to endeavour to unravel it. So delicate are the fibres in some tissues that they can only be detected by resorting to artificial colouring." (*Bioplasm*, p. 93.)

An important element in the differentiation of diverse tissues, according to Virchow, is the time consumed in the incubation, if we may use the term, of the cell that alone induces it to evolve various characteristics; besides, we know that the various tissues were not synchronous in the evolvement of the series of animal organizations, nor are they in the ontological life of the individual organism. The tissue, also, in its early stages differs much in character. Virchow says:—" In one class of formations the divisions proceed with a certain regularity, so that the ultimate products from their very beginning exhibit a complete correspondence with the parent structures, and the young structures at no time deviate in any remarkable degree from the parent cells. In another class the development proceeds in such a way that divisions certainly take place, but make very rapid progress, and produce cells which gradually decrease in size, and ultimately, in some instances, become so small that they can scarcely be distinguished to be cells. The proliferation may cease at this point, and then the cells severally begin to grow and to become larger, and under certain circumstances a structure may in this case again also be produced, analogous to that in which the development originated. Generally, however, the young small cells pursue a somewhat different course of development, and a heterologous structure begins to form." (*Cellu. Path.* p. 403.) The same modifying element, time, is also observed in all after developments as being one of the primary elements in diverse differentiations. " In the development of the embryo the different organs of the ovum run through their phases of development with different degrees of rapidity, and especially those parts which are destined to form the higher organs run through their individual stages with much greater celerity than those whose lot it is to form the lower tissues. In a similar

manner in pathological formations also differences occur
in reference to the time occupied in their development.
Whenever the development of the cells takes place with
great rapidity, we may be sure it is a more or less heterologous development.   An homologous hyperplastic formation always presupposes a certain tardiness in the process
which give rise to it, the cells generally remain of a larger
size." (Cellu. Path. p. 404.)

As the higher mental differentiations in all cases proceed
from the individual exaltation of the higher faculties, so
we shall equally note the physical advances are manifested
under special states of exaltation. We have seen that
Dr. Foster ascribes the primary differentiation of tissues to
the special exaltation of one power out of the plasmic
unity, each of the common attributes becoming specialized
in various tissues. So in like manner Virchow intimates
to us that the special effect of exaltation is to induce
more rapid action where the result aimed at is a higher
evolvement. We shall subsequently find that in all cases
exaltation precedes advance in differentiation, whether in
the production of organs, faculties, or mental qualities,
and also that in the series of animal progressions time is
also an important element.

The first of the homologous powers to differentiate is
that of elementary reproduction, when the cell, by excess
of food substance, becomes expanded to its natural fullness,
the granules of plasma become compressed, and consequently exalted, and we may naturally anticipate that
the relations of the particles are altered by the induced
heat, that the plasmic movements are quickened, until by
the extension of the envelop in the line of least resistance
the centripetal movements generate the extension of the
nucleus and nucleoli in the same direction, and thus two
centres of movement are induced. These separate the
nucleus and nucleoli, and the division, by the action of
the double centripetal movements continuing, absolute

separation ensues, and two cells result from the one cell.

Co-ordinately with this induction of the primitive generative differentiation we may infer that the preservative differentiation of food ensues. Exaltation in movements appear to be the *modus operandi* of that first stage in progress, and it would appear that the storage of food power resulted from the same cause, the early hardening of the cell envelop. We have seen that its failure in continuous power of retention led to the creation of two centres of growth, but when the envelop was firm against the inward pressure, caused by the innergrowth of the plasma, it is evident that the accumulation of plasma must be stayed or the more abundant production, instead of being retained in building up more living plasma, must be condensed into a quiescent store for future contingencies. Such is the origin of the fat cell and the higher corresponding sebaceous glands. The fat was first stored in the single cell as stored nutriment for its own plasma, then as these differentiated the special power of converting food material into fat became the property of certain adipose tissues, cells, and glands. Even the mammary gland in the higher vertebrates is only the highest differentiation of the primary granules of fat in the unicellular organism, as nutriment at first for itself, after for its descendants. Haddon says:—" The protoplasm in the ova usually has the power of storing albuminoid matter as a reserve food material by a differentiation of its own substance in the form of yolk granules. The amount of food yolk varies greatly, in some few instances none appears to be differentiated, often only a little is formed, more frequently there is a considerable amount."

In following the primary evolutions from the simple plasma which give rise to the various tissues, we find that besides the generative and assimilative special exaltations in cells, there are the separation of plasmic elements into pro-

tective, as the cuticle and its after products. Of the free
volitional powers, so markedly common to simple plasma, to
even in the single cell this quality being specially assigned
to one part or product; and more, however low we may deem
the sensibility or mental force in the undifferentiated plasma
we are assured that such must exist as a common element
in all its granules. On the elementary state of these special
powers Gegenbaur says :—" It cannot be denied that in many
cells there are envelops differentiated from the protoplasm,
yet this condition is never found in the earliest life of the
cell, but is always the result of an advanced change and of
the passage of the cell into a differentiated form. Automatic
movements of the protoplasm of the cell are such common
manifestations of their life that they are always definitely
apparent as a property of all cells which are not highly
differentiated. In free cells, and such as are not enveloped
by firm membranes, this phenomena of movement produces
locomotion. Even in cells that are not free movement may
be observed, consisting partly in a change in the form of the
surface partly in a change in the position of the granules in
the protoplasm. That there are properties also resident in
the protoplasm which we may attribute to sensibility of a
very low grade, results from many experiments and observation." (*Gegenbaur, Elements of Compar. Anat.* p. 16.)

That the common epithelium of the cell early manifests its
sensibility to light and other influences, both by physical
response and general perceptibility, is apparent in the changes
that ensue therein when from the common surface it becomes
concentrated in parts, and ultimately gives origin to sense
cells. Of the nature and origin of these we cannot do
better than quote the words of Professor Haddon :—" The
origin of the nervous system and the sense organs from the
epiblast is one of the best attested embryological discoveries.
Nerve and sense cells have arisen in response to a stimulus.
But protoplasm in its very nature is irritable, and this inherent
irritability is common to all cells, in some this becomes greatly

differentiated " (p. 164); that is, the sensibility is *exalted* and more especially uses up the common energy ; the stimuli of heat, or light, or sound, or touch, act most strongly on their surface. The result is the specialization of a sense cell, but if the same had been exalted by the food preserving *impulse* being excited most, then it had become a fat cell. The sense cell responds to certain stimuli, because it is in accord with them. The response is *not the result* of external causation but *internal differential exaltation*. The stimuli would have received no response from a fat or epidermal cell. No doubt the habit of user converted the sense cell into a sense nerve, and every additional state of exaltation enhanced its special character.

Of the process by which the common sensibility of the plasma became the combined consciousness, Professor Haddon says:—" It is now demonstrated that the cells of the tissues of the Cœlentrata are connected with each other by means of very delicate usually branching root-like processes which serve for the contraction and general co-ordination of the parts or whole of the organism. The sense cells form no exception. The nerve cell retains connection with the neighbouring cells by its root-like processes and thus may be united with a sense cell on the one hand and with a glandular or muscular cell on the other. By this double connection a nerve cell may receive a stimulus from a sense cell, and by the excitation of its own irritability may transmit the stimulus in an intensified form to the distant cell, and the latter will be stimulated to perform its special function. The foundation of a distinct nervous system will be thus laid, and the multiplication and localization of sense cells and nerve cells has probably been effected to a large extent independently in the different groups." (*Ibid.* p. 166.)

Section 5. *Differentiation of Organs and Functions.*— The individualizing of the general forces inseparable in the plasma was rendered possible by its breaking up through the differentiation of the various tissues in aggregations of like cells. By this process not only was the special force in each cell exalted, but, as a necessary consequence, the influence of the now co-ordinate cells was also exalted and manifested ; a new character inducing a form of individuality, that of organs, consisting of like differentiated cells, asso-. ciated together and manifesting special distinct powers.

Not the least important change induced by segmentation was the production of tissues. These exist independent of sexual influence, and persist to manifest their powers, even with heightened effect, after the development of sexual powers. In their primary incidence they are mere apparatus evolved in growth, mechanical forces aiding and conducing to, and even marking the modes and forms of growth. Under the conscious presence of the appreciative mental powers evolved through the principle of sexual conjugation, the tissues have become æsthetic as well as practical. To every power of sensibility, as formed, they have modified their nature, they appeal with passionate but yet un-conscious endurance to every capacity evolved; themselves the mere evolvements of growth power, they have by the selective aptitudes of the sexual instincts become endowed with qualities that appeal to every mental state.

In the conversion of the tissues into vital faculties, to each special tissue is apportioned its special place and duties in the compound organism, and as these continue to differentiate, each faculty itself becomes broken up into divisions. All these diverse changes ensue under the con-joint action of the individual co-ordination, and rarely, if ever, even amongst the lowest differentiated organisms, can a function be evolved without the co-operation of the other primary principles, and so conjoint are the powers that if at any time a faculty fails to be capable of con-tinuing its duties, others attempt to supply the deficiencies of its active attributes.

The earliest functions are of a low character, but the

texture of the tissue, by which they are manifested, is ever of a primary type; in some cases we find it at times difficult to distinguish textures, attributes, and powers. We have to proceed some distance in the line of organic evolution before we can with certainty distinguish definite muscular tissue, and still further to be assured of the presence of the simplest substance characterized with the attributes of nerves. Even the epithelial character progresses at every stage in evolution, becoming more and more varied in nature and in attributes, so that in the scale of progress we ever advance in quality as well as in function.

The epithelial integument in its simple form is seen in the unicellular structure, it may be said to form the first tissue, as in the common integument it forms for the lower many-celled organisms. As it is the first to come, so it is the first to differentiate; it grows into cilia, it secretes coriaceous and calcareous coverings, it forms hairs and processes, and before we meet with muscle or nerve tissue, much less bone and brain structure, it has become elaborated into many parts with secondary attributes. These early tissues in their simple character have only the same individuality as ordinary compound cellular organisms. In the higher animal forms they act as mediums for many of the developed functions, but they always retain their own individuality as mere mutiple cell tissue. This is proved by their capacity of continuing their special simple vitality until in grafting, by the interposition of the living plasma and the cellular leucocytes, they become conjugated not only to another entity of the same race, but even to another animal form.

As each group of multiple cell organisms differentiate into their special tissues, they co-ordinate under distinct arrangements, every one of the principles severally contained in the cells becomes most expressive, and gives a special character to the ensuing tissue. Thus the motive power in the plasma becomes converted into the contractile power in muscle tissue, and the vague and uncertain sensivity of the single cell is exalted to the mentally expressive force that marks the special character of nervous tissue. So ever as the outer surface of a cell differentiates into the primary epithelium, the protecting envelop of the enclosed plasma, in like manner, when the epithelial cells form groups and become tissue, the same characteristic principle marks their after life modes of procedure; ever they are the protective members of the compound organism, whether simply as an epithelial epidermis, or converted into a scaly, coriaceous, hairy, or feathered covering, or when, becoming simple faculties, they take the forms of horns, claws, nails, talons, or protective excrescences. They in their higher manifestations become bracts as with the sinophors, teeth and tusks with mammals, beaks with birds. To support these various parts they become modified into sebaceous glands, fang glands, and glands of various kinds, and, in like manner, co-ordinate with the other tissues for the common purpose of defence. Now with the bone and muscular tissues in forming weapons for attack and defence, now with the delicate nerve tissue blending to express exquisite sensibility, and in infinite ways the various tissues are attached and mutually combined to protect the undeveloped germs put forth by the generative cells, and thereby enable them to develop into like complex individuals.

The corneous tissue alone is simple, all the other tissues form parts only in combination one with another, nervous tissue does not by itself form a nerve, but only in combination with conjunctive tissue and blood vessels. Some of these compound tissues are distributed through the body, others are limited to certain parts. (*Van der Hoeven, Zool.* I. p. 16.)

Each of the tissues has its own special character, and is evolved according to its own formative law from the primary cell. Thus the epidermis consists of flat cells, each with its nucleus; these in some cases become cylindrical or conical, and carry cilia. In cartilaginous tissue the cells form layers or plates of fibres crossing in all directions. In osseous tissue the cells become small oval corpuscles. Muscular tissue has a two-fold character, as it evolves in connection and in response to the conscious ego, or subservient to the reflex forces unconsciously manifested by the co-ordinating vital energy. The muscles of voluntary motion consist of bundles of fibres and fine transverse stripes, the others are constituted of coarser fibres, not varicose, and without transverse stripes. In elastic tissue the fibres are of unequal size in a serpentine course, dividing and re-uniting frequently. (*Ibid.* I. p. 11.)

When we become conscious of the presence of functions and faculties, they are ever of the lowest type. Specialized nutrition begins with the inversion of the hypoblast, the cavity of which forms the stomach and represents at the same time the whole vascular system. We even note that not only does its surface serve the purposes of respiration in association with the epiblast, but the ova fulfill their first vital processes in connection with it.

Ever the various tissues begin to combine co-ordinately, and wherever one fails singly to fulfill the special duty others come forward to assist; hence it is rarely we meet with an object attained singly, muscle aids nerve, and cartilage and bone serve as mechanical supports for both, and in their archiform constructions sustain the secretory, excretory, and reproductive organs. It is no uncommon thing in the higher organisms to note one part doing duty for another, still more in the lower types of life we meet with many instances of common activity for the same object. Still, essentially the character of the muscles is to be contractile; of the epithelium, according to position, to be protective and secretory; of the nerves, to be automatic and sensitive; the generative parts, reproductive; the lymphatics, store-keepers; and bone and cartilage, structural.

For these primary purposes they are all self-productive, and in their early stages more or less are self-contained under the abiding influence of the common plasma that permeates the whole organic entity. By its aid they all can renew their waste, repair damages, and even, in serious cases, blend with any like foreign graft. Such qualities are also retained by like parts even in the higher organizations. These never lose their special individuality.

Functional differentiation in the embryo commences with segmentation, and is co-ordinate with the amount of food yolk contained in the protoplasm ; it even depends upon it, as without this store of energy no segmentation takes place. Segmentation is rapidly followed by the definition of the three organic layers : the epiblast, the hypoblast, and mesoblast. At first the developing organism has the one external integument only, this by the inversion of part of the surface creates the hypoblast and converts it into a common nutritive sac. At this early period, functional parts are differentiated in the two layers, the hypoblast and the epiblast. There is, however, little organic change, as the one part may readily assume the duties of the other, as in the introversion of the hydra ; there are as yet no absolute specializations, no breaking up of functions into special duties, the homogeneousness of the organic substance is still practically retained. The mesoblast is only found in a fully developed condition in forms more highly organized than the cœlenterata.

Muscular tissue is first seen in the hydroid polyps, the cells of which give off flattened processes which form a continuous layer of contractile fibres. Each individual ectoderm cell concerned in the formation of this layer of fibres represents a sensory apparatus which stands in direct continuity with a contractile apparatus. (*Gegenbaur*, p. 39.) As the muscular layer of the body becomes differentiated, the ectoderm becomes the principal organ of sensation. The differentiation of a nervous system is due to the development of a portion of this layer as a sensory organ; this at first is superficial in the ectoderm, and as it becomes differentiated from the ectoderm, it sinks down in the body. These ultimately, by subsequent division of function from ganglia and the nerves, continue the external connection. (*Ibid.*)

Respiration is at first a function of the integument. Nutrition begins with endosmis, this is afterwards the duty of the digestive sac, aided by cilia and feelers, the one entry serving both for nutrition and excretion. Among the cœlenterata an anal orifice is differentiated, and by subsequent division of function the alimentary system, stage by stage, is evolved. Skeletal structural supports begin as epidermal secretions, then, as in porifera, as solid separate deposits in the tissues. Cartilaginous tissue is found in the medusæ. "In the lower forms of life the nerve fibres are so very delicate as to be, under ordinary circumstances invisible. In the arm of an actinia among the muscular fibres delicate fibres can be discerned, so also on the suckers of the star-fish, the skin of the oxfluke, and the true skin of the leech and earthworm." (*Beale, Bioplasm*, p. 169.)

The writer last quoted shows that though some of the parts early evolved differentiate their functions, there are others that through life retain their individual characteristics. He says:—"In vertebrate animals there is not an organ in the adult but retains not only the form which it assumed at an early period, but some of the very same tissue which was active in early life, remains in an unaltered but deteriorated state. Every adult organ may be said to contain, as it were, the imperfect skeletons of organs which were active at an early period of life." (*Biop.* p. 105.)

CHAPTER III.

Phylogenic Sexual Forms in the Human Personality.

Section 1. *The Asexual Characteristics in the Human Personality.*—Life is duplex. There are two forms of being: the organic and the mental, one is the result of asexual continuity, the other of sexual conjunction. Asexual vitality is the primary status of the organic power, and the higher manifestation is derived from combinations of the lower form. Every organism begins in asexuality, and sexuality, in all cases, has to arise now out of the same conditions as primarily. Not even man inherits it; he has to attain it.

The elementary germ of the ovum and the spermatozoa are, as far as we can judge, identical, and it depends on nutrition whether such germs will be anabolic or katabolic, nutritive or reproductive, male or female, and so long as these powers remain separate so long will the higher organic qualities remain undeveloped.

In the lower animal series certain cells, independent of accessory organs, even when isolated, evolve into ova and spermatozoa. In the higher animal series groups of cells are set apart as reproductive glands, and subsequently special parts to convey them and special recepticulums in which they may evolve are developed.

So from the parent organism the ovum derives directly its primary sustaining nutriment, or it becomes, as Balfour says, invested by a special layer of cells which constitute what is known as the follicle; its function seems to be to elaborate nutriment for the ova. When no store is prepared thus for sustenance, as in so many of the early vital phenomena, a crude super-abundance of germs are given forth, and before the sustaining principle is evolved the early ova feed on their *confrères*.

Spermatogenesis corresponds with ovagenesis. "The primitive sperm cells arise from tissue corresponding to that which gives origin to the primitive ova." (*Haddon, Embry.* p. 11.)

The highest of the asexual reproductive processes are the following. Dr. Gruber describes the process of fission in a protozoa, *Stentor caeruleus.* Spontaneous division commences in the median line of a dividing Stentor by the evolvement of a vertically placed stria of cilia, which gradually blends into an arc and ultimately forms a circlet of cilia, which constricts off a portion from the rest of the body. Then one end of the stria sinks spirally into the interior of the body, and thus forms the mouth and the œsophagal funnel. Dr. Gruber states that if at excision the nucleus is lost, through the cut opening, the parts continue for a time a vegetative life, but cannot renew the excised portion. That can only be done by the intervention of a portion of the nucleus. *Amœba proteus* has only a single nucleus; if this be divided so that the nucleus is all in one half that will regenerate all absent parts, but the portion without a nucleus will die. What is superinduced in all protista, and generally in every cell, by the want of a nucleus is its incapacity to renew lost parts, to produce new structures. (*Ann. Nat. Hist. 5th Series*, XVII. p. 486.)

Gruber found that in division when the two halves were combined by a small uncut space, the two animals had co-ordinate movements which lasted as long as they were partially united, even the thinnest thread of plasma sufficed, and the half with the new cilia continued its movements in accord with the part having the old cilia moving in the same direction in unison, the two changing their movements simultaneously. When the plasmic thread is ruptured then each acts independently. (*Ibid.* XVII. p. 492.)

The same united energy, not of will but growth, is seen in a *Volvox globator* sphere, which may consist of many hundred individuals. The sphere swims forward and backwards, turns in a circle, remains still when necessary if some obstacle is in its way, the same as a cataleptic man. Thus all the individuals in the colony seem governed by a common will, but break it up and the parts show that the united energy was simply the necessary result of the vital conditions, and each in the new state acts in accord with the energy persistent in its being.

The difference between the activity of an asexual and sexual organism is seen in the following description:—"An infusorian, *Clymacostomum vireus*, had swallowed a single-wheel animalcule, which was rushing about in the parenchyma as if mad, stirring up everything, and sometimes pushing out the cortical zone, sometimes drawing it in by means of its rotatory organ. The Clymacostomum, however, swam about quietly and uniformly; other infusoria thus devoured were digested in a quarter of an hour, but the wheel animalcule remained alive twenty-four hours, it lay quiet, but still the rotatory organ was in motion. (*Ibid.* XVII. p. 494.)

We may quote the case of the conjugation of *Asellicola digitata*, an acineta, as illustrating the highest form of asexual generation. A swarm bud is evolved from a mature individual, it separates from the parent organism, swims about with its cilia for a time, then attaches itself to a suitable dwelling place. It then in growing loses its cilia and pushes out delicate tentacles. After a time, when ready for conjugating, it throws out a conjugate tentacle

which moves to and fro until it touches another like tentacle
of a neighbouring Asellicola, when they join at their ends,
grow into one another as a graft, and the combined part
often grows longer than all the other parts of the animal;
a common canal pervading the entire process. But the two
are then no more one being than is the graft and stock, for
on the least disquietude the cells of both parts moving
freely in the canal separate from each other, leaving the
middle of the canal void. After a time, the associate conjugation taking effect, the nuclei of both individuals migrate
into the canal of union and approach each other. After a
time of reciprocal influence they migrate to their old positions, the plasma returns from the canal of union, which
becomes narrowed until it finally ruptures and the remains
of it are retracted by the respective individuals. Thereon
some unknown change of substance having taken place new
nuclei are formed, and in time the process is repeated after
new buds are evolved. Dr. L. Plate says the conjugation
of the infusoria represents a sort of foreshadowing of the
act of fecundation. (*Ann. of Nat. Hist.* 6th Series, II.
p. 217.)

The results of the asexual conjugation are by no means
yet satisfactorily known. The general affirmation is that
two unisexual organisms are mutually drawn into contact;
that then, as in a graft, the parts come into special relations
and induce a generative change, in which an interchange of
organic characters takes place by which the subsequently
evolved organic buds obtain some special qualities from the
other conjugating cell not identical with those it derives
from the immediate budding cell.

As illustrative forms of asexual conjugation we quote
the following:—*Euglypha alcolata*. In an animal which
has already formed the necessary shell lamellæ, in its
interior the protoplasm is obtruded from the orifice in the
form of a small bud covered with shell lamellæ. This
flowing forth of the plasma continues until the mass

outside the original shell, now covered with the new shell lamellæ, has attained the same volume and the same shape as the original animal. During this process the nucleus also divides, and one half of it passes into the newly produced individual, and these soon separate to live as individual animals. Sometimes after a division has taken place, and the nucleus of the new individual has occupied its ordinary position at the bottom of the new cell, the protoplasm is retracted. The writer then describes two of these individuals conjugating, the plasma and nuclei blending, when a single animal, agreeing with them in structure but exceeding them in size, is produced. After the process of budding is repeated. (*Ann. of Nat. Hist. 6th Series*, I. p. 35.)

With another asexual organism, *Noctiluca miliaris*, the adhesion of two individuals is effected by means of a viscous structureless jelly secreted in a thin layer of the body wall. The nuclei do not at first fuse, but after a time they advance towards each other, and, uniting, do not undergo any change of structure, but the newly-formed nucleus performs small amœboid movements. The tentacles of the pairers usually disappear at the commencement of the conjugation, either cast off or withdrawn. Swarm buds arise from the projections of plasma above the surface of the globule. (*Ann. of Nat. Hist. 6th Series*, III. p. 23.)

The sexual cells arise as germ cells in special follicles in the maternal organism. They may exist as attached cells drawing their nutriment direct from the mother, or they may lay in groups parasitic in her organism, either feeding on her plasma or on one another. This period may represent a considerable asexual duration. It is affirmed that in a girl of six years of age are already evolved all the germ cells she can ever present, hence the asexual life of some of these cells may last forty years. The period from germ formation to conception is chiefly passed in a coma or cyst state.

The powers manifested in simple cell life when present in the higher animal forms (the ova) are most varied. Thus A. C. Haddon (*Embryol*. p. 6) writes :—"It not unfrequently happens, as with many hydrozoa insects, and some vertebrates, that certain of the primitive germ cells feed upon neighbouring germ cells. In most platyhelminths are yolk cells which may be regarded as germinal cells, which have lost the power of reproduction but retained that of forming yolk. Either the ovum or embryo in due course feed upon this reserve of food." The same writer says the protoplasm in the ova usually has the power of storing up albuminoid matter as a reserve food material, by a differentiation of its own substance, in the form of yolk granules. The amount of food yolk varies greatly ; in some few instances none appears to be differentiated, often only a little is formed, more frequently there is a considerable amount. (*Embryol*. p. 7.) This food yolk is stored up in the primitive hypoblast of most vertebrates, sometimes to an enormous extent. During its development the embryo digests and absorbs the yolk by means of the surrounding hypoblast and the vascular splanchnopleur. (*Ibid*. p. 95.)

The same writer further says :—"The ovum is developed either from one cell out of a layer of cells, or from one out of a number of cells segmented off from a nucleated mass of protoplasm not divided into cells. In both cases they are called germinal cells. The change which the ovum undergoes in the course of its growth consists in the absorption of other cells. Thus germinal cells which do not become ova are assimilated by the ovum much in the manner of the amœba" (I. p. 16).

Of the nature of the ova Weismann writes :—"The egg cell of most animals during the period of growth is by no means an indifferent cell. At such a period its cell body has to perform quite peculiar and specific functions, it has to secrete nutritive substances of a certain chemical nature and physical constitution, and to store up this food material in such a manner that it may be at the disposal of the embryo during its development. In most cases the egg cell forms membranes which are often characteristic of particular animals." (*Weismann, On Heredity*, p. 213.)

Balfour summarises the changes in the growth of the ovum and the fusion of the spermatozoa, in the following processes:—"1. The transportation of the germinal vesicle to the surface of the egg. 2. The absorption of the membrane of the germinal vesicle, and metamorphosis of the germinal spot and nuclear reticulum. 3. Assumption of a spindle character by the remains of the germinal vesicle. 4. Entrance of one end of the spindle into a protoplasmic prominence on the surface of the egg. 5. Division of the spindle into two halves, one remaining in the egg, the other in the prominence, the prominence at the same time being nearly constricted off from the egg as a polar cell. 6. The formation of a second polar cell in the same manner as the first, part of the spindle remaining in the egg. 7. Conversion of the part of the spindle remaining in the egg into a nucleus, the female pronucleus. 8. Transportation of the female pronucleus towards the centre of the egg. 9. Entrance of one of the spermatozoa into the egg. 10. Conversion of the head of the spermatozoon into a nucleus, the male pronucleus. 11. Appearance of radial striæ round the male pronucleus, which gradually travels to the female pronucleus. 12. Fusion of the male and female pronucleus to form the first segmentation nucleus." (*Bal. Embry.* I. p. 70.)

These asexual germs have a life history in which are developed the constituent powers of the cell that it afterwards presents. As yet it has been assumed that life begins in the blending of the male and female pronucleuses, but there is an antecedent period that represents the asexual life of the protozoa, the elements of which continue to form a great part of the vital force in the sexually developed organism. Not only do the leucocytes in our blood and lymph, the cells and tissues, express the continuance of the asexual potentiality, it is present in every organ and function that is evolved by germination, and, moreover, it not only precedes ganglions and brains, but the first stages of the sexual germs are wholly dependant on its sustentation.

All that constitutes the unconscious life of the organism, whether functional or aiding development, whether combining the parts or balancing their relations, in short, all that constitutes the silent, unobtrusive vital forces, working with a definite purpose for a definite end, sometimes present to the consciousness but more often acting under unrecognizable powers of monition, are manifestations of the primary vital force that anteceded the sexual phenomena. Its expression is so dominant in the highest organisms that it represents, even in man, the greater part of the vital manifestations; all the nutritive, sustaining, and growing powers are due to its workings. So unconscious volition and unconscious cerebration, even if due to the state of consciousness resulting from sexual combination, have from their active been remitted to its passive control.

That the intellectual life of men and animals are due to their sexual secondary combination is apparent in the constant fact of these qualities being blended thereby. In the general deduction that the offspring exhibit the characteristics of each parent, we recognize the mode by which these mental forces have been evolved, they are due to the more exalted status induced by the combination of two germs, each of which must have had some characteristic, may be acquired, and which accompanying the act of generation became like psychic instincts, inheritable. As with intelligence, so with the feelings. These not only express the relations that result from sexual association, they create the very sentiments, and embody them in principles. In asexual life there are no moral instincts any more than intellectual responses; every cell, whether solitary or combined in aggregates, or living under the guidance of a higher intelligence, can but act through its own unselective undiscriminating growth-forces, combining by the accident of association, and being assimilated or assimilating other organic cells by their quantitive or qualitive plasmic conditions. They have no *morale*, no choice, no knowledge, no perception even of their own activities.

Hence, we perceive the existence of two distinct working principles in organisms, the one constituting all we can know or express under the designation of the vital forces, the other constituting all that is comprehended under the terms intelligence and feeling. The one manifested in all asexual developments, the other through all sexual combinations. The one is single and simple in all its incidences, the other not only has a double origin, but its continuance is ever dependent on the two distinct but blending forces.

We have to premise that of the origin of these distinct principles; we now take no heed, we cannot conceive of the conditions under which they arose, and we will not assume the origin of relations we have no means of investigating.

But though we may not enquire into the racial beginnings of the vital and mental forces, we can investigate many, if not all, the incidences of their original expression in the individual. In this respect we may be held back by the same ignorance of first causes, but in following the life history of the germs of the pronucleus, male and female, and the results of their after combination, we shall have the development of their distinctive phenomena present in their relative forms of origin.

We have said that the primitive vital germ is a cell, and we recognize in the primary state no distinction in the cell that lives only an asexual life, or the cell that may become one of the elements in the sexual congress, an ovum or spermatozoa. The life history of the asexual cell has been amply discussed; its processes of multiplying by division or budding, its forms of aggregation and fission, and these active or latent, are present wherever its elementary vital forces are manifest, they never leave it, and, however it may be associated with the after results of sexual conjugation, these powers are never wholly lost, and in the highest organisms ever as the conditions call for their manifestation, they awaken into activity.

The life history of the ovum and the spermatozoa is more complicated, and they lead to differentiations of vastly greater significance. Though they both begin life in the same elementary form as the asexual cell, it is evident by the resulting changes that not only is their potentiality different from the asexual cell, but their powers materially differ in themselves. Hence, while in some respects the evolution of the ovum and the spermatozoa are identical in general character, they soon widely differ.

Practically, until they blend the characters, they represent modes of living nutrition, and volitional activities are the same as characterize the asexual cell. This affinity is manifest in their form; in the materials of which they are constituted, the plasma and the nucleus; in their vital manifestations, as in the movements of the plasma and the nature of their nutrition; and the formation of the cell wall. All these forces act independently in all the primitive cells, and they continue the same general activity when combined in any organism. Without perception or consciousness, they live on any food products within the range of their activities, and what they do not immediately require they store for future needs. Without feeling or passion; they eat and are eaten; their existence the mere instinct of being vital unsconscious energy, responding in harmony with its surroundings. If the conditions are affirmatory, the cells coalesce; if discordant, morbid antagonism vitiates the vital principle.

Such are the forces present wherever asexual life is

manifest; such are the forces which constitute the substance of every higher organism, and which, though
possessed by its own intellectual and conscious ego, have,
in addition, this manifestation of vital phenomena, over
whose workings it has no immediate consciousness, no
primary and essential control. These constitute the double
lives of all the higher vital organisms, each of which has
its own processes, laws of growth and action, and the life
of each essentially depends upon the relative nature of the
associate dependence.

We have seen the primary unity of these forces; we
will now follow the lines by which sexual power becomes
manifested, and, as the result thereof, consciousness, intelligence, and feeling became the prerogatives of the
higher forms of being.

There are a series of growth movements in the virgin ovum
that manifest all the ordinary characteristics of cell vitality.
In the case of the *Asterias glacialis*, Balfour describes the
following series of changes in the independent ovum cast
unfertilized into the sea :—" As soon as the ovum reaches
the sea-water the germinal vesicle undergoes metamorphosis.
It exhibits frequent changes of form, part becomes absorbed,
the outline indented, and, to a certain extent, the contents
confounded with the vitellus. The germinal spot loses its
outline and gradually disappears. Then a star-like form
appears near the place of the germinal vesicle; later on
there are seen a horizontal spindle with two terminal stars,
below which is seen a round body; later on the stars and
spindle become erect, and the point of one star appears to
pierce the surface. The spindle which projects into the
prominence on the surface of the egg divides into two
parts, one in the prominence, one in the egg. The prominence then becomes constricted off from the egg to form
the polar body; the portion of spindle in the egg becomes
converted into vesicles, which unite to form a single nucleus."
(*Embryol.* I. p. 62.) These important series of operations

are presumed to be caused in the egg itself for the purpose
of removing some of the superfluous plasma to make room
for the spermatozoon, facilitate its entry into the ovum,
and prepare the bride and bridal chamber. All this is cell
life, and the drama proceeds with like manifestations of
individualisms. " At the moment of contact between the
spermatozoon and the egg, the outer layer of the protoplasm of the latter raises itself as a distinct membrane,
which separates from the egg and prevents the entrance
of other spermatozoa. At the point where the spermatozoon entered, a crater-like opening was left in the
membrane, through which the metamorphosed tail of the
spermatozoon might at first have been seen projecting.
At whatever point the spermatozoon may have entered, it
gradually travels towards the female pronucleus, the latter
remains motionless till the rays of the male pronucleus
come in contact with it, its repose is then changed for
activity, it rapidly approaches the male pronucleus apparently by means of its inherent amœboid contractions,
and, eventually, fuses with it. Selenka says the female
pronucleus sends out protoplasmic processes which embrace
the male." (Balf. Embry. pp. 65, 66.) As the spermatic cells
originate from cells indistinguishable from the primitive
ova, the fusion which follows is the fusion of morpho-
logically similar parts in the two sexes. (Ibid. I. p. 69.) In
other words, the difference is only the distinct differentiations that have supervened in the two organic elements
during their special evolutions; they have been exalted on
distinct lines, and the result has been to induce the special
sexual lines of progress that accrue in the multiform forms
of sexual evolution.

In following the life history of the ova and the sperm-
oids up to the process of conjugation, we have phenomena
presented to us whose analogues may be seen any day, with
a good microscope, in the changes present in many minute
forms of cell life; they grow, they divide, they cast off

buds, the plasma in them has its special form of volition; they assimilate nutriment, they cast forth excreta. So it is with the like primary forms of vitality in our own, as well as every animal organization. The vital penetration of the wall of the ova cell is of identically the same nature as the penetration of the walls of the capillaries, even in the human organism, by the leucocytes; for a functional purpose the polar cell penetrates the envelop of the ovum; and, for a like functional process, the amœboid leucocyte passes through the vascular tissue. So, in like manner, all sexual activities work for given purposes in our system. As the result of the vast series of high differentiations, the movements of the vital plasma and the leucocytes are kept in given channels, and impassively, the resulting state is more controlled by the absorption of nutriment; the forms of volition and the powers of excretion are identical in their nature in all independent cells, and in the cell life of the higher organisms, with the primary cell life of the germinal vesicle, whether an ovum or a spermoid. All these primitive powers express simply vital energy or growth assimilation, and continuance by division. There is no expression of consciousness, no output of mental power, no concept of thought or feeling; there is neither the glow of joy, nor the depression from failure. As we have said, they are equally indifferent to the result whether they eat or are eaten.

There are two points in the life history of the ova and the spermatozoa that we would wish to refer to. The one regards the purport of the expulsion of the polar bodies, and the other the vital processes by which the ova and spermatozoa are brought into conjunction. Regarding the first, much ingenious speculation has ensued on their connection with heredity. It has been assumed by Weismann that the purport of such expulsion is to make room for the male pronucleus, but this, and all the ingenious results deduced therefrom, are demolished by the statement of Balfour, that in some instances the expulsion of the polar body takes place after impregnation. We have seen that a like phenomena often takes place in the human capillaries, but we do not deduce a wide scheme of heredity from such a simple vital process. Secondly, the passage of the ovum and the spermoid do not mainly depend upon themselves. There are two natural and equally unconscious and unthinking forces at work to bring about a necessary consequent result. These forces are situated respectively in the parent organisms, and in the ova and spermatozoa themselves. In each case the modes of action, and the means employed, belong to the simple series of asexual energies. Even the ova and spermatozoa are moved by their own amœboid volitions, or by asexual ciliary volition on the parent's part. The fact is, these phenomena of growth of vital energy characterize the early organic state, whenever and wherever it is presented, but the asexual results are so combined in the higher organisms with sexual changes and parts that betimes it is difficult to distinguish the conditions to be allotted respectively to the two great series of causes; but whenever we see an activity in a higher organism corresponding with one in an asexual being, we may be sure the presence of the power in the higher form is the result of its survival from the undifferentiated organism, to which primarily it owed its being.

When we take a retrospect of the many forms in which the reproductive elements exist, the vast diversity of the conditions and places in which they arise, and the still more infinitely varied processes and adaptations that have ensued to bring them into association, every one of which incidental variations has given origin to other and more complicated reactionary conditions, so that it seems we are, as it were, investigating the laboratory of nature, penetrating its arcana of mysteries, and looking on not a designed and purposive result, but at a series of experiments whose incidents pass beyond the prescience of the investigation, and bring about results antagonistic, derogatory, or disorganizing.

Thus, if we take the general processes of ovatation, in many cases it is not easy to see how the ova, once liberated into the parent's body cavity, find their way safely into the small opening of the discontinuous oviduct. In frogs the tracts are ciliated, which propel them correctly. In reptiles, birds, and mammals the open end of the oviduct is widened and fringed, and lies close to, even touching, the ovary. Muscular fibres there aid it. The oviduct once reached, the downward progress of the ovum is ensured by the epithelial lining. It may be so in many of the higher forms, but not in all. The ova, even in man, are exposed to many detergent conditions. The general equilibrium of living organisms only ensuing from the great fruitfulness of the reproductive energy. We do not now speak of the battle of life, but of the contingencies that intervene before even birth in the primary asexual life of the ovum and spermoid. How little assured, even in man, is the destiny of the ovum; they may escape to, or be carried into every part of the body cavity. In how many cases have they not been found even in the abdomen, and matured there only to perish, the parent's life only being saved by an operation. In other cases they have remained in the ovary, and given rise to ovarian cysts that have destroyed both parent and embryo. In like manner they have remained in the fallopian tubes, or have even found their way into the bladder or rectum. Nor is this all; escaping these many contingencies, have they not become blended with other ova, sometimes as integral portions of the common being, at others associated in distinct individualities, or as mere parasites on or in the body cavity, or any part of the muscular system; now the full organism, and anon a mere foetal fragment.

In the lower forms of animal life the destiny of the ovum and spermatozoid is still more precarious. We have seen from Balfour that the germ of the young Ascaris is cast into the great almost fathomless ocean, there to work out its destiny and become impregnated by chance; others, like the ova of many fish, are deposited in set places, to which an instinct of formation, not intelligence, directs them. In the case of the Bonellia of each mass of possible ova, we are told that only the one adjoining the stalk, and, therefore, near the source of nutrition, becomes a differentiated ovum, all the others perish by atrophy. (*Ency. Brit.* XX. p. 414.) Often, as we have remarked, the ovum only continues its life heritage, like besieged citizens, by preying on its fellows. Sometimes, for security, an ovum forms for itself a kind of nest among the surrounding cells. We will not dilate on the many odd, intricate, and experimental processes used by various animal forms to secure their helpless young—here placing them in a nest, there stowing them away in a pouch, or carrying them about in a bag, as the Australian widow carries about the bones of her dead husband. Some, like frogs and certain toads, stow the eggs on their backs, or if evolved, like some snakes and fish, carry them about in their mouths; and others, like the larvæ of the Cecidymia, develop into larvæ in the parent's body. All is experiment, all a vague search to work out a new want; it is just such a state of things as mere vital energy, unconscious growth, would work out in the pressure of the blind unscience of its force. The active energy, like the unpent waters, works wherever its growth-pressure can find room, and accepts every resulting condition undesignedly. Ever as a necessary result, betimes unnormal conditions ensue. Thus in animals, and more especially in humanity, menstruation is an unperfected function; it has not, like so many functions, worked to a bettermost principle. In its inition it is not only personally unpleasant, but a source of great pain, of mental and physical irregularities, not to say its offensive influence on man ; among savages driving her, during its period, from the common association of the tribe. The general theorem has been that it is merely a mechanical preparation of the uterus wall for the coming ovum. May it not represent the highest working of the same principle we found existing even in the primitive cell, the great law of reserved energy that, in infinite modes, stores food and nutriment for the sustenance of the vital co-ordination ?

It is this storage of energy that everywhere in organisms represents the endurance of the asexual vitality, and in the higher forms of being it is equally necessary in sustaining both the asexual and the sexual vital co-ordinations. It is the full embodiment in woman of the asexual energy in her nature, that unconscious principle which co-ordinates all the vital as well as mental phenomena. Its full evolvement is found in every normal organism, and it must be expended as formed. The child casts it forth in play and sport, and wild displays of futile energy. So the mature woman evolves more life-forming stamina than is necessary to sustain her own organism, if this is not used up to feed her embryos it must be cast forth ; her nature does not admit its conversion into a store of fat for future claims. Such is the necessary relation between woman and the phenomena of menstruation. It is evident that it was evolved under conditions that were purely animal, a mere organic form of excretion that took no account of the mental and æsthetical attributes that sexual evolution was destined to produce. More, it is evident that mind-power has no influence to modify the nature of the formative forces, but must endure their working without any power to direct them into another channel, or carry them off in a less personally offensive manner. The energy of growth creates its own laws and evolves its own forms, and the higher mental nature resulting from sexual conjugation is powerless to control them. When the power of reproduction ceases, as the energy of the organism abates, the faculty we have been considering also ceases. It is the same with man, and though the phenomena differ, the result is the same, the extra vital energy has to be dissipated.

Section 2. The Sexual Co-ordination.—We have seen the higher classes of vital organisms have a life history identical in its nature with that of the lowest forms, and that the various special phenomena are common alike to both, for a time only in the one class, but as the permanent status in the other. Up to the sexual congress, the life of the ovum and the spermatoid represent the continuous vital state of the cell, defined, as we have seen, by the characteristics of vital energy, growth, and cell aggregation, without consciousness.

These primary cell-organisms may differ among themselves integrally; they may also differ in the circumstances which surround them, and in the forms as the result of those circumstances which they present; they also have a developmental history, and may be present in any of its stages. We have seen also that the sexual germs had a common origin, and were at their beginnings in no way to be distinguished from the ordinary cell, either in form, or in the phenomena they manifested. Hence, our first object, before considering the results of sexual conjugation, is to discover the origin of the distinctions in the sexual germs.

To speak as Minot does of primitive hermaphrodism is to beg the solution of the whole question, for by hermaphrodism is implied the possession of the binary organs that give origin to sex, the separation of which would be a natural process in fission; we know there are no such organs in the leaf that brings forth a bud, or in the bud evolving from a cell in its primary state, we only recognize plasma having the power to assimilate nutritive matter. It

may exist without expressing reproduction, and when it
does so we recognize only the breaking up of an overgrown
mass of plasma, no special differentiation of substance or
organs. Even when we or accident bring two cells into
juxtaposition, one of two results may ensue: the lean
cell may be assimilated by the fat cell, or the two may fuse
into a common mass of plasma.

As yet we have no effective theory of the origin of sex,
any more than we have a determinative hypothesis of the
origin of life. The geological record intimates that there
was a time when life was not, and the same paleography
informs us that for untold ages life existed without sex.
We know that given vital substance the powers of assimilation and those of fission, and under favourable sustaining
conditions, life may multiply, and even through the
distinctions of conditions it may essentially vary. We
know there are what have been termed anabolic and katabolic states, but we must not let ourselves infer that
distinct terms induce distinct natures. We may express
the surrounding conditions of two distinct manifestations,
and recognize special differences as associated with those
special conditions, but we must not infer, any more than in
the case of Tenterden steeple and the origin of the Goodwin
sands, that the two circumstances have any necessary
relation. The fact is that regarding primary origins we
know nothing. All we can do on the nature of sex is to
show where it is not and where it is present, the nature of
the conditions in which the two elements are existant, the
apparent modes of their relations, and, still more important,
the nature of the results of their conjugation.

We may, even in unicellular life, note distinctions of
character and form; we may distinguish changes through
growth and affinity; we may classify them into groups;
but when we have done so we are nowise apparently nearer
the solution of the problem we have propounded, though
we find that some vary but little in form and substance,

while others concentrate and become ciliated, or amœboid and diffused. We may even trace an affinity in the cyst to the ovum and in the ciliated cell with the spermoid, but any further deduction is quite hypothetical. The nutritive or anabolic set of conditions may result in division or in cyst, and the katabolic or energy expanded state into a corresponding vital or spermoid-like organization, and into being devoured by the more powerful assimilative powers in the highly nutritive cell; but that the two should begin a new life cycle by mutually fusing implies not individual activity or conquest, but, as we have described in the conjugation of the two elements in the ovum from Balfour, a purposive series of mutual operations; in fact, it is the first evidence of mind or choice of which we are cognisant in organic life.

If the origin of sex was no more than the simple processes of growth as leading in one direction to anabolism and the other to katabolism, why is it in the innumerable elements unicellular thus existing now that we do not discover new sexual origins? Our rivers and ponds, even the rain puddles, not to mention the great ocean, are full as it were of them. If the sum of the operations to originate sex were so simple as Geddes propounds (*Evolution of Sex*, p. 132), why do the lower cellular conditions exist? So, in like manner, how came it to pass in the long geological period we have referred to, that no sex life existed when the conditions to give it birth were so prominent and the organisms capable of being so transformed were so numerous? No; the origin of sex was not likely to be a contingency depending on chance association. It represents not a beginning only of a new function, but the introduction of all consciousness, all mental power, all sentiment and feeling in the world. It exists not simply as a necessary consequence of life, any more than life itself exists not as a consequence of matter. We are assured that life was once an original and unique phenomena, and we all recognize that all living organisms are the result of that primitive phenomena. So, in like manner, the introduction of sex was an unique and original phenomena, and one that has never been repeated, though it may be varied and interchanged by conditions and by human revision. We ever follow the principle of heredity back, back to its primary origin. Sex is. eternal, the same as life is eternal, by the law of succession.

In the long primary geological epoch we had life without sex, life that only represented growth nutrition, assimilation with the necessary unconscious power of excretion, and division itself a mere form of growth. All the mental phenomena, all the powers of consciousness, all feeling and sentiment, were *non est*, they were unexistant, and thousands of generations passed, myriads of organisms lived and never matured sex, never manifested consciousness, thought or feeling. Yet when and how sexual life began, how it gave origin to consciousness, thought and sentiment, we know not, we may never know. Yet that these several powers are due to its presence, we are assured they never exist without it, and their growth and manifestation ever correspond with the development of sexual distinctions.

As we divide the life of the world into two epochs, the unconscious and the conscious, the asexual and the sexual, so in like manner we divide the life of man into the same corresponding series of epochs. Man is primarily asexual, and, in the first period of his being, before the conjunction of the sexual elements that gave him conscious being, his parts existed separate, manifesting no more individuality than the phenomena of growth accorded. These in the ovum and the spermatoid states were simple unicellular beings, and had a life history analogous to the life history of any indifferent unicellular organism, devoid of faculties both physical and mental. By the sexual fusion the two elements, the ovum and the spermoid, became united into, not two natures with limited powers of growth and unconscious states of existence, but into one compound organism, having one system of vital parts but of a double nature. Like the primary cell, it had a growing life, a life marked by the inception and expression of energy, the same as all asexual organisms, but, in addition, it acquired the capacity in growth to manifest the powers of consciousness, and evolve to every condition that the ancestor powers of its germs were able to manifest, and every mental and physical faculty that they could express. As cellular organisms their powers were absolutely limited, in a few moves, a few transitions, they would have reached the possible length of their tether, and whether they began their existence in the infancy of vital organization, or were budded or fissioned in these later days, they could only present the limited destiny that for ever encompasses undifferentiated asexual organization. Not so when the sexual fusion occurred. Thus united all the possible perfectibilities of the advanced organization were theirs, unfused they could but have lived and perished as mere cell organisms. They may have individually possessed all the inherited possibilities of their parents' organization, the great mental attributes, the stores of instinctive prescience, habits inherited commensurate with every faculty they might thereby have evolved, yet without fusion all these treasured inheritances would pass away without result, without a record. It was so when sex first began, it is so now. To each individual organism the power is powerless. It must reciprocate with its opposite, become with another being a single nature, and the fused individuality is immortal in its results.

The new individuality thus engendered has a capacity so transcendental compared with the primary cellular vitality, it may not only advance to the status, mental and organic, which its parent organizations possessed, it has inert, undeveloped powers that may raise the standard of its racial manifestations to a higher grade than any ancestral organism exhibited. More as a result of the fusion of two lines of organisms, it becomes surcharged with all the attributes ever possessed by any of this double line of ancestral organisms. We have submitted two unanswerable problems, the origin of life and the origin of sex, and we have to associate with them the origin of heredity.

Among the thousands of indifferent acts and conditions that accompany the existence of each organic life, why one special act, set of conditions, accident, or purposive volition should become attached to the germs which it casts forth for futurity, and all other special like volitions, thoughts, or impressions be atrophied, lost both for time and eternity, we cannot tell. We know that an insignificant hair, a blur on the visage, even betimes an accidental infliction, may be inherited, while other more vital changes, additions or distinctions pass away and carry no sign thereof into futurity. So it is with morbid specialities, intellectual and moral specialities, some may become inherited powers, faculties or forms, and others pass away like the shadowy gleams of sunset. We know that in the lottery of life some of the special tickets turn up prizes, but why or wherefore none can tell.

Much has been written, not only on the forms, but to account for the very principle of heredity. It has been assumed that organization is a mere chemical composition, and through the inception of the cell theory, it has been affirmed that homœpathic infinitesimals of each constituent element, be it a part, a faculty, a mental quality or tone of feeling containing in them all the powers and principles that the mature energy of each is capable of expressing, course through some underground railway, as fugitive slaves in America were wont to do, to reach and combine with the one generative element, and through its instrumentality, these myriad powers and susceptibilities attain, not singly, but may be in shoals, the capacity to multiply innumerable organisms having all the attributes of the parent organisms.

Weismann says heredity is brought about by the transference, from one generation to another, of a substance with a definite chemical and, above all, molecular constitution. He supposes that in each ontogeny a part of the specific germ plasm contained in the parent egg cell is not used up in the construction of the body of the offspring, but is reserved unchanged for the formation of the germ cells of the following generation. In other words, that the individual being the result of the sexual conjunction builds up its own body and mental forces out of a portion of the bi-parental entity, at the same time storing up a treasured quantity of this complex ingredient, and which treasured quantity multiplies itself into as many generative elements thrown away, waste, useless and effective, as during the individual's life pass from it, each and every one of which combines with a similar selected store of the all-creating ingredients that the individual's own organism gives forth. As we have said, the human female has been estimated to have thirty thousand such elements of ova, and we believe no one has ever attempted to compute the possible spermoid powers of the male. In the lower forms of sexual animal life the powers of fertility infinitely surpass human capabilities.*

In treating on the germ elements, it is so common to consider them in the case of the effective transactions only, on account is taken of the enormous amount of failures, and as all the failures represent the same primary constituent energies as the very limited number of successful results,

---

* The duration of the asexual life of the spermoid is undetermined. We have no data to prove the extent of the period from the inition to the expulsion of the spermoid, but the germ of every ovum in the human female is evolved before she is three years old, hence the asexual life of the ovum may be from nine to over forty years in duration.

it is evident, on Weismann's theory, that in the second
generation the treasured elements, which it is supposed to
convey from the first generation to make the atavism
survivals in the third generation, are bewildering in their
profusion. Instead of taking chemical homœpathic molecular infinitesimals as his primary elements, he might have
conceived that the aura breathed as it were from generation
one in the sexual conjugation, would have continued to
possess generation number two, and with its own aura, and
have been inherited by generation number three. Or the
same series of results, requiring no special vehicle of transportation, for the material essence of past beings might
have been expressed in the nomenclature of the imponder-
ables, and positive and negative, latent and polar, could
have been made to express all the phenomena of successional
interchange.

But need we mechanical or quantitative terms ? Instead
of speculating on theoretical first causes, a mode of argu-
ment as old as language, and which has never yet solved
any proposition, let us simply take cognisance of the
actual physical phenomena that the interchange of life
qualities presents, and catalogue in due order and sequence
each specific inherited attribute. We may never know how
it came to be a continuous phenomenon, but of its actual
continuousness, and the nature of its manifestations, we
may be absolutely assured.

In noting the process of fertilization, we become conscious of a double series of processes marking the asexual
life of the ovum and the spermoid, and which were wholly
unknown only a few years ago. The various phenomena
are even now very inadequately investigated, and hasty
deductions have been drawn of the purport of some. The
phenomena of the polar bodies have been commented upon,
their nature and purport ; and one embryologist refutes the
conclusions another has drawn, may be too hastily, therefrom. All agree in the nature of the ovum, the entry of

the spermoid, and the subsequent fusion of the latter with certain ingredients in the former. As to what passes out of the cell or ovum before the spermoid enters, we know nothing, and may, therefore, safely leave the purport of that change for future discoveries, being content only to read those phenomena that are patent to all investigators.

Firstly, then, what are the contents of the ovum when it first proceeds on its more or less independent series of life adventures? We know that it contains a germ, the maternal germ charged with all the accredited ancestral attributes, the personal qualities, the mental endowments and sentiments of the mother's race. In like manner we accept the proposition that the spermoid contains an equal assemblage of like inducing attributes as manifesting the ancestral specialities of the father's race. We know of no other elements of being derived through the father, though others may yet be discovered; but in the ovum itself we recognize other ingredients than those affirming the maternal ancestry. To begin with, the yolk bag, or yolk cells, they have a history and purport of their own. In many cases, the maternal and paternal stores of personal beauties and mental qualities would have had little chance in the battle of life, had not the asexual formative instinct in the ovum, or the vital formative instinct in the mother, equally unconsciously have prepared this store of nutriment for the after developed sexual germ, and of the nature of this food on the compound organism, as yet we have no means of judging. But, besides this food store, the polar bodies in the egg are derived from the mother, but it is affirmed that similar polar bodies are given off by the spermoid; as, however, their purport is an open question, we need only now mention their existence. There are, however, other elements in the egg derived from the mother more especially, the free plasma, which induces all the early vital movements in the ovum, vital movements that only represent the principle of asexual vitality, as does the yolk. We accept the hereditary ancestral theory, both through the father and the mother, but these other independent ingredients, derived necessarily from the mother's personality, present a medium through which the new germ may acquire other characteristics than those common to both ancestral lines. Of the nature of the germ material we say nothing, for we know nothing, but every new organism has, besides ancestral germs from both sides, qualities which it has inherited distinct from those of the maternal and paternal lines, and which may have become inherited from the mother herself. This new class of inheritance, let us call them acquired, will naturally differ from the male and female series. Those in each new generation can only express the same forms, tones, and feelings as in the past, their origin necessitates their undeviating unchanging nature; they may atrophy, they may lie dormant, but if they manifest their instinctive vitality, it can only be in the forms of past experiences. But the nature of each new germ may be exalted on independent lines; it may manifest powers the world never knew before; it may give origin to a new line of formative or mental attributes that will be superadded to the ancestral lines, and which new attributes themselves will mark the line of all mental, all physical progress. Now, have we any evidence the offspring derive any characteristic or attributes specially from the mother, more particularly those that denote advances outside the ancestral *rôle*?

Jevons, in reviewing Ribot's *Heredity*, specified three sets of formative elements: first, Ordinary ancestral inheritance. Second, The influence of the environment on the growth and the formation of character; and third, Spontaneity. Of course, the full environment affects all the elements; they withhold, restrain, or modify the inherited ancestral qualities; they influence what we should term the immediate influences of the mother, as well as any source of spontaneous energy that might arise in the organism through the influence of its consciousness on the sum of its vital energy. The possibility of modification thus affects all the initial forces in the individual, and these, we hold, are first, the ancestral qualities, male and female; second, the asexual energies, its element of growth; third, the special plasma, in addition, derived beyond the ancestral germs from the mother, this would be Weismann's somatic plasma; and lastly, the spontaneous ebornments derived, by its own consciousness, from the conflicts of these varied impulses in evolving the new co-ordination. We can deduce no possible evidence of the origin of a new or exalted impulse from either ancestral line or from the asexual elements. We must look for a new force, a more exalted special manifestation as being derived either specially direct from the mother's plasma, or self-evolved in the individual's growing plasma.

Both these sources of change may be accredited with new special results. We know that new forms of thought, new creative powers, mechanical, and mental, and artistic, are far more fully evolved by the male than the female, that it is possible the nutritive commands in her system may absorb all possible higher results, yet there is no reason to infer that the germs of original thought in her spontaneity may not have been conveyed to her sons maturing under the influence of their greater energy and fuller co-ordinate control. It has been a common observation for ages, that great men, great from the original superiority of their intellectual powers, whatever their nature, have had clever mothers. This has been affirmed in proverbs, in legends and myths, even divine personages have derived some of their prestige from the great mind-powers evinced by their mothers. Michelet said that every son takes after his mother. Galton admits the vast creative influence of the mother's mind. We must also recollect that in generation there often occurs, as Bain says, a transmutability of nervous and mental forces,

and, as under similar conditions, one abnormal form may
be transferred to another abnormal state, a change constantly present in disease. It is not necessary that the
son's mental exaltation should assume the same character
as that of the mother.

But whatever may be the origin of the new elements
that are the seeds of progress we know they can have no
connection with the ancestral germs and must be derived
direct from the mother's organism or initiated *de novo* in
special co-ordination in the individual's own personality.
Our object has been to show that there is a possible source
of germ-power in the ovum which cannot be exhibited by
the spermoid.

That betimes special physical and mental exaltations are
presented in the individual co-ordination of whose antecedent
source we have no evidence, but which are familiarly now
expressed as individual spontaneity most are assured. We
have seen that a new co-ordination or arrangement of all
the elements, physical and mental, are gradually evolved in
every sexual organism according to the type of the being.
The status and exaltation of each of these primary powers
is settled in its own ontogeny by the distribution of its
vital energy, and as every organic being starts into existence
with a definite though variable quantity of energy, and which,
physical and mental, has to be sustained by nutrition and is
dissipated by work, physical and mental. We have expressed
our ignorance of the origin of various vital functions, so in
like manner we are ignorant of the mode by which in each
individual this stock of energy is distributed; how and why
with some it is mainly devoted to the physical capabilities,
with others to the mental. Sometimes one faculty alone is
specially distinguished, at other times another or others.
In some instances, even when limited, the distribution is so
unequal that whilst in the individual a single faculty—say
music among idiots—is so exalted, all the formative energies,
all the rest of the mental energies are more or less atrophied.

We need not say that individual consciousness does not select the mode of this distribution, nor that any external power has any charge thereof. The control of the energy and the nature of its co-ordinate results are the expression of the vital—not conscious—forces; they start on a certain definite line, but the nature of the co-ordination may be altered; subsequently the quality of the energy in the individual may be transferred from one faculty to another, whether normal or abnormal, but what the nature of the power in the individual that thus exalts or depresses the special faculty may be, we know not. We are only now beginning to perceive that there is a special co-ordinating power in each organism, but its relations with the whole series of faculties and with the conscious ego remain yet to be defined. We have read of duplex sovereign powers in several political states; we have yet to define the nature of like controlling forces in vital organisms. It is evident that the organic force is not due, like consciousness, to the sexual power seeing that it exists, though of a lower class, in all asexual organisms.

The asexual attributes are diverse. They consist of special substance differentiations, functional as the specialization of parts for distinct duties, formal as growth in definite lines. These severally represent growth, nutrition, reproduction. Growth as a vital character is always a-conscious; we know no more of its procedure in the highest animative than in the lowest vegetative forms. We may recognize the change in our own persons but the actual quality of growth appeals to no perceptive power, no form of volition. Nutrition itself is primarily unvolitional; the organism, if so circumstanced as to receive nutrient materials through the physical action of its surroundings, passively absorbs it, though it is equally indifferent whether the matter it grows over is digestible or not; if the former, its constituent fluids act upon the organic textures; if the latter, it simply grows out of it, and later on evolves the habit of expelling it.

Habits of growth evolve into instincts of growth, which, while becoming more complex, exhibit no conscious perception. It is the same with volition; at first the mere unconscious impulse of growth, then it becomes growth discriminative, passing over objects noxious or unnutritive and absorbing those suitable to its vital forces. Then, like the pseudopodias of the amœba, it grows towards objects flowing around them, and ultimately parts grow into organs from continuous habit of growth; and unconscious and motiveless like the pulsations of the heart, the cilia pulsate drawing objects freely flowing within the nutritive range. In like manner primary reproduction is mere growth. The absorption of extra plasma produces a mechanical strain on the integument of the cell, around the weakest axis a constriction takes place, a double series of centripetal movements are induced, the nucleolus and plasma become extended, then divided, and the constriction finally separates them into two organisms with like asexual powers. Or it may be that the cell integument is weak at only one place, this limited place becomes by extension a bud, and as the centripetal force brings a portion of the nucleus and plasma into the new expansion, it gradually evolves into a distinct cell germ. Whatever the origin of the new organism it excites no perception, no consciousness either in the being which gave it birth or in the matter of its own body cell, it simply represents the energy, the material impulse of growth; it knows no distinctions, it recognizes no differences, and, no more than as in our own bodies, the growing parts fail to manifest consciousness of self or externals, so the asexual cell has no recognition of relations.

The sexual state may be conceived as beginning in a mere process of growth. By the juxtaposition of two cells the portion of their special integuments in contact would lose the force that induced its formation; they would be thereby weakened, and, as they were differentiations of the

respective plasmas, they would be amenable to become
again plasmic. Thus they would attain new relations; the
plasmas would, through their centripetal forces, blend, and
as the junction enlarged the two nucleuses would in like
manner fuse. If we admit that each separate cell contained
its special series of growing powers and that they might
severally be distinctive, it is evident that by amalgamation
each germ force would be enlarged, exalted, and as the
separate elements exhibited certain powers the fused parts
having the attributes of both cells might induce conditions
not possible in either separate.

The first element of consciousness, the presence of distinctions, would be thus excited. The fusing elements
would act and react on each other as distinct forces,
producing a new series of growing impulses, objective
and subjective polarities, and these changes continuously
repeated would make common heredity of all the qualities
contained in all the cells conjugating. It is evident that
the sum of the powers in the asexual could never exceed
the inherited powers of growth and those acquired by the
individual cell, but in the conjugated and often cross-
conjugated cells every growth element became common
to all conjugated cells. The difference between the two
individuals is so vast that we should anticipate that new
results, new powers, would be produced by the aggregation
of the forces. But little change was possible in a series of
years by the simple addition to the asexual cell of acquired
attributes, but in the conjugated cells the new attributes
would be innumerable, even in each successive series. The
one represents addition by units, the other multiplication
by compound quantities, and ever increasing in a geo-
metrical ratio. That the aggregated forces should induce
the evolvement of new powers, new differentiations, seems
consistent with the results of combined activities even in
the physical world. Exaltation as a preliminary step ever
begins with the specialization of parts, and as a necessary

consequence the specialization of duties. This series of
organic operations begins in the asexual cell, but in
the organism possessing multiple forces it is immensely
enlarged; and, while the asexual independent cell differentiates only to a limited extent, the asexual cell under
the guidance of the sexual germs evolves into all the
various tissues, organs, and parts in the higher organism,
and has associated as a necessary consequence with it all
the varying and distinct impulses these special organs and
functions represent—in short, all that constitutes the ego
and its associate forces.

The germ budded from conjugated cells manifests
powers special and distinct from those that any independent unicellular organism presents.

Conjugation appears to exist under several modes.
Balfour says many protozoa have the capacity of temporarily or permanently fusing together without an immediate
act of reproduction. Thus in Actinophrys the simple
coalescence of two or more individuals gives a sufficient
amount of extra vigour to their product to compensate the
race for the loss of the individual members. In Vorticella
a free swimming individual conjugates with, and is permanently united with, a fixed one. Drysdale and Dalling
described the conjugation of a monad in the amœboid
condition with an ordinary monad. The results of conjugation are as yet very inadequately known. As Balfour
writes: in some, as the Vorticella, the fused organism becomes
exalted, and budding or fission ensues, necessarily adding
the compound qualities of the fused individuals to the new
division. But with many protozoa, as Flagellata and
Gregarinidæ, the fused body becomes by the act of conjugation converted into vital germs or spores, in some preceded by a resting state or cyst. The series of changes thus
have some resemblance with the stages in Arthropoda, the
larval, pupal and imago, save that in the one case each stage
denotes many individualisms, in the other a single person.

The distinction of evolving at once into many individual germs, or of giving origin to one only at a time, though the successive continuance of the power may produce an almost infinite series, appears to mark the great distinction between the two systems, and implies a distinct character and distinct origin. Simple fusion by the blending of the contents of two cells in accidental contact may have led to all the forms and results of conjugation, even ultimately to all the granules in the fused being, becoming spores or reproductive germs; the change simply implies that through many conjugations the nucleus and plasma of the primitive cell, instead of increasing by simple division through the whole cell, had differentiated the power to all the nucleus and plasmic granules in the mass, each of which assumed the attributes once restricted to the whole. The asexual product is the blending of two individuals, and their then breaking up into a mass of germs; the sexual requires that a portion of each of two individuals shall blend to make a new organism, the parents continuing independent organisms as before, and according to their general characteristics able to continue to cast off in conjunction new individuals. Various theories have been propounded to account for the bridging of this gulf, but the fact remains that only once has this been done in the life history of all organisms—every higher animal form being derived in succession from this special exaltation—and which act has never been renewed, or we should have other ranges of derivative organisms.

There are numerous instances of references to the modes in which sexual organisms exhibit reversions to asexual characteristics. These, however, are not in all cases correct; thus it was supposed in spring that the queen bee laid eggs unfecundated, but Von Siebold found that the queen stores in her own ovipositer the sperm cells of the preceding summer and with them fertilizes the eggs as she lays them. Drone eggs, however, may be laid by unfertile queens, and

even worker bees. (*Packard*, **Guide to Study of** *Insects,*
p. 118.) Parthenogenesis exhibits, as in Aphis, a return to the
cyst state modified by sexual attributes; the **same is** also
characteristic of the pupa stage in insect life, and **of the
resting spore** or cyst in many forms of parasitic life. **The
silk moth sometimes** lays fertile eggs without sexual union,
but out of 58,000 eggs unimpregnated, though many
passed through the early embryonic asexual states, **only
twenty-nine became** caterpillars. Asexual eggs are laid
by *Nematus ventricosis*, *Cynips spongifica*, *Sphinx ligustris*,
Smerinthus populi, *Telea* Polyphemus, *Psyche apiformis*,
and *Bombyx mori*, **but how or whether these are** fertilized
by other means than copulation direct, we know not.
Wagner observed asexual reproduction in the larvæ of
Miastor metraloas, **and Meinert in** *Oligarces paradoxus*,
but, as in the case of the queen bee just noted, we **have no
means of** determining in many instances whether or **no
the** fertilizing element may not have retained the power
for a period to be productive under subsequent conditions.

More, there is a source of acquired attributes not due to
either of the parents, thus it happens that the impression
of a previous male influences the **mother's** uterus and
conveys to her after offspring **characters** that neither its
own father or mother possessed. **Thus, in** Lord Moreton's
park an Arab mare was paired with a male quagga; after
with a black stallion. Each succeeding foal by the black
stallion was more like the quagga than the first was, but all
had quagga markings. So children by a second husband
take after the first. (*Lancet*, 1883, II. pp. 437-526.)

THE mental results affecting a graft. In the case of extensive skin grafting quoted page 18, we show that from whatever source derived the graft skin assumed the characteristics of the local skin which it replaced; the inference in this case is that the special power of differentiation is not contained in the local part, but is expressed by the associate influence of the co-ordination. This suggestion starts a new series of practical investigations into the nature and source of the special powers, organic and mental, presented by each organic personality.

The general inference is that the newly-acquired tissue accepts and becomes responsive to the forces presented by the co-ordination. Thus the new skin, whatever its source, loses its previous attributes, and takes those present in the co-ordinate personality; in cases wherein a foreign nerve has been grafted, after a short period the newly-grafted nerve, whatever its previous mode of action or the influence it presented, these powers become dormant, and it becomes naturalized to the functions of the lost part it has replaced. Thus a portion of the sciatic nerve of a rabbit was transferred to a man, and in the *Lancet* (1887, II. p. 102), are two cases of nerve grafting, one the graft of the sciatic nerve of a dog. In a case of transplanted muscle (*Brit. Med. Journ.* 1891, I. Epitome, p. 43), it is said that the transplanted tissue undergoes degeneration and is then invaded by new tissue from the indigenous muscle, so the transplanted portion merely forms a nidus for the growth of muscular fibres from the neighbouring parts.

In Appendix A we more fully illustrate the whole question of organic co-ordination, both normal and abnormal.

CHAPTER IV.

The Co-ordination of Faculties and Functions constituting the Human Personality.

THE nature of the individual has been often considered, and many have questioned the limits of the powers it represents. Dr. Laycock summarised the modern deduction in the following observations :—"Goethe said every living being is not a unity but a plurality. Even when it appears as an individual it is the reunion of beings living and existing in themselves. Duges terms that group of co-ordinate organs which can maintain an independent existence an organism or zoonite, while the combination of organisms into a socialistic unity is an animal. M. Moquin Tandon is of opinion that every five segments of the medicinal leech may be considered a distinct organism, as they have a nervous system with its œsophagal ring, a digestive system, organs of circulation, locomotion, and reproduction. He said it has two kinds of lives, a general one, or that of association of the separate individuals, and a special one, or that inherent in each zoonite. Each ganglion, he held, the brain of each zoonite, the general harmony secured by the commissural cords which run between the ganglia. The anterior zoonite, being in relation with the organs of special sense, is the ruler. He proved it ; as each zoonite when separated from the others ed and died independently of them. **Duges** said each lateral half of the segment of an **invertebrate is a zoonite**. In the articulata they are placed not serially but in pairs, laterally in radiata. Divide an holothuria, he said, into five parallel strips and they constitute an asterias. Unite the five limbs of an asterias by their contiguous margins, and you have an echinoderm. As integration advances the life is more concentrated in the organism, and the independent vitality of the zoonite elements is lost." (*Mind and Brain*, II. p. 244, &c.)

Goethe, with his exalted preceptive and reflective powers, took a more general introinspection of the attributes of vitality than were common in his day, hence he often anticipated after deductions. On this question of individuality, the microscope, the discovery of many of the special laws of vitality, vivisection in connection with experimental research, and a more extended investigation into the life history of many animal forms, have placed us even in advance of the prescience of a Goethe. The materials before us, and many preliminary scientific discoveries by investigators, both in Europe and America, give opportunity now for more systematic deductions, and we cannot but consider that a living organism represents a much more complicated entity than it was formerly and is now generally considered to be.

The evolution of a series of progressive formative types was deduced in the genetic history of organisms in like manner. The ontogeny of the animal also expresses the same general formative series as accruing in the life of the individual, and we now affirm that each co-ordinate organism, according to its status in the evolutionary scale, possesses in its various parts existences representing all the powers its ancestors have possessed, denoting the special forms of their individuality.

In the first stage the general powers were all homogenous; in the substance of the plasma there was no differentiation. In the second stage the living substance was limited to the cell in which the differentiation of the epidermis was the preliminary process, which, by converting the motive power from being general to be specially limited, induced differentiation of the homogeneous substance into a nucleus and nucleoli. Growth, which previously was only in mass, was now, by the exaltation of the limited growth in the cell, converted into cell multiplication, in the two forms of fission and budding. The third stage, represented by the aggregation of cells according to the exaltation it presented of the primary homogeneous power, took the form of special tissue, and we have to remember, as Dr. Foster has so ably shown, that the enlargement of one power in the cell, or multiple of cells, did not signify the total cessation of the other homogeneous powers in the same cell, for whatever may be the nature of the special exaltation, even in the highest differentiation, every living cell retains the elements of all the other vital principles, even though they may be only latent. Cell differentiation only expresses the fact that in the co-ordination of the cell one power has appropriated the greater part of the vital energy that was at first common to all the members of the co-ordination. It has become the leading member of the associated principles.

Modern discoveries into the evolution of the ovum have shown that cell division, even in the ovum, precedes fertilization, and the polar bodies formed in the ovum by its own process of growth before the entry of a spermatozoon, as Balfour shows, originate by cell division, and have the value of cells. They are independent of impregnation, and are the final act of the normal growth of the ovum. (*Embry.* p. 62.) All cases of parthenogenesis, and alternate generations in like manner, are the continuous survival in higher organisms of the primary generative form—the division of the cell.

Even in man, as well as with all the higher animals, we have evidence of this primary vitality and individuation of the ovum before impregnation.

In tracing the development of the co-ordinate individuation the three lowest states, that of plasma, the cell, and cell aggregates, the organism is more or less homogeneous, but when the segmented cells differentiate into tissues homogeneity is lost, and sooner or later functional activity and the specialization of parts bring into active vitality various distinct powers having specialized duties and betimes becoming antagonistic. We begin with the organism as an individual, then it becomes a family, and at last a state. In the highest co-ordinate development, man, we have integrated the most diverse powers, functions, and parts. Some are wholly under the guidance and control of the conscious ego, and are only manifested by introspection; others are the mental response to external impressions; some, even of mental influences, are outside the active interposition of the consciousness, and are manifested through the instrumentality of some unconscious influence by special cerebration. Akin to these are the reflex cerebrations outside the presiding will, and the reflex nervous activities, some of self origin, in the organism, some in answer to external impressions, and beyond these are the vital functional forces that build up and sustain the physical and psychical powers in the organism regulating growth, sustentation, reproduction, and every reciprocal co-ordination.

Without reference to the physical organism may be for the time unconscious of its presence, the higher mental powers pass out of their individuality, out of the surrounding world of externals, closing the windows of the soul to dwell for a time in a state of solemn abstraction, or through the scintillating gleams of many memories and many impulsive feelings, build up the realms of fancydom and ideal dramas of mystic significance. Or may be, the con-

scious ego, responding to its volitional impulses, is full of
doing and daring, not only controlling its own physical
organism, but guiding, ruling, and influencing in innumerable modes other individuals, and the vast series of forms
and powers about it. Yet, at the same time, whether it
dwells on the living world or seeks to penetrate the
mysteries of the unknown, without a personality, without
even a name, there is ever present, ever working in its own
organism, a presiding and, in many respects, a dominant
power to which unconsciously it sometimes appeals, but by
which, in many respects, its motives and actions are commanded. This great vital energy, that works unceasingly
night and day from the first segmentation in the ovum
until organic life ceases in the individual, rules every
physical part and function; appealing, when necessary, to the
conscious ego for its active assistance, and, like a prudent
ruler, storing in the organism the necessary supplies to
sustain every independent member, every associate individuality. It apportions to each its special task, and so
arranges that even unconsciously the ego must work in
accord with the many co-ordinate powers. So silent, so
powerful, so influential are the workings of this great ruler,
yet not a function, not a member, not a tissue, not even the
humblest individual in this co-ordinate organism, the
almost homogeneous leucocyte, but moves, acts, and is in
all respects subservient to its guiding influence. Even
when abnormal influences tend to disintegrate the harmony,
ever it steps forward to induce one part to take up the
duties of another part, one function to supply the failing
powers of another function, to sacrifice or cast off any
detergent member, may be exalting or depressing any
part or function for the common good, and endeavouring
by increased activity in parts, or the transfer of abnormal
conditions from one part to another, to reinstate the normal
co-ordination. Nor does it look only to the immediate; it
converts every extra product into stores for the future, and

so balances income and expenditure that it may ever have a reserve of energy. With the same judicious forethought it nourishes the germs of future generations until they compel the conscious ego to become the nurse and guardian of their future destinies. These, and infinitely many more unobtrusive, silent, yet equally important workings, are ever evolving in the organism unknown of the conscious ego, every one of which is necessary for the due arrangement of the co-ordination; and however free and individual may be the life of the many parts, even that of the leucocytes imprisoned in the vessels, all under normal conditions proceed in due accord, like the many classes and interests in a well-regulated state.

Such as is man, so correspondingly according to the status of its development is every animal organism. Step by step, as we descend the long roll of vitality, ever we find differentiation after differentiation involving and becoming more and more simple until they are all lost in the homogeneity of the primitive plasma. It is but one system, one record, one chain of being, every member of which bears imprinted in his organization the history of his advancement and the status of his race; more, each has within him, latent or active, every power the ancestors of his race have been cognizant of, and his members are built up of all the simple and compound vital energies that they have manifested. Not one vital organism is simply a single individuality. Every one has plasma and lymph and blood corpuscles, all of which are necessary to sustain the vital functions, yet any of which, under suitable conditions, may live on any other animal. So with the tissues, whether simple or multiple, they may form part of one organism to-day, of another to-morrow, without forgoing their individuality. Important members and functions may continue to live long after the general vital force has succumbed, even the power of reproducing parts is proportioned to the differentiation of the member. Some functions are so absolutely necessary to the existence of, the co-ordinate individual that it perishes if their mutual relation is disturbed, while others may entirely perish, and the co-ordination will continue to exist, either restoring the lost parts or contriving to do without them.

Though in the higher organisms, we are so familiar with the subsidiary character of the members and functions as to consider them as parts only of the complex individuality, we have to remember that in many forms of life some of these functions and powers represent distinct personalities, and in others one or more of these faculties may be absent, showing that such are not an essential part of the individuality. To enumerate the parts of human beings that may be absent, or the functions that may be in abeyance without the individuality being lost, were to record all but the later centralized powers contained in the brain, heart, and lungs.

All the limbs of a man have been amputated, many visceral and generative parts have been removed, we have even read of a considerable portion of the brain stuff, both of the cerebrum and cerebellum of men being destroyed by disease or lost by accident without any appreciable effect; the individual may be still the same save in the physical capacities of lost parts and functions, as in the powers of generation and the use of limbs.

The life of a part may be sustained artificially when the other parts of the body in an individual are dead. Dr. Lauder Brunton says :—" After death has occurred and circulation has ceased in the body generally, we are able to maintain the functional activity of isolated parts by means of artificial circulation ; so that the lung retains its vitality, the muscles their conductivity, and the glands their secreting powers for hours, or even for days after the rest of the body to which they belong are dead. On the other hand, if the circulation in any organ be arrested by contraction, plugging, or pressure upon the vessels supplying it, its function is quickly abolished, although the other parts of the **body are perfectly healthy.**" (*Brit. Medical Journal*, 1889, **II. p. 88.**)

We have seen that **parts** and even functions may be lost after manifestation in the co-ordinate individuality without loss to the general co-ordination, save in the special functional activity. So in like manner individuals may be born with superfluous parts, functions and powers. There may be an extra limb or limbs, or supernumerary parts of various kinds. Through the coherence, or natural grafting in the womb, one fœtus may have super-added to it any portion of another fœtus, so as to possess extra parts in the one co-ordination. Or two co-ordinations may be blended in one compound organism—there may be two heads, two wills, four arms, and but **two lower** limbs; the viscera may be single or blended in various proportions. Thus we may advance in the multiplication of parts, from the addition of **nails, digits, horns, and** doubtful excrescences of various kinds—extra glands, even additional mammary glands in various parts of the body. Mr. Wood showed that there may be extra muscles of various kinds and extra bone structures. Meckel also describes cases of the growth of extra muscles.

In like manner there are many cases of arrested development of parts, even of their total absence; and yet, as far as all the other co-ordinate characters may be marked, the individual loses nothing of his special individuality, save as foregoing the functional adaptability of the lost parts, the mental co-ordination, thought, feeling and sense being still normal. All that marks him out as a man through the three periods of his vital existence are never lost, though they may be shortened or extended.

In the *British Medical Journal* (1889, III. p. 525), we have the case of a child born without limbs—a mere head and trunk. Miss Biffin was minus the upper limbs from the shoulders. A Venetian was devoid of arms and legs, the hands being attached to the shoulders and the feet to the hips. There occur instances of deficiencies in the viscera and generative organs, and one part may supply the functions of another. In all these the remaining parts not only have their own individual characters, they have their own individual powers; and though in the normal state these are subservient to the will of the conscious ego and the energy of the unconscious co-ordinating power, they manifest not only independent growth but a seeming vital independence that may be continuous under abnormal states.

Thus the special tissues in considerable aggregates as muscle, epithelial of various kinds, bones, and even nerve, as living structures may be removed—that is, absolutely severed from their connection with one part of a man and applied to replace like lost structure at some other part; and like parts of other men, or even of certain animals, may in like manner be separated from an individual man or animal and attached to and become a living part of the man to whom they may be attached.

It is certain that the living personality, whatever its nature, in skin, muscle, bone or nerve, must be continuous; as it was on the individual on which it grew so it was when separated, and so it continued under its new attachment. Whether animal or human its differentiation and attributes were the same; the plasma and the leucocytes in the graft and in the parts to which it became attached were in affinity and blended—all were in harmonious accord, as if it was only simple, self-induced growth that was proceeding in the new development, not the junction of the parts of two distinct organisms.

We will take note of some instances of grafting before enquiring into the nature of the co-ordinate results they present, premising that the many successful operations that have been presented during late years intimate that the same class of tissue substance may be taken from another part of a man or other animal indifferently, and that it is not only possible to graft human muscle, tendon, skin, and nerve on another human being, but that like portions of one animal may be grafted on another animal or on man. Thus a lost bone, ligament, nerve or muscle, or wasted skin may be replaced in man by removal of corresponding tissue from the higher animals. A laundress, aged twenty-three, had an arm crushed in a mangle, with great loss of muscle. The injured parts took several weeks to heal, then she had practically lost the use of the fingers. For the purpose of grafting, a raw surface was secured by cutting off the ends of the contracted and paralysed muscles; then a muscular substance, four inches long and two inches wide, was instantly transferred from the thigh of a dog and planted in the open arm. The experiment was quite successful, as in little more than three weeks the young woman was able to move her arm with little difficulty; she also regained the use of her fingers. (*Medical Times*, 1885, II. p. 33.) The same publication also records the successful grafting of tendon from a sheep and dog to a rabbit, of like parts of a rabbit on to a dog; also grafting tendons of birds upon mammals, as those of a duck or turkey on a rabbit and rabbit on a fowl. The tendons so grafted preserved their mobility and their normal resistance. (*Ibid.* 1885, II. p. 851.)

In the *Lancet* (February 5th, 1876), is a case of skin-grafting after amputation. One hundred pieces were placed where granulation had commenced, most of which began to grow in forty-eight hours. A like case of grafting the skin of one horse on the bare parts of another is referred to in the *Standard* newspaper (September 11th, 1876). Cases of tendon-grafting from the hand to the arm of a weaver (*Lancet*, 1889, I. p. 1084), and of the transplanting of skin-flaps from other parts to the nose and cheek. (*Lancet*, 1889, I. p. 1131.) In another case we have an instance of nerve-grafting at Vienna. The place of the excised nerve was supplied by a piece of the sciatic nerve of a freshly-killed rabbit. Two months after sensation was gradually returning to the anæsthetic areas. (*Lancet*, 1889, II. p. 1220.) In like manner several cases are described in which the injured conjunctiva of the human eye was repaired by conjunctiva from the eyes of rabbits. (*Ibid.* II. p. 1282.) In the same publication we have the case of the testicle of a child being successfully transplanted from the perineum to the scrotum. (*Ibid.* I. p. 272.)

The *British Medical Journal* gives several instances of special grafting. One of tendon-grafting—in place of the common extensor of the index. The hand could be pronated and supinated, and he could move the thumb and index finger. The graft supplied was four and a-half inches long. (1889, I. p. 1229.) A case of bone-grafting. A boy of thirteen, at tin works, had the ungual phalanx of his right thumb pushed out by a punch; a wedge of bone cut from a Newfoundland puppy was inserted. Five months after he had a very useful right thumb, almost as good as the fellow on his left hand. (*Ibid.* II. p. 88.) Another case of fractured bone in a soldier, removed by trephining and the successful insertion of a new bone in the place. (*Ibid.* II. p. 133.) Dr. Nesterovsky relates in the same medical paper four cases of old standing intractible, extensive and deep ulcers of the leg, foot and thigh, where after all ordinary means had failed, the transplantation of the skin of frogs was invariably followed by a permanent healing in from nine to fourteen days. (1889, I. p. 1246.) Even a supernumerary bone may be grafted by accident. A fragment of a vertebral bone of a hare, through a blow of the hand in killing it, was fixed unconsciously on a man's finger and grew. At first it was only considered to be a swelling, but, becoming painful, it was cut out, when the fact of its being accidentally grafted became apparent. (*Ibid.* II. p. 1331.) Dr. Macewen transplanted a portion of one of the flat bones of a canine skull into a gap in the skull of a man. Two-thirds of the graft remained in the tissues, apparently becoming incorporated with them. In another case, three wedges, forming three-quarters of the humerus of a boy, inserted and growing. (*Pro. Roy. Soc. Lond.* XXXII. pp. 234-244.)

It is certain that these various grafts—whatever their origin, whether from other men or from dogs, rabbits or frogs —at first were no part of the man's personality, and yet after junction they became integral parts of the organization, and the personal co-ordination was manifested as fully by them as any other portions of the organism; they even, as in the case of nerve-grafting, came into direct relation with the mental consciousness, conveying information to it and fulfilling its volitional commands.

Grafting and fusion are early vital characteristics. The granules of plasma may be separated and reblended into a homogeneous mass; the cell may graft and blend with a fellow cell; and in the ovum the male and female elements fuse and blend into an united entity. In the fœtal state the accidental grafting and blending of distinct organisms, or only parts of such, is by no means a rare occurrence. It is evident though such phenomena in some circumstances are abnormal, in others they are naturally normal, and it is only by the possibility of such association that the higher organizations can be evolved. Every primary organ and function, though usually attached in sets, may, and do in some cases, exist not only as parts of an individuality, but possess themselves special though limited individualities. There are individuals like the Lernæ, in which the male function, absolutely separated from the nutritive, manifests a distinct individuality. A limited individuality is seen in the male bee and the neuter bee; and total absence of nutritive organs marks the mature stage of butterflies.

In the Stephanomia the various functions are individualized in special buds or offshoots springing from the common associate stem. In these animal forms one is the volitional function actively seizing the prey, another digests the food so obtained, while a third carries on the aeration of the circulating fluid, a fourth member is the seat of the visual power, others carry on the necessary generative functions, and locomotion is induced by a co-ordinate distinct set of organisms which, by a process of dilatation and contraction, propel the colony of parts.

Van der Hoeven says the " Siphonophoræ are compound animals or colonies connecting the hydroid polyps with the acalephs. They consist of a stem to which appendages are attached, which differ remarkably in form and function. Some of them are suctorial tubes or stomachs; others, motive organs; others, feelers and prehensile organs; others, again, protective laminæ (bracts) and sexual capsules. Great differences prevail with regard to the number, arrangement and development of these parts in the different families. Those constant in all Siphonophors are the stomachs, the prehensile apparatus, and the sexual capsules. The stem is muscular and hollow, the interior forming a canal in which the nutrient fluid moves with rapidity. The swimming apparatus is either passive or active; in the first it is a bladder filled with air, when active it consists of swimming bells variously grouped. These are formed on the plan of a medusa. All the appendages of the stem have a system of vessels communicating with the internal cavity of the stem, the only other external openings are the mouths of the digestive tubes, the food from these passes into the stem cavity, and partly by its contractility, partly by means of cilia, it is carried to all the appendages." (*Handbook of Zoology*, I. p. 102.)

The animals having these functional individualities are very numerous, and vary greatly in the nature and the number of members constituting the group. Rhizophysa have no swimming bells, and bracts and feelers are wanting. Agalmopsis has two rows of bells, and Hippodius has no swimming bladder; and others, as Agalma, Physalia, and Physsophora, differ in other respects. The arrangement of

the parts vary. In the Siphonophors the suctorial tubes or
stomachs have no tentacles round the mouth, at the base of
the stomach are the prehensile apparatus with thread cells,
the sexual appendages have swimming bells, medusa form,
the protective bracts are more solid than the other organs,
the feelers are vermiform, often in constant motion. In the
Stephanomia the swimming bells are numerous, forming a
conical column which surrounds the stem with many spiral
turns. The polyps are set on the stem with long contractile
pedicles, the feelers are pediculate and affixed to the stem.
The bracts or covers are not confined to the stem, but
surround the base of the polyps as the calyx surrounds the
flower. The prehensile filaments are at regular intervals.
The sexual organs are in bunches close to the feelers.
One Stephanomia was seen four feet long, with twenty
spiral turns, ten to twelve bells on each turn. Three
feelers, two on pedicles, one sessile; the male and female
organs being in close proximity.

An interesting question is the nature of these organisms,
and much discussion has taken place on the character of the
individuality they represent. K. Brooks, in the *Memoirs of
the Boston Natural History Society*, refers to the general
opinions thereon. He says :—" Gegenbaur and Balfour tell
that the medusa is not an organ but a person, homologous
with a whole hydroid not with a part of it; that the separation of the community into sessile nutritive hydra persons
and locomotor reproductive medusa persons, has been
brought about by division of labour ; that the hydra
community is older than the medusa; that originally all the
members of the community were alike; that gradually
certain ones became set apart for reproduction, and that
finally these latter were set free and, acquiring reproductive
organs, became locomotor medusæ, and that this was
brought about in order to secure the diffusion of the reproductive elements." (III. p. 412.) Balfour (*Embryo*. I. p. 135)
says :—" By Huxley and Metzchnikoff the various parts—

nectocalyces, hydrophyllia, hydrocysts, polypites, generative gonophores, &c.—are regarded as simple organs, while Leuckart, Haeckel, Claus, and others, regard them as so many different individuals forming a compound stock."

Brooks's view of the origin of the group is "that the remote ancestor of the hydro medusa was a solitary swimming hydra or actinula with no medusa stage, but probably with the power to multiply by budding. That this pelagic animal gradually became more and more highly organized, and more perfectly adapted for a swimming life, until it finally became converted into a medusa, with a swimming bell and sense organs developing directly from the egg, without exhibiting during its growth the stages through which it had passed during its evolution. After, the larva derived some advantage from attachment to other bodies, the sessile mode of life was perpetuated till it lost the tendency to become a medusa and remained a sessile hydra, giving birth by budding to other larvæ. That in this way sessile hydra communities, with medusa buds and free sexual medusæ were evolved, and these became polymorphic by division of labour." (*Memoirs Bos. N. H. Soc.* III. p. 411.)

If we take a general survey of the evolution of the vital functions and parts, we shall be better in a position to estimate the due relations of the members in a community of Siphonophors, as well as many other anomalous forms of vitality. We have seen that what we term functions and powers were primarily united in the plasma, which was homogeneous. That by differentiation these powers were separated, and each manifested distinct characters and specially worked out its own cycle of differentiations, sometimes more or less in accord with some of the other functions. Generation, which at first began by division only, then extended to multiple budding, after by fusion became sexual, and in both male and female elements continued to possess the same multiple process as in budding; hence, each germ consisted of many vital elements, and

each vital element contained all the powers expressed in
the homogeneous plasma. Hence, potentially we may
consider each germ as a cell, and as they proceeded in
differentiating their elements or powers, whether we term
the process division of labour or specialization of function,
matters not, but ever the breaking up of the germ specialized
the powers, then each power became again and again
differentiated by the fuller unfolding of the sub-divisions
of functions and the necessary concurrent evolution of
powers as yet latent in organization, and only possible of
manifestation under the new and enlarged conditions,
limited only to the numerous class of animal forces now
existing with their greatly varied and specialized powers.

Each of the organisms in this vast series of beings has
in it the same sort of functions as were contained in the
primary homogeneous plasma, but specialized according to
the stage its class has attained in differentiation. Each
individual animal, instead of the primary potentiality of
indefinite budding, has multiple generating powers; each
germ resulting thereform is capable of becoming a perfect
organism of its kind, but, more, according to the differentiation it has undergone are the nature of its functions and
their relation to one another. Thus the parent animal in
every case, whether it be an ovosphere or spermosphere,
or their ultimate fusion, consists of a number of individual
germs. Secondly. These germs each consists of as many
functions or divided functions as belong to its animal type.
In ordinary normal generation these are presented in the
normal form with the special normal powers. But in the
ovosphere or in the ovary, in the more highly developed
in the uterus, these parts may combine by partial fusion
after the breaking up of any of the developing germs into
any possible living combination of diffused members, orders,
or functions, or parts. Even with humanity not only may
two perfect fœtus's be combined as one individual, but they
may bo fused in any order of position, parts even being

atrophied; or a fœtus may break up into its parts, functions, and members, and these severally may obtain a parasitic existence in the mother's organism or be attached as superfluous parts to another fœtus, and after live as parasitic attachments on or in it. A case of a fœtal femur imbedded in the body of the uterus. (*Brit. Med. Journal*, 1872, II. p. 161.)

Such cases as we have referred to in human beings are purely abnormal, but they serve to demonstrate that even with them the parts of an organism are limited individualisms. In many cases a developing germ may normally hold many other like germs of functions; in this manner we may explain the phenomena of parthenogenesis, neuter bees, and other like vital phenomena; not the least special manifestation of this aggregating and integrating of parts and functions are those exhibited by the class of organisms of which the Siphonophors are the most typical. In them the two processes of budding and the production of sexual germs are continuous and common, so that the common polyp may be an isolated individual, it may be a set of associated germ cells, it may be several of these with their after-evolved bud germs. But the more specialized individuals of this class consist of aggregates from the breaking up of an ovosphere, of any series of fragments of many individual germs; there may be any number of generative parts, of motile parts, of digestive parts, and of protective parts, each of which has its own limited individualism, and each of which lives its own functional life.

The higher organisms, even men, are individually but aggregates of like functions to those that make a Siphonophor, and, like those compound animals, each special function is in association along the line of growth natural to the organism. The special attribute of the Siphonophor is not that it consists of a single set of functions as man, but that it is constituted of varying aggregates of each special function. We know that in the case of the human fœtus if there are duplicated members attached to any portion of a fœtus they must be derived from another fœtus during the ontogenetic evolution. In an article by Dr. Allen Thomson in the *London and Edinburgh Monthly Journal of Medical Science* (IV. p. 480), it is shown that supernumerary fingers, toes, ribs, teeth, muscles, vertebræ may be found added to the ordinary co-ordination of the fœtus. That the following parts may be double or multiplied, as the tongue, gullet, cœcum, spleen, pancreas, mammæ, ureters, testicle, and other parts of generation, the uterus, kidney, and heart. The parts added to the living human organism may consist of a whole duplicate fœtus, any great or lesser portion, any individual part, any fragment or fragments of any tissue, any cystous cell. Thus in some instances, as in that of the Siamese twins, we have two perfect organisms coalesced; in other cases the organisms are blended or so fused as to have a double upper or lower portion fusing into a single other portion. Sometimes attached to the one perfect organism is observed, in a twin pregnancy, an embryo that fails to develop a heart and vascular system, subsisting in the womb on its twin fellow's placental system, and growing into a shapeless mass in which all trace of the human form is lost; in some cases the viscera is alone absent, in others no head is visible. (*Ency. Brit.* XVI. p. 765.)

Occasionally the closure process in the human embryo is defective, and it is born with the parts exposed, somewhat as with Siphonophors. A case in the *British Medical Journal* (1888, II. p. 1044), in which closure of mouth imperfect, there being double hare lip, the abdomen was divided from sternum to pubes, the liver and the intestines lying outside the abdominal cavity. The brain was also exposed; there were other organic defects intimating the deficiency of the co-ordinating energy; it attempted to breathe. In another case recorded in the *Lancet* (1889, I. p. 324), there was an opening in the

abdominal walls from the epigastrum to the left iliac fossa,
through which the viscera protruded, the liver about two
inches, to the left of which could be seen the stomach
pancreas and transverse colon; the diaphragm was absent,
the anus imperforate; it lived thirty minutes. The
co-ordinating impulse may be defective in developing any of
the special powers at the same time that the other forces
continue their appropriate parts in the ontogenic evolution.
A singular case in point is given in the *Lancet* (1888, II.
p. 112), in which certain developing forces were stayed in
the invertebrate stage, while the general formative differentiation was continued on the human type. A fœtus born
dead is described as being quite soft to the touch, and
curiously swollen in the limbs. No bones could be felt in
the head, body, or limbs, and on holding the legs and arms
up to the light they were found to be almost transparent,
and not showing any signs of bones. An incision made
in the left arm showed that it was composed of a sort of
firm jelly; no trace of bone could be found. Dissection
was not permitted.

As further illustrating the individuality of the parts of
germs, we would refer to the many instances in which the
growth of fragments of a germ have taken place in the
ovaries not only of married but virgin women. In J. B.
Sutton's work on *Dermoids* many of these are described.
They consist of epithelial growths in general, and that is
the first evolved tissue from the differentiating cell, and
evolves segmentation, even in the higher organisms, before
the fusion of the sexual parts. What are now known as the
polar bodies carry on the primary process of asexual
development. These dermoids are like asexual growths.
Sutton describes them as containing teeth, bone, spurious
mammæ, with nipple; one, a cutaneous process with a nail
horn; one contained a lock of hair twenty inches long.
These living individual parts, whose principle of co-ordination antecedes the evolution of sex, may not only continue

their individuation in the unfertilized ovum, but when it is fertilized they may become attached to the growing fœtus, and continue parasitic on it during the whole course of its life. Essentially this is the origin of many tumours, moles, and dermoid growths on the human conjunctiva of common cuticle. Sutton gives the case of a sheep in which a similar phenomenon occurred. This was covered with wool (*Dermoids*, p. 28), as might have been expected, being a fragment from another sheep germ. In a similar case from an ox it was hairy skin. (*Ibid.* p. 30.)

The phenomena of the regeneration of lost parts, an individual speciality common to many forms, and which extends not only to the growth of new limbs, but new heads and other important parts, is a quality whose manifestation depends on the amount of general differentiation the animal represents. Each cell, by division, can produce a like cell, and any fragment of a hydra is able to evolve into the perfect animal, and what individuality it possessed was multiplied, as it ever is, by segmentation, but as animals possessing this quality have no memory, the individuality is but momentarily continuous. So, though each fragment of a polype becomes a perfect organism it lives only in the immediate present. It has no past, can conceive of no future, and consequently the conscious individuality has no continuity of mind force.

Between this full reduplication and that of a single limb, we may specify the regenerative powers in the annelids and their expression of individuality. In the *Annals of Natural History* (1867, p. 358) we read: " A great number—perhaps all annelids—can reproduce the anterior region, including the head. M. de Quatrefages demonstrated the fact in Eunice, and Dalyell observed the reproduction of a head and branchiæ by the posterior extremity of a sabella. ' 'I,' says Professor Claparède, ' have frequently met with marine annelida (Etone, Nepthys, &c.) which had undoubtedly reproduced their anterior regions.' "

This renewing of parts is a province of the co-ordinating energy, and the two developing powers in the higher individuals are distinct though associate. The conscious Ego is the result of the sexual fusion, but the asexual budding and dividing energy is much older. It exists in the primitive plasma, and is never wholly lost even in the higher differentiations. The conscious ego, which in all its forms in vitality induces by its active interposition the evolution of all sexual combinations, has no perceptive knowledge of, or control over the many processes of asexual development always going on in its own individuality, whether the budding of a leucocyte, the formation of a new limb, the multiplication of the segments of an Echinoderm, or the creation of a new head to a Nais.

So vast is this asexual power of reproduction by budding in some vital forms, as in the instance of the *Triton cristatus*, which has been observed to replace its tail and feet sixteen times in one summer, that 687 new bones were produced. This in a vertebrate animal is an extreme case, but among invertebrates the capacity asexually in some cases is co-extensive with the whole vitality. Trembly cut the fresh-water polypi in all directions, and into many-shaped pieces, yet each piece developed into the perfect animal. The head of a snail has grown again after being cut off, and the eye of the water newt has been restored after being taken out. A single ray of a star-fish has, according to Sir J. Dalyell, developed the other four rays, and then itself being cast off, the new star-fish has developed a new ray in place of the one that started the new co-ordination.

The Holothuria will apparently voluntarily cast off its tentacula, the dental circle, mouth œsophagus, lower intestinal parts, the ovarium, leaving the body an empty sac, a mere memberless cyst, yet in three or four months all the lost parts are regenerated.

Tubularia indiva has had its head fall off and decay several times; it lengthens the body at each loss of the head, then a new head is formed by a process of budding. This has been observed to take place four times, and as it is the only mode of growth, each segment may be regarded as an individuum, and counted the same as we count the age of a tree, by its circles of growth. In like manner the *Nais proboscidiœ* can reproduce their heads. Lewes experimented on two, cutting their heads off, and in a few days they grew again; when these were quite perfect he cut them off again, and they grew the second time. He cut them off the third time, but only one made a new head; that he cut off, but after the fifth operation it never grew, the energy failing. Duges, according to Muller, has shown that the planaria after being cut into eight or ten parts, each part is able to reproduce a perfect individual. In winter this took twelve or fourteen days, in summer time only four days.

In the lower vertebrata the reproductive powers in the general organism are much more developed than in the higher; thus the larva of the salamander if its extremities, gills, lower jaw, or eyes be removed, will redevelop them; as is the case also with the crustacea. A crab had seven of its limbs taken off by another crab, and yet when it cast its shell some time after it had the full complement of limbs.

In the higher vertebrata the reproduction of parts are more limited, though even in man all the tissues if destroyed or injured may be replaced, as well as hair, nails, and skin. In the disease named necrosis, the bone dying a new one forms and expels the dead parts. In speaking on grafting, we showed that portions of muscle, nerve, and even bone, as well as skin, may be taken from the individual himself, another human being, or any animal, and inserted, and supply efficiently the place of the lost part.

The individuality of functions and parts is also proved by the vitality of the part not necessarily ceasing with the death of the conscious **ego. Neither men nor** animals die all at once, but **the** parts according **to their** conjoint relation to the general co-ordination. Thus, **according** to **Muller,** the head of a decapitated kitten continued to suck. **The** uterus continues to contract a quarter of an hour after death, **and** the fœtus, in some cases, is expelled after **the** death of the mother. (*Muller, Physiol.* p. 716.) Dr. Magendie **found the** lacteals fill again, after being emptied by pressure, **two hours after death.** The gastric juice is secreted after **death.** Mr. Bell, while dissecting very carefully and **minutely the poison apparatus of** a large rattlesnake that **had been dead some hours,** observed **that** the poison **continued to be secreted so fast as to require to** be **occasionally dried off with a bit of sponge.**

Walckenaer decapitated a wasp, *Cerceris ornata,* entering the nest of a humble bee, **it** still **continued to** move forward, and when turned round endeavoured to resume its position and enter the hole. A decapitated salamander retains the power of motion some hours. Birds after being decapitated flap their wings; frogs sit. The finger introduced into the pharynx of a **decapitated** animal is tightly seized. (*Muller, Phy.* p. 716.)

According to M. Quatrefages:—"If the head and posterior segments of a praying **mantis be** removed, the prothorax which remains will live for more than an hour, although it now contains only a single ganglia. If you attempt to seize it you will find that the aggressive feet of **the** animal **will be** directed towards your fingers, in which **it will** bury **its** powerful **hooks.** The abdominal ganglion **which** alone animates the **ring** has, therefore, felt **the** finger, has **recognized the part** compressed **by a** foreign body, has **wished to free itself,** and hence **has** directed towards the **point that has been** attacked its **natural** arms, and co-ordi-**nates their** movements. This ganglion, although **com-**pletely isolated, comports itself like a perfect brain." (*Rambles of a Naturalist,* II. p. 183.)

"Whilst examining a terebella," says Mr. Lewes (*Seaside Studies*, p. 56), "I observed that one of its tentacles had been torn off and was wriggling with independent vivacity. I bethought me of trying how long these organs would live separated from the body. So cutting them all off I placed them in a phial. This was on the 21st of May; on the 25th some died, but to-day is the 27th, and there are still several vivaceous." Again, the same observer writes:—"The filaments of the actiniæ will live for some time, like tiny annelids, crawling in the water." (*Ibid.* p. 57.)

That functions and members often have an individual vitality superadded to the common general vitality, is demonstrable by the facts that occur in all the various metamorphic changes in the individual vitality. In the process of evolution from the larva to the pupa and from that to the imago, old members and parts, and even functions, are altered or discarded altogether, and new functions and parts, by a process of budding, are evolved. It is even a question whether in alternate generations the distinct individuums are not mere buds capable of throwing off sexual buds.

Portions of a being may perish and yet not all the being. Some members and functions are cast off periodically, as deer cast their horns, serpents their skins, and crustaceans their shells. In like manner star-fish cast off their rays, and many insects their wings. Hair and feathers are also seasonally shed. Teeth are discarded: even the function of reproduction ceases.

Special functions perish, but the individual exists. The eye may cease to see, the ear to hear; all scents may be powerless to the nostrils; the power of motion may be paralyzed, that of feeling dead; limbs may be severed, an ulcer or cancer may eat up any muscle, and yet the mind of the ego will be the same as before. The sightless brain will be conscious of luminous spectra, the deaf auditorium hear sweet melodies, and the inner perception be conscious of mental fragrances. Though the limb is gone, the man will still feel that he has toes and aver he can move the fingers long since cut off and reduced to dust.

We have, in speaking of monstrous births, spoken of the various blending of individualities that thereby accrue. The brain may be duplex, and two conscious ego's having diverse powers may be present to us only conjoined by the external integument. From this simple human polypodom we may pass to all the various possibilities of blended members and functions common to the two ego's—the vital energies in some distinct for each; in others, common to both. From these more or less double individualities we pass through a series in which the one conscious ego exists with more or less superfluous, wasted, lost, or fragmentary parts and functions; where even the anencephalous organism has no conscious egoism, and the aborted organism manifests only some of the functions of an almost vegetative existence, there being no conscious ego, and in the wreck of the co-ordination no central energetic vitality.

Such are the series of discordinations that may occur in men and in the descending scale of organisms, each has its typical normal representative. Life ever arises from stored energy, is ever renewed by energy, and multiplies itself from the products of energy. In its primary stages it is asexual, and in all the functions and parts of individuals, however highly organized, they all arise from asexual development. The whole asexual series, whether rising to the dignity of individual organisms or retained only as functions and parts of organisms, represent no mental power, no consciousness, no will. Every such whole or such part is the product of and sustained by the vital unconscious energy. Not until by the fusion of distinct germs or cells sexual combined vitality is evolved, can we recognize the presence of sensibility, consciousness, mind-power. The two series of sensible and unconscious growths are absolutely distinct,

distinct in their origin, distinct in their actions, distinct in their resultants. The one proceed in unalterable, unchanging lines, the other are as inconstant and variable as the mental will. There is no choice in the working of the forms of unconscious life. Under given external conditions it must bud, it must grow, it must combine into tissues and parts. The other complex force can only be induced by choice, it can only exist by the purpose of an active will, and the extent of its power of choice denotes its living and mental status. In the lowest forms of organic life we recognize beyond the mere substance, only growth and energy; they are the mere passive instruments of destiny. But no sooner have two cells blended and fused their elements into one organic entity than the new power mind is created, lowly at first and only manifested by the humblest volitional capacity, centrifugal and ciliary. But when, by the differentiation of the power of reciprocal fusing to special cells, sexual germs were created the many higher manifestations of will, and sense, and thought, were only questions of time. If one will was depressed another was exalted, and new mental and, as a necessary result, new vital dispensations became assured. The energy of multiplication, that in the cell made two of one then four of two, under the new power of will became profusely unlimited; there is not a sexual organism but has the elements of thousands of individualities, some that of millions. Why, even humanity whose absolute productiveness, by the necessity of care and its long period of development, seems limited to a dozen or more offspring, has in its ovaries no less than thirty thousand germs all effused by its initial energy before the third year of the young life.

Necessarily from the existence of the two forms of individuation, we have two series of vital manifestations, the conscious and the unconscious. These co-ordinate homogeneously in the lower order of beings, but in the higher will and consciousness ever tend to evolve an ever continuous series of differentiations, and these co-ordinate under the influence of the double series of powers in their nature. Under the influence of the energy of mere growth the lower organisms pass through their vital series of differentiations; while the higher class of organisms, ever developed by the same power, have their special workings modified, in some measure controlled or rendered betimes nugatory, by the presiding consciousness that rules over them.

Hence, in the co-ordination of all the higher organisms we have to specially mark the range of these two respective powers of growth and will. In normal man we have them both in full efficient working order. In the ovum and in embryonic life the mere energy of growth is manifested— the movements represent energy, not will; and in the adult human being the two activities, vital energy and consciousness, work associately but independently. Under normal conditions every vital function proceeds without the consciousness interposing : the heart beats, digestion proceeds, the various glands fulfil their respective duties and growth ensues ; the thousands of cellular, plasmic and tissue modifictions go on uninterruptedly, unknown. It is only under morbid conditions or when the interrelations are mutually responsive, as in the calls of hunger and excretory conditions, that the two powers acting in affinity require the interposition of the ego. Pain in its many forms is the felt but silent expositor of the failing bodily co-ordination, the appeal from the unconscious to the consciousness to endeavour to redress some faulty conditions. In some measure they may be said to stand in the same relations as the telegraph posts and wires to the electric current that follows their track, it may be weakened or their connections broken or deranged, and the co-ordinate harmony be lost.

We are quite assured that of the physical and vital workings in our organization, the ego is not the originator or conductor ; yet, while distinct in origin from all the mental impulses, we know that they have many interrelations that imply connection, adaptation of one to another, mutual interchange, the transfer of powers and states of being. We are conscious of an oneness of purpose in these mutual affinities, and that the harmonious co-ordination is not due to the ego. More, we know that the parts associated in a co-ordination, though generally normal, may vary considerably, and that this tendency to vary is equally common to all animal life, and demonstrates not only the unity but also the tendency to variability in all vital forms.

In the affirmation of the many facts thus presented, we recognize the human or animal co-ordination as consisting of associate faculties, parts, and powers acting conjointly as an individual, but each of these, according to its nature and grade of differentiation, presenting its special individual aspects and denoting various series of individual aggregations.

BOOK II.

THE FORMS OF THE MENTAL AND ORGANIC CO-ORDINATIONS.

ORGANIC life is present to us in its two great attributes, organic conformation and mental activity. These, when in co-ordinate relations, are manifest in various healthy conditions, but when, by any deranging influences, this harmony is lost, the more or less antagonistic powers exhibit diverse disruptive forms. The forms of co-ordinate expression are both active and passive, the last in various degrees. These we characterize as normal, and those exhibiting discordant relations as abnormal. The abnormal states are, first, those representing structural derangements, and, secondly, those denoting mental disorganization.

CHAPTER I.

The actively Wakeful State.

IN this state are displayed the active energies of the individual organism; both mind and body manifest their relative co-ordinate influence, and thought and volition are in co-ordinate harmony. The organic functions are all virtually in a healthy working state, the conscious and the unconscious performing their due parts in sustaining the equilibrium, and in the exposition of all the needful powers. So with the mental powers, according to the demands of

the ego are their reciprocating advances.   Like a carefully
arranged machine, every wheel, spring, lever and other
parts work in harmonious accord in integrating the common
result.   It is in this genial state that the inner as well as
the outer productiveness of the being are essentially most
fully present.   The nutritive, the respiratory, and the
reproductive faculties jointly maintain the race and the
individual, in sustaining the perfect working of all the
social, emotional, mental, and even exalted powers.   This
is the profitable active state of all the functions of mind
and body, whether the organism is sexual or asexual,
conscious or unconscious.   That, according to their status,
individuals differ in the force of the movements and
volitions when in action is apparent to all.   There are
invertebrates in their wakeful state so sluggish as scarce
to move beyond the pace of the shadow on the dial, and
there are others whose wakeful state is expended in endless
gyrations—as the wheel rotifer.   So it is in a great
measure with some of the higher animals; as many reptiles,
whose awakened volitions are simply expended in obtaining
a new store of nutriment, that they may once more wrap
themselves up in the lethargy of slow digestion.   The more
intense, the more active the wakeful powers, the greater the
call for a continuous supply of nutriment.   The smaller
birds, and many insects, always on the wing, are eating
and digesting all the day long, and while thus energetically
employed never seem satisfied.

Wakefulness may be abnormal, as well as normal, and
the unhealthy condition of insomnia presages the breaking
up of the co-ordination in the individual.   In vain may he
have recourse to opium and sleeping-draughts, these only
for the time influence the result, the cause of the derangement is outside their possible activities; they only may
stay the invidious deranging influence which, unless changed
by altered conditions or direct mental intervention, threatens
to destroy the co-ordination.

Normal wakefulness may be asserted of the average man under the average healthy conditions, and it is marked by the general regular activity of the mental and bodily functions. The senses are in full play, judgment, attention, and imagination actively occupied on the ideas and objects presented to their consideration; and in corresponding unison the nerve powers and muscles display their active proclivities. These conditions express the average working humanity in its multiform phases of intelligent doing.

Depressed wakefulness, expressed by *ennui*, inactivity, vacancy of thought-power, restless inattention, exhaustion, or the repose of some of the faculties of the body or mind, expresses the wonted necessity of repose to give again full tension to mind and body.

Morbid wakefulness, due to mental or bodily excitation, through fevers, inflammation, or other special disorganizing bodily conditions, or mental stimulus by anger or revengeful feelings, or resulting from stimulants or narcotics, may express only unhealthy mental and bodily states; or if only locally expressed may result in passion, in illusions, in hallucinations or monomaniacal tendencies—in all cases implying that the excitation has broken the balance of the mental moral forces.

The æsthetic wakeful state is only possible to minds possessed of special powers; it leads to distinct manifestations in lines corresponding to the higher special powers that influence it in different directions, so that fixing the attention on distinct ideas or objects the full force of the mind-powers are evolved in marked channels. In the lower form it is expressed by the love of hobbies, fancies, and special habits; in its higher evolvements it expresses research, genius, the unswerving pursuit of predominate ideas, resulting in all that denotes the elevation of man above the brute.

CHAPTER II.

The state of Quiescent Repose—Sleep.

SLEEP is an organic necessity to give repose to the substance of both nerve and muscle ; the strain of active tension being withdrawn, the tissue cells are enabled to restore the lost power by acquiring renewed energy. The mind becomes tired as well as the body, and cessation of or change of work re-invigorates the exhausted capabilities. Hence the two phases, the wakeful and the sleeping, are the only essential states of being, and, if normally succeeding each other, we can suppose they would represent the only conditions present in the cycle of vital powers. But such harmonious successive co-ordinations are broken and often rendered nugatory, by antagonistic phenomena evolving in or acting upon the delicate affinities of both mind and body, and inducing states of irregularity in the activities often abnormal, and in the best but the inefficient exposition of the normal states. These create many intermediate states of conscious mental and bodily activities, and certain faculties, organic and mental, may be in repose, whilst others manifest various ranges of active expression, as in reverie, somnambulism, dreaming, and semi-wakeful attention.

The primary change from wakeful exertion is denoted by the unvolitional desire for repose being forced on the passive will by the exhausted physical and mental powers.

The eyelids close and refuse to open without an act of will, yawning ensues, the head droops, and the half-closed eyelids are for a moment fixed; the inspirations accommodate themselves to the new conditions, and from varying in intensity become slower but deeper—the lower jaw relaxes as the state of repose extends, the mouth opens, the limbs become supine and recline in co-ordination with the line of the body; thought becomes vacant, the word but half uttered, and the ear, like the eye, and the other senses, fails to heed their co-ordinating impressions. All but the vegetative and organic functions cease : the will loses its dominancy and becomes inert, and, more or less, every impulse, every mental faculty, from attention and memory to judgment and idealization, become dormant; the unconscious powers of body and mind alone in their quiescent passivity seem to continue—the brain and the body work without a call on the reserved physical energy, brain matter and nerve matter ebbing and flowing, as in the tidal motions, that they seem almost material in their nature, mere accompaniments of the laws of gravitation. We cannot count their changing aspects of rest and activity, we cannot follow the unconscious cerebrations that so often occur in the depth of sleep, so manifest in the higher mental powers, as Dr. Carpenter shows, and in the needful organic repairs, as C. Creighton affirms; a power of unconscious work, never at rest even in the deepest state of repose, explained by Dr. Wigan as the alternate activities of the double consciousness, but which to us is the mystery that links the two distinct states of being in one individuality. That these phenomena do take place we know, but we can no more realize their active dispensations than we can those of the vibrations that in one range of action appeal to the sense of sound, in another to that of sight, whilst in others they may possibly mark other mental activities, linking together in harmonic relations other mental and organic manifestations.

In the dark silent hours of night and sleep, when nature, as well as the human soul, abide in quiescent repose, still the great physical laws present their mighty pulsations, still the heavenly orbs continue to revolve in their courses, the power of gravitation never sleeps; so in the microcosm of the human organism, the living forces never relax in their activities, the pulsating heart works without intermission, save in the unmeasurable period intervening between the vibrations. Nor is the respiration the only other faculty that continues to work, they are reduced in intensity, for the active will no longer demands their expression at full pressure, so in like manner the secretions are reduced in quantity, digestion goes on slower, the bile comes with less energy, the milk in the woman's breast partakes of the same reduced activity, the peristaltic motions are lower in tone and force, and the blood circulates in a more venous state, partaking of the common repose and lowered activity. The nutritive and generative activities from the organic necessities never cease, but they too become reduced in power from the granulating cell reproducing structural loss to the embryo evolving in the mother's womb.

Of the never sleeping, never dying power, that sustains the entity and oneness of the individual, we have not now to speak—that unnamed, silent, all-sufficient mind-supplementing power, that Dr. Carpenter so ably demonstrated as acting as another self within us, guiding, without our knowing how, the silent course of the higher cerebrations in unconscious persistency, and which also guides, controls, and balances the always unconscious organic functions. It never sleeps; and, as Mosso found, there "are frequent adjustments in the distribution of blood, even during sleep. Thus a strong stimulus to the skin or to a sense organ, but not strong enough to awaken the sleeper, caused a contraction of the vessels of the forearm, an increase of blood pressure, and a determination of blood towards the brain;

and, on the other hand, on suddenly awakening the sleeper, there was a contraction of the vessels of the brain, a general rise of pressure, and an accelerated flow of blood through the hemispheres of the brain. So sensitive is the whole organism in this respect, even during sleep, that a loudly spoken word, a sound, a touch, the action of light, or any moderate sensory impression, modified the rhythm of respiration, determined the contraction of the vessels of the forearm, increased the general pressure of the blood, caused an increased flow to the brain, and quickened the frequency of the beats of the heart." (*Ency. Brit.* XXII. p. 156.)

The sleeping, like the wakeful state, has its predominating phases. Normal sleep is denoted by the repose of the bodily powers usually most active in the waking state, and the apparently absolute dormancy of the mental faculties; yet, as the heart continues to beat, and the digestive and other functions never cease to act, so it may be that some special mind-powers continue, unconscious to the ego, to fulfil their duties, even to working out trains of ideas and solving problems, afterwards presented to the re-awakened thought by the memory. Still, as a general fact, normal sleep is dreamless.

The state of sleep may be induced by a certain position of the head, by a full stomach, a dull book, monotonous repeated sounds, fatigue, rocking motion, singing, by mesmeric action and hypnotic influence, and by drugs. But these forms of sleep vary in character, and in the status of the great essential faculties. In aught but true self-induced sleep, there are abnormal conditions which withhold some of the bodily or mental powers from participating in the general repose. Thus as Sir H. Holland says:—"Mesmeric sleep is exceedingly various in kind and degree, from the vague state of reverie or half trance, in which impressions are still received from the senses, to that deeper trance in which, as in coma and other anæsthetic states, even violent stimuli applied to the body fail to awaken or produce any obvious effect. This is a condition evidently remote from common sleep, yet differing, as far as we can see, only in degree." (*Sir H. Hol. Mental Philosophy*, p. 18.)

Even healthy sleep is not a constant, but a fluctuating state. As Maudsley says :—" There are degrees of sleep, not only of the cerebro-spinal system as a whole, but of its different parts—so many intermediate steps. Between it and waking we graduate through a twilight waking into imperfect sleep, and from light slumber into profound unconsciousness. One sense goes to sleep after another, each sinking gradually into a deeper slumber, then the spinal cord ; and last, the respiratory centre in the medulla oblongata, when the man dies." (*Pathol. of Mind*, p. 5.)

Sleep, Sir H. Holland writes, must be regarded not as a single state, but a succession of states in constant variation, not only in the different degrees in which the same sense or faculty is submitted to it, but also in the different proportions in which these several powers are under its influence at the same time. We thus associate the bodily acts of the somnambulist, the vivid trains of thought excited by external impressions, the occasional acute exercise of the intellect, the energy of emotion, to that of profound sleep, in which no impressions are received by the senses, no volitions exercised, and no consciousness or memorial left on awaking of the thought or feeling which have existed in the mind." (*Sir H. Hol. Ment. Phy.* p. 16.)

As showing the relations of the mind with the sense impressions in the transitionary states, it has been remarked that by the inhalation of ether or chloroform we observe that the person hears after he can no longer see, and that the senses of taste and smell are lost before those of hearing and touch ; so in natural sleep there are similar stages of unconsciousness, even a lightly sleeping person will sometimes hear apt questions that are cautiously put to him in a familiar voice, and make a reply without awaking. So in regard to volition—a man will sleep on horseback when the muscles of the back must be in action, even also in walking as recorded of so many somnambulists, and their volitionary powers are most diffuse, not only do they in sleep manifest the active instinctive equipoise of the body, they may walk, and run, and ride, and there are instances of sleeping persons swimming; besides, the arms and hands may be used in any ordinary work or manipulation, and the organs of the voice carry on a discourse.

Of the various intermediate forms between the wakeful and sleeping states, attention is the principal factor. This, constrained by the will, may be devoted to one train of ideas; then the attention, and with it the senses, more especially the general common sense, are almost dormant. In this mental status men are unobservant even of the ordinary life-preserving impulses, as if they were imbeciles or maniacs. Such was the incident so often quoted of Archimedes and the soldier. Carneades had to be fed by his maidservant to prevent him from starving. Cardan was wont, on a journey, to forget both his way and his object. Socrates once stood a whole day and night engrossed with the consideration of a weighty subject. The mathematician, Vieta, was sometimes so absorbed in meditation that he seemed for hours more like a dead person than a living, and was wholly unconscious of everything going on around him. Pinel relates that a priest in mental absence was unconscious of the pain of burning. Budgell, in the *Specta-tor*, represents Will Honeycomb throwing away his watch instead of a pebble, and Bruyere describes a similar character as swallowing the dice and throwing his glass on the table. (*Eclectic Rev.* I. p. 604.)

There are many forms and phases of sleep beside the profound; in that all the personal powers of the man are dormant, both physical and mental, and in the perfect wake-ful state all are in action or prepared for action, only waiting the call of the ego—but in the intermediate phases there may be as many distinct forms of quasi sleep as may be represented by the dormancy of any one or any combination of faculties, either physical or mental. Attention may be at rest, memory inattentive, the eyes may be open and we may not see, the ears passive and we fail to ear, judgment may be dormant and volition in any of its numerous forms quiescent. Even all these may be at rest and imagination only active, wildly discoursing of the shadowy impressions it has appropriated. So many and so varied are these intermediary phases, that we can but dwell on those activities that seem to mark generic affinities; of the rest, the consciousness we all possess of the experiences in our minds will aid us in conceiving both their nature and varieties.

CHAPTER III.

The State of Reverie.

REVERIE differs from abstraction in this respect: that it represents rather *ennui* than activity; while abstraction implies the all-engrossing activity of one form of thought which fills the mind and, as it were, casts all the other mental impulses into a state of coma. It may consist of one predominating conception, or a train of like ideas, striving to arrange themselves in their appropriate places in the mind; whilst in reverie, the listless fancy, allied to a more or less quiescent organization, allows the shadowy semblances of its many impulsive activities to pass in vague meanders athwart the idle, almost unconscious brain. Abstraction is allied to the hypnotic one-idea of soul concentration. Reverie, on the contrary, is the listless mind playing with repose in fitful, fading gleams. In this passive state of being any external object, sound, or impression, or idle, vague thought, may, for a time, cause a momentary impression, itself to pass away as the next wave of feeling impinges on the soul; and these flitting changes may succeed each other until the mystic attention dies away in sleep, or one or more emphatic ideas arouse the mind from its listless state of *ennui*.

Sufficient attention is not always paid to the distinct qualities implied in reverie and abstraction; they are often spoken of as the same, and yet they are widely diverse, and not only represent distinct phases of the mind but imply essentially distinct mind attributes. The one is the fantastic visionary seeking only the momentary gratification of its varying feelings in the phantasmagoria of its many thoughts, yet in its state of exaltation these may grow, as in dissolving views, to scenes of beauty, or shape their vague parts into orderly compounds that evolve into rhythmic legends that may never die. The other represents in its preliminary phase intensity of purpose. It calls up a single form or set of forms of thought, and these fill its soul with the profoundest sense of their all-sufficiency. Heedless of all else, it would work them into cohesion, trace their affinities, reconcile their seeming distinctions until they become a tower of mental strength in its soul. What was life to Archimedes in the presence of such a thought? With Newton, the bridal symphonies failed to impress his mind when a great problem stood in the way.

There are mental states that seem to present phases of being intermediate between abstraction and reverie. The religious enthusiast has his one predominating series of ideas, as has the mathematician. Like him, he would cast away all external objects and feelings. But how different their modes of proceeding; the one fills his soul with the great truth or truths he has to resolve into order, the other may be like the Yogi or the Monk of Mount Athos, who, prefiguring the modern hypnotist, only acquired the needful state by steadily gazing with both his eyes on his own nose or abdomen. May be, with the Buddhist priest, he reached the same soul quiescence by the never-ending repetition of the holy word. But these were merely forms for fixing attention, the which many devotees can assume by an act of the will; but in all cases when this state is brought about it differs from that of the reverist, in that his is a state of ever-varying change; the thoughts may be vague, but they are endless in character, and they differ from the mathematician's state of abstraction, whose purpose is ever to educe order out of disorder. Not so the devotee. His one idea may not be questioned, cannot be changed; it is holy, perfect, and fills his soul with the august presence of an unchangeable eternity.

The secondary characteristics of all forms of abstraction and reverie are most varied, and as diverse as are the pursuits, feelings and minds of men. One merely idles an hour or two in listless, almost apathetic ideality of a common, pleasing nature—an after-dinner sleepless reverie; another, tired with sport or pleasure, a long walk, or even social chat, wiles away the afternoon in his easy-chair or on the sloping bank by the brooklet's side, in listening to his own breathing or flitting the butterfly thoughts in his idle brain. From these we may pass to the higher workings of the poet's reverie, selecting and arranging his fleeting thoughts into harmonious symphonies, that fill his soul with pleasure, and after, through all time, re-echo in men's hearts. There are some who allow the false *ennui* to grow into their being, until, like all monotonous states, it overmasters the mind that allows it to predominate. These become abstracted at all times, in company, in the street, in the assembly; they read books, and derive no fixed ideas therefrom, the incidents pass through their minds as dreams, and the converse of friends is recordless. Their utmost aim is to lounge in idle *ennui*, allowing mere passing scenes or thoughts to flit in vague illusions across their sensoriums, until at last the ever-relaxed energy of will loses its tension, and cannot be restrung. Such conditions of mind may be more or less familiar to all; but Dr. Crichton records a case in which the unbroken abstraction became a mental disease. He was a young gentleman of large fortune, but of a rather unsocial disposition. Hence, he loved to be alone, without pursuit of any object or seeming purpose in life; he would willingly sit nearly a whole day without moving, and if his countenance were attentively watched it was easy to discover that a multiplicity of thoughts were constantly succeeding each other in his mind; at times he would laugh heartily, then in a moment the expression of his countenance would change, and he would again sink into a deep reverie. In time he became so remarkably inattentive that even when pressed by some want he would, when after having gotten half through a sentence, suddenly stop, as if he had forgotten what to say.

Dr. Darwin, in his *Zoonomia*, describes the case of a young lady, who, after a nervous attack, fell into a reverie about an hour every day. She conversed aloud with imaginary persons with her eyes open, and could not for an hour be brought to attend to the stimulus of external objects. In these reveries she sometimes sang over some music with accuracy, and repeated whole passages from the poets. She never could recollect a single idea of what had passed in the reverie. In this case the reverie was passing into the exalted dream state.

There is much in reverie that reminds us of dreaming and the actions of somnambulists. Like Dominie Sampson, the reverist may have only one train of ideas; like Mr. Cargill, in *St. Ronan's Well*, he may be oblivious of externals. There may be insensibility to all but the prominent impressions, an imperfect awakening to practical life, a dream-like absence of surprise at anything which chimes in with the prevailing idea.

In reverie we become oblivious of the hours, and time seems nought; at others, as in dreams, a world of ideas may pass through the mind in seconds of time.

In the first stage of limited activity the predominating idea may be so active as to nullify the presence of the other faculties, so that, except for the object in hand, the perceptive, reflecting, and remembering powers are dormant. In some persons this is known as absence of mind and want of forethought. It has been notable among many persons possessed of great abstract, artistic, constructive and inventive powers. The mind in them is so absorbed with the one set of ideas that it fails to recognize things, persons or events that are passing about it.

CHAPTER IV.

The Dream State.

THE reverie may pass into passive and thence into profound sleep, or the mind may from a state of reverie pass into that of dreams. The same images, the same ideas, may continue in the mind, but the influences that co-ordinate them have become changed. The will, even in its almost quiescent state, no longer has any control over their natures or activities, only the still waking mind-powers have influence over the nature of their manifestations, and these morally and personally have no relation to the sentiments that influence the organism in its wakeful state. Some intimation of the coming change is present in the reverie: the will is less dominant, the moral faculties are less prominently manifested, we may not be actively cruel, but we are passively indifferent. Of the great moral change that comes over the mental activities in dreams we shall have afterwards to take cognisance, suffice it that now we have to record the fact that the sleeping, dreaming man and the wakeful man are not, as far as the attributes of character delineate, one and the same being. We do feel and suggest actions in our dreams that are most abhorrent to our waking thoughts, and this arises from the fact that the nature and co-ordination of the mental powers are distinct in the two states, and as each represents a diverse combination of the mind-powers they are necessarily diverse in their active results.

Dreams are induced by various influences, and are modified by many distinct causes. A preliminary state, disturbed sleep, may arise from the action of any stimulus on the organism either as a whole or on special members or parts, or by internal excitations, as by prevailing mental ideas, by morbid conditions of the body, by stings, bites, and so forth. These disturbing states may simply be manifest by more or less unconscious restlessness, or take active forms in the various kinds of dreams.

Dreams generally arise from increased cerebral circulation brought on by any of the predisposing disturbing causes; producing a chain of irregular, often miscellaneous ideas, may be partly induced by impressions in the memory, often heterogeneously blended, partly arising from or taking a definite character from immediate external influences which modify and transpose the original excited ideas.

No dream image is ever other than the mind might derive from images presented previously to the attention of the sensorium. Hence, the born blind never in dreams perceive visual forms, their impressions of dream objects only express the active memories of the other senses. So with the born deaf. The will may be, to a certain extent, active in sleep, as when the attention is called to waking at a certain hour, or to the active expression in sleep of any thought or duty, as in the instances given by Dr. Carpenter of the influence of previous waking ideas and obligations on the minds of the Telegraphist, and others.

Dreams are induced by various causes : as the revival of previous impressions, by present external impressions, accidental or intentional, by morbid bodily and mental states, by temporary exciting conditions. Proximate causes are the recurrence of ideas erroneously assorted in the mind. Sympathetic causes of dreams are previous intense thought, repletion, fatigue or depression, excitement or grief, joy, dyspepsia, &c., the position in slumber of head, body or limbs, bodily exposure or perspiration.

Normally healthy dreams only represent moderately increased organic excitement affecting parts of the brain and the great nerves, and through them certain mental and bodily functions. These produce ideas, sentiments, or scenes in accordance with the special mental character of the individual: pleasing, humoursome, friendly, or affectionate, or illustrative of his or her usual daily duties and associations. Often incidents but lately impressed on the sensorium, or which were prominently active in the previous wakeful condition, become modified in their characteristics and associated with persons and incidents not possible in the wakeful state to the individual. These are usually of a quiet and grateful character.

Beyond the simple commonplace dreams of our ordinary humanity, mere illusions of a mental character, denoting the more or less active wakefulness of the faculties most prominent in the mind-powers, and which, in connection with a partially awakened memory, rehearse or combine the prominent mental tendencies in more or less natural though heterogeneous illusions. Hence, the child is often at play in his dreams; sentiments of vanity, social visiting, the play of the affections, daily duties and associations, impress other minds. With men: self-esteem, the desire of action, influence, sport, or ordinary, literary, or business, or friendly pursuits characterize the dreams. If the dreamer has a hobby, a special pursuit, a prominent feeling of obligation, in some way, however bewildering, it will give a tone to his dreams. With women the feelings and emotions are most marked in the dreaming state. Dendy said:—" If it were possible to find a creature so wretched as to be endued with no external sense from his birth such a being would neither dream nor think, he would lead the life of a zoophyte. On the opening or restoration of his senses all his associations would be erroneous." (*Phenom. of Dreams*, p. 43.)

1. *Dreams, the result of previous impressions.*—Dr.

Macnish held that dreams are uniformly the resusci-
tation or re-embodiment of thoughts which have, in some
shape or other, formerly occupied the mind. He took
special note of some of his dreams and analyzed them, so as
to discover the elements on which they were founded and
the ideas that tended to give them their special character.
That he took a too-restricted conception of the origin of
dreams will be apparent from the facts we shall present.
We know that dreams may be built on circumstances and
persons of a bygone time, and that they may be the products
of the perceptions or observations but of yesterday. Even
events, persons, and objects, which our sensoriums have no
recollection of ever having been presented by our senses,
may afterwards come to the mental presence, as is the case
with an observed image on the retina the brain never took
cognisance of. A long forgotten event may return to the
mind as if explained by an apparition, the whole of which
has simply been the blending of the circumstances and the
persons into a dramatic incident, as apparitions recording
the places in which lost wills have been deposited.

Even the wildest, maddest dreams are mainly built up
out of the materials stored by the memory in the sensorium.
Every incident in the wild, visionary phantasies of the
opium eater, as recorded by De Quincey, are but the ordinary
pictures of life and nature intensified by an exalted brain-
temperature to a status far beyond the realities on which
they were founded. No doubt there are elements of truth
in all dreams if we could but separate the real from the
adventitious. Every dream has to be considered on its own
merits and in connection with the circumstances and persons
introduced therein. From crude narratives, often mystified,
we may not always become conscious of the inducing causes ;
or how some little incident omitted, or the mental state of
the dreamer, how much the result was often due to forget-
fulness or emotion.

Thus, dreams of apparitions of mysterious figures, having

special marks or performing special acts, are due to personal memories and emotional incidents, and these, if accepted by fear or pious resignation, act sympathetically on the mind of the dreamer and induce the result his own mind had primarily suggested. Thus, out of a number of cases of presentments we will quote one from De Boismont. A man in a dream saw the figure of a relative many years dead, who, in the usual manner, came to him, and announced that he would die that day ; but the waking man, as we show, is not the same moral and emotional being as he is in his sleeping state. So this gentleman, capable of initiating a super-natural mystic sentiment in his sleep, was not prepared to accept it when awake. Being of a strong mind, he told his dream, saying if it were to be—no matter. But doubting that it was only an illusion produced by the way in which he laid he followed his ordinary occupations and, of course, without any unpleasant catastrophe; but, as he said, in so many cases of others, if he had been weak enough to believe the dream and give way to emotion, he would really have died, as the men recorded by Procopius. (*Hist. Halluci.* p. 198.)

We are told that King James II. of England, at the time of the plague, had a dream that his eldest son, who was only a child, appeared to him as a full-grown man with a bloody cross on his forehead, and in the day he heard of his death. It is evident that the King saw the figure of a man with the red cross on it, the sign of the plague, and it is certain, knowing of his son's illness, his mind would be in a state of nervous trepidation, and he associated the remembered figure of his dreams with his son, but if there had been any connection with the two ideas as a presentiment, then his son would have died, not as a child, but as a full grown man. The incident illustrates how the mind, prone to the marvellous, accepts the most incongruous deductions.

Another incident recorded by Boismont is explainable by the circumstances surrounding it. A lady dreamt that her mother appeared to her in a dying state. The next morning when she told her dream, her uncle, in whose house she was staying, said it was true her mother was dead. The illusion was deemed of a spiritual nature. But afterwards the lady found a letter thrust into a corner which contained all the incidents that were presented to her in the dream. The only reasonable inference is that she had seen the letter when her uncle put it down, being unwilling to disturb her with the mournful news, that she slept on the news, and in the strong emotions after the dream, forgot the inciting cause, the circumstance that the particulars in the letter were identical with those of the dream strengthens this solution of it.

2. *Dreams are often the reflex action of the influence of external impressions on the mind of the sleeper.*—This has long been known, and Abercrombie gives the case of a gentleman volunteer and his wife full of the idea of the French invasion anticipated at that time, both dreaming of it as a reality, the dream being caused in both cases by the falling of a pair of tongs, which their sleeping sensoriums accepted as the signal gun denoting that the French had landed, being fired at the castle at Edinburgh.

Dreams of a particular character have often been produced by whispering names in the sleeper's ear, or by making special noises, they have been also due to odours, as from a laboratory, and by the smell of burning in ironing. Hot water bottles, put in the bed to keep the feet warm, have induced dreams of fires or volcanoes, being seized by brigands and tortured by burning the feet. One dreamt of being a bear and dancing on hot irons; another that the house was on fire, and the heat of the floor was burning the feet; and a third having a lighted candle put near his face, dreamt of burglars. To be absolutely assured of the influence of externals in the dreaming state, M. Maury caused a series of experiments to be made upon himself through the senses, and he recorded the resulting dreams.

Thus, tickling the lips and the inside of the nostrils produced the dream of a mask of pitch applied to the face and torn roughly off. A pair of tweezers struck by scissors near his ear produced a dream of bells ringing and the tocsin sounding. A bottle of Eau de Cologne held to his nose produced the sense of perfumes and visions of Eastern adventures. When a burning lucifer match was held close to his nostrils, he was at sea, and the magazine on the vessel blew up. Pinched slightly on the nape of the neck he dreamt of a blister, and this idea recalled to his mind the impression of the physician who gave him one when he was young. A piece of red hot iron held close enough to give the sensation of heat produced a dream of robbers, fire, and burning feet. Words of a special character sounded in his ear produced vague dreams of bees and conversations. A drop of water on the forehead produced a dream of drinking wine in Italy. Lastly, a light surrounded with red paper produced a dream of a stormy tempest accompanied with lightning.

Macnish recognized the influence of external impressions in causing dreams. He says :—" Dreams often originate from impressions made upon the body during sleep. Thus if the clothes chance to fall off us, we are liable to suppose that we are parading the streets in a state of nakedness, and feel all the shame and inconvenience which such a state would in reality produce. If we lie awry, or if our feet slip over the side of the bed, we often imagine ourselves standing upon the brink of a fearful precipice. A smoky chamber has given rise to the idea of a city in flames. The sound of a flute in the neighbourhood may invoke a thousand beautiful and delightful associations." (*Phil. of Sleep*, p. 58, &c.)

3. *Dreams arise from morbid bodily conditions,* even

from the position of the body in bed. Winslow records
the case of a gentleman who appeared during the day
free from any acute hallucinations, but who could never
lie on his back without being distressingly harassed by a
number of frightful imps, whom he imagined to be dancing
fantastically round him during the night. He was consequently forced to sleep in an arm-chair in consequence of
these symptoms. (*Obscure Diseas.* p. 498.)

A large class of dreams are due to morbid bodily conditions: as affections of the heart, aneurism of the large
arteries, affections of the brain or spinal cord, diseases of
the digestive or urinary apparatus, even the menstrual flow
has been caused by the collar of the nightgown being too
tight, or the special position of the head on the pillow, and
the angle of the body. In these instances the immediate
cause was the blood in circulation not being sufficiently
aerated. Neuralgic attacks cause the suggestion in dreams
of being stabbed with daggers, cut with knives, or torn to
pieces. (*Hammond on Insanity*, p. 259, &c.)

On this cause of dreams Macnish writes :—" The dropsical
subject has the idea of fountains and rivers and seas in his
sleep, jaundice tinges the objects beheld with its own sickly
hue, hunger induces dreams of eating agreeable food, an
attack of inflammation disposes us to see all things of the
colour of blood; thirst presents us with visions of parched
oceans, burning sands, and unmitigable heat." (*Phi. Sleep,*
p. 69.)

Even when disease is not openly manifest the nature of
the dreams indicate the morbid bodily state. Thus, as
Hammond writes :—Dreams indicate a coming physical
result, as of apoplexy and its subsequently following the
dream. Conrad Gesner dreamt that he was bitten in the
side by a venomous serpent, and in a short time a severe
carbuncle came there, of which he died. Many other like
local derangements are given by Hammond as expressed in
dreams. Forbes Winslow records many similar cases. Thus,

a barrister before an attack of cerebral paralysis was in the
habit of awaking in a state of great alarm and terror.
Persons who have been attacked by epilepsy, paralysis, and
apoplexy, have had for some period previous to their seizures,
distinct recollection of dreaming of these affections. If a
person sees in dreams frightful figures making grimaces, the
person is menaced with an intestinal malady or an affection
of the liver. Diseases of the internal organs cause in dreaming painful sensations which relate to the parts affected.
Apoplexy is preceded by dreams in which the person believes
he is in danger of perishing. (*Obscure Diseases*, p. 504.)

4. *Dreams in like manner arise from morbid mental states*,
as from over-work of the brain, from intense emotional
activity, from overweening moral fears, from great religious
or devotional excitation. No matter what the subject the
mind dwells too exclusively upon, the result is the same ;
the disturbing influences of dreams whose images take the
attributes of the subject-matter that has induced them. In
these dream-forms the natural bias of the mind is expressed,
and propensities and impulses that in the wakeful state are
under the moral control, often in dreams have full activity,
and if from any cause they are in a state of excitation, the
dream partakes of a lascivious, selfish, dominant, or other
immoral character.

Morel' says that many patients before becoming completely insane, have frightful dreams, and appear as if they
were conscious of being on the eve of losing their reason.
Some almost dread to go to bed, so horrible in their dreams
are the apparitions. Pinel observes that ecstatic visions
during the night often form the prelude to paroxysms of
maniacal devotion. It is also sometimes by enchanting
dreams, and a supposed apparition of a beloved object,
that insanity from love breaks out with fury after longer or
shorter intervals of reason and tranquillity. (*Winslow*,
p. 505.)

5. *Temporary exciting causes* often produce special dreams. Such were the old oracular dreams, dreams arising from sleeping in temples, at holy fanes, or under influences specially exciting to the mind. In this class may be included the mystic dreams of devotees and saints, the visions resulting from partaking in sacred rites and mysteries, all and every class of influences which, working on an excited brain, may present images either of adoration or terror.

The condition favourable to this class of dreams may be the result simply of mental or emotional excitation, it may be brought on by fervid devotional exercises, by partaking in scenes and incidents of an exciting mental character, and which fill the mind with illusory images or stimulate the imaginative powers. In many sacred festivities these exciting causes are supplemented by partaking of intoxicating drinks, drug solutions, and other means of stimulating the mind powers. We find these stimulating materials now in use by the Shamans in Asia, by the North American Indians in their religious festivities, and by the negro tribes in their fetish observances. It may be said that to bring on these ideal religious dreams all the intoxicating drugs and drinks were introduced. Wine in the Bacchic and other festivals of the Pelasgians, soma in the ancient Persian and Hindoo rites, kava in Polynesia, and hydromel in Druidic mystic devotions. These still form the general exciting media among the nations, supplemented by opium and other drugs, and distilled spirits of various characters. We only refer to these drugs and alcoholic infusions as secondary causes used to heighten the religious expressions; of the states of mental and moral derangement induced by them we shall have subsequently to speak. Now we only refer to the associative and other mental influences that bring about religious reverie and religious dreams in which the dream-excited mind runs riot in prophetic visions and ideal hallucinations.

CHAPTER V.

The State of Somnambulism.

WE have said that the various co-ordinate forms of the physical and mental powers glide into one another, and are introduced by grades of differentiation that alter their expressive attributes. Thus we tone down into deep sleep, thus we arouse to full wakeful volition. A like series of graduated changes accompany that large class of perceptive excitations which create dreams through the forms suggested by memory, bodily and external suggestions, and these, too, vary greatly according as the various volitional powers are in active affinity with those of the imagination. In the many dream states, some of the mental powers alone may be awake, the senses being quiescent; or one or more of the senses may be awake, or at least capable of receiving its special impression which, according to external conditions, blend with and modify the fantastic imaginings of the dreams. So likewise the will may be partially active or any of the nerves of voluntary motion be in a wakeful state, and these various forces, combining in endless proportions, induce most varied manifestations.

Somnambulism expresses not one but many forms of mental stimuli. Besides the common excitation of the memory in dreams, the vocal volitional powers may be under the control

of the will and the sleeper, subject to their influences according to the emotional tendencies, gives varying expressions of
the idealisms acting on the physical organization. A
common form of somnambulist activity is to talk in sleep,
this is to be accounted for from their greater general activity
and the habit of continuous speaking, with some almost
instinctive. Whatever the subject present to the mind of
the dreamer with such a tendency, it becomes dramatic; it
may only rise to interjectional expressions, mere call notes
or vocal symbols, or it may ascend to monologues descriptive
of the images passing across the brain, or questions addressed
to the most prominent figures. Others, with logical astute-
ness, will carry on a continuous dialogue or disputation with
an imaginary controversialist, their own minds supplying the
arguments both pro and con, though usually with a mental
bias to their own tones of thought. There are instances
recorded in which the volitional impetus takes the form of
singing, and the mental stimulus has full effect through the
harmony of sweet sounds, need we say that on these
occasions, when no sense of diffidence, no emotional reserve
can intervene, and in which all the energy of the mind is
concentrated on the present idea, that the exposition is
usually of an exalted nature.

As with the vocal powers, so also with those of bodily
volition; they have become almost instinctively expressive.
Awake, we know we need not direct our general
movements by the will, through habit they have become
almost automatic, whether applied in the actions of walking,
in the use of special tools, in the fingering of musical
instruments, or any other manipulative operations. Hence,
the sleeper actively impelled arouses from his bed, and from
the sense of habit proceeds for a walk. He opens the
window, looks out on the quiet aspect of nature, then unlocks
his door, and, as is his common course, passes downstairs and
out into the cool morning air. Knowing from habit each
road and lane, his course is very simple. He visits the

favourite haunts, may be sits down on the wonted seat, and, if all is as usual, returns and goes to bed without any active consciousness of the feat he has performed. But if things are not in their usual places, or he is not fully habituated to the succession of impressions he has to meet, then he stumbles, may be runs at a gate, a post, a wall, and is awakened to a consciousness of his mental state.

Betimes, the matter of the dream gives congruity to the volitional conditions, and the senses become so far active, or the general sensibility sufficiently acute, to carry the enterprising sleeper through any difficult undertaking he may be induced to pursue. The incidents as portrayed in "La Somnambula" have been again and again the realities of that mental and physical state. Men and women have not only walked out of the house windows on to the roof, but have passed unconscious and uninjured over rocky passes and along dangerous defiles without detriment, the instinctive powers that uphold the body and balance the moving organism being more exalted and independent of the nervous conscious fear that more often renders the precarious position the most dangerous.

It would almost seem from many recorded instances that anything that it was possible for a man to do in the ordinary waking state, he could as equally well perform in the somnambulic condition. Felix Plater relates that he often fell asleep playing the lute, which he continued in his sleep until it fell from his hand and woke him. He also states that a friend fell asleep whilst reading aloud, and read an entire page whilst sleeping. Habits that are habitual by day are most frequently re-enacted by night. Some men will then descend the shafts of mines, others ride on horseback, walk past dangerous places, which they could not accomplish when awake, or perform the most complex mechanical arrangements. Some will even swim in sleep. Dr. Franklin relates such an instance of himself, and Macnish gives the account of a man who walked over a rough and dangerous road nearly two miles, and then plunged into the water, where he swam a mile and a half before he was picked up, still fast asleep. Horstius relates the case of a boy who dreamt that he got out of bed, and ascended to the summit of an enormous rock, where he found an eagle's nest, which he brought away with him, and placed under his bed; but the whole was an actual event, and the nest was found in the precise spot where he imagined he had put it, and by the evidence of those who had seen his perilous adventure it was confirmed.

A Signor Augustin was accustomed to perform a variety of acts in his sleep. He would saddle his horse, have a gallop on it, then return to the house, knock at the door, go then to the billiard-room, and motion as if playing; afterwards go to the harpsichord and play a few irregular airs, then go to bed with his clothes on. One Negretti, a house servant, would repeat in sleep the accustomed duties of the day. He would carry trays and glasses about, and spread the table for dinner with great accuracy. His sense of sight was imperfect, as he struck against the doors and objects put in his way; so was his taste, as he would eat cabbage for salad, drink water for wine, and take coffee for snuff, without appearing to detect the substitutes. (*Eclectic Review, New Series*, I. pp. 79-81.)

One of the most extraordinary instances of the use of the various faculties in somnambulism is that quoted by D. H. Tuke, in his work on *Sleep Walking*, of a series of experiments performed by M. Mesnet on a French sergeant, subject to the habit of sleep-walking. "He came in contact with a table, then opened a drawer, took out an open paper and an inkstand, which he placed on the table. Then he got a chair, and began a letter to his general, commending his own bravery, and asking for a medal. Whilst the sergeant was employed in writing the letter, to test his capabilities, M. Mesnet placed a metallic plate so as to completely intercept his vision. He did not cease writing the line he had begun, but wrote a few words, the strokes jumbled together, then stopped. When the plate was removed he finished the line and began another. Whilst he was writing water was substituted for ink; so long as the pen made marks he continued, but when there was nothing but water he stopped, rubbed the pen on his coat and tried again, with the same result. When commencing, the sergeant had taken ten sheets of paper, and while writing on the first it was quickly removed, and so with the next, unto the fifth. In all cases he continued writing, as if all he had written was on the one sheet of paper. When done, he took up the last sheet of paper, read it, as if all he had written was visual on it, when it actually only contained his signature, moving his lips to every word, and correcting errors of spelling on the blank paper in their due position in the series " (p. 25).

There are some circumstances in the above case as illustrating the nature of the mental powers that we shall have subsequently to refer to. Of the general condition of the mental powers in the state of somnambulism, Dr. Carpenter draws the following conclusions :—"The somnambulist may hear, though he does not see or feel—he may feel, while he does not see or hear. The muscular sense is always active, and many of the most remarkable performances, both of natural and induced somnambulism, seem referable to the extraordinary intensity with which impressions on it are perceived, in consequence of the exclusive fixation of the attention on its guidance. Sometimes the somnambulist's attention is so completely fixed on his own train of thoughts that he is only conscious of such external impressions as are in harmony with them, and a definite sequence of ideas is not unfrequently followed out with a steadiness and consistency which contrasts very strikingly with the strange incongruities and abrupt transitions of an ordinary dream." (*Ment. Phys.* p. 592.)

The continuity of the mental perceptions thus manifested

in the semi-wakeful state, is brought prominently before us
by the many instances in which their exposition has been
marked by special exaltations.   On these Dr. Carpenter
says:—"A mathematician will work out a difficult problem;
an orator will make a most effective speech; a preacher
will address an imaginary congregation with such earnest-
ness and pathos as deeply to move his real auditors; a
musician will draw forth most enchanting harmonies from
his accustomed instrument; a poet will improvise a torrent
of verses; a mimic will keep the spectators in a roar of
laughter at the drollness of his imitations.   The reasoning
processes may be carried on with remarkable clearness and
accuracy, so that the conclusions may be quite sound, if the
data have been correct and adequate." (*Ment. Phys.* p. 592.)

   Dr. Tuke describes a patient who in his sleep was capable
of carrying on a conversation with anyone.   A young lady
who had fits of singing songs and hymns in her sleep in
quick succession, and could not be aroused, paying no heed
to questions until the attack, which usually lasted from four
to six hours, was over.   She sang better during the somnambulic attacks than when in her ordinary condition, as Dr.
Bastian reported, who attended her. (*Sleep Walking*, p. 34.)
Of the general mental state of sleep-walkers, Dr. Tuke
writes that with some the hearing is dormant, with others
fairly active; so with the sense of smell, one patient in his
sleep was always smelling the escape of gas.   In like manner
the sense of touch is variously manifested.   Some are insensible to pain, while the muscular sense is acutely alive;
so motility is active, the sleep-walker unfastens and fastens
doors, and fetches anything he may require.   Of exalted
manifestations, he gives the case of a young school girl
getting up in the night and learning her lessons, memory
and attention being fully occupied, while the conscious ego
was almost dormant yet not absolutely so, as when taking
her books in the morning she became conscious that she
knew her lessons.   A like instance is also given of a boy

working a problem in his sleep. The teacher, in the night going his rounds, saw him kneeling on his bed as if working the problem on the blackboard. The next morning, in answer to his enquiries, the boy said that he had worked the problem ; he dreamt it, and in the morning remembered the solution. (*Ibid.* pp. 29-30.)

Other instances of somnambulists giving active manifestations of their wakeful faculties are recorded by Dr. Carpenter. In one, a Scotch lawyer had been harassed with a difficult case, and in his sleep he got up, went to his desk, worked out the question, put it in a drawer, and went again to bed. In the morning he told his wife of his dream. Then his wife who had watched his proceedings in the night showed him the memorandum he had placed in the drawer. In another case, at a seminary at Amsterdam, a student had worked at a difficult problem without success until far into the night, when he went to bed. In the morning he found that he must have got up in the night in an unconscious state, have dreamt the solution, and written it out, as he found it laying on his table when he got up. (*Mental Phys.* p. 594.)

Dendy in "*Philosophy of Mysteries*" says that Louisa Vinning, the infant Sappho, at the age of two years and eight months sang repeatedly a melody perfectly new, and so perfect that it was written down from and entitled the "Infant's Dream." During all this the little creature was in such a state of apparent abstraction, that it was believed that she walked and talked in her sleep (p. 361).

The following cases illustrate the influence of emotional feelings inducing the hypnotic state of somnambulism, and of the revived mental perception of ordinary duties :—A young lady, as the result of excitement, loss of her mother, and grief, showed at first symptoms of chorea, the muscles of the face being in constant action. After this she began to talk in her sleep, and at length one night was found endeavouring in her sleep to open the street door. From

that day she became a constant sleep-walker. In this state
Dr. Hammond saw her rub a match several times on the
underside of the mantel shelf until it caught fire, then
turning on the gas, she lit it. She then threw herself into
an armchair and looked fixedly at a portrait of her mother.
Her eyes were wide open, and did not wink when the hand
was brought suddenly in close proximity to them. The
muscles of the face, which in her usual state were in constant action, were now perfectly still, the pulse regular, the
respiration slow and uniform. A book held between her
eyes and the picture on which her attention was apparently
directed did not prevent her continuous gaze as if no
obstacle intervened. She never noticed motions as for
blows, and Dr. Hammond was entirely satisfied that she
did not see at least with her eyes.

A lighted sulphur match under her nose produced no
irritation, and perfumes failed to make any impression on her
olfactory nerves. Lemon juice passed into her partially open
mouth and a solution of quinine failed to make any impression
on her; applied on bread, they were slowly chewed, and
instinctively swallowed. After this she rose from her chair,
paced the room, wrung her hands, sobbed and wept violently.
Led back to the seat she soon became calm. Scratching the
back of her hand, pulling her hair, and pinching her cheeks,
excited no sensation, and tickling the soles of her feet produced no laughter, though the feet were drawn up. When
awake she had no consciousness of anything that had passed
in the somnambulic state. (*Mental Derangement*, p. 4.)

In another case noted by the same writer, Jane Rider, a
young lady of seventeen years of age, who from having
been subject to headaches had passed into a state of chorea
followed by sleep-walking. She dressed herself on one
occasion, went down stairs, prepared for breakfast, arranging all the things with precision. She then went into the
pantry, skimmed the milk, pouring the cream into one cup,
the milk into another, cut the bread, dividing the slices

with as much precision as in open day, though her eyes were closed, and there was no light, except from one lamp standing in the breakfast room to enable the family to observe her operations. During the whole time she was unobservant of those around her, though when they purposely stood before her, or placed chairs in her way, she avoided them with an expression of impatience. She then quietly went to bed, and in the morning enquired, when she saw the breakfast prepared, why they had allowed her to sleep and another to do her work. She had no consciousness in her wakeful state of what she had done in her sleep. (*Ibid.* p. 6.)

Fosgate records a special instance of volitional excitation in sleep. A woman would sink down as if fainting, then becoming insensible she would commence preaching in a loud voice for from two to three hours. She had periodic spells of this state for five or six years every two weeks regularly. When she first commenced talking she appeared to be choked with frothy saliva; she preached in a clear, distinct voice. Sometimes her appeals would be most pathetic and eloquent. After preaching she continued insensible fifteen or twenty minutes, awaking by yawning. While preaching she could neither see, hear, nor feel, not being disturbed by any noise, and if pricked she did not flinch, whilst all the time her eyes continued closed. · (*Fosgate on Sleep*, p. 127.)

A case of exaltation is also given by Macnish. (*Philosophy of Sleep*, p. 159.) A clergyman used to get up in the night, light his candle, write sermons and correct them with interlineations, then retire to bed again, being all the time asleep. He also records the case of a man who had been dumb for many years, in the terror of a horrid dream, like the son of Crœsus, calling out in his sleep, and thus recovering his speech. (*Ibid.* p. 72.)

It is necessary to be very cautious in drawing general deductions from a few individual cases; thus, Dr. Carpenter wrote that nothing which occurs during the state of somnambulism is ever retraced spontaneously, or can be brought back by an act of recollection. But Dr. Tuke, who instituted an extensive series of enquiries, came to the conclusion that some sleep-walkers when awoke voluntarily or otherwise, had no remembrance of any act they did in their sleeping state, that some remembered them slightly or some circumstances in them, others only remembered them if awoke during the act, yet there were others who were fully conscious of all their sleep-walking volitions. (*Tuke, Sleep Walking*, p. 39.)

We have quoted succinct accounts of very many cases of sleep-walking, our object being not to supply interesting or exciting narratives, but to note the many varied illustrations they present of the fact that any one or more faculties of the mind may be dormant in sleep whilst the others are actively occupied; so in like manner any nerves of motion may be under the direction of the corresponding mental powers, whilst the remainder are in continued repose. One general deduction remains, and that is, that not only may the sleep-walker express all the mental attributes of his wakeful state, but that the whole energy of his mind may be expended on the few wakeful faculties, and that these may produce a moral status in the ego wholly distinct from the sum of the wakeful impulses. Of the deductions these facts present for our interpretation of the mental elements we shall afterwards have to enter into.

CHAPTER VI.

Induced Mental and Physical States.

In all the co-ordinate mental and physical states we have been considering, the ordinary mental and bodily faculties worked out among themselves the various states that have been presented, and thus produced a seeming definite equipoise in the ego. But there are other conjoint bodily and mental states of which the inducing power is not the general mental personality, and these within a certain range cannot be called morbid. These states may be induced by the intense concentration of the individual's own power of attention; they may be due to the influence of other minds controlling the individual's will, or they may arise from special physical agents controlling the mental will and the bodily faculties.

Thus sleep other than the simply natural may be induced by the attention being concentrated purposely on a single object, and all thought held in abeyance but on the one inert perception. An individual may be thus self-mesmerised, hypnotised, pass into an ecstatic sleep, or into a cataleptic state, as was the case with Colonel Townsend. Various instances of such self-induced sleep and dream-forms are on record; some remarkably indicating the power of the will through the attention. Thus Dr. Brodie records the case of a gentleman of his acquaintance of a very sensitive and imaginative turn of mind, who informed him that not unfrequently when he has had his thoughts intently fixed for a considerable time on an absent or imaginary object, he had at last seen it projected on the opposite wall, though only for a brief space of time with all the brightness and distinctness of reality. (*Psychol. Inquir.* Part I. p. 84.) Second sight, as Dendy says, was induced by fixing the attention on something during the dark hour until the imagination evolved a train of thought, often in connection with powerful unsatisfied waking thoughts, which then fashion themselves substantially, until the self-mesmerised eye and ear feel the presence and sound of things they deem prophetic.

A young lady, subject to somnambulism and fond of study, had acquired the power of producing hypnotic sleep by taking up some one of the philosophical works she was in the habit of studying, selecting a paragraph which required intense thought or excited powerful emotion, read it, then close the book and fix her eyes steadily but not directing the foci so as to see any particular object, and then reflect deeply on what she had read. From the reverie thus occasioned she gradually passed into the somnambulic sleep. During this state she answered questions, read books behind her, described scenes passing in distant places, and communicated messages from the dead, with all the qualifications of a clairvoyant or medium. That she, in her self-induced sleep-speaking state, assumed the reality of the images and thoughts present in her mind is apparent, but the supernatural illusiveness of character and subjects so readily inferred in the minds of the lovers of the spiritualistic wonderful, became mere figures of speech under the careful observation of one well acquainted with both normal and abnormal manifestations. Tested by Dr. Hammond, of New York, she only exhibited ideas of persons and things that had been but lately impressed on her mind. She had been reading Plato and Bruno and she saw their spirits, and then absorbed suggestions presented to her, so as to convert them into incidents in connection with her visions. (*Journal of Mental Science*, XVII. p. 132.)

Of the influence of general attention on the mind Taine gives an illustration in the case of Balzac, who, when he wrote the story of the poisoning of one of his characters in a novel, imbibed so distinct a taste of the arsenic used, in his mouth, that he vomited his dinner. This we might associate with the like intensity of attention in Charles Dickens, as recorded by Lewes, causing him to actually seem to hear the words his characters spake.

We are told of natural sleep being induced in infants by their attention being concentrated on one perception. In Nepal an aged female is appointed to watch a number of infants whilst their mothers were engaged in agricultural operations. The infants are wrapped up like mummies, laid on their backs, and from a number of spouts a rillet of water is made to fall upon and flow over the heads of the children. The most refractory, when tied up and his head bathed by the stream, will, in a few seconds, fall into a voiceless slumber. (*Lloyd and Gerard's Trav.* p. 272.)

Concentrated attention, allied to the hypnotic state, is often manifested in religious ecstacy. The symptoms, as Dr. Maudsley says, are very much alike in all cases, after sustained concentration of the attention on the desire to attain communion with heavenly things, the self-absorption being aided, perhaps, by fixing the gaze intently upon some holy figure, or, perhaps, upon the aspirant's own navel; the soul is supposed to be detached from the objects of earth and to enter into direct converse with heaven; the limbs are then motionless, flaccid, or fixed, general sensibility is blunted, the special senses become insusceptible, the breathing slow, the pulse low. (*Maudesley, Pathol. of Mind,* p. 70.)

Many illustrations of self-induced attention aiding the purpose of the visionary might be quoted, but the following

will suffice to show low forms of the application of the
power. In Smyth's *Aborigines of Victoria* we read that it
is the custom for a man to sleep at night on the grave of a
deceased friend to be freed from the fear of future apparitions, for during that fearful sleep the spirit of the deceased
would visit him, seize him by the throat, open his mouth,
take out his bowels, which the spirit would replace, and
then close up the wound. (II. p. 271.) To fix the attention
is the great secret in most rustic mystic supernaturalisms,
thus:—"Maids and bachelors in Oxfordshire, on a Friday
night, bring every one a little flour and a little salt, then
everyone blows an egg and everyone helps to make it
into paste and lay it on the gridiron; everyone turns it
and everyone breaks a piece and eats one part and lays the
other part under their pillow to dream of the person they
shall marry, all to be done in serious silence, without one
word or smile or else the cake loses its virtue." (*Aubrey,
Gentilisme,* p. 65.)

It is, however, under the form of hypnotism that an
attempt has been made to reduce the power of self-induced
attention to something that approaches seeming scientific
precision, and thus at first by the individual's own act, after
by the influence of the mutual attention of subject and
object, to educe various important modifications of the
mental and physical co-ordination.

Mr. James Braid, in his *Hypnotic Therapeutics,* describes
the process by which the hypnotic state was evolved. At
a conversazione, sixteen out of eighteen went into the
condition by gazing fixedly and abstractedly on the rood of
a chandelier. At a lecture, five deaf and dumb patients,
and a paralytic patient, all put themselves in a similar state
by gazing at inanimate objects (p. 3).

Generally, the hypnotic state is induced by the individual's own attention without the aid of a second person,
it being concentrated on a small, single object, sufficiently
distinct, yet unsuggestive, so as to command the fixedness

of the eyes without supplying matter for thought. An article of metal or glass is thus placed about a foot from the eyes and above the line of the forehead. Then, as the eyes and eyelids endeavour to accommodate themselves to the shortened focus and the raised position, the pupils relax, and as the concentrated attention is continued, the object becomes a dazzling, vague sensation, .the ducts supply moisture to the eyes, waves and circles of light become confused and undefined, and the abstracted mind passes into a dormant state.

Dr. Garth Wilkinson described the primary hypnotic state as that of mere abstraction produced by the fixed gaze upon some unexciting and empty thing. Abstraction continued tends to become more and more abstract, narrower and narrower it tends to unity, and after to nullity. Heidenhain considered that the hypnotic state was the result of the perverted action of certain parts of the cerebral nervous organs, and not by any occult forces.

Primarily, the psychical, or spiritual phenomena, as well as the associated sympathetic affinities, of which we have many historical instances, taking the forms of mental and religious epidemics, have uniformly been induced by the intensified attention being concentrated on one idea, one state of emotion, one form of feeling, not usually resulting in a cataleptic state, though a form of coma sometimes prevailed, but more often the excited sensibilities were awake to the one series of emotions, the other mental and physical faculties being more or less abstract and dormant. The long narratives of the Revivalists, the Convulsionaires, the Stigmatics, and other self-induced emotionalists, present us with the same partial insensible state of the religiously-excited organism. As in true somnambulism, the subjects are as insensible to temperature, to pain, to bodily discomfiture as the hypnotised patient. Special nervous centres may be in convulsive vibrations, or the subject may roll uneasily, or lie in listless apathy. While many faculties are thus dormant, the concentrated attention may be so intense as to induce in some parts increased sympathetic affinities such as are recorded on the bodies of the Stigmatics. We do not, and cannot, suppose any other than special-induced mental and bodily activities; and, no doubt, in many cases, the increased excitability of the skin in sympathetic reflex activity was supplemented by the often unconscious manipulation of the feverish parts by the hands of the morbidly excited subject. We shall be more prepared to fully realize the nature of the assumed supernatural or spiritual conditions and powers when we have worked all the forms in which mental and organic forces are manifested. At present we only intimate that all the conjoint expressions only represent a common law that any bodily or mental powers may pass into dormant states without affecting the continuity of the associate phenomena.

Certain organic and mental conditions are necessary accompaniments of the various hypnotic forms. Bertram instances a particular nervous temperament, this is manifest in all religious ecstatics, in mesmeric or spiritual mediums, and, as Mr. Baird found, in being susceptible of the hypnotic state, and, as has specially been noted, in those subject to the attacks of somnambulism. Sometimes the suitable status is induced by the course of certain diseases, and by great mental exaltation. These conditions have been described as the natural, the symptomatic, the induced, and the ecstatic. But whatever the controlling influence, similar phenomena, more or less intense, mark all the states.

Highly nervous individuals may be found, who, without formally inducing the hypnotic state, pass into its illusive phase whenever they apply their attention intently to one idea that prominently acts upon their emotional feelings. This may be considered as the half-way stage to mania, and the lower manifestations of many ecstatics, the cases of Tasso, Blake, Nicolai, and Charles Dickens all illustrate the gradual passage of the mental idea towards the diseased illusive form. In all, the attention is prominently directed to one subject of thought, or one object.

Mere attention suffices to induce this state, as Mr. Hammond shows in several instances. Thus, a lady, of a highly excitable nervous temperament, one day intently thinking on her mother, and picturing to herself her appearance as she looked when dressed for church, happening to raise her eyes, saw her mother standing before her clothed as she imagined; in a few moments it disappeared, but she soon found she had the ability to recall it at will, and that the power existed in regard to many other forms, even those of animals and inanimate objects. She could thus reproduce the image of any person on whom she strongly concentrated her thoughts. At last she lost the control of the operation, and was constantly subject to hallucinations of sight and hearing. (*On Nervous Derangement*, p. 81.)

In another case, the same scientific observer says:— "A young lady has recently informed me that she is able to bring visually before her the images of the characters contained in any novel she has been recently reading, or in any striking play she may have witnessed." (*Ibid.*)

Nor is the power of the attentive will only manifest directly on its own co-ordinate mental organism; it is equally manifest in the influence another's will may exert on the individual consciousness. For a century or more this, as a direct force inherent in certain individuals, has been made a matter of public demonstration in the forms of mesmeric, magnetic, hypnotic, and psychic excitation. But the power that one will possesses of influencing another is as old as the race, and is even manifested by many animal forms. Nor is it only expressed by direct impact, by the determined look, or intense dominant attention; it is manifested in general attractiveness, in social

sympathy, in emotional influences of all kinds. Beauty of
form, energy of purpose, attractiveness of habits, even the
expression of the feelings, have their several influences, and
when these are associated with like mental sympathies,
political, social, or religious influences, the individual
controlling power becomes most energetic.

These mind-controlling influences in all the ordinary
affairs of life are vague and general, and are induced
often without any purposive impetus, as the result of
social, mental, or emotional conditions, not as special
manifestations.

In all ages there have been social and religious expressions of dominant mind-powers to permanently impress on
the minds, more particularly of the young, central, general
sentiments which are intended to educe permanent social
and religious ideas in their minds. Such is the principle
affirmed in the North American Indian youth going forth
in silence and alone into the forest, there to wait and
watch, hope and fear, until his illusive imagination presents him with the dominant idea of his after life, his
sacred mystic medicine. We have the same intense
attention, the same tenacity of purpose, often continued
for weeks and months in the holy rites of puberty, both
in the case of boys and girls, among all barbarous and
semi-barbarous races, and ever after continued as the
discipline of the attention among all the higher races,
thereby to instil special social, moral, and religious
doctrines.

But in addition to these set institutions, whose object is
to concentrate the developing attention in definite lines,
there is the accidental and occasional influence of special
phenomena and thoughts on the attention, which often
become epidemic and induce even the derangement of one
mind to be sympathetically expressed by many. Such
have been the influence of sympathetic fear in exciting
panics, even without a perceptible cause, such the effect of

natural special phenomena sympathetically working on the imagination of **many**. Earthquakes and eclipses, new forms of disease, even the mental visions of one have worked on the co-ordinate sympathies until they have produced an epidemic of chorea, sometimes of mania. Still more so has this been the case when the sympathetic affinities have been associated with supernatural or religious impressions, and corresponding with the impossibilities of proof are the intensities of the feelings.

In the long narratives of possession and witchcraft, in the wide influence of the dreams of ecstatic girls and wild enthusiasts, in the absolute prostration of body and mind among devotees in all countries, we have the results of the common attention of many being devoted exclusively to one set of ideas, one tone of feeling, until it produces in the minds of those under its influence all the characteristic marks of morbid mental manifestations.

Nor was it only in the ordinary affairs of life, or in the special communal excitations to which we have referred, that the common general attention was expressed. The laying on of hands, and the holy benediction among the Christian Fathers, only expressed the same influence of the more exalted will on the lower as was commonly presented in the initiatory rites of religion among all races of men. These were often associated with sleeping in the temples, sacred dreams, of hypertrophying the resisting will, until both body and mind were prostrated. The records of these customs and institutions are so familiar that we need not dwell upon instances.

Even in the old world there are evidences of this power of the individual will of one man over the mental and bodily activities of others. The mantle of Elijah might fall on Elisha; the spirit of Eli pass in the anointing into David, as the robe of Gamaliel encompassed his disciples. There was the same priestly initiation in Egypt, and Babylon, and Old Mexico, as we now observe among the

unredeemed Papuan and American and Negro races; ever
the ancient dispenser of divine favours inoculates with
special rites the young acolyte, who wins the guerdon of
the sacred mysteries by fasts and prayings, physical endurance, and mental self-negation.

Every age has had its special forms of divine interaction,
as men in all times can but apply those forms of activity
special to their ordinary experiences. The dream-state from
its universality is pre-eminently the medium between the
divine and human natures; but in addition to that common
mode of supernal manifestation, the sentiment finds other
modes of expression according to the habits of the times:
here it is a fetish intermediary, there it is a mystic animal
form; the chance medley of the volitions of bird and
animal life, or the accidental or ritual opposition of any
objects and phenomena may be signs and manifestations
from beyond the skies, more or less associated with mystic
charms and omens. A new field of psychic energy was
evolved by the scientific discoveries of modern times. The
many forms of the imponderable gradually passing from
scientific toys to world-wide manifestations of heretofore
unrecognized forces became new links to explain the ultra
mysteries of being. The affirmations of psychic force,
animal magnetism and mesmerism induced polar influences; and the telephone and telegraph gave a plausible
significance to telepathy and thought-reading; and in an
age when mechanic force was utilized to superinduce every
volitional expression we might have reasonably expected
that the wit and ingenuity of man would have been
employed to devise machines through whose instrumentality the assumed spirit-nature could be brought into
co-ordinate affinity with the human. Have we not in
response had the Odometer of Dr. Mayo, the Magnetometer
of Mr. Rutter, the arts of writing and drawing in black
and in colours exhibited on material forms by divine
natures? Has not the awe-inspired medium seen the supple

human fingers guided by an unseen presence, evolve words of warning or contrition, or unfold the mystic glories of another world ? Have not forms, radiant with grace and beauty, gradually risen in innumerable shades and tints on blank paper, wrought by unseen hands in the presence of the spiritually devout ? In other cases, have we not appeals to human thoughts and sympathies in the shorthand of heaven: jagged and curved lines expressing divine dynamics, and aspirations reduced to human signs?

Nor can we help noting that considerate apparitions uniformly embody in their bodily and mental natures, the local characteristics, religious and social, and the special prejudices and fashions of the race ; even the divine harmonies accord with the music of the times: here expressed in tom-toms, there in the trumpet's roar, with others in the pealing organ's flow of music.

The natural history of ghosts has yet to be written. To the savage they ever come in the form of his fellows ; robed in skins with the Esquimaux ; naked as born with the Australian aborigine ; ever a black man with the negro. With the Roman and Greek it bore the shady form of the statues of their gods and goddesses. The Virgin or Saint of the ecstatic either was in accordance with the paintings in the churches, or the blue and gold divinities emblazoned in the missals. Many a ghost has presented itself in doublet and trunkhose, with farthingale, frill and hoop, or, like the spirit of Maupertius, in knee breeches, with stockings and silver buckles.

On this subject Dr. Maudsley observes :—" That apparitions, seen in different times and places, have always been in keeping with the ideas or beliefs of the age and people. Those of barbarous people are different from those of savage people, and those of cultured people are different from those of savages ; they change in character with the changing phases of intellectual development. Apparitions of Satan were not uncommon in the Middle Ages, though they seldom or never occur now. Luther's notions of the doings of Satan were very much on a par with those of a Saxon peasant of his times, he having no doubt whatever that witches frequently had carnal intercourse with their familiar devils ; he was not surprised, therefore, to see the devil come into his cell and make a great noise behind the stove. But is there an instance on record of Greek or Roman seeing the devil? Or did ever ancient Greek or Roman, by private bargain, sell his soul to him for earthly pleasures and prosperity as so many persons suffered death for during the Middle Ages? The Satan whom Luther assaulted by throwing an inkstand at his head had not then been invented." (*Nat. Causes and Supernatural Seemings,* p. 203.)

One cannot help but noting the want of congruity, and even manners, manifested by the denizens of the spirit world. They do not appear to care for the inconveniencing of those they visit, nor do they by any means object to present themselves in the most ghastly and repulsive forms. A maudling girl would usually act more sensibly and discreetly than do half the ghosts. Essentially they are stupid silly things, with a lackadaisical effrontery, or they come, like mutes at a funeral, with tongueless abjectiveness. Can we have a more melancholy illustration of wonder run wild than in the *Report of the Dialectical Society on Psychic Facts in* 1869. Sounds of a varying character apparently proceed from articles of furniture, the floor and walls of the room, the vibrations accompanying which are often distinctly perceptible to the touch. It is possible that those who heard these, as they assumed, mysterious sounds, had never heard of the Cock Lane ghost, or of the many instances in which servant girls, with long hairs and wires, have rattled the crockery on the shelves—often to the serious loss of their masters and mistresses. These admonitory signals were sometimes accompanied by the consciousness that the poor dumb dogs

could recognize the spirit appearances when their masters
and mistresses were wholly unconscious thereof, as they (as
Mr. Varley informs us), on the approach of the spirits,
would howl, bark, and run under their owners' chairs.
Then, it appears to have been a favourite amusement of
these spirit-ghosts, by way of interlude, to have a little
horseplay with those they were inspired to communicate
with; such as lifting tables, twisting people round on their
chairs, or making heavy bodies, like Mahomet's coffin,
remain suspended in the air without visible support.
Sometimes, in their spirit-fun, they played a game of
hide-and-seek with their mortal victims, touching them
by some invisible agency; and, as spirits are well up in
languages, they understood all that was said to them,
whether in Latin or Greek, French, German or Hebrew,
and touched any part of a person thus designated to them.
After these little familiarities, and others, such as raising
some of the ladies and gentlemen of the company several
feet from the ground, the spirits would demonstrate their
presence in various definite ways.   Hands and figures
would be seen dancing and flickering about in the air with
perfect mobility; even bodiless hands would touch or grasp
the communicants, and red hot coals, or what seemed red
hot coals, would fly about the room, bobbing on the hands
or noses of the doubters, but without producing pain or
scorching.· Betimes, the spiritual visitors would entertain
the mortals by invisibly playing on invisible instruments,
the bodiless strings and wires twanging with notes as full
as those derived from catgut or steel.   At others (but this
must be in a darkened room, as Captain R. F. Burton
affirms), heavy bells and tambourines were seen floating in
the air, and the worthy Captain felt a dry, hot, rough hand
on one occasion on his face, his moustache was pulled, a
cigar from the mantelshelf being placed in his mouth, and
his head patted.   Surely, these spirits must have been a
merry lot, and cried " hail, good fellow," to the Captain.

Nor was this all. Even spirits have to think of more serious matters — so they take to writing letters and drawing faces on slates held under the table; or playing at guessing the signification of certain knocks and raps, so as to establish a code of signals for communication between the outer and the inner worlds. Eight witnesses stated they had received precise information through rappings, writings, and other ways. Three witnesses were present when drawings, both in pencil and colours, were produced in so short a time as to render human agency impossible. In one case they admit a precise and detailed statement was delivered, but the spirit, like Saul's, was a lying spirit, and it proved entirely erroneous. But to make up for this, six witnesses declared they had received information of future events, accurately, foretold, days and weeks before they happened.

Now, is it not a little singular, in all this spiritual verbiage and amid all the striking details of things and events occurring, that neither acolytes nor mediums, or spirits, have manifested any concept of a great idea, an important work, a great social discovery. Our ancestors talked about the devil in a night attempting to cut through the South Downs. Cannot some of the mediums so familiar with the spirit-world suggest an emprise equally denoting power, and far more useful to man?—say, cutting through the isthmus of Panama, or debouching the Atlantic into the Zahara, or getting some poetic spirit to indite a new Iliad—not the wretched twaddle that has yet arrived from the spirit-world. Surely, some St. Cecilia might be induced to present us with spiritual harmonies far beyond the highest products of mere mortals. Moreover, is it not possible that great discoveries as yet unkent of in mortal mind, might be brought direct from the heavenly chancery? It appears as if all the spiritual ambassadors waste their potent powers in bewildering a few nervous lovers of the marvellous among

men and exciting ecstatic phrensies in hysterically inclined
women. That the exalted nervous state is bad, all know.
The experimenters all complain of loss of energy.
Mr. Varley after a *séance* had great loss of power, and
felt a difficulty in only supporting himself; while Mr. Home
fell on to the floor in an almost fainting state. (All the
data in the above remarks, from *Psychic Facts*, by
H. Harrison.)

We may well pass from these aberrations of the individual will to those more immediate dispensations of a like
controlling influence that mark the exposition of will-
power in modern days. In mesmeric, biological, hypnotic
and psychic expositions, we have the manifestations of the
same might of a dominant will, with the more intense and
immediate subjectivity of the supine individual volition,
than the highest of the old hierarchical influences exhibited.
We may not give full credit to the pretentious assertions of
psychic force and hypnotised sensual impressions any more
than we bow our wills to the illusive presences and mytho-
logical incidents that made up the old spiritual might. As
much that was fallacious and aberrant in the old world
histories have been reduced to normal affirmations of
co-ordinate natural laws, so we deem it feasible that the
extreme pretensions of psychic and hypnotic powers will be
found to be in accord with the more enlarged expositions
of the laws of the natural world, save in those instances in
which human frailty has enunciated and accepted impossible conditionings.

The simplest form of secondary influence on the attention are those in which the dormant or other forms of the
attention are induced by the directions of another's will.
In all those cases of hypnotising, as recorded by Mr. Braid,
in which the individual directs his attention to a cork
fastened on the forehead, or merely gazes at a bright or
other object within a short range of his eyes, or, as with
some, by looking down the sides of his own nose; we have

little or no direct manifestation of the influence of another's will on the subject. Not so when the influence is directly personal, as by the attention being intensely concentrated on the eyes of the hypnotiser, when passes are made either before the eyes or over the head or limbs of the mesmerised individual, even when it is brought about by the conscious susceptivity of the subject to the declared will of the operator. Some men can by a look, under ordinary conditions, overawe even the rebellious will of another; how much more easy must the reciprocity be when the subject is specially nervously sensitive, and looks up to the operator with a consciously submissive will. As to the nature of the force that coerces the sentient will, or overawes the animal brute, we have yet no need to consider, we only have to discover the nature of the present facts.

Of the method of procedure and its results, Dr. Maudsley says :—" The magnetiser attracts attention by making a few gentle passes with his hand, or by holding some bright object before his eyes at a little distance from them, or by merely looking fixedly at him. After a short time the person falls into a trance-like state in which the ordinary mind functions are suspended, his reason, judgment, and will being in complete abeyance, and he is dominated by the suggestions which the operator makes to him. He feels, thinks, and does whatever he is told confidently that he shall feel, think, and do. If he is assured that simple water is some bitter and nauseating mixture, he spits it out with grimaces of disgust; if assured it is sweet and pleasant, though bitter as wormwood, he smacks his lips as though he had tasted something pleasant. If he is told he is taking a pinch of snuff, he sniffs it and instantly sneezes; if warned that a swarm of bees is attacking him, he is in the greatest trepidation, and acts as if he were vigorously beating them off. He is very much in the position of an insane person, who believes that he smells deleterious odours, tastes poison in his food, or is covered with vermin, or of a dreamer entirely under the imaginary perception of the moment.*

Mr. Braid describes the hypnotic state as essentially a state of mental concentration, in which the faculties of the mind of the patient are so engrossed with a single idea or train of ideas as for the nonce to be dead or indifferent to all other considerations and influences. In consequence of this, concentrated attention to the subject in hand, therefore, intensifies whatever influence the mind of the individual can produce upon his physical functions. Moreover, words spoken, or other sensible impressions made on the body of an individual, by a second party, act as suggestions of thoughts and actions to the person impressed, so as to draw and fix his attention to one part or function of the body, and withdraw it from others; and whatever influence such suggestions or impressions are capable of producing during the ordinary working condition, should naturally be expected to act with correspondingly greater effect during the nervous sleep when the attention is so much more concentrated. (*Hypnotic Therapeutics*, p. 4.)

The phenomena exhibited by the hypnotised subject depend wholly on the will of the operator, as his mental and bodily faculties do not respond to or originate in his own mental impulses, but represent, or are imitations of, the active mental and bodily powers of the operator. Thus, common food may be taken as medicine, onions eaten as fruits, and suggestions made by the operator may simulate any form of volitional activity, as riding on a chair as if on horseback; the muscles may be made rigid or flaccid, or assume any character and position the operator may suggest. So any state of sensation may be induced, and any emotional influence created by the agency of the operators will; even

---

* *Maudsley, Pathol. of the Mind*, p. 52.

the very opposite sentiments that would mark the active intelligence of the subject.

On these bye-plays of the dominant will we need not dwell; but trace out the nature of the higher powers claimed in connection with mesmeric, hypnotic, and psychic conditions. Of these the most prominent is the conversion or transference of the special senses of the subject; his taste, touch, or sight may be wholly at the will of the operator, and any special sense may be transferred by the action of the dominant will to any part of his body. Thus, as Mayo says :—"In many cases of waking trance the patient does not see with his eyes, hear with his ears, nor taste with his tongue, and the sense of touch appears to have deserted his skin. At the same time the patient sees, hears and tastes things applied to the pit of the stomach, or sees and hears with the back of the head or tips of the fingers. So in imperfect mesmeric trance, waking sensuous impressions appear to have entirely deserted his own body and to be in relation with the sentient apparatus in the mesmeriser's frame, for if you pull his hair, or put mustard in his mouth, he does not feel either, but is actually alive to the sensations these produce on the mesmeriser; realizing not his own, but the mesmeriser's sensations. Hence, on this subject it is claimed—1st: That the special sensations may be transferred from their natural positions to any other part of the subject's body; or, 2ndly: that they may be rendered dormant and replaced by the sensations of the operator." (*Truths in Popular Supersti.* p. 165.)

Before attempting to illustrate or account for these phenomena of the senses, we have to take cognizance of the general law of animal nature that the loss or negation of any one faculty implies the transfer of some of its special powers to the other faculties; and, as a necessary corollary, that the intense use of one faculty enhances its powers at the expense of the other faculties. We have these compensating phenomena manifested in the case of blind people, in the increased delicacy and power of their senses of hearing and touch, so in like manner the special continuous use of one sense intensifies it, as is familiar in the increased powers of scent, hearing, and sight in the chase, and in viewing objects at long distances, or hearkening for far off sounds.   On this subject Professor Gregory said that under the influence of magnetism "smell and taste become astonishingly delicate and acute, vision so irritable that patients are able in very dark rooms to distinguish not only the outlines but also the colours of objects where healthy people cannot distinguish anything at all, and that patients hear and understand what is spoken three or four rooms off."   (*Researches on Magnetism.*)

A variety of instances of transfer of the senses and increased tension are recorded in the *Truths of Popular Superstitions.*   Thus we have the case of one who could read with her skin.   If she pressed the palm of her hand against the whole surface of a printed or written page, deliberately, as it were, to take off an impression, she became acquainted verbally with its contents, even to the extent of criticising the type or the handwriting.   She called this sense-feeling; contact was necessary for its manifestation.   In another case the patient is said to have heard at the pit of the stomach.   One gives an inventory of the contents of the pockets of all in the room.   Another case of a Miss Catherine, who, when with her eyes she could not distinguish light, yet read and read distinctly by carrying her fingers over the letters.   She thus read in the daylight or in the profound darkness printed pages out of the first book that came to hand, or written passages.   Other instances are given of like powers, both in the mesmeric and in the somnambulist state.   (*Mayo,* pp. 112-161.)

Such instances are recorded of individuals in the experiments on the influences in *Animal Magnetism.*   They have been familiar circumstances in mesmeric lectures, in spiritual manifestations, in the hypnotic and somnambulic

states, and powers of a like nature have been claimed in
illusive manias. That in these various mental phases, all
more or less marked by hallucinations, the subject should
accept a suggestion or impression and affirm to special
powers, is a well-known circumstance. It is common in
every form of illusion—morbid or simply exalted. The love
of the marvellous is so great, the idea of personal notoriety
or the possession of supernatural power, so readily accepted
by the excited ego, as well as by onlookers, that even in
sense exaltations it is necessary to be very circumspect in
admitting any beyond the known extensions of sensual
power, more, as there have been unaccepted test challenges
on this subject prominently before the public, both in this
country and America.

Mr. Hammond, in his work on *Mental Derangement*,
relates the case of a lady, quoted, who was able, by her
own intense attention, to induce the hypnotic state, and in
that state answered any question, even if it implied prescience, put to her. The worth of this assumption will be
seen in the following:—Thus, in answer to the question, Who
would be the first patient to enter Mr. Hammond's office
on that day week? she answered promptly: "A gentleman
from Albany. I see him now. He is pale and weak. I think
he is paralyzed." The first to enter on the day in question
was a lady from New York, suffering from nervous headache.
Asked where her father then was (second sight), she
answered: "He is at the corner of Wall Street and Broad-
way, looking at the clock on Trinity Church," when in fact,
during the whole of that hour, her father was in Brooklyn
(p. 14). We may not be certain what suggested the ideas
or illusions of her replies; whether their origin was external or internal; of one thing we may rest assured, that
in the hypnotic state she accepted any idea that was
presented to her. For immediately after, though she was
conscious of being in New York, yet when it was suggested
to her that she was on a ship in a storm, she immediately

accepted the situation, wrung her hands, expressed great
fear, and cried : "O save me ! save me ! " More, the supernatural power of the hypnotist was tested by reading a line
in a closed book, and telling the time by a watch held to
the back of her head; but though she always made some
answer, she was never once right.

As denoting her mental state, Dr. Hammond states:—
"That certain parts of her nervous system were inactive or
dormant, whilst others were capable of receiving sensations and originating nervous influences. Images were
formed, hallucinations entertained, and in these respects
she was in the condition of a dreaming person, for the
images and hallucinations were either directly connected
with thoughts she had previously had, or were immediately
suggested to her through her sense of hearing. Some
mental faculties were exercised, while others were quiescent. There was no correct judgment or volition. Imagination, memory, the emotions, and the ability to be
impressed by suggestions, were present in a high degree."
(*Ibid.* p. 15.) In the hands of a judicious medical attendant,
the true character of her hallucinations was at once
apparent; had she fallen into some other hands the world
might have been startled with a series of new revelations
from the spiritual world.

On this subject of exalted, even supernal, manifestations,
we need but quote the words of Dr. Carpenter :—" It is
affirmed of spiritual mediums, as of mesmeric clairvoyants,
that they occasionally give information as to matters of
fact which they cannot conceivably have become aware
through any ordinary channel, so that they must be
credited either with the possession of some psychic force,
or with the reception of their communication from another
sphere of existence. In regard to a large proportion of
these cases, it may be unhesitatingly asserted that they
would break down altogether if submitted to the same
searching enquiry that has been bestowed upon others of

their kind. The writer has had numerous opportunities of
observing the readiness with which occurrences have been
caught at by sympathising witnesses and worked up into
marvels, some of which were obviously the result of
suggestions sometimes designedly made by himself, while
others were mere guesses, often very wide of the mark,
which were made to fit the facts by progressive though
unintentional modifications." (*Hum. Phy.* p. 629.)

Very largely these *outre* cases, passing beyond the
ordinary incidences of life, are manifested under the
illusive stages of mesmerism, psychic forces, and hypnotism. In all these cases there may be delusions on one
or both sides, there may be conspired trickery, or one may
be the dupe of the other, but the inter-actions and inter-
positions of operators, mediums, and attendant spirits, give
many opportunities of adaptation, pausing, and for tact to
be displayed, not present to a single illusionist. Yet in all
ages, in many countries, and more especially by religious
enthusiasts, powers and actions far beyond the ordinary
have been assumed; we know also that in many forms of
mania, men now claim powers of a synonymous character.
In our asylums divine personages are always to be found,
and individuals claiming preternatural powers. So the
lowest Australian savage believes his medicine man, like
the angekok of the Esquimaux, has been up into the sky,
or has descended into the sea—the forms may differ but
the same supernal attributes are common to all.

All these sentiments and ideas must have some specious
cause for their enunciation—the impulse to be something
else, to do something other than ordinary, must exist before
the idea becomes an image or takes a living form. The
wildest sentiments of the dreamer, the somnambulist, the
hynotist, or the maniac, must have arisen in his will before
they became living illusions or stood forth as realities on
the excited brain. By habit they come and go, until by
numerous repetitions they assume the place of fixed ideas.

Now, there are many phases in the state of being, many incidents in the life of all organisms, that cannot be explained by the ordinary theories of natural changes. These prepare them to note like incidents among their fellows, such as *sudden* changes in the individual, the occurrence of diseases, the influence of one man on another, the power of fetishes, charms, and the occult powers derived therefrom.

The health-destroying and disease-curing powers are always esteemed to imply mysterious and occult powers. In one form or another they prevail among all men; they have been marked characteristics of those claiming mysterious or divine powers in all ages, and now they form an important feature in all the expositions of the commanding power of the human will. As in the olden time so now, the only preparation needed is the absolute submission of the will of the subject to the supernal afflatus. The cures thus affirmed are due to faith, the strength of a great will calling on a nervously feeble will to do and it does. It may be in relation to possession, to paralysis, or weakened nervous energy stimulated to manifest renewed vigour; it may result from concentrated attention to one part of its own body, to one sense, or to the action of the heart, intensified by submission to the commands of a dominant will. We are assured that in high mental excitement the lethargy of brain, nerve, and muscle become exerted to the utmost, and again renew the normal organic state held in abeyance by detergent causes. If the expression of the will in the lower forms can renew lost members, in the higher forms of being it at least can renew the dormant vigour and vitality of individual parts.

It is by such influences we account for the accredited cases of the dumb speaking, the paralyzed regaining the use of their limbs, and every power of the body being stimulated to renewed activity. Braid, in his *Hypnotic Therapeutics*, says:—"I have produced full vomiting in

hypnotised patients simply by giving them a mouthful of
water to drink, and then suggesting to them in audible
language that they had taken an emetic, or simply by
moving my own lips and jaws which they heard and
imitated, and on my suggesting that they had taken an
emetic, the idea alone was quite adequate to produce
vomiting " (p. 24). He further illustrated this form of the
power of attention by cases in which, through a few passes
of the hand, a flow of milk when the woman's breast was
dormant was produced, also like cases of opening the
bowels and causing the menstrual discharge. He looked
for no divine or occult influence but self-confidence
renewing the organic faculties, mere mental impressions
causing renewed physical activity. More, he considered
that many homeopathic cures resulted not from the
fractional quantity of the medicine taken, but by their
minds being confidently and persistently concentrated on,
and engrossed with a lively and expectant idea as regards
a particular result. To the same class of mental influences
he ascribed the cures effected by charms, spells, and
amulets, by sacred relics, and various nostrums, all of
which corroborated the influence of mental faith in the
result. The same he also affirms of the cures effected at
the grave of the Abbé Paris at Medard in Paris, which
in like manner afforded clear proof of the influence of
mental and moral causes, in changing physical action
according to the expectant idea in the mind of the patient
at the time. (*Ibid.* p. 34.) Mr. Braid narrates several cases in
which the influence of hypnotism cured a great variety of
diseases, not only nervous but chronic, as gout, spasm,
tetanus, muscular contractions, and various affections of
the larynx. (*Ibid.* p. 17-19.)

We might refer to similar cures being effected by
mesmeric passes, animal magnetism, metal cures, the
powder of sympathy, and a whole legion of like nostrums,
not forgetting those by royal touch. Most of us know

personally of some cases in which by the alteration of
medicines innocuous substances have effected important
cures. Of the power of imagination to discard disorderly
symptoms Dr. Hammond gives us an illustration. A lady,
subject to neuralgia, came to him; to test the temperature
of the two sides of her head he applied to each cheek a
thermo-electric pile in connection with a delicate galvano-
meter. She could have had no sensation beyond that of
the contact, but seeing the needle move she at once exclaimed that she was decidedly better, and another contact
would complete the cure. It was done. The pain was gone
by the strength of the imagination righting the nervous
irregularity. (*Nervous Derangement*, p. 226.)

We might notice here that there are cases in which the
power of the will becomes paralyzed by its want of co-
ordination with the organic faculties; not only cannot
another influence the volitional powers, the individual
himself cannot control his own volitions. Mr. Hammond
gives various cases of this failure of mental and bodily co-
ordination not due to nervous atrophy. One is the case of
a notary, who if he desired to go out could not exert his
will to that extent. A second could not command the
power to sign his name. With a lady the task of putting
on her bonnet was beyond her will; another could not
summon resolution enough to get out of a carriage; a third
said she could not unbutton her coat if the salvation of the
world depended upon it. A still more singular instance
was that of a gentleman who had two beds in his room, and
slept sometimes on one, at others on the other. Often he
said he had passed the whole night vainly endeavouring to
decide, and ending in a thoroughly exhausted state, falling
asleep on a chair or the floor. (*Insanity*, pp. 525-529.)

Nor is this phase of mental force seen in the power of a
commanding will, and the influence of personal attention
limited to man. Wherever there is mind the qualities that

distinguish mind are present; so the hypnotic force can be
as readily applied with the self-same results on animals
as on men and women. It is an old tale, that of the
fascinating power of snakes and of basilisks striking the
looker-on dead with a glance. The prey of the great
carnivora often perish before they receive a wound.

Mr. Hammond, in his work on *Nervous Derangement*
(p. 19), says :—" So long ago as 1646 Kircher found that a
mysterious influence could be produced on the mind of a
hen. He tied its feet together, laid it on the ground,
where it struggled for a time, then became passively
submissive when Kircher drew two lines in chalk on the
ground, one from each eye, and uniting at an acute angle
at the front of the head. He then loosed the band from
the legs, but the bird, though free, remained still, and
could scarcely be moved out of its position." Kircher's
experiment, as copied by Czermack, is narrated in the
Popular Science Monthly (1873). He made passes with his
hand from the tail to the head on craw-fish, which at first
resisted, then gradually became calm, then finally stood
erect on their heads, remaining motionless as if asleep.
Czermack found that the tying and the chalk mark were
unnecessary in the case of the hen; it could be hypnotised
by merely placing it in position.

Mr. Hammond writes :—" I have repeatedly performed
Czermack's experiments, using young lobsters, frogs, hens,
geese, and ducks, with scarcely a failure. All that is
necessary in the case of a frog is to hold it firmly for a
minute or two by the sides of the body just behind the
forelegs, and then gently lay it on its back. So profound
is the hypnotism that the blade of a pair of scissors may be
introduced into the lower part of the belly, and the animal
cut open the whole length without its moving or apparently
experiencing the least sensation." He experimented in
the Fulton market in the same manner on crabs, and in a

few minutes had more than a dozen motionless, on their heads. Crabs in the hypnotic state may have the claws, legs, and fins successively cut off with a stout pair of scissors without evincing any signs of sensation. Pigeons may be hypnotised if something, as the finger, is held before their eyes so as to attract their attention; the same result is produced by a piece of glass, a cork, or small candle, or other lifeless object. Mr. Hammond also says there is no difficulty in bringing dogs, rabbits, and cats fully under the hypnotic influence. (*Nervous Derangement*, pp. 19-24.)

The Rev. Mr. Bartlett, in the *Zoist* (1850, p. 293), says :— Descending a mountain road between two stone fences, a bull in an angry mood followed me, tearing the ground with his horns, and bellowing fiercely. When he came to a high gate, as I approached I looked him steadily in the face, catching his eye. In another minute a trembling of the eyelids arose, and after three or four minutes the eyes gradually closed, and the bull remained as immovable as if chiselled by the hand of the sculptor. Hypnotising by the eyes is a favourite mode of gaining control over any savage animal it is desired to render tame. Sullivan used to reduce the wildest horses to obedience by whispering in their ears.

We will conclude this part of our subject by instancing some asserted animal cures of the same nature as those we detailed on men and women. In the *Zoist* (No. 12, p. 522) Mr. H. Thomson contributes an account of the cure of two horses, one of an eye sore, the other of an inflamed leg, by passes made over the diseased parts. Miss Martineau sent to Dr. Elliotson an account of a cow taken ill, and the Cow Doctor said he could do nothing with it. She determined to have it mesmerised, when, after the process, in a few minutes it became easier, and before morning it was relieved in all ways.

Further on, in treating of the mystic powers expressed by self-suggestion and suggestion by others, we shall more fully illustrate and account for many of the higher supposed occult manifestations, as affecting the individual co-ordination.

CHAPTER I.

The law of Variability in the Human Personality.

Though each individual consists of a special series of mental impulses acting on the special organization and constituting its representative individuality, the result is not a continuous absolute identity, but that varies according to the special influences, internal and external, that affect and modify its parts. Thus there may be daily and hourly changes of character in the expression of the mental forces in an individual. We are also assured that normally there is a progressive growth and definition of the general mental attributes, a gradual cohesion and modification of the special impulses in every human being from infancy to manhood, and so to senility. These changes may be the simple expansion or contraction of each impulse, or they may denote the greater tension of some of the forces by excitation or their failure in full exposition by special depression.

All these forms of change come within the range of the healthy association of the organic and mental forces; they in no way necessarily denote disease, mental or bodily, or take away the moral responsibility of the consciousness. Yet the expressed characters of all men result from the infinite series of such changes which constitute the tones

and tendencies of all minds in the play of the passions and
the varying influences that denote each man and woman,
and induce those changing manifestations that are the
material on which the novelist dilates. No human being is
at all times the same personality—we change in the nature
of our pursuits, in the nature of our associations, in the
moral influences that guide us, often in the very purpose of
our lives. We not only follow the evolution of character
in the child, we trace it in our associates and friends,
likings and dislikings alter, and the change of impulses
guiding the individuals are noted, they become distant and
often cease to take interest in persons, things or events
that heretofore were watched with genial cordiality.
Betimes the alteration of character becomes more marked :
the genial become morose ; the sympathetic, indifferent ; the
excitable, staid ; even the trim, careless and reckless. Do
not our police reports often exhibit the moral delinquences
of once honourable and trusted members of society ?

But beyond this vast range of changing and developing
distinctions of character, we have another large class of
manifestations which pass beyond the normal activity of
mind and body, and denote morbid phases in the individual
activities. These may range from mere hobbies to
characteristic impulses, from eccentricities to morbid tastes
or pursuits, until they culminate in the perversion of the
impulsive and perceptive powers.

From these many varied considerations it is evident how
vast are the distinctions of character in men, not only in all
men, but in the same man in all times. Of the little varying
distinctions which healthy general humanity present, we
have not now to speak, they constitute the province of the
historian and the delineator of the varying attributes of
men. We have to consider now only those mental results
which have led men to draw concepts of relative conditions
of being and influences outside the province of physical
being, and the co-ordinate mental manifestations, and on

which have been founded the various phenomena and powers of the supernatural world.

Accompanying the various stages in the normal evolution of the series of co-ordinate phases in the individual, there often ensues special timal discordinations. Necessarily, at each stage, the new set of conditions being evolved greatly disintegrate the unity of the organism, and in the struggle of the various faculties and powers to assimilate, it often happens that derangements ensue of a morbid character, and which betimes affect the permanent co-ordination of the organism or result in the deterioration of some of the parts.

We have to remember that each of the great changes marking the successive stages in the human individuality are real metempsychoses, not physically so marked as those of the insect, the crustacea, or even the medusa, but mentally equally important, and we must not forget that the more highly differentiated parts in the human organism represent an exalted set of functional changes : in the alteration of dietary with the babe from milk to solids, in the output of the teeth, and in the general volitional evolvement in which all the organic and mental powers have to be brought into new harmonious relations. It is the same when the milk teeth give place to the permanent, when the physical powers become more fully enlarged, and the mental manifestations evolve into harmonious accord. Still more striking are the organic metempsychoses that ensue at puberty, when special parts assume sexual powers, and virtually the mind-forces seem to express a new state of being. Nor can the human organism cease growing and assume the state of maturity without being liable in the change of every faculty to various morbid influences. The same also accrue when in the change in the body the generative functions cease, and lastly, many detergent influences arise to prevent the co-ordinate being from passing to the final simultaneous decay of its various powers through

senility ; from the cradle to the grave ever some morbid conditions threaten the continuity of the co-ordinate individual.

Even before birth the due co-ordination of the physical
organism and the mental faculties may fail to accrue by
reason of fright or other mental and physical influences
acting through the mother on the fœtus, or by the influence
of drugs taken to produce abortion. So in like manner a
tedious or abnormal labour may affect the organic integrity
of the infant to such an extent as for ever to prevent its
faculties exhibiting the normal characteristics. Should this
period in the life of the young being progress without any
marked derangement of its parts during the period in which
the first teeth evolve and when the nervous system is more
immediately differentiating, its various functions may not
proceed in accord. In all these successional early periods
in the life of the organism it is not so much the derangement of some of the bodily functions as that of the whole
harmonious co-ordination that is to be feared. Then the
common result is more or less fatuous idiocy, marked as
equally by physical as mental degradation. The American
Journal of Insanity in explaining the causes of idiocy, says
seven were made so by their mothers using powerful drugs
to produce abortion. (VII., p. 75.) Bucknill and Tuke in their
Manual of Psychological Medicine give the case of M. R., one
of a large family of healthy children but born after a tedious
labour testifying to pressure. After birth it did not cry
for some hours, could not suck, for several days had twitch-
ings and spasm. Could not walk till three years old, then
unsteady. Only acquired a few monosyllables a year after,
and became a typical idiot, feeble in his mental powers,
ineducable, could not articulate distinctly. Yet with all
these degraded powers he could play on the piano any tune
(p. 56). Of later reversions to idiocy we quote the following
from the American *Journal of Insanity* :—" A child had
convulsions when three weeks old. At the age of one year
it was always restless and screaming, and pressing its hand

to its forehead. At two years old it was continually endeavouring to tear its own face, or push other children into the fire; died in convulsions." (VI. p. 304.) In another case in the same work the child was first healthy and learnt to walk and talk after it had convulsions, hydrocephalus ensued, and tho mental faculties were gradually impaired. For a time speech was partial, then thero followed other convulsions, and the vocal organs were severed from tho influence of tho brain and thero was no comprehension of language, but the appreciation of musical sounds continued. After a year or two ho attempted to whistle, articulating in connection with musical sounds. Music brought speech, the co-ordination was restored, and he afterwards learnt to read and write. (XXIV. p. 18.)

On the influence thus affecting the child Dr. Carpenter says :—" The period of dentition is sometimes one of considerable risk to the infant's life. The pressure upon the nerves of the gum is a fruitful source of irritation, producing disturbance of the whole system, and giving origin to convulsive affections which are not unfrequently fatal. An existing malady or abnormal tendency is pretty sure to be aggravated during the cutting of the teeth." (*Human Physiology,* p. 1017.)

In the *Journal of Psychological Medicine* is quoted the case of a girl at Melun who had no peculiarity at birth, dentition was completed at three years of age, then general development was arrested. She is now twenty-seven and has the intelligence and tastes of a child of four or five years, plays with a doll. She has no sentiment of modesty, cannot learn, and scarcely counts to twenty. Her physical organization participated in the mental derangement. Her height is only three feet, her head elongated and flattened, the tongue thick, the nose flat, mouth large, lips thick. Second dentition commenced only at eighteen and is not yet completed. The mammary glands are only rudimentary, she does not menstruate and evinces no sexual sensation.

(XI., p. 650.)   Maudsley records a somewhat similar case of a girl who developed normally to three and a half years, after which no growth took place until eighteen and a half years old, her bodily and mental condition being that of a child of three and a half years.   At four she increased a little more in size, then remained unchanged the rest of her life.   (*Pathol. of Mind*, p. 180.)

To how low a state the discordinate powers in the born idiot may be reduced we may observe in the two following cases as given by E. G. Howe, of Massachusetts:—" E. J., aged eight years, is in form and outline like a human being, but in nothing else.   Understanding he has none, and his only sense is that which leads him to contract the muscles of his throat and swallow food when it is put into his mouth.   He cannot chew his victuals, he cannot stand erect, he cannot even roll over when laid upon a rug, he cannot direct his hands enough to brush the flies off his face. He has no language, none whatever; he cannot even make known his hunger except by uneasy motions of his body. His habits of body are those of an infant just born. He makes a noise like that of a very sick and feeble baby, not crying.   There is no nervous energy, nothing to brace the muscles, no more power of contractility than in a person who is dead drunk.   The involuntary muscular motions are properly performed, the organic life goes on regular, the heart contracts and dilates, the peristaltic motions of the bowels is regular."   (*Jour. Psychol. Med.* II. p. 370.)

In another case reported by the same intelligent educator of the imbecile:—"The boy has no muscular contractility, he cannot stand, nor sit upright, nor even turn over if laid upon his stomach, he paws and kicks until turned over on his back, which position he likes best.   He has no language, but seems to understand some simple sentences.   He can feel flies on his face and brush them off.   His habits are those of an infant."   (*Ibid*. XI. p. 371.)

Of the physical discordinations in genetous idiots, Ireland says:—"The most common are hernia, wad-shaped fingers, one or two toes of abnormal shortness in each foot, squinting, rolling of the eyes, fissures of the iris, strange shape of the ears, clubfoot, the testicles occasionally wanting, hair on pubis scanty." (*On Idiocy*, p. 51.) These are also often accompanied with dwarfish stature and irregular proportioned members. In all these physical abnormalities, as well as in the mental referred to, we seem to observe a total failing in the amount of the organic energy out of which the organism was constructed. This capital fund to sustain the organic vitality is variously disposed of, here it is expended in a co-ordinate scale, the organism being in all its parts generally reduced; in another individual the organic faculties are fully matured, the mental only being dwarfed; whilst with others certain bodily members or mental powers are supplied inefficiently, and they only show the discordinate conditions, fingers are webbed, toes shortened, feet clubbed, some physical sense fails, intellect is deficient, or wanting, moral sentiments not manifest. Often this deficient co-ordination is represented in the susceptibility to organic and mental disease, to perturbed functions, growth instead of being continuous and the organic evolutions in timal order are irregular, the being evolves by fits and starts, and sometimes certain faculties and powers are never evolved. Lastly, the entity deficient in nervous energy, and unable to recruit the staple power, is prone to rapidly degenerate, age may come on at the usual period of adolescence or at the normal period of maturity, and death from senility ensue long ere the normal average of life is attained.

The new co-ordinations effected in the organism at the several periods denoted by the alterations in the generative powers, as at puberty in females, at childbirth during the organic changes, and at cessation of the generative power in both sexes, are marked by the exposition of morbid

symptoms. The subject is treated of in all expositions of
the forms of insanity. In 235 cases of dementia Esquirol
found fifteen due to disorders at menstruation, and thirty-
five by derangement at the critical age. A writer in the
American *Journal of Insanity* says :—" In nearly one-fourth
of all the cases of insanity occurring in both sexes, the
disturbance of the generative organs was so marked as to
be regarded as the primary cause of the mental derangement. Whether the primary cause in these cases had its
seat in the cerebral or the generative system is a question
no less interesting than difficult of solution, and whether
the preliminary link in the chain of morbid sympathies had
its seat in one system or the other, it is none the less
important in relation to the reciprocal influence of the
two." (XII. p. 306.) The same publication also says :—
" In the female in gestation by the peculiar change wrought
in the female economy, and the train of inexplicable nervous
symptoms which result, give rise to insanity, and there are
cases on record of females who have been positively insane
during the whole of each period of uterogestation, but who
have recovered their mental health and strength soon after
delivery. The cases in which some slight mental or moral
disturbance during gestation has been observed are
numerous. Of the menstrual period, intelligent females
have said that they then possessed far less control over the
moral feelings than at other times, and were more excited.
In some the whole character changed during the menstrual
period, and from being cheerful, kind, firm, patient, and
decided, they have become morose, taciturn, wayward,
fidgety, impatient, and nervously irritable." (*Ibid.* XII.
p. 307.)

Of the moral disorganizations that ensue during the
evolution of the sexual powers, Hammond gives many
painful descriptions. The feminine moral nature becomes
wholly perverted : affection, kindliness, the sense of duty, of
obligation, of reverence, of purity and chastity, are wholly

lost. Though educated under the most refined and moral influences, they exhibit a coarseness of manner and language, and an immorality of ideas that shock all. They become filthy and obscene, strip themselves naked, and blush at no abuse, and all this betimes passes away, and body and mind are restored to the natural modest purity, solely by the natural secretion being normally restored. (*Insanity*, pp. 480-490.)

These are often the extreme results accruing from the physical disorganization, but the mental deteriorations are far more common, and affect both sexes. The new bodily conditions, the organic excitement, and the consciousness of new sensations often unhinge the moral self-control, destroy the natural delicacy of sentiment, and excite the mind and passions to habits of self-abuse, which, in their fearful reaction on the co-ordinate powers in the organism, deteriorate the physical powers, and degrade alike the intellectual faculties and the moral sentiments; the perverted manhood and womanhood passing away in atrophy of the bodily faculties, and dementia in the mental powers.

On the new co-ordinations effected at the several changes in the organism we have referred. Other organic faculties participate in the new process of integration, which have no special affinity with the organic parts in transition or the new sentiments evolved. Joseph Adams refers to the case of the Lecomptes, who saw clearly until sixteen or eighteen years of age, when some, without any apparent cause, became dim-sighted, and grew gradually more so, till all became dark. Such had been the case with a certain number for three generations; and those who passed safely through that period retained their sight through life. In Mr. Bass's family, at Peterborough, the defect of hearing was manifested, in the same manner, at the same age. He also instances cases in families in which the tendency to elephantiasis, hydrocephalus, and angina pectoris was in like manner manifested in several of the family at puberty, and who if they passed the critical age escaped altogether the disease. He, in like manner, refers to the susceptibility to madness occurring at the period of catamenia, pregnancy, and the cessation of the generative functional activity. (*Heredit. Dis.* pp. 19-23.)

Prichard says the predisposition to various diseases shows itself in particular families at certain periods of age. Thus, phthisis may appear in many or all the children of the same parents at the seventeenth or eighteeth year; in other families at a more advanced age; so with epilepsy. (*Nerv. Dise.* p. 97.)

Dr. Savage classified the mental derangements severally occurring at the transition periods in human organic life into those of infancy as idiocy and imbecility; those of childhood, as mania, melancholia and moral perversion; those of adolescence, as sexuality, phthisis, mania, melancholia, and hypochondriasis; those of maturity, as mania, melancholia, dementia and paralysis from excess; of the climacteric, as delusions, persistent hallucinations, hypochondriasis, and visceral derangements; and those of age, as mania, melancholia and dementia. (*Insanity*, p. 11.)

Morbid discordinating influences not only affect the after development of the individual by stoppage of growth, by the loss of faculties and functions, they affect the normal stability of the organism. To fully describe them is beyond our purpose; they may affect every faculty and power—the vascular, the digestive, respiratory, and generative functions, as well as the nervous co-ordinations.

In the capacity to acquire new habits, mental and bodily, both by men and animals, we trace the origin of all the varied forms and powers characteristic of animated beings. Without the self-contained power to grapple with various conditions, and through the mind-impulses bring the organization into accordant harmony with surrounding conditions, the possibilities of life had been limited to the primary elements. But from the period of its first origination to the present day, not only have races been modified, but individuals also have been modified; variety is the one great and universal law of nature, and as no man is in all respects ever like another man, so like essential distinctions of form and character give a personal individuality to every organism.

This mental organic law, as old as the hills, now dominates all vitality, and the myriads of beings every hour of the day and night commencing the heritage of life, are marked with the same distinct characteristics as the manifold generations of the past. Nor are these distinctions merely genetic; from birth to death surrounding conditions, internal as well as external, mould the supple and plastic entity according to the sum of their differences, and as the result of the many interactions, more and more varied conditions of being, more and more diversified forms of existences, higher and higher manifestations of mental force, have induced the mighty series of organic structures, the vast range of perceptive and reflective powers that now distinguish living beings.

We know by the structural relics of past ages that this law of change has ever dominated on the earth, and we can feel and record its changes in our own personalities, and behold it ever working at the present day among our fellows and in every form of life inhabiting the common earth.

Of the nature of this persistent universal principle we have now to enquire; trace its mode of action, and the special means of influencing mind and body alike, whatever their state in development, whatever the form or attributes they present, that is thereby evolved. Primarily it will be necessary to remember that variety, not uniformity, is the law of being, and that species only exist through the laws of association limiting the range of individuals. So while, on the one hand, we meet with natural and human selection limiting and defining organic and mental characteristics, these guiding principles are themselves ever in antagonistic relations to the universal tendency to variation.

It appears as if this vast and influential law of variation has not impressed itself fully on the minds of those investigating the nature of living organisms, therefore we cannot be surprised that general humanity has somewhat overlooked its importance. Formerly the whole tenor of science was to look for affinities, and the general idea was satisfied to associate animal forms through the crudest resemblances, and even now the popular mind dwells most on real or assumed family resemblances, affinities of status or place, and is indifferent to the general range of divergent characters. Charles Darwin while dwelling most fully on adaptive variations in his numerous writings, could not but express the important part that variability played in the differences of beings, and the little attention that had as yet been bestowed on them. He says :—" I am convinced that the most experienced naturalist would be surprised at the number of the cases of variability even in important parts of structure which he could collect on good authority. It should be remembered that systematists are far from pleased at finding variability in important characters, and that there are not many men who will laboriously examine internal and important organs and compare them in many specimens of the same species. It would never have been expected that the branching of the main nerves close to the great central ganglion of an insect would have been variable in the same species, it might have been thought that changes of this nature could have been effected only by slow degrees, yet quite recently Mr. Lubbock has shown a degree of variability in these main nerves in Coccus, which may almost be compared to the irregular branching of the stem of a tree. This same philosophical naturalist has also quite recently shown that the muscles in the larvæ of certain insects are very far from uniform." (*Origin of Species*, p. 47.) Charles Darwin himself did not fully appreciate the nature of these organic variations, he saw in them the result of circumstances, modifications by conditioning, heredity rather than an universal law controlling and modifying organization.

We know that personally if we take note of the expression, form, features, modes of volition, nature of mental and even unconscious activities of the various individuals now or who ever have been present to our consciousness, that we never have found the same characteristics ever blended in two individuals, and if it were possible to trace the emotions influencing them, modified as they are by social acquired aptitudes, or with the scientific anatomist compare the various organic functions and parts, we should find that those nearest approaching in affinity would be both mentally and structurally widely divergent.

To describe individual isolated cases of structural variations in men would only tend to multiply references. We will content ourselves on this part of the subject by specifying the important variations in all parts described in *Meckel's General Anatomy*, and refer for their conformation to the deductions of Mr. John Wood, the eminent Demonstrator of Anatomy at King's College. Thus, to commence with the osseous structure, M. Meckel notes the following variations :—Deficiency of vertebræ and parts of vertebræ, the change of one vertebræ into another, deficiency of a rib. Abnormal ribs arrested in development at the mammalian, bird, and reptile stages. The occipital bone in several pieces arrested in the reptile and fish stages. In the arm, deficiency of bones, as the humerus absent. In the hand, rudimentary, defective, and superfluous fingers. In the leg, patella bone wanting in father and son. (*Holland's Medical Notes*, p. 33.) Of muscular variations M. Meckel specifies a considerable number ; some revert to ape, mammalia, fish and bird forms, others are wholly absent or take new characters. There are extra muscles on the arm and hand, and a tendency for the muscles of the phalanges to double. In some cases the hand takes the muscular character of the foot. Various important muscles are betimes wholly absent, thus the diaphragm is deficient, the quadratus femoris absent, the sartorius absent, and the pyramidalis absent.

We may more readily denote the class and range of muscular variations by denoting the deductions that Mr. J. Wood was led to make from his extensive investigations on the muscles, which are contained in the *Proceedings of the Royal Society*. In one session he dissected thirty-two subjects, and in these Mr. Wood found one hundred and thirty-two variations of the muscles, not mere trivial distinctions but of importance, and implying absence, bifurcation, alteration of character, of insertion and notable departures from the ordinary type. Again, in another session in dissecting thirty-four subjects he found no less than two hundred and ninety-five abnormalities, giving an average of over nine specific modifications in each individual, and from this important fact we may judge how wide must be the range of muscular alterations. Like M. Meckel, he found many of these reversions to forms permanent or characteristic of the same parts in apes, bats, pachyderms, and ruminants. One individual had no less than sixteen muscular abnormalities, twelve of which were in the arm ; another had nine muscular abnormalities in the arm. He also found that some muscles were specially liable to variations, thus the lumbricales were irregular in nearly half the number of subjects. (*Pro. Roy. Soc.* XV. p. 529.)

Dr. Macalister in an important article in the *Transactions of the Royal Irish Academy*, V. p. 25, describes an extensive catalogue of anomalies in human anatomy, as the absence of ordinary muscles, the doubling of muscles, new muscles being evolved to work new co-ordinations, enlarged muscles and undeveloped muscles. Also slips of muscles going in other than normal directions, others manifesting abnormal insertions, sometimes accessory slips are split into four parts, sometimes partial severance of a muscle occurs.

Under new conditions new muscles are developed. Thus in the case of a double thumb, an undescribed muscle passed from the metacarpal bone of the proper thumb to the basal phalanx of the supernumerary digit. (*Ibid*. XXV. p. 99.)

As illustrating the range of variations, Dr. Macalister observes that Prof. Turner of Edinburgh has given an analysis of fifty specimens of the unions of the flexor tendons in the foot, and he found that no two were alike. (*Ibid*. XXV. p. 120.) As typifying the variations, we quote the following:—" Flexor brevis digitorum has been seen with (1) absence of the little toe tendon with no substitutes. 2. Its place supplied by a small fusiform muscle. 3. The substitute arising by two fusiform bellies. 4. A slip of perforans for the middle toe. 5. A long slip of the perforans tendon joined the flexor brevis. 6. The same from the accessories. 7. The muscle has been seen with only three tendons. 8. With five tendons. 9. The little toe tendon not perforate. 10. Or lost in the interior fascia of the toe. 11. The little toe short flexor has risen from the long flexor tendon. 12. It has been found separate, and arising with one head from the external intermuscular septum and from the flexor accessorius. (*Ibid*. XXV. p. 128.)

We cannot but pause to note the nature of these special variations. Thus, one class are mere reversions to lower evolutionary types, another are exaltations both in number of members and the nature of their aptitudes, and the origin of these we may justly refer for their primary source to mental influence. All are familiar with the fact that the ordinary appliances of the hand and arm by men were very limited in distinct activities among savage men, and that every great social advance has extended the range of special muscular movements. Machinery, tools, musical instruments, often of a complicated character, call for innumerable new co-ordinations or special movements of the muscles. Now these are primary mental concepts before they are acquired as muscular activities, and their origination is mental, not organic. As the result of the greatly varied movements thus made special in the arms and hands we should expect that those local muscles would manifest the greatest tendency to variation, and accordingly we find that the more varied use of the arms and hands have induced the greater number and most important muscular variations in those members. On this subject Mr. Wood observes that "notable departures from the ordinary type of muscular structures run in definite grooves or directions, which must be taken to indicate some unknown factor." (*Ibid*. XV. p. 242.) Can it be that these many new departures in the forms of the muscles of the arm and hand indicate, may we say, a new variety in human, mental, and structural attributes ?—We might supplement this observation by noting that as new ideas tend to create new muscular forms, so the degradation of parts follows the decreased mental activities used in their adaptations. All are familiar with the many hand-like flexibilities of the toes among savage races, and even among the lower class Hindoos and Negroes, while the higher races less variously using their feet, and generally encasing them in non-pliable boots, lose even the general volitional flexibility of the toes ; as a necessary result it is found that structural variations in the foot are degeneracies. Thus the *lumbricales pedes* are apt to be absent. (*Ibid*. XV. p. 538.) And in seven subjects Mr. Wood found that the tendon of the little toe was absent, and in six out of seven on both sides. In most no substitute for the missing tendon was found. Meckel has marked the frequent deficiency of this tendon in the human foot. (*Ibid*. XV. p. 538.)

Other important structural variations in man affect the heart by arrested development, the arteries vary in position, in size, they double, they pass through different vertebræ,

they vary in number, volume, and branch ; in some cases
they take the character of the lower animals, so in like
manner the veins vary. (*Meckel, Gen. Anat.* I. pp. 393-519.)
The nervous system likewise varies. The brain is deficient,
it is modified in every possible way; so is the spinal cord.
The bilateral nerves are irregular and the cerebral nerves
differ in volume, form, and origin. (*Meckel*, II. pp. 88-136.)
On the variations in the nature and power, and even forms
of the organs of sense, we need not enlarge ; they are familiar
to the ordinary observation. So, in like manner, the
digestive, respiratory, and reproductive systems manifest
a wide range of variations.

This great law of variation is present to us in two aspects :
in one it represents degeneracy, reversion, the falling back
into pre-existent types, in the other it denotes exaltation,
an advance to new mental concepts, new structural conformations. In its normal activity the law of heredity tends
to continue the same mental and structural types from generation to generation, and, as a necessary sequence, disease and
malformation act upon the same lines, and if the individual
or race cannot sustain itself at the proper standard it falls
back by reversion to previous organic stages, conforming as
much as possible to the mental and structural aptitudes of its
normal station. Not so the power of variability, it tends to
mental exaltation in every direction, and the bodily parts
bend and grow and change in the direction the will leads ;
the impulse may be from within due to the individual exaltation in special mind-powers, it may arise from circumstances
of a physical nature or from outward mental influences, but
whatever its inciting cause, it is free to extend in every
direction. We are conscious that through the vast geological periods it not only passed upward and higher, raising the
type of animality, like a many-storyed tower, to higher and
higher affinities with its spiritual heaven, but it cast out
lateral branches in many directions, each ever progressing

to more varied mental and structural results, until we had
the vast range of vitality now present on the globe.

Thus while the law of variability throws out of gear
and, as it were, dissipates the organic and mental primary
affinities, the law of heredity by drawing them into
special inter-relations brings them again into unison. More,
the two principles are to vitality what the centrifugal and
centripetal powers are to the universe of matter. Of the
primary nature of variability we have not yet to enquire, we
are but tracing the element that induces habit, and to do so
it is necessary to show that the organism has in itself the
power of change, and that this law of variation arising the
mental forces create new habits which react on and modify
the structure, and thus evolve new definite instincts.

We have seen that the law of variability is strongly
marked in the structure of man and that if we set up an
hypothetical organic model it would be difficult, perhaps
impossible, to find one human organism, wholly true to the
type. Now is the same law of structural variation equally
true of other forms of life as of men. Meckel in his *Manual
of General Anatomy* says :—"The organs of man do not
present a single anomaly which is not similar to what is seen
in animals " (p. 80). Vasey on *The Ox Tribe*, shows that
the various species of the genus Bos vary not only in the
number of the vertebræ they possess, but in their arrangement; thus the dorsal are sometimes thirteen, at others
fourteen, the lumbar either five or six, the sacral either
four or five, the caudal vary from twelve to twenty-one. In
like manner he shows that the periods of gestation vary
from nine to twelve months (p. 152). C. Darwin has
collected the records of variations in the breed of dogs.
De Blainville has given deviations in the number of the
teeth, and has shown that it is not always the same tooth
which is supernumerary. The Turkish dog is very deficient
in its teeth, sometimes having none except one molar on

each side. The appearance of the permanent teeth differ
in different dogs; thus the mastiff assumes its adult teeth in
four or five months, whilst in the spaniel the period is
sometimes more than seven or eight months. The ears
vary in size, and with their greater development the
muscles become atrophied. The caudal vertebræ vary, and
the mammæ vary from seven to ten. Dogs have properly
five toes in front and four behind, but a fifth toe is sometimes added, and F. Cuvier says when a fifth toe is present
a fourth cuneiform bone is developed, and in this case sometimes the great cuneiform is raised and gives to its inner
side a large articular surface to the astragalus, so that the
relative connection of the bones, the most constant of all
characters, varies. The skulls of dogs, according to Cuvier,
differ more than do those of the species of any natural
genus. (*Varia. Anim. &c.* I. pp. 34-36.) Of the horse the
same writer has collected instances of individual variations.
Thus there are sometimes eight permanent incisors instead
of six. Male horses alone properly have canines, but they
are occasionally found in the mare. The number of ribs is
properly eighteen, but Mr. Youatt has not unfrequently
found nineteen on each side. There are several notices of
variations in the bones of the leg, this we should expect
from the various mental aptitudes inducing diverse paces.
Mr. Price speaks of an additional bone in the hock, and of
certain abnormal appearances between the tibia and astragalus. Horses sometimes possess a trapezium and a rudi-
ment of a fifth metacarpal bone, a reversion to the foot of
the hipparion. Horn-like projections sometimes occur on
the horse; these have occurred on individual animals and in
various countries, varying in length from two to four inches.
Mr. Waterton records of individually evolved varieties, the
instance of a mare which had successively three foals without tails. In Paraguay horses are occasionally born with
hair like that on the head of a negro; this modification of
structure extends to the manes and tails, and even the

hoofs have a peculiar shape like those of the mule. Reference in regard to variation in the horse may also be made to the tendency to become striped, probably a reversionary character. (*Ibid.* I. p. 50, &c.)

The modifications induced in the pig are many and important ; the whole of the exterior of the skull in all its parts has been altered, the orbits have a different shape, the auditory meatus has a different direction and shape, the incisors in the upper and lower jaw do not touch, the canines of the upper jaw stand in front of those of the lower jaw. Some of these changes have been shown by Malthusius to result from altered habits in procuring food, structure accommodating itself to mental aptitudes. Pigs also vary in the period of gestation, in the number and place of the vertebræ, in the structure of the feet, in the number of the toes, in the possession of jaw appendages, in striping, and in the texture of the hair. (*Ibid.* I. p. 71, &c.)

We might quote other like variations in domesticated animals arranged by C. Darwin, but in general they refer to racial conformations, though in some instances we have the records of individual variations ; thus (*Ibid.* I. p. 120) he refers to an extra lumbar vertebra occurring in two distinct races of rabbits, and to various individual variations in vertebral forms in rabbits, in variations in the teeth, &c. Of fowls, Mr. Darwin says all the bones of the skeleton showed great variability, except those of the extremities. (*Ibid.* I. p. 268.)

We have to remember that the general purport of Mr. Darwin's writings was not to exhibit the heterogeneous individual variations, they are only mentioned incidentally. In his writings his object was to show how some of these peculiarities by natural and human selection evolved into races, and thence inferred a like origin of species. When we consider that formerly any deviations in the human structure were treated with indifference, or not observed until they became extreme, and were then considered as

monstrosities, we cannot be surprised that the after discovery by anatomists of an infinite variety of human
structural differences excited some astonishment ; but even
as yet few have followed Mr. Wood's systematic enquiry
into the nature of the structural changes, and that of the
whole series of anatomical enquiries into the structure of
the lower animals we have so few comparative details in
reference to members of the same species. Such researches
have in general been physiological. What we want are
in each case, whether of man or the lower animals, to
institute a typical standard, and then each case to be
referred by comparison to its type, and the deviations
recorded. More, we want to attain some concept of internal
and external influence, to have the conditions of the life of
the being attached to the description of its variations, that
we might separate the accidental from those that are
congenital; and more, trace the growth of the changes
where new habits have tended to produce special forms.
We want special investigations, like those of Mr. Wood,
on the miscellaneous town people dying in a London
hospital, carried on upon those who have lived under many
varying habits of life, as special savage races of hunters,
of tree climbers, those frequenting the sea, agricultural
races, and any class of specialist workers with hands, arms,
feet and the general body; so of the various races of
domestic and wild animals, not merely to discover affinities,
but especially to discover anomalies, and, where possible,
define any mental influences, self-generated or externally
applied, that tended to influence the process of structural
conformation. We have seen that Sir John Lubbock
found even the ganglion of a bee to exhibit an important
variation. Like enquiries in the whole series of animated
beings would tend much to illustrate both structural and
mental origins.

Observations made on man without intentional research
have shown innumerable cases of individual variation, even

in the most important internal parts; they have been found not only varied in conformation but displaced, even so far as to be situated on the opposite side of the body. Every pathologist knows how varied are the symptoms among his patients; every accoucheur is acquainted with the structural differences that affect his operations; even the effects of re-agents affect in every possible way individuals. We have not only general differences common to many, and special differences only manifested in the individual, we have timal differences only observable under special conditions, and varying with climate, habit, food and association. In like manner, the medical practitioner becomes acquainted with the vast differences that temperament, the emotions, customary usances, food, and habits have on his patients, so that in no case are the conditions he has to treat identical.

So when we individually note the characteristics of those we associate with we are often startled with the wide divergencies of character that they present, the differences in their perceptive powers, and their capacities of doing. One man cannot observe the differences in objects and conceptions that are immediately self-evident to others. Nor are these differences limited to the perceptive powers. There is not an intelligent, moral, æsthetical or devotional power but has the same tendency to vary in its nature, energy or attributes. There is every shade and grade in the power of reasoning, in the mode in which deductions are brought about, and in their nature; and these, too, have a special character dependent on the individual. So with all imaginative conceptions, all applications of wit and humour, all processes of moral discrimination. Some men appear to delight in torture, and, like Tippoo Saib, make music out of the groans of a man torn to pieces by a tiger, whilst others, like Las Cases and a Howard, make the whole purpose of their lives to alleviate the sufferings of other individuals. With some the sense of right pre-

dominates; they could not wrong, ill-use or take advantage
of another, whatever the inducement or opportunity; but
other men luxuriate in having outwitted their fellows—they
must steal, even if the article be useless to them; they
delight in chicanery; they must ever manœuvre, earn,
cheat, act the hypocrite, lie, and deceive all with whom
they have dealings.

The religious propensity is as varied as the moral powers.
One man feels the presence of the Deity in everything, it
modulates his thoughts and actions, and mellows and bathes
his feelings in a halo of reverence, while others would
spurn the presence of such sentiments, they care nothing
for saint or martyr, they feel no veneration for temple or
godhead.

Need we point out how the pursuits of men differ not only
as men from habit, but as boys. One is up with the lark
and away to the field or woodland to duty or natural taste,
whilst his mate sleeps on until the unwelcome bell rouses
him. One is all joke, fun and frolic, observing every incongruous act or expression, making humour of the commonplace, and puns and laughter out of every incident; whilst
others, sedate and self-contained, wonder at or despise the
littlenesses that fill his soul with merriment. Here one is
prim and methodical, whilst another is as wild and shaggy
as an unkempt bear.

The shades of differences in character form a fertile field
for illustration to the novelist. The motives that influence
men are diverse, their actions are diverse. Men have
become poets, orators and statesmen without knowing how;
words of beauty have come from their lips, harmonies of
sound have penetrated their ears. The capacity to execute
form in the flat or in the solid is attempted by them, and it
is done almost as instinctively as the bird builds its nest,
the bee forms its cell. Tact and administrative power come
without tuition, circumstances call for the display of special
faculties, and a Cromwell, a Napoleon, a Washington is found

naturally prepared. He may be like Masaniello, a fisher-
man, like Spartacus, a slave.

From what source can we deduce these multiform varieties
of power, character, and organization ? If we mix two or
more chemical ingredients under like conditions beforehand,
we can predicate the result, define its nature, and affirm the
qualities. We may do this as often as we please and the
different results will be in co-ordinate harmony. But who
can predicate the form, mental character, æsthetic attributes
and moral disposition of the new-born babe. We know
that under the law of heredity it may have its father's eyes,
its mother's mouth, it may be brown-haired like one parent,
large-boned like the other. It may follow its father's
character in business prudence, its mother's in childish
petulance. Even in trivial things it may exhibit its hereditary affinities, in odd hairs, in high cheek bones, thick lips
and special gait and movements. Even the ancestral
blood may endow it with ancestral diseases and sundry
specialities once manifested by distant progenitors. There
is not a characteristic bodily or mental faculty of any
predecessor in blood that it may not possess. It may
be all that oxygen and hydrogen are associate in any
atomic proportion, but it may be varied in any and every
direction which the result of their combination never can
be.

In the young child, or the grown man or woman you may
see an eye, a nose, a set of features that you seek for in
vain in any of its ancestors. Not in any agnate can you
detect that indomitableness of will, that firmness of spirit
manifested in their descendant. We may say the ancestral
roll is incomplete, and we may through reversion carry
bodily and mental types, carry variations to diverse animal
forms, yet we may become conscious that the child or man
has one or more special phenomena of character, may be of
organization, that could not have been derived from any
preceding source. We may become conscious that it knows

what no man heretofore knew, can do what no man had hitherto done, that it can create ideas that were never created before.

If we were told that oxygen and hydrogen in certain relations after having for ages produced by combination only water, had now in a similar combination resulted in becoming the metal mercury, we could not be more surprised than we ought to be when informed that after ages of peasants a Giotto was born, that village rustics gave a Shakspere to the world, or that petty Corsica had sent a master among mankind.

In considering the origin of mind variations, we may well ask whence came the soul of poetry, in what alembic was the spirit of music evolved, who fashioned in the human brain the first concept of beauty, who enunciated the idea of law, who first conceived of moral right? These abstractions once were not, and we are assured these and ten thousand other forms of thought had their origin in a single human mind, and are due to the exaltations of the intellect manifested under the law of variation by diverse men.

Had heredity alone prevailed and variation only ensued from surrounding conditioning, then Lully had ended his days among the adjuncts of the scullery, and Metastasio continued a macaroni dealer. Nay, it matters not what impedients may be in the way of the aspiring intellect, it makes its own circumstances. A mere collier, James Brindley, became the architect of mills, the constructor of canals. George Stephenson, seemingly destined to lounge over a sheep farm and only be familiar with a collie, taught us alike the power of steam and the power of a self-confident will. So all the substantial entities of our time, like the great discoveries of the past, owe their conception to individual men. The creating mind differentiates the new power out of the mysteries of its own soul, out of the variation of mind-power it originally possesses.

We have seen that variations in the individual are

infinite, and that for one that becomes a fixture thousands pass away. So it was and is structurally in the evolution of form, so it still is in the evolution of mind. Has not Charles Darwin shown us how these forms of variability pass away and are forgotten, and how only a few under favourable natural conditions or special human selection, grow into habits and become, through the law of heredity, confirmed structural characters and special mental idiosyncrasies.

The various modifying principles arose under several inducing causes. Thus structural variations may be due to the exalted nature of the primary impulse in the individual, inducing mental habits in special directions, and to whose continuity of manifestation the organic structure accommodates its forms of growth. Local not mental influences betimes draw the mental activities in special directions, they may affect the nature and due supply of food, personal security, modes of life and social adjuncts; some structural changes are due to accidental circumstances, natural phenomena, the influence of individual wills, incidences that affected the organism before birth or during the period of growth, and thus altering its structural conditioning reacted on the mental forces with special influence. The mental variations which primarily distinguish one individual from another, and which may or may not have a marked action on the structural organization, arise distinct and special in the organization of the individual mind; by exaltation in special directions they pass outside the influence of heredity itself, but assume forms of development, which may be stayed at any stage in the individual evolution and become the source of higher manifestations, and without whose special activities higher forms and natures had not been possible. Other mental variations of a less marked but important character are due to the influence of other men to, social conditions, and the nature of the local circumstances that affect the individual's existence.

The character of the variation is distinguished from the ordinary general evolution by the tendency it induces in the individual to repeat its special manifestations, until they grow into the very nature of its being in the form of personal individual habits.

We now propose in the following chapters more fully to define the general forms of co-ordinate variability, and those that mark the large series of failures in co-ordination.

CHAPTER II.

Variations in the co-ordinating powers, Mental and Physical,
resulting from Transference.

ONE of the most remarkable phenomena that affect the
nature and character of the co-ordinate organism is that
expressed by the term Transference. It expresses a class of
phenomena almost unknown to the metaphysical school of
philosophers, and one that never called for their special
attention. We may look in vain in scientific manuals and
text books for its exposition, and yet we hold it represents
a class of influences which materially tend to elucidate, not
only the nature of the mental forces, but their relations
with the organic functions. The only individuals who as
yet have ventilated the subject are those popularly known
as the "mad doctors," many of whom, from their intimate
relations with patients who manifested its most striking
attributes, could not fail to observe and recognize the
remarkable changes that their varying habits, sentiments
and forms of thought expressed.

Dr. Prichard was one of the first to speak in general
terms on the subject, and since his day most writers on
Insanity have recorded some of the variations of character
and sentiments it denotes, more especially the singular

illustrations that were betimes presented to them of the metamorphosis, as it were, of one kind of mental or physical morbid state into another.

Our first purpose is to note and classify the many forms of change, and then to endeavour to discover the relations these have with the general co-ordinating organic powers, and at the same time enquire into the influence they have on the exposition of the nature of the mental forces.

The forms of Transference, that the instances we will quote display are, firstly, the transfer of one form of morbid bodily condition into another. Thus a disease of the brain is converted into a disease of the stomach, so that the morbid symptoms are transferred from the head to the digestive faculties; in another case, mania of an exalted kind, arising in the cerebrum, or a fever of the blood, pass away and the disorganizing symptoms become manifest only by gout in the toe. The second class of co-ordinate changes are those in which physical disorders are converted into mental, or mental into physical. That is, morbid symptoms of a mental character only, pass away and in their place we observe some form of organic disintegration; and *vice versa*, organic disease heals in some remarkable manner, while at the same time it is accompanied with some mental idiosyncrasy. In our third class the change is simply the conversion of one mental characteristic into another.

The Transference of physical conditions.—Dr. Prichard says:—"Persons who have partially recovered from a recent apoplexy are often assailed by convulsions which display most of the phenomena of epilepsy, and fits of the genuine epileptic character frequently occur after an attack of hemiplegia. On the other hand, victims to repeated fits of epilepsy perish under all the symptoms of apoplexy, and others who recover from a severe fit, or from frequently repeated fits of epilepsy, are often found to labour under hemiplegia, or other modifications of palsy. Sometimes persons who have suffered under epilepsy lose this disease

and become permanently paralytic. (*Prichard, Diseases of the Nervous System*, p. 59.) The same writer also observes:—
" One kidney performs the secretion of urine when the other has become obstructed or otherwise diseased." (*Ibid.* p. 12.) Apoplexy and hemiplegia betray an affinity to mania. Maniacs are very subject to expire suddenly under an attack of apoplexy; in other cases, after a violent paroxysm of delirium, the patient is found to have lost the power of voluntary motion on one side. Paralytics are subject to various appearances of impaired intellect, as fatuity or imbecility, but maniacal delirium is by no means a rare occurrence under similar circumstances. In very severe and inveterate cases of epilepsy the paroxysms of this disease are often followed by attacks of maniacal delirium. (*Ibid.* p. 62.) Hysteria is a disease which in turn puts on the form of almost every individual distemper of this class. Sometimes it causes an apoplexy which terminates in hemiplegia. Sometimes it causes terrible convulsions, very much like the epilepsy. (*Ibid.* p. 65.)

Other cases are quoted of Transference by Dr. Prichard. Thus, "An old woman subject to ulcers in her legs for many years has been cured, and then becomes troubled with an affection of the head." (*Ibid.* p. 217.) Another like case resulting in epilepsy. (*Ibid.* p. 218.) A case of "Delirium, the result of the *translation* of erysipelas." (*Ibid.* p. 219.)

Forbes Winslow records several instances of the transference of organic disintegrations of various kinds; as idiocy in a child up to thirteen years of age being cured by a fall from a height, on his head. A man suffered from a paralysis of memory following a severe blow on the head. He was fortunate enough to have a repetition of the physical injury, and as the effect of this accident, his memory was immediately restored to its original strength. Petrarch records that Pope Clement VI. found his memory wonderfully strengthened after receiving a slight concussion of the brain. Father Mabillon is said to have been in his younger days an idiot, continuing in this condition until the age of twenty-six. He then fell with his head against a stone staircase and fractured his skull. He was trepanned. After recovering from the effects of the operation and the injury, his intellect fully developed itself. He is said to have exhibited subsequently to the accident a mind endowed with a lively imagination, an amazing memory, and a zeal for study rarely equalled. (*Obscure Dis.* p. 370.)

Esquirol quotes an instance of remarkable physical transference. "A young girl brought into convulsions by the horrid conduct of her father, after taking several drugs had varied and peculiar physical changes. She was successively blind, deaf, and dumb, and incapable of walking or swallowing. This state persisted sometimes for hours, at others for a day, and even two days in succession. Sometimes her tongue projected two inches from her mouth and was tumefied. At others the patient could not swallow, whatever efforts she might make. In one instance she passed several days without taking anything. I have seen her fall at full length upon the floor, now upon her back, now upon her face. I have seen her turn round and round for an hour without it being possible to prevent her. She had a blister on the left leg, and when she became blind, or deaf, or mute, or incapable of motion, the application of a single drop of vinegar upon the blistered surface, suddenly restored her sight, hearing, speech, or power of motion." (*Insanity*, p. 259.)

Of special transferences by heredity we have already quoted instances. Dr. Maudsley says insanity in any form in the parent may be represented in the offspring, either by a similar affection, by sensory disorders, by epilepsy, by hysteria, or by the vague and undefined weakness or perversions of judgment, capacity, or will, which we call unsoundness of mind. Dr. Elam, in a *Physician's Problems*, remarks that the offspring of the confirmed drunkard, rich or poor, will inherit either the original vice, or some of its protean transformations (p. 88).

Dr. Carpenter gives the case of two first cousins possessing a strong family idiosyncrasy, but no definite taint, having married, four children were born, each of which was distinguished by some marked defect of organization or perversion of function, one being deaf and dumb, another scrofulous, a third idiotic, and the fourth epileptic. (*Human Physiol.* p. 905.)

We may form some concept of the nature of these forms of transfer from the following illustrations of the specialities that follow in the ordinary course of the transfer of diseases, from the *Proceedings of the Royal Society.*

" It has long been known, and it is now a well established fact, that various eruptive fevers and blood diseases from which the mother may suffer, can be communicated to the fœtus in utero. There is evidence also that a disease may be transmitted to the fœtus through the mother, who is herself insusceptible to contagion, as in the case of a child having been born covered with smallpox eruption, the mother being quite free from it."

"A healthy woman pregnant by a syphilitic man, may give birth to a syphilitic child, and still remain healthy herself. Syphilis has been found incapable of communication to the lower animals."

" Anthrax. The fœtus of a rabbit in utero may be impregnated with the anthrax bacillus, but neither the mother or any after embryo rabbits, gave any evidence of the bacillus. The mother subsequently inoculated with the blood of an animal dead of the anthrax, and swarming with bacillus, does not succumb, but is found to have received protection—even eight months later the same animal re-inoculated with anthrax blood, was proved to be still protected." (XLV. p. 152.)

Referring to the physical changes in the human organism induced by mental derangement, Esquirol observes that " the vital forces acquire an exaltation which permits them to resist influences most calculated to affect the health, but this exaltation is not so general as is commonly believed.

Some insane persons experience an internal heat so intense, that they throw themselves into water and even amid ice, or refuse all clothing at the coldest season of the year. With others the muscular system acquires an energy the more formidable as force is united to audacity, and their delirium renders them indifferent to danger. We have seen madmen pass many days without food or drink, and preserve all their muscular energy. Maniacs and monomaniacs do not sleep; insomnia continues for several months. If they sleep they have the nightmare, with frightful dreams, and are awoke by surprise. Some are troubled with a constipation which persists for eight to twenty-one days. Some retain their urine for from twenty-four to one hundred and twenty hours, while others pass them involuntarily. All the secretions acquire a penetrating odour, impregnating the clothing and furniture, which nothing can remove. The vital propensities are also changed, the physical and moral sensibility—the faculty of comparing and associating ideas, the memory and the will, the moral affections, and the functions of organic life, are all more or less impaired." (*Insanity*, p. 27.)

Nervous energy, that is, the power of doing or vital force, depends first on the supply of food taken; and, secondly, on the muscles and nerves, as well as all the general faculties having their due periods of repose. Under normal conditions each organism is sustained with suitable food, and recuperative sleep recoups the energy lost in the daily occupations. Hence the balance of the vital force is sustained, and the individual being presents a certain average amount of physical power to withstand differences in temperature and other climated conditions on physical energy, in the capacity to fast, and in every inter-action of his bodily organization. But this co-ordinate harmony altogether fails under mental disorganizations. Every treatise on insanity notes the extraordinary muscular sense of maniacs, their remarkable powers of endurance of

cold or heat, of want of food and drink, of repose and
sleep. A slender girl has taken four powerful men to
restrain her, and men and women have in mania abstained
so long from food, that it would have been death to have
done so in the normal state. So with sleep; we know how
deleterious is the loss of one night's sleep to the energy of
the individual, but Forbes Winslow mentions the case of
" a deranged person who was not known to have closed his
eyes in sleep for the period of three months; he was in
the habit of walking long distances, greatly excited during
the day, and at night he never ceased talking to imaginary
persons." Dr. Wigan had a patient who did not sleep for
fifteen days. He was in the habit of getting up in the
night and tiring three horses with galloping, in the vain
hope that excessive muscular fatigue might induce a disposition to sleep. In another case, "a patient rarely closed
her eyes in sleep for ten consecutive minutes for nearly a
year." (*Obscure Disea.* p. 496.) Equally opposed to the
possibilities of life under abnormal conditions are the
instances in which the insane have endured privations and
exposures of all possible kinds. Wintry blasts, cold water
and ice seem to have no effect upon them ; they rarely are
frost-bitten, and endure personal exposure to cold and wet
such as would rapidly break down the constitution under
ordinary conditions. So wounds and bruises, broken ribs
and dislocations heal, or are healed, without their apparently
enduring much, if any, discomfort therefrom. Hence we
conclude that in the discordinate physical and mental status
the vital energy has other characteristics than under normal
conditions, and that thereby the nature of the various
mental and physical powers are altered, the disorganization in the mind is transferred to the organic parts so as
materially to affect all their physical attributes.

Of the nature of the mental and organic activities and
affinities we as yet know but little. Dr. Prichard found
that in many cases the brain had undergone injuries and

apparent disorganizations altogether surprising, and yet during life the sentient power and the mental faculties in general appeared to have sustained no material injury. (*Dis. Nerv. Syst.* p. 11.)

We know that the general opinion is that " at the present day we are in possession of a sufficient number of positive facts to render it certain that there is, and can be, no intelligence without brain substance; that when brain substance exists in a normal condition, intellectual phenomena are manifested with a vigour proportionate to the amount of matter existing; that destruction of brain substance produces loss of intellectual power; and, finally, that exercise of the intellectual faculties involves a physiological destruction of nervous substance necessitating regeneration by nutrition here as in other tissues in the living organism. Mind is produced by brain substance, and intellectual force can be produced only by the transmutation of a certain amount of matter." (*Flint, Physiol. of Man,* IV. p. 326.)

These sweeping generalisms partake too much of the dogmatism of the schools that once accounted for all mental phenomena by the transmission of animal spirits, the vibrations of the particles of the brain or the motions of a nervous fluid. That most of the propositions are the general deductions of all observers does not suffice to account for those many instances of observations that do not agree therewith. Thus while it is true that the mass and quality of brain stuff imply corresponding mental powers, and that waste of brain stuff is synonymous with mental loss, yet there are many cases in which foreign substances have been lodged in the substance of the brain, in which the matter of the brain has become very extensively decomposed, or in which by accident, suppuration, or other circumstance there has been great loss of matter both from the hemispheres and cerebellum without any corresponding deterioration or loss of mental power. We say the impressions received by the senses are conveyed to the brain, and yet there are many cases recorded of destruction, waste, and deterioration of its substance, even to a great part being lost, many instances of which are recorded in the *Edinburgh Review*, XXIV. p. 447.

Even Dr. Flint found it judicious to insert some saving clauses in his positive deductions. He says :—"Experiments clearly show that the brain is less important as regards the ordinary manifestations of animal life in proportion as its relative development is smaller. If we remove the cerebral hemispheres in fishes or reptiles, the movements which we call voluntary may be but little affected, while if the same mutilation be performed on birds or some of the mammalia, the diminished power of voluntary motion is much more marked." (*Phy.* IV. p. 329.)

Again, Flourons found that the complete removal of the cerebral hemispheres in living animals did not take away the general sensibility, though, as he conceived, they were deprived thereby of the special senses of sight, hearing, smell, and taste. This, however, as Dr. Flint says, was afterwards found to be erroneous ; both sight and hearing were retained after the extirpation of the hemispheres. (*Ibid.* IV. p. 331.)

The fact is, our knowledge of the point of impact of the mental and physical forces in the organism is but little, if at all, in advance of the facts known to Dr. Abercrombie. He very judiciously withheld himself from making any assumptions thereon, observing :—"We do not know whether impressions made upon the nervous fabric connected with the organs of sense are conveyed to the brain or whether the mind perceives them directly as they are made upon the organs of sense." (*Intell. Pow.* p. 54.)

We may never know what the co-ordinating principle in the organism is, and yet we may classify and arrange all the phenomena connected therewith ; and the more fully we multiply and arrange the facts bearing thereon, the nearer and truer will be the deductions that will be present in our minds. The doctrine of transference introduces a new class of phenomena to us as intimating the nature of the relations of body and mind. **By** transference, as we have seen, **the** active energy present in any **portion of** the organism may be transferred, whether normal **or morbid, to another** part or faculty **of the** organism; and, as **we shall show,** the **nature of** the physical faculties and **the** mental attributes are so in affinity that the special state of an **organic** part may be transferred to any impulse or emotion **or to** the general perception or judgment; and more, that any possible variation of one mental force may be transmitted to another. These phenomena we shall now illustrate by various instances.

First, we have to observe that any break in **the** harmonious relations of the co-ordinate mental and physical **parts,** as well as any great disintegration, **is** marked **in the organic** world by the same phenomena **of** deranged relations as **in** the material world. Storms and tempests and violent disruptions mark the one series until the forces re-balance in the new co-ordination. So is it in human eruptions. There are physical inflammations and mental inflammations, depressions and exaltations. Dr. A. Morison says :—"The delirium of mania is evinced by confusion and incoherence, succeeding each other with morbid rapidity and without **connection.** The perceptions are erroneous and frequently accompanied with violent passions, **as contempt,** suspicion, **anger,** and **hatred ; the** attention **cannot be** fixed, **the** memory is confused, and consciousness of existence seems lost, the imagination is excited, the judgment is erroneous, and the efforts of volition are vague and **unsteady.** There is an irresistible inclination to motion, **the muscular** power **is** frequently increased, and there is a strong disposition to act from the impulse of the moment." (*Cases of Mental Diseases,* p. 11.) Other both physical and mental **phenomena** mark the transition stage, some of which **the cases** quoted indicate.

Dr. Falconer mentions the case of a gentleman who had such a morbid state of sensation that cold bodies felt to him as if they were intensely hot. A gentleman, mentioned by Dr. Conolly, when recovering from measles saw objects diminished to the smallest imaginable size. Another, mentioned by Larry, saw men as giants, and all objects magnified in a most remarkable manner. A similar enlargement of objects was noted in a gentleman when recovering from typhus fever. (*Aber. Int. Pow.* p. 60.)

There are many absolute physical transferences perpetually going on in our organism; an excitement of a nerve on the right side is being continuously transmitted to the left. One eye or one ear does duty for the other. When Sir Isaac Newton produced a spectrum of the sun by looking at it with the right eye, the left being covered, upon uncovering the left and looking upon a white ground, a spectrum of the sun was seen with it also, which must have been transferred from the other eye.

The transference of the mental value of one sense to another is a common occurrence on the loss of any special sense. Dr. Abercrombie says :—" Blind persons acquire a wonderful delicacy of touch, in some cases, it is said, to the extent of distinguishing colours. Mr. Sanderson, the blind mathematician, could distinguish by his hand in a series of medals the true from the counterfeit with a more unerring discrimination than the eye of professed *virtuosi*; and when he was present at the astronomical observations in the garden of his college, he was accustomed to perceive every cloud which passed over the sun." (*Int. Powers*, p. 50.) Dr. Moyse, the blind philosopher, could distinguish a black dress on his friends by the smell. An individual, according to Mr. Boyle, distinguished black by touch, as having the greatest asperity, and blue the least. Dr. Abercrombie had known several instances of persons affected with that extreme degree of deafness which occurs in the deaf and dumb, who had a peculiar susceptibility to particular

sounds by an impression of touch or simple sensation.
They could tell of the approach of a carriage in a street
without seeing it before it was taken notice of by persons
who had the use of all their senses. (*Ibid.* p. 51.)

Dr. Carpenter, observing on the transfer of sense-power,
says that Laura Bridgman unhesitatingly recognized her
brother by the feel of his hand. He had repeatedly seen
hypnotised patients write with the most perfect regularity,
when an opaque screen was interposed between their eyes
and the paper, the lines being equidistant and parallel, and
the words at a regular distance from each other. He has
seen an algebraical problem thus worked out with a neatness
which could not have been exceeded in the waking state.
(*Mental Phys.* p. 143.)

Dr. Abercrombie refers some of these sense impressions
thus corrected to habit. He says habit regulates the
perception by the two eyes as a co-ordinate object, habit
converts the impression received by any number of nerve
points on the hands through the means of the ten fingers
co-ordinately, and if we alter the form of co-ordination we
fail to receive a true impression of the object, as in crossing
the fingers and then rolling a pea between them. But it
surely was not the effect of habit that enabled Sir I. Newton
on the first attempt to convey the impression of the spectrum
from one eye to the other. We may, by habit, correct a
false impression, as in the case of the pea, and ascribe it to
its true nature, but not habit, but actual transference of
power only explains the transmission of one sense-power to
another, one nerve action to another, one emotion to another,
one form of sympathy to another.

That a physical form of the common energy can be
transferred to mental expression and *vice versa*, we have
innumerable evidences. It may be an exalted or depressed
characteristic, it may be a morbid state, it may occur in
disease, in sleep, in somnambulism, it may take place in the
individual direct or be transferred by heredity while in the

embryo stage to other physical or mental powers diverse from the status of the parent.

The mental manifestations may be changed by altered though normal physical conditions. Esquirol says a lady had several attacks of insanity, and each attack ceased as soon as the patient became lean in flesh. The intermission continues two years, then she increases in size, and when she seems to have obtained the maximum of health, delirium suddenly bursts forth, is prolonged for months, and its intensity lessens only when emaciation begins, it ceases when she becomes very lean." He also cites another like case. (*Insanity*, p. 57.)

Dendy (*Philos. of Mystery*, p. 78) gives the case of a domestic servant who lapsed into complete idiocy. Some time after she fell into typhus fever, and as this progressed there was a real development of mental power. At that stage, when delirium lighted up the mind of others, she was rational because the excitement merely brought up the nervous energy to the proper point. As the fever abated, however, she sank into her ideopathy, and this continued till she died."

Mauchart (*Feuchtersleben Medic. Psychol.* p. 237) speaks of a girl who, when young, had the smallpox most severely, by which she lost her sight, but acquired an extraordinary memory, she repeated perfectly on her return home a sermon which she had heard during her journey.

Mental disorganization may be transferred to physical forms of disorganization. Savage gives the case of a gentleman insane having all sorts of hallucinations, attempting suicide, refusing food, believing he was to be vivisected, that detectives were watching for him, and other delusions; one morning he told the doctor that he had got the gout, and was all right in his mind. (*Insanity*, p. 434.) A similar case is given by Dr. Wigan (*Duality of Mind*, p. 78) of a gentleman whose friends proposed confining him in an asylum, a delay was allowed for the night, in the morning it was found that his great toe had swelled to an enormous size, all his delusions had vanished, and his reasoning powers had become extraordinarily acute.

Even dementia may be only a condition depending on transference of the common energy. "The child of an eccentric father was so weak in mind that his education was all but given up. He was never expected to be more than an imbecile, and about fourteen years of age was utterly uneducated. Then for the first time he had fits of an epileptic nature, and from that time he developed at first slowly and then more rapidly in mental and bodily power, till at eighteen he had attained a good education, and lost his fits. He gained an open scholarship, and is now a promising student at one of the Universities." (*Brain*, IX. p. 454.)

As illustrative of the transfer of physical conditions to mental in the normal state, we quote the following from the *Journal of Science*. A gentleman was making a pedestrian tour along with two friends in a beautiful but thinly peopled country. They crossed a mountain ridge at a wrong point, and entered a region perfectly destitute, where for at least thirty-six hours no food was procurable. They were not only hungry, but the most prominent point noted, was the alteration which want made in their dispositions. The one theme of conversation was vicious recrimination. As the second day wore on we all began to see or fancy nonexistent objects, which vanished or took other shapes when we drew near. (VII. p. 59.)

Dr. Wigan says:—"I knew the wife of a clergyman in Lincolnshire, a woman of a very excitable and nervous temperament, who during the hot paroxysms of ague was always preposterously and ridiculously insane. An hour afterwards when the sweating stage came on she recovered the entire possession of her faculties." (*Duality of Mind*, p. 134.) An interesting case of transfer is recorded by Dr. Rush. A farmer's daughter in the low stage of typhus fever, and rapidly sinking, was aroused from the depressure of her present state to healthy mental concepts of a pleasing kind by the visit of one who had been a companion of her girlhood, and who roused her latent energy by his presence and the simple phrase "the eagle's nest." Thus reviving the pleasing memories of her early life, and under the new stimulus she recovered.

In the many various forms of altered powers of men we have the more common effects of the transfer of physical conditions to mental. The physical failure, whatever its nature, may be converted into the following changes in the powers of memory. There may be a total loss of the languages, words, and even memories of the later life of the individual, and a simple return to the knowledge of early youth or childhood, or there may be a loss of the early forms, and retention only of the later acquired forms of speech and memories. There may be without other change a revival of early ideas, knowledge and words. There may be a loss of the memories of a certain period, may be that of certain days, months and years, or of all personal reminiscences during a certain period of excitement or depression. There may be present alternate states in the same individual, represented by disease, or sleep, or somnambulism, in which the memory recalls only the incidents of a like state, and is wholly unconscious of all that occurs in the intermediate periods. There may be only a temporary loss and then recovery of the knowledge of all or only special incidents, or there may be the total loss of all acquired knowledge of persons, things and events. The defections of memory may be limited in some cases to names and nouns only, in others simply to misapplying words, in some to loss of names only when spoken, but conscious of them when written, in others to the loss of the power of words, both spoken and written. Of these various forms of mental deterioration as due to the transfer of physical conditions we will quote a few cases.

Thus Abercrombie gives the case of a lady he attended

on account of injury from a fall from a horse. During
the first week she was in a perfect stupor, she then gradually
revived, so as to be sensible to external impressions, and after
some time to recognize friends, but ever after she had no
memory of the visits and incidents that occurred before her
perfect recovery. (*Intel. Powers*, p. 137.) In a case of pro-
tracted fever in the delirium stage, there occurred intervals,
often of several hours' duration, when the patient was quite
sensible. Of this period he remembered no persons, no
passing of time, no distinction of day and night, no sleeping
or waking, or hearing, seeing, smelling, or tasting anything,
only the impression of a long, dull, horrible, indescribable
dream, during which he was sensible to external objects.
(*Ibid.* p. 138.)

Of recoveries of memory, Abercrombie gives several
cases, as of a Frenchman who lost the language of his
boyhood for many years, but recovered it through an injury
to his head. A lady speaking in the dialect of Brittany in
her delirium, a language she had derived from a nurse girl,
and never heard or spoken since she was a child. A German
woman who forgot her husband's language, which she had
alone used for many years, and spake in her childhood's
German. A woman from the Highlands, the same in her
illness, spake only in Gaelic. Dr. Rush gives the case of an
Italian in a fever, as it progressed he spake at first in
English, as that passed from his mind, in French, and in the
delirium, in Italian only, the language of his childhood.
(*Ibid.* p. 142.)

Of memory remaining in abeyance we quote the following:—
A boy at the age of four years had a fracture of the skull,
for which he underwent the operation of trepan. After
recovery he retained no recollection of the accident or the
operation, but when fifteen years old in a fever he described
the operation, the persons present, the colour of their clothes,
and other minute particulars. In another, a gentleman in a
slight delirium sang Gaelic songs with precision. In his

ordinary state he had no turn for music, and though he had in his youth known some Gaelic it was supposed that he had entirely forgotten it. (*Ibid.* p. 143.)

Cases of altered feelings and the loss of word impressions are very frequent in both mental and bodily diseases. Patients lose all particular regard for their relations, or towards those persons to whom previously they had been the most affectionately attached; they even manifest a decided hatred and antipathy towards them. In other instances the temper has been so much altered in consequence of some diseased condition of the body, that persons formerly of the most happy and cheerful dispositions have become habitually sullen and morose, others extremely irascible and easily excited into paroxysms of rage. (*Prichard, Dis. Ner. Sys.* p. 36.)

One of the most remarkable cases of mental transfer is that of Mr. Simon Browne, who from being in a state of religious excitation desisted from his ministerial duties, inferring that he had fallen under the sensible displeasure of God, who had caused his rational soul to perish and left him only an animal life in common with the brute. That therefore it was improper for him to pray. In a work of his on the *Religion of Nature*, he describes himself as once a man, and by the immediate hand of an avenging God his very thinking substance has for more than seven years been continually wasting away, till it is wholly perished out of him, if it has not utterly come to nothing. None, no, not the least remembrance of its very ruins remains, not the shadow of an idea is left, nor any sense. (*Gentleman's Mag.* 1762, p. 454.)

A similar case is recorded in the *American Journal of Insanity*. A patient said :—" The Lord has abandoned me. He has taken from me my immortal soul and made my body immortal, incapable of pleasure, and sensible only to pain. I now only have the brain just as a dog or elephant has a brain." (III. p. 232.)

The necessary result of the concept of the withdrawal of the soul is to induce the doctrine of Metempsychosis, when the soul is absent from the body the spirit of any other man or being may take possession of it and control its actions.

A patient at York Retreat gave this description of herself:—I have no soul. I have neither heart, liver, nor lungs, nor anything at all in my body, nor a drop of blood in my veins. My bones are all burnt to a cinder. I have no brain, and my head is sometimes as hard as iron and sometimes as soft as pudding. (*Bucknill and Tuke, Phy. Med.* p. 201.) Benvenuto Cellini records the case of the governor of a castle every year having different hallucinations. At one time he conceived himself metamorphosed into a pitcher of oil; another time he thought himself a frog; in a third state he fancied himself a bat, and used gestures with his hands and feet as if going to fly. (*Ibid.* p. 200.)

Dr. Morison records the case of a woman who says she has lost all the feelings of a human being, and resembles a brute. Another of a woman in fear of being burnt or tortured begging to be changed into a quadruped. Another who conceives that a Kaffir got into his body when he was at the Cape of Good Hope, and is still there, the author of all his troubles. A man of fifty had the fixed idea that a cloud had fallen upon his head, and is still there, abusing his mind and altering his feelings to his wife and family. (*Mental Diseas.* p. 82, &c.)

Dr. Adriani, of Perugia, cited a number of cases where recovery from insanity supervened upon typhoid fever; in one, an idiot of eighteen years, who had never uttered any word but mama, after an attack of typhoid fever from being of a sad disposition, became gay, and he learnt to express his ideas in various ways—to sing songs and to keep in mind the names of things and persons. (*Brain*, I. p. 397.)

Every variety of weakmindedness, Dr. Savage says, may

bo the result of apoplexy. I have known a man who was
a fluent speaker recover with an ability to write and to
understand as well as ever, but with inability to express
himself with freedom of speech. Probably emotional insta-
bility is the most common result of apoplexy, the person
becoming loquacious, irritable, and tearful. A patient
who was formerly quiet and reserved is now talkative and
communicative. (*Insan.* p. 355.)

Chronic alcoholism may be slowly replaced by some
moral perversion, so that an apparently good wife who has
been a secret drinker may take to hate her children and
maltreat her husband and servants. (*Ibid.* p. 425.)

Esquirol says, as the result of melancholia, the character,
affections, habits, and mode of life change. He who was
prodigal is now avaricious; the warrior is timid and even
pusillanimous; the laborious man no longer wishes to
labour; libertines with grief reproach themselves and
repent; he who was the least exacting cries out treachery;
all are diffident and suspicious. (*Insanity*, p. 209.)

Regarding the transference of the normal character
through disease, Dr. Savage says:—"I have known a man
come into an asylum with a history of good conduct and
strictly moral behaviour. He has had a short, sharp
attack of mania, followed by a slight period of depression,
but from that time, although sent from the asylum as
having recovered, he has been an entirely changed man,
and instead of being sober and moral, has now become
intemperate and vicious. I have seen at least a dozen cases
in which the patients have become kleptomaniacs after an
attack of insanity, and they will act with the utmost
deliberation and with apparent power of calculation and
combination to effect their purpose." (*Insan.* p. 271.)

Nor is the change always to lower mental characteristics,
to lower moral states. The same writer says:—"I have
known a husband come, years after his wife has been
discharged recovered from an attack of insanity, and say

that not only has his wife remained well since her attack, but has been a changed woman, being more amiable and self-sacrificing than she was before. This is no single instance, but represents the change I am referring to, to a moral change, a change in temper and disposition succeeding an attack of insanity." (*Savage, Insanity*, p. 271.)

Nor is it only under abnormal influences that the character, habits, tastes, and moral sentiments of men and women change. We know that such changes are continually occurring to individual members of families ; they cease to keep the same associates, evince the same desires and pursuits, to think and express the same sentiments as heretofore ; the chaste become lascivious, the morally just pecuniously dishonest or far-reaching, the mild and forbearing irascible and domineering. It seems as though the very being is changed, and the eyes of affection, with trepidation, note that with the growth of coarser forms of expression there are evolved coarser lines in the features —the physical organization taking its new tone from the influence of the altered mental impulses. It would seem that the co-ordinate affinities constituting the individual which had so long travelled in one direction had now diverged in a lateral course, and had assumed other co-ordinate conditions—in fact, denoting other types of personality.

Nor is it only under great morbid changes, or in the process of growth, that alterations of character may supervene. All are familiar with the fact—many of us by our own experiences—that in the hallucinations occurring in sleep, the natural moral character of the dreamer is, for the time at least, altered. In the few minutes that may have intervened between the moral wakeful state and the dream illusion, the mind of the sleeper may pass from the type of moral rectitude and active benevolent energy to that of an erotic kleptomaniac, or lower still, to the impulsive state of a barbarian or savage, even to the expression of mere animal appetites. More, the phenomena that mark these lower types pass equally rapidly away, leaving the awakened dreamer morally aghast with the tenor of illusive sentiments and actions retained in his memory.

As in dreams, so in somnambulism. The moral character may, in a like manner, have changed, and the individual commit acts repugnant to his wakeful nature.

Lastly, we have to refer to the changes induced in the hypnotic and other like mental states, the transference of mental impressions, the sense of special flavours, thought transference, and the transference of ideas and even mental pictures.

The claims asserted under mesmeric phenomena were popularly expressed by Dr. Mayo many years ago. The greater part of the powers assumed, we have seen, may be generally expressed by individuals in morbid conditions; but now, no more than in Dr. Mayo's time, can they be affirmed as claiming any scientific expression ; more, whatever truth they may contain, but illustrate the same phenomena of transference on which we are now treating.

The points affirmed by Dr. Mayo are—1. That in many cases of waking-trance the patient does not see with his eyes, hear with his ears, nor taste with his tongue, and the sense of touch appears to have deserted his skin. At the same time the patient sees, hears, and tastes things applied to the pit of the stomach, or sees and hears with the back of the head and the tips of the fingers. 2. In imperfect mesmeric trance-waking, sensuous impressions then appear to have entirely deserted his own body, and to be in relation with the sentient apparatus in the mesmeriser's frame. 3. The entranced person displays no will of his own, but his voluntary muscles execute the gestures which his mesmeriser is making, even when standing behind his back. 4. If the trance faculties continue to be developed the entranced person enters into communication with the entire mind of his mesmeriser. His apprehension seems to

penetrate the brain of the latter and is capable of reading
all his thoughts. 5. In the last steps the apprehension of
the entranced person appears to have left his own being
and to have entered into relation with the mind or nervous
system of another person. 6. In the last state the
entranced person displays the power of revealing future
events. (*Truths of Popul. Supersti.* p. 165, &c.)

It will be noted that the varied phenomena we have here
presented of transference intimate the possibility of any
co-ordination of the faculties possessed by a human personality being possible, and that in every form of expression
some powers fail to combine and must be outside the personality, even though continuing in the organism when they
relatively have only the status of the free leucocytes in the
organism. Such facts demonstrate that every power,
faculty, and part in the individual expresses distinct sub-
personalities.

CHAPTER III.

Variations through growth in the Human Personality.

THE human organism begins its personality as sarcode, it develops an inclosing membrane, it aggregates by cellular division, asexual at first but sexual by fecundation, when it becomes a binary compound representative sexually of one of its binary predecessors. In physical growth it is the typical exponent of their many stages of evolution, and these, as Dr. Weismann beautifully explained, though they make their appearance in the last stage of the ontogeny, are by the successive introduction of other typical characteristics thrown more and more forward in succeeding developments, that though at first only expressed in the mature stage, they become ultimately thrust forward to the foetal stage. Thus it happens that the typical stages of not only the invertebrates, but those representing many vertebrate orders, occur in the human organism in the foetal stage. The higher vertebrate types are expressed by the babe's first impulses, and it is some time before it attains the emotional activities of the monkey, and its subsequent advances express the states of savage childhood, barbaric childhood, and lastly, that of the childhood of the lower civilised races, each of these being in accordance with the higher evolved status the babe inherits. So whether we apply the organic law of growth as expounded by Dr. Weismann to the position of the markings on the segments of caterpillars or extend them to the mental affinities as evolved in humanity, every such advance throws all preceding differentiations into the earlier stage in the ontological life of the organism. No doubt the same law marked the differentiation of the cell as now marks the differentiation of the man.

As Dr. Weismann says, the development begins in a state of simplicity and advances gradually to one of complexity. New characters first make their appearance in the last stage of the ontogeny. Such characters then become gradually carried back to the earlier ontogenetic states displacing the older characters until they disappear. (*Studies in the Theory of Des.* p. 274.)

The fœtal stage.—The early periods of the human fœtal life are representative of but not similar to the fully matured forms of the lower classes of organisms. The influence of the law we have just quoted has materially tended to limit the expression of the earlier typical characteristics. The later developed types push out and reduce the expressive natures of the early forms. Thus the notochord whose evolution dates long after the presence of special sense powers were known and succeeded the ascidian type, yet in the human fœtus its plan is laid down when the yolk sac is differentiated.

As in all animate forms we begin with vital energy in sarcode. This develops the simple cell, and that process is followed by the series of differentiations that produce the mulberry group of evolved cells. Then gradually the vital germ contained in the many celled organism separates from the co-ordinating elements associated with it. These become its nurse-parent and associate nutritive function, acting as intermediary between the vital germ and the mother organism, whose organic function is to protect and support the fœtal stage of the vital germ, and the latter retains the store of nutriment, the first is the allantois, the last the yolk sac.

The vital germ, at first but a single cell, increases by segmentation, and divides into a group of cells the germs of members and functions, at the same time it is elevated above the surface of the yolk sac, on which it is located. Then gradually by growth and contraction the germinal membrane is converted into an open sac-like structure in which the various functions that are afterwards to distinguish its physiological nature are differentiated from their elementary cells. The germinal membrane separates into two layers, an internal and an external. At an early period these parts, already manifesting the mammal type, have cilia, and we read of rotatory motion, analogous phenomena to those manifested by Protozoa, while in the open and simply aggregated arrangement of the unenclosed physiological functions we have a typical characteristic of the Siphonophore colony.

It has been said that the human embryo at one period resembled a radiate animal; at another a worm, then a fish, an amphibian, and lastly a typical mammal before defining the human form. Each class of vital organisms is projected on its own type, and when the type is hereditary, according to the law promulgated by Dr. Weismann, it is obvious that in every vertebrate advance the ontological type would advance a stage in the organic evolution, hence it follows that in the higher mammal organisms it would displace and crouch forward all anterior forms. Thus it happens that the radiating and segmenting characteristics of the earliest animate types are converted into the vertebrate plan, so the resemblance is transferred, not to the primary form, but the primary powers.

At the end of the first month of fœtal life the formative germs of the extremities become manifest, a cavity marks the future mouth, the trunk is open, and the viscera are severally attached members, and though no independent digestion has to be manifested for a long period the preliminary conformation of the parts has proceeded, and we have, as in Ctenophora, a continuous gastric tract with apertures at both extremities.

During the second month the intestine commences its series of convolutions in the presentation of the preliminary loop, ossification also commences, and the rudiments of the muscular system are evolved. Gradually the heart is covered in, the aortic arches are reduced in number, and the glandular viscera take their preliminary forms. Even as early as this period in the evolution of the organism, the organs of generation, so important and yet so long to continue latent, are projected, as also are the elementary organs of the special senses. Thus, though presenting but a crude plan of the after form, all the essential elements of the full organic powers are now detailed.

The after ante-birth period of the fœtal life is occupied in perfecting the various functions and parts, in including them in the protecting trunk, in developing the special senses, the extremities, and each and every distinct member and function of the organism. In the sixth month the fœtus manifests independent volition, such may breathe, but cannot sustain independent life; but one of the seventh month, with great care, may live. In the eighth month the testes reach the scrotum, and the type of the full organism is complete.

Of the progress of the fœtal mind we can have no knowledge, nor have we any records which illustrate the early exposition of the mental powers in a seven months' living child as distinct from those on record of a fully developed babe. The only mental expression antecedent to birth is that of personal volition, but of its nature and actuating force we have no knowledge. Our mental judgment of the mind of the babe at the period of birth are founded on the nature of its after manifestations.

Child Life.—Perception through general sensation may

have been present for a long period. That a seven months' child can live, implies that consciousness, though of a low grade and volition and general sensation, are then definite mental characteristics of the fœtal mind. Perez says that from the fourth month the nervous system begins to re-act and reveal the vitality of the different apparatus of which it is made up. That from this period the fœtus is sensitive to the action of cold, and that we can develop its spontaneous movements by applying a cold hand to the abdomen of the mother. It executes spontaneous movements to withdraw from pressure that constrains it and brings its sensibility into play. We may fairly assume that a long time before it is born a child will have become acquainted with pain and pleasure. It will have experienced a great number of lesser sensations, which must have had some sort of echo in its already formed consciousness. (*Preyer, First Three Years of Childhood*, pp. 1-7.)

Up to the moment of birth all the vital functions were carried on in the child as secondary to those of the nurse-mother. Its first instinctive impulse was evolved in the act of breathing, an impulse controlling the will, and which will cease only with life. Preyer says :—" As soon as its head comes in contact with the air, it pours in torrents down the delicate tissues of the respiratory organs, and the successive movements of pulmonary respiration are not affected without painful shocks." (*Ibid.* p. 7.) At the same time, its delicate skin is suddenly enveloped in an atmosphere which is icy cold compared to that which it has just left, and instead of the one common organic sensation, its un-defined special senses are "battered by repeated shocks of strange impressions." No wonder that the instinctive wailing cries become continuous, and it is not until habit reconciles it to the many new sensations, and the digestive sense of comfort induced by the instinct of suction, bathes the young being in its first slumber, and admits of the several co-ordinate functions through repose to recruit their wasted energy that the change is complete. Then the influence of habit becomes manifest, the repetitions of the same states are followed by the same results, until the young organism not only recognizes but expects the successional conditions. When this balance of the co-ordinate functions and powers is attained, then memory and attention direct the young consciousness to the use and influence of its special senses.

Born deaf and blind, we might esteem it as representing a lower organization than the Cephalopod, were it not that we know that the same law which regulated the principle of its co-ordination affirmed the period when each function and power should become manifest, and these expositions are never attained until in the normal subject the whole co-ordination is in harmony with their expression.

The newly born babe cries instinctively, thereby expressing its sense of discomfort, for as yet it knows not that it cries, as it is not capable of hearing, as the external ear is not yet open and there is no air in the middle ear. Gradually the sounds from externals become cognizant to its perceptive powers, may be indefinite and vague, and many impressions of such must have reached its auditorium before it learns to classify and localize them, distinguishing those of its own production from others and assigning them to their due places and causes. So it is with the sight, at first a mere blaze of discordant light impinging on the non-co-ordinate eyes, and creating a confused mass of impressions. By serial stages, out of the mass of discordant sensations, it gradually educes perceptive order, colour, form, distance, shades of light, order, and oneness of impression. Days and weeks are spent in these incipient mind-workings before the concept of general powers and general harmony is attained.

So with the manifestation of the will. Through volition some feeble efforts in this direction must have been apparent to its consciousness long before birth, but they were probably more reflex sensations than conscious co-ordinations, yet that at birth it had the mind to will and power to execute its volitions is immediately apparent in its many movements, partly reflex, partly voluntary, as screaming, kicking, yawning, stretching, sneezing, hiccoughing, and sucking, followed by vague incoherent movements of the arms, legs, and facial muscles, aimless striking right and left without any definite object. Preyer says there are no deliberate voluntary movements in the first three months after birth, then it gradually acquires a definite control over its muscles, moves them co-ordinately, and evinces imitative powers.

Dr. Maudsley, in a series of articles in the *Journal of Mental Science*, traces the growth of the mental powers of a child in their typical relations to the series of evolved mental powers in the various classes of animals. "There appears," he says, "to be a short period in the infant's early history—a moment as it were—in which not yet awakened up to a reaction with the world around, its existence may be described as sensational, when an impression on its limb produces only the feeling that of a body that is part of itself; when it may have the sensation of sound without any perception of an external cause of it. In this state it reflects the purely sensational life of a certain portion of the invertebrata. The sense of touch has apparently advanced to the recognition of a not self, even before sight and hearing exist at all. There are multitudes of animals which are not conscious of any sensation, and which correspond to the reflex activity in man, so there appear to be multitudes more which are conscious only of a sensation which feel the affections of their own organisms without any consciousness of an external cause, and which correspond to the sensational stage of early infancy. The next stage in the development of mind through the animal kingdom is that in which the animal appears to have a dull consciousness of something without it as causing the one or two sensations of which it is capable, but in which it nevertheless forgets the sensation the moment it is delivered therefrom, as is the case with the sucking babe and the Gasteropod." (*Jour. Men. Sci.* VII. p. 474.)

The evolutions of the mental powers are expressed not as principles, but as modes of impulse. The child evolves the character of its mental relations with its own organism and with the external world in the modes it manifests activity, and the special character of its first impulses. Primarily the special senses and the muscular sense occupy in their manifestations all of mind it can present, save those general emotions common to it and the animal world, as irritability, irascibility, the undefined sense of fear, the impulse of volition, crude and imperfect in its undeveloped organic powers. For a few days after birth it exhibits only the general characteristics of low animal life. Its first impulsive activities are all purely instinctive ; its movements are responsive to externals, its early sense activities are purely reflex, attention grows into action under the stimuli of sensuous impressions, then from merely reflex they become voluntary, and it questions the qualities and attributes of all things present to its consciousness.

The babe, like the animal, has the sense of fear first aroused through the ear. All animals depend more upon the ear than the eye for safety. In most of their cautious recumbent positions the eye is of but little service, and whether burrowing in the earth, hid in a cleft in the ravine, among the high grass, buried in foliage, scudding over the moor or on the open hill side, the pricked up ears evince how much more extensive are their powers than those of sight. The babe inherits this sense of fear by unexpected sounds startling the sentiment long before it can have any knowledge of their purport. Like the animal, the babe exhibits the same impulse of resistance, the same irascibility and savage struggles. Unable to discriminate between the outer and the inner it gives vent to the same modes of resistance, the same screams and struggles at any sense of internal discomfort, any bodily pain, as if attacked by a dominant foe.

The higher animal impulses and the lowest human propensities equally are presented in their due courses in the new impulses that are gradually unfolded in the child's mind.   There is a definite period in the babe's evolvement when it first exhibits mischievous, noisy, and destructive tendencies.   These characteristics, unknown to the lower mammalia, are first present in the often wanton destruction by the carnivora, but they are fully manifest in the highest animals, the Simia.   These, like young children, love to tease, worry, and annoy their playmates, a spice of cruelty is continually observed in the play of children, and, like monkeys, when the immediate present gratification of possession is satisfied, the child, no more than the Simia, has any concept of putting an object by for another day.   It is immediately pulled to pieces and scattered about or thrown irritably at its fellows.

The first, the instinctive stage of the babe's life, is thus illustrated by Perez :—" When after birth we see a little babe feeling after its mother's breast, and co-ordinating the movements of its mouth, head, and neck so as to suck in the milk ; when it combines the actions of the tongue, palate, and pharynx, which co-operate in the process of deglutition; when, a little later on, it presses its little fingers and fists against the breast in order to facilitate the passage of the milk ; when the combined and harmonious action of all these numerous organs produces respiration ; when the eyelids close if the conjunctiva be touched, or if too intense a light disturbs the retina, or a violent sound shocks the ear; when irritation of the face, ears, or tongue causes contraction of the muscles, &c., we know that neither experience nor reason have taught the little creature these movements, which are accomplished with a precision far superior to what we find in actions where the will intervenes." (*Perez*, p. 45.)   The same writer conceives that the animal instinct of fear gives obscure intimations before birth in the tremblings produced in the fœtus by any sudden terror in the mother. (*Ibid.* p. 62.) In like manner the active manifestation of the instinct of suction, he says, precedes birth, thus the chicken consumes the white of the egg, the child sucks up the water of the amnios, as do calves; and further, he says, it is an ascertained fact that calves lick themselves before birth, pieces of their own hair having been found in their stomach with the water of the amnios. Such being the case the sense of taste naturally becomes first expressed in the babe, and it is the first sense appealed to, and that which, in conjunction with the common muscular sense of warmth, first excites the sense of pleasure. From the first every object goes to the babe's mouth, and long after it can appreciate their nature by the other senses this is from habit appealed to, as with its toys, even though in the contact with the sense of taste they are found offensive.

In the second, the more advanced state of the child's mind, all the perceptive powers are in full activity, and all its waking volition is used up in again and again feeling, trying, sounding, and looking at each and all. Thus it comes to comprehend colour, rotundity, space, distance, and weight. So intense are these mental manifestations that the child can brook no stay to its interchange of perceptions, but wants every object the instant it perceives it, animal irritability is excited unless immediately gratified, but the irresolute will is no sooner attracted to another object than the first is either torn, or disfigured, or cast aside.

In early babyhood, taste is the most predominating sense, after that of sound becomes very marked. Young children, like young monkeys, love to make a noise, no matter how discordant, how harsh, how tumultuous—they shriek, they laugh, they halloo; even before they can stand they kick and beat with their hands their toys, or any object they can get possession of, and later they parade and stamp, and beat with sticks, and join in a wild chorus, and if they can produce any detonating sound they are more than pleased, they are exalted. In all this they present the peculiar phase, not only of the savage, but of the higher races of animals whose mental forces tend in the same direction. Houzeau says the love of making a noise is as common with monkeys as with children. The noise of the monkeys is produced intentionally; they will make a noise for the love of the noise, and as a means of amusing and exciting themselves. The black chimpanzees of Africa will assemble together as many as twenty to fifty, and amuse themselves not only with uttering shrieks, but by beating and thumping on dead wood with small sticks held in the hands and feet.

So the leading social characteristics of the child harmonise with those of the monkey. Wild rough play, tricks, mischief, the desire to do strange things, to break, tear, and destroy, are seen in both, often with a love of cruelty and indifference to the condition of its fellow. Children, as Maudsley says, like brutes, live in the present, their happiness or misery being dependent on the impressions made upon the senses; the idea or emotion excited does not remain in consciousness and call up other ideas and emotions, so modifying the sense of present pleasure or pain by memories of what had been felt before. (*Pathol. of Mind*, p. 265.)

By the time the child has acquired its full volitional and oral powers, the whole of its physical and mental co-ordinations have entered into general harmonious relations, the mere animal have in most cases been replaced by early human aptitudes. Speech, that grand faculty, soon elevates the child out of the limited range of capabilities and sympathies that denote the animal co-ordination. As Blandford says, by the time the child is three it manifests human as well as animal mental powers, he can convey ideas in speech, he can retain words and facts in his memory, he can reason, and in some measure estimate acts. The volition becomes bent on pleasurable emotion, both mental and bodily, it would run about and eat, its mobility will not allow it to passively take its food, it would run and eat, play with things and eat, and satisfy the perceptive, the volitional, the appetitive instincts at the same time. It cannot do anything long, it rapidly feels, and moves, and sees, laying down the object as soon as taken up, rolling, throwing, testing the nature of each. The handsomest, rarest toy is no better than a piece of broken crockery, a fragment of Berlin wool is as serviceable as a figured toy, each gratifies the mind for a short time, and is tested for its capabilities in every possible way. Out of each it learns something, acquires some definite idea, or through it throws off some false judgment. Hence it is ever feeling, eating, running, playing, shouting, and finding amusement, and, unconscious thereof, instruction in all things. These, more-over, form a background for all its emotions which rise into dramatic incident and change from comedy to tragedy, and back to comedy or indifference, alternately manifesting anger, fear, jealousy, hatred, love, wonder, pain, personal assumption, or bashful retirement.

Of the preliminary steps marking this great advance in the child's powers, Perez says :—"Towards the end of a year, when a child begins to be able to walk, its sphere of personal investigations becomes rapidly enlarged, and the additional . faculty of speech supplies its curiosity and wishes with the means of endless variety. All the observa-tions formerly made with the eyes are now made with the hands and mouth ; he darts hither and thither, crawls or toddles from one thing to another, opening things, breaking them, knocking them and mixing them. He pours his broth into his grandfather's watch, puts the gold fish into the doll's bed, and the doll into the water of the fish globe. In short, he commits a whole series of incon-gruities, and all from a desire to know what the things are, what can be done with them, and from the need of fresh sensations. A little later the mischievous tendencies become still more numerous. The child seems to be everywhere at once—in the kitchen, in the garden, in the drawing-room, with eyes and ears wide awake hearing and seeing everything, without seeming to do so; asking endless questions, and storing up in his memory all the most striking details." (*Perez*, p. 84.)

The advances we note in the child's mind at this period correspond with those mental features which distinguish the savage man from the higher members of the animal kingdom. These are in the relations of things, their common personal nature, their consciousness and amenability to the ordinary influences that affect itself and fellows. With the savage and the child every object as well as person is an independent actor; what it does or is done through it are questions of conduct; it has responsibility and is subject to penalties. The deodand was demanded of the stone on which a man fell and was killed, of the tree whose broken branch caused his death. The savage and the child immediately execute judgment on the unconscious floor, on the fetish that fails to protect. They suppose that the powers they are conscious of in themselves are common to all things; with them nothing dies, and any fragment contains the whole. Hence the broken horse, the headless doll, are cherished; the child sees no incongruity in talking to a battered and misshapen figure, or in putting the rag doll, without senses, limbs, or parts, comfortably to bed.

The child's imagination scarcely reaches to the fetish concept of the advanced savage; but it is as full of wonder as he is. He has no failure in belief, no conception of incongruous power or association. As it will place its toys anyhow, and accepts any quality that they seem to possess, so it will accept any tale that is told to it. The savage who accepts at once his medicine-man's assertion that he had climbed into the sky, is akin to the child who gives full credence to the adventures of Jack up the beanstalk; neither the one or other are conscious of the physical impossibilities of the feat. Herbert Spencer says of primitive men:—They accept what they see, as animals do. So it is with the child. What it sees has every attribute that it seems to possess. The doll lives and has the same living nature as itself: it can do wrong, and the doll equally does wrong. It knows nothing of the distinction between the spiritual and material; to it all things are material. What it knows of duty and doing are as much properties of its toys, of the chairs, floor, and tables, as of itself and companions. They are naughty, and as conscious of punishment as it is.

The affections of the child, like those of the savage, are transitory, its sympathies are continually on the change; and like with the savage, the dog or cat that it played with one minute is teased the next, or more cruelly treated. Like the lowest animals, the young babe knows no dissimulation—it has no cunning, no doubts; it never lies in act or impulse. Not so the child. As it grows and passes through the mental stages of the higher animals and savage men, deceit and the want of veracity grow in its nature. We cannot say that lying to the child is instinctive; yet, like the higher animals, it acts lies for security; and more, like the savage, it lies without a motive. To deceive in the interest of the ego, is the great object with all the higher animals, and the impulse has been continuous to the present social standard. The child presents a bold front, or uses dissimulation to abstract anything its appetite impels it to seek. They hide themselves to do what is forbidden, and they call it play or fun when detected helping themselves, or defiantly storm to assure possession. There is much of cunning in their play, and the child who hides its eyes, making believe it cannot see, fails to draw the distinction between a playful fib and a covetous lie. Amplification is the natural result of the exalted nature of its ideas. As it would have things so it esteems they are ; it cannot detail proportions, and without any moral intention in this case to deceive, it would have you estimate the object or narrative by its own magnified standard.

Perez says that all the egotistical feelings of a child, as we know is the case with the savage, conduce to lying. A child who has had some good thing to eat will say that he has not had it, or that he has had very little, in order that he may have some more given to him. Indifference will induce both lying and laziness. A child is given a book to take to his uncle, who is sitting in the garden. He reluctantly leaves his playthings, hesitates before starting, walks as slowly as he can, and when out of sight he drops the book into a bed of flowers, and runs back to his toys as if he had executed his commission.

In the history of lying we may advance from the secret cunning of the animal, the deceptions it practises, and the art manœuvres it executes, to the more mature active lie of the savage or his open-word falsity. In this respect he applies all the cunning in his nature, all the trickery of language, all the dubious qualities of words, all the bold effrontery of an impassive physiognomy to mislead. He will not answer a straight question, lest in doing so you should gain or he lose some advantage. He grows at last to love a lie for itself, and the more force in the deception the greater his estimation of his own cunning. Not a few parents can follow a like series of immoral growths in their children. Truthfulness is an acquired quality, it grew out of the consciousness that honesty is the best paymaster. Exaggeration may have been put down by the accuracy of scientific data, but trust and truth are commodities from out the dealer's wattle.

Property is an acquired characteristic; with some few animals it became an instinctive propensity, but there is ever present the contention between the individual claim and the common right. So the child, like the savage, wants everything it sees—no matter whether of use or not to it; and after holding it for a short time, it becomes indifferent thereof, or delights in pulling it to pieces. Possession soon palls on it, and a new object is sought.

Imitation begins in the child when instinct tends to become dormant. There is little imitation among the lower animals, one never copies another, and it is not until cunning is evolved that imitation is appealed to, first for security. In the savage state of humanity the impulse has passed beyond this phase, and the desire for new sensations, novel movements, set the stimulating faculties at work in mimicing movements, actions, objects, and sounds. The child attempts to do what it sees its elders do, and later on, like the savage, to mimic sounds and physiognomical expressions. Some forms of mimicry are sympathetic, by sympathy we feel the desire to eat when others are eating, so by sympathy we imitate actions and words. The impulse is manifest as soon as it can be profitable for use or pleasure both with the child and the savage.

Of the growth of the higher mental forces in the child, much has been written. On these we propose rather to treat of general results than trace the special exposition in individual children.

Attention is the reflex manifestation of the ego to outward stimuli, it induces the conscious state, rousing the ego from the cataleptic apathy of non-perception through vague impressions—which stimulate the latent energy, the working capital of the co-ordinate organism, and call up the as yet unexpressed powers to their primary manifestations. We speak of the mental qualities as powers, not that they represent distinct persons or forces, they are only the various phases of the reactions between the outward and the inward co-ordinate and inseparable. They all blend into each other, and the ego itself is but the sum of their effects. The personality of the babe begins with sensation, it advances to perception, the images through multiple impressions, unsought, uncalled for, excite attention, essentially an evolved habit, and the primary form out of which instinct was evolved. Memory itself is a habit evolved through the energy of attention, and through it the ego becomes conscious of ideas. All beyond is growth. The multiple images call into play the powers of distinguishing and discriminating, of observing similitudes and distinctions. From considering things present it passes to their relations with its remembrances, out of these evolve the vast range of simple and compound abstractions, the capacity to reason, the power to generalize, and the concept of the universal.

The babe manifests the faculty of attention first through the influence of its function of digestion. It sucks until the monotony of the sensation and the sense of comfort induces sleep, then it wakes, roused to attention by the stimuli of its sensations, and they call forth all the active energy of the young ego, exciting emotions pleasurable and painful, and these gradually bring into activity all the impulses inherent in its nature, which only require the due timal period of growth to manifest the enlarged nature of its mental capacities, as like physical phenomena define in due course its physical attributes.

The quality of attention is of a very low character at first in the babe's mind; as Perez says, it is not a continuous mental activity, but a series of attentive acts, which by habit become consecutive. The researches of Horace Grant and Edwin Chadwick have taught us that after five or six minutes in the case of infants, and from thirty to forty-five in the case of elder scholars, the attention becomes fatigued, and intellectual effort fails. (*Perez,* p. 117.) But what power the child ceases to express by continuity, it makes up in variety, the versatility of its attention is unbounded. It turns from one object to another, from using one faculty to applying another, eye, ear, hands, and legs rapidly alternate in their evolutions. It is a very savage in the quickness of its sensibilities; its limited powers are ever at attention.

Necessarily attention stimulates volition, but the will is developed out of the emotional impulses, they themselves being called into activity by the common and special sensations. At first the will is manifest through instinctive cries, by vague and incoherent movements in the arms, legs, and facial muscles. Gradually the young will learns to feel its powers, to gain by habit co-ordinate movements which become definite in their workings, but it is a long time before it acquires a steadiness of purpose, or is able to grasp any object in its fulness. As it is with its attention and will, so is it with the faculty of memory. It gives itself no time to see an object properly, but takes it in, in detail, in parts, hence its first memories are vague, it is some time before it acquires the actual memory of any object or person. When it does so, then memory of the same or diverse objects induces comparison, and the young intellect is fully prepared for the mental researches that will become the work of its life. All after is simply progress, progress in perceiving fulness of expression, fulness of relation, in gaining higher and longer ranges, deeper introspections, fuller generalizations.

The Period of Youth.—We need not dwell long on this important period in the life of humanity; its changes, both physical and mental, are steady and continuous. Growth, simple growth, is its marked characteristic, it excites no violent change and induces no special powers. Up to this stage the body and mind of the organism have attained all their leading qualities, save those specially induced at puberty, and all they have to do now is to grow, expand, and gain fulness, bringing to the fore any marked characteristic, thus defining the individuality of the being.

Essentially the physical endowments of the child-age are the acquisition of the first teeth, the change from fluid to solid food, the acquisition of volitional powers, and the early forms of speech. The period of dentition, as Dr. Carpenter writes, is sometimes one of considerable risk to the infant's

life. The pressure upon the nerves of the gum is a fruitful
source of irritation, producing disturbance of the whole
system, and giving origin to convulsive affections, which are
not unfrequently fatal. Any existing malady or abnormal
tendency is pretty sure to be aggravated during the cutting
of the teeth. (*Human Physiol.* p. 1017.) More, as we shall
subsequently observe, this, like other great co-ordinate
changes, is a period that risks the general stability of the
organic entity, producing idiocy, and laying the foundation
of great organic disorganizations. Youth may be said to
commence with the second dentition. This extended over a
much longer period, necessarily induces no sudden changes
in the organic entity, and being slowly spread over many
years, the organic parts passively accept the change without
any great irritating effects.

Growth, as we have said, is the essential purport of this
period in the young life. All the visceral faculties acquire
their varied natural developments, the muscles expand and
ever continue to gain tension, and the nerves and brain
substance acquire enlarged capacities. Ever the mental
forces act on the bodily organization, and continuous action
gives power, precision, and firmness to every act of volition.
The slowly acquired evolutions are marked in the osseous
character now assumed by the bone structure, in the greater
firmness of the flesh, in the full growth of the hair on the
head, and the acquisition of all the general athletic powers.
As yet there is little but conventional distinction in the
physical powers of boys and girls; left to themselves they
will equally climb and run, and sport in every possible way
with their limbs. There is not a movement of the higher
animals but they will, when permitted, respond to, running,
leaping, climbing, swinging, struggling and rolling in wild
sport on the sward. They may sexually vary somewhat in
the nature of their sports, but essentially they manifest the
same impulsive origin. And it is well it is so, muscle and
bone and tendon and nerve thus not only gain present

powers, but lay by a store of energy that in the after calls of puberty and maturity, and under the range of altered activities enable the individual beings to withstand the worry, the *ennui*, the sedentary or exacting duties of their after life, and ever by repose to regain somewhat of the alacrity, the hilarity, the energy of youth.

Beside the vast gain in the bodily powers which begin to present the fulness of the human form we behold, accrue a corresponding extension of the simple mental forms in the child. As every physical power during this period prepares for the after purposes of its physical life, so the mental forces attain vigour, and school themselves for the exposi-tions it is their purport to manifest. Not the least among these extensions is the work of memory, in the preservation of the infinite varieties of perceptions and arts of doing, more especially in the retention of words and their application for this purpose, talk becomes unceasing, and the young voices, like the young legs, are always at work. Whatever the eye sees or the ear hears, or the hands can handle, the young mind questions the why and the where-fore, it is never satisfied with a crude answer or a vague put-off, but questions and re-questions until its simple nature is satisfied or the excitement of a new idea awakens its attention to another subject.

It is towards the close of this period that, self-conscious of the unlimited powers of its bodily and mental faculties, there awakens in the youthful mind the sentiment of its individual capacities, as physically it would dare and do anything, and first manifests the desire for unbounded self-volition. So full of adventure, resolution, and the sense of endurance, it desires new fields of action, new sources of perception and sentiment; it would penetrate the unknown. In like manner as the physical powers pass from the immediate to desire the unknown, the beyond, so the mental forces essay to express their own individuality. Beyond what they hear and read and know, they build up in their inner consciousness concepts of original relations of new powers of application beyond the known. As physically they aspire to find new scenes, so, mentally, they search for new motives, new purposes in life. It has been said that the basis of all human improvements, all great works, is first evolved at this stage in the life of the organism; of this we feel assured, that if long after they attain the power of doing at this period, the impulse for all future activities is first created. The want is then felt that time matures at first into the concept of a power, and then makes a present fact.

Puberty.—As growth marked the age of youth, so at puberty, besides the special evolution of the generative race-continuing functions, we note the consolidation and fulness of all the organic powers as constituting the perfection of the organizing work. This double series of changes affect body and mind alike, a series of new sentiments of vague or distinct ideas and of strange impulses present themselves to the consciousness. They obtrude themselves under all circumstances, they qualify every expression of the mind. They call attention to the bodily faculties in a way never felt before, until through the physical changes and the new aspirations covering a wider field in the present, and grasping the conditions of the future, the ego itself becomes changed and enters on an essentially new phase in its existence, the old ideas, hopes, fears, and pursuits more or less pass away, and the new concepts and feelings become an integral portion of the ego; the self-consciousness undergoes a radical transformation, and, after great mental commotion, the exposition of various morbid tendencies in general, a new co-ordination ensues.

The physical change, essentially marked by the active state of the generative system, now for the first time, by the speciality of function, denotes the distinguishing attributes of sex. Secondary physical developments and

changes accompany the maturing of this important function, the sexual impulse arouses the mental faculties and
moral feelings, and the new status of the individual evolves
with its special sexual tendencies. In the boy's nature,
when the change becomes manifest, we note the enlarged
sense of responsibility and duty evolved through the new
impulses. He questions the future, he plans and designs
new relations, new associations; he must do; he must
acquire more earnestly than ever. Higher sentiments of
honour animate him, and while new selfish motives act
intensely on his mind, the old personal selfishness of the
boy's nature is converted to an extended selfishness that
includes in its grasp both associative and kindred influences. In like manner his relations with the sex become
more restricted and more emphatic, he becomes bolder and
yet more shy, his confidence is checked, he doubts his
resolution, and appeals again and again to the same mental
influences.

Previous to puberty, it has been said the mind of a
young girl is the mind of a child, merry, thoughtless, volatile.
Occupied by childish trifles, delighted with toys, playing
with her brothers, and differing from them mainly in some
little feminine tastes, and in being less boisterous. After
menstruation a great and rapid change is observed, womanly
tastes and womanly feelings have sprung into existence,
thought, feeling, and reflection are substituted for her
former levity, her expressions become more refined, more
reserved, and indicate deeper sentiment; her affections
are warmer, yet more finely tempered, her pursuits more
elevated, her tone of mind more serious, her sympathy
more deep and earnest, her joy, though less buoyant, more
intense, her tastes finer and more delicate. Like the
young man, her thoughts dwell on the future, she advances
and yet holds back, hope and imagination being busy in
her mental concepts.

Maturity.—At this stage the vital organism, male or

female, attains its maximum co-ordinate efficiency ; all the
powers, bodily and mental, save those which express fulness
of duration and the predominance of multiple impressions,
have now arrived at the plenitude of their manifestations.
The organization is most complete, the parts most in harmony ;
there are now no incipient forces, but each and all of the
attributes constituting the organism have accepted its
assigned place, manifested the nature of its powers, and
combined with the others in co-ordinate harmony.

If we survey the organic activities, we observe that they
not only have consolidated, but manifest their full vigour
and energy, and that in their conjoint nature they have
greater powers of endurance and of resisting disintegrating
forces than at any previous or even subsequent period in
the life of the co-ordination.   It is during the continuance
of this state that the organism in its duplicate sexuality
fulfils the great purport of its being, the preparation of new
vital elements to continue the race.   Out of its consolidated
energy new energies are differentiated, and the mortal
attains a seeming immortality, racial if not individual.

During this period each of the sexual activities has and
accepts, as a general rule, its appointed status and duties,
the male founds and guides the home, and becomes the
external exponent of the new family relations, while the
mother is the inner supporting and sustaining power, the
nurse and emotional leader of the new generation ; co-
ordinately, they represent the perfect humanity, and constitute the unit out of which the State grows and the fulness of social life is embodied.

Each according to their sexual characteristics exhibits
the same fixedness of attributes; growth, as denoted by
elongation, has ceased, the fulness of the vital energy not
absorbed in building up the new generation is expended in
consolidating the general structure and in storing up
physical resources for future calls on the common energy.
The muscles thicken, stores of nutriment are laid up in

appropriate cells, the supporting bony structure becomes more consolidated, and the union of the epiphyses with the several osseous members gives firmness to the main organic structure. Many as yet separate sets of bones as implying previously unfinished growth now coalesce, as in the sternum, the cranium, and the limbs. The whole structure takes the character of a garrison prepared to sustain their unity and resist any inner or outer deranging forces.

Necessarily some changes must accrue,—the emotional sensibility is more under the command of the moral power, and the wider presence of duties withhold the previous fulness of the observing powers, their former pre-eminent activity is filled by the moral and intellectual collaborations which work in definite lines and by modes which have become habitual to them, and thus ensue continuous, unchangeable, and unvarying deductions, thereby new modes of doing are rarely acquired, and previous attained processes work in their habitual lines without effort and almost instinctively.

As regards the expenditure of the natural energy, Flint says the appropriation of new matter is a little superior to dis-assimilation up to about the age of twenty-five years, but between the ages of twenty-five and forty-five these processes are nearly equal; at a later period the nutrition does not completely supply the physiological waste of the tissues, the proportion of organic to inorganic matter gradually diminishes, and death ensues.

The Age of Human Declination.—The earliest sign that the human vitality is proceeding on its downward course is present in the weakening and loss of the procreative power, now no longer capable of continuing the race, and all the physical energy is employed in sustaining the individual co-ordination. In woman the period of cessation is more exact than in man, the change in her is more definite, there are no longer any calls upon her generating and nutritive resources, they are all transferred to sustain and uphold her own personality. Not so man, he can no longer, like woman, participate in the sexual relation without the expenditure of vital energy, hence he wastes sooner than woman, and the decline of the one power with him is the decline of the manly co-ordination, hence he wastes more rapidly than woman, and is subject to earlier decay and death than is her usual lot.

The process of the decline is ever accompanied with a gradual diminution of the vital powers of the organism, both formative and sustaining. As Dr. Carpenter says, the tissues become effete and are no longer replaced in their normal completeness, while degeneracy of substance, fatty or calcareous, mars the general working of the organic parts. Then follows a weakening in both the mental and corporeal energy, the mind is less active, the senses lose fulness and become dull, the feelings fail or tend to be obtuse, and the only power that sustains its presence for a time is judgment, upheld to its fullest manifestation by the greatly extended acquisitions of the memory, but later on, when the memory becomes turgid, and the later and therefore highest deductions slip out of recollection, the earlier and therefore more fixed only coming forward in response to the will, or by unconscious cerebration, then the mind recoils on itself, and judgment fails in its most important characteristics, until it is absolutely lost in the decrepitude of senility.

In old age the muscular movements gradually become feeble, the bones contain an excess of inorganic matter, the ligaments become stiff, the special senses usually obtuse, and there ensues a diminished capacity for mental labour, with more or less loss of mental vigour. In old age, as Flint remarks, it frequently happens that some organ essential to life gives way, or the old person is stricken down by disease. It is so infrequent to observe a perfectly physiological life, but we sometimes observe a gradual fading away of vitality in old persons, who die without being

affected by any special disease. In general, however, some
faculty or power, either from inheritance or by morbid
acquisition, is below ordinary tension; there are few but
have a lesion in some faculty, and this is so long sustained
and upheld as the common energy can come to its aid, when
that fails the weakest, as in the social compact, goes to the
wall. In all cases the organism wastes by atrophy, it loses
nervous tension and becomes palsied, the blood flows slower
and more irregularly, the digestive demands become less
and more selective, the respiratory powers lose tone and
fulness, the secretive fail in some measure, or become
intermittent, until by the consensus of discordinations the
vital accord is lost, and death ensues. As the co-ordinate
organism is built up of distinct individualities, they die, as
shown, in succession.

CHAPTER I.

Abnormal Physical Co-ordinations.

WE recognize in each living entity two forms of active power, one manifested by the conscious ego, and expressing will, thought and perception, the other expresses growth, structural change and physical development. The last, while admitting of the restricted special vital activities of plasma and cell of segmentation and the formation of tissues, controls all these special organic forces, apportioning them to parts and functions, and endowing each of these with still more subsidiary duties. More, when from external or internal cause morbid symptoms ensue, it acts as a guiding and controlling power, fills up every void, supplements every weakened manifestation, and modifies for that purpose all the local conditions. Nor is this all, it not only influences the individual will that expresses in a like manner the mental attributes of the co-ordination, but it so arranges that when by abnormal conformation two physical wills, a duplex series of faculties and parts more or less complete, are brought into union, even though the addition to the co-ordination may only be that of an isolated organic fragment attached to a normal organism, that all work in harmony. So when there are lost or aborted faculties or parts it induces in the reduced personality by modification of energy and various transferences of functions or powers, the best working of the local powers that the disablement permits.

Abnormal forms by excess and by defection working in co-ordination.

1. When two individuals, twins, possessing all the normal parts are combined by simple fusion of the integuments or external muscles, such as was the case with the Siamese twins. This was probably due to simple grafting, arising by accidental contact after the embryo's were very fully developed. The result of such an association, besides the simple unity, may only be the fusion of the integumentary, perhaps the muscular cells, and the anastomosing of the smaller capillaries, a mere partial interaction of the nutritive fluid. In this state all the functions and parts are individual, the minds and the bodies of each being influenced by their own ego's. Each may be indifferently in a state of active thought or mental repose, awake or asleep, and all the bodily functions act individually independent, no necessary connection, more than the sympathetic influence of suggestion, which accrues in like manner to separate organisms. The Siamese twins in all their relations with others deported themselves as having different mind-powers, likes and dislikes, individual feelings, and individual impulses and tastes. As distinct individuals they were married, each had his own wife, and each exhibited distinct affections for their own families. The ailments of life to them had no necessary connection, not only might their tempers at the same moment differ, but one might have a headache, or be disordered in the bowels, without the other being in a like condition; even the death of the one had no immediate influence on the other, save as suggesting, and, therefore, predisposing the mind for a like fatality. Hence, they were, however organically attached, two distinct mental and bodily personalities.

2. From simple integumentary fusion we pass to those instances in which not only do the muscles blend, but, besides the interchange of the capillaries, some one or more distinct parts or functions blend, organs may be fused or common to both, or betimes acting now conjoint, now individual. In these instances the mental ego's express special personalities, mental states, tempers, passions and feelings are distinct, the sympathy, owing to the intimate union of some functions, is more direct and more absolute; the bodily condition of one reflexes on the other, simply as the mental reply to deranged function by external influence. Necessarily if the reflex connection affects a vital function the death of the one induces the death of the other.

One of the most remarkable instances of this fusion of the bodily functions was that of Millie and Christine, the Carolina sisters, of negro parentage, and united at the lower part of the back; they are described as feeling hunger and thirst, and a call to evacuate the bowels or bladders simultaneously, neither knowing whose organs evacuated. But while the bodily powers were thus co-ordinate, the mental were distinct. One might be talking and laughing to other persons, while her sister was sound asleep. One alone might have a slight headache, but, if severe, so as to affect the common organism, it was felt by both. The nerves of sensation being anastomosed, if the lower extremities of one were touched the other felt it, but could not locate the sensation, so as to describe whether the foot or leg was touched. (*Boston Med. and Surg. Jour.* 1869, III. p. 414.)

A special enquiry into the nature of the two ego's in this case by Dr. Buchanan, of Glasgow, and the result of his examination as contained in the *Lancet* (1872, I. p. 273) is first, That each sister has in her own person the functions of the nervous system quite complete, having in particular perfect sensation over the whole body and full command over all the voluntary muscles. Second, That each, in addition to perfect sensation in her own person, had passive sensation all over the lower limbs of her sister, acquiring thus a sense of touch, of pain, of heat and cold, and movement, which states of consciousness are transmitted to her as vaguely felt, not specially localized, not discriminated. He considers this special faculty arises from the fusion of the lowermost invertebral and sympathetic ganglia, each ganglia being the common centre to the same nerves on the right and left limbs alternately of the two sisters, and that every impression made on the nerves of the lower limbs follows a single tract to the ganglion, where, divaricating, it passes by two commissures to alternate sides of the two cords. Hence, each sister has perfect sensation, voluntary motion, and direct reflex action in her own limbs, while over the limbs that do not belong to her she has no voluntary power of motion, and derives from them only passive sensation and cross reflex action. Dr. Buchanan considers that this passive sensation has nothing to do with the brain; the mind, though cognisant, does not heed it, but in discriminative sensation the attention is aroused, the mind directs the sentient organs, and volition and judgment are exercised. In his experience among animals Flourens found that without brain there was no discrimination of sensation, but that passive sensation was exercised by the spinal cord.

This fact is important in considering the steps in the development of the mind-powers. There may be only the mere nerve reflex, beyond this a vague undiscriminating passive state of sensation which progresses through various stages of discriminating power, as present in many of the invertebrata, to the full delicate mental recognition of external influences so exquisitely manifest in the higher developed special senses.

More, there is another deduction present to us in this case illustrating the mode by which the compound individual may be built up. There may be aggregation without fusion in which the parts are only held in affinity, like segregated cells, by the intercommuning plasma, or the simple cell walls may fuse and blend. Beyond this state the muscles may reflex, but when the nerves anastomose, common sensation is felt though not specialized, as in the case of Millie and Christine.

The two sisters, Helena and Judith, exhibited at the Hague in 1708, and afterwards in London, were of the same class of two distinct individuals joined at the sacrum as the Carolina sisters, but the blending was fuller, the urethra and anus were single, and they were misplaced, not being in the middle line of either, but situated between the two bodies at the front and back of the junction. The only information we have of the nature of their sensations is that at the place of conjunction they have feeling in common. (*Phil. Trans.* L. p. 311.)

Instances representing the interblending of two embryo's by the union of one or more of the vital functions of both are common in anatomical collections; the two hearts may be fused, the livers and hearts fused together, there may be only one heart between both. (*Descrip. Cat. Warren Anat. Museum, by J. B. S. Jackson*, pp. 115, 116.) In another case the livers were fused, and there was but one stomach. (*Ibid.* p. 128.) Of these the one in which the two hearts were fused lived a quarter of an hour. In another the two hearts were united, and there was but one auricle. (*Ibid.* p. 297.) A more remarkable case, united above and separated into two distinct sets of members below the umbilicus, the pharynx œsophagus and stomach were in common, while the other parts, including the heart and respiratory organs, were double. In all these cases fusion was by contact in an early stage when the functions were forming outside the body cavity. In these, and in all those cases where more or less of the one or both bodies were abrogated, it would appear that the lost parts had been absorbed by the other members or by the leucocytes, and used for the common sustenance. This may occur in any stage in the evolvement; dead or non-active parts are always used up or expelled by the common energy.

A case of a duplex formation—the two organisms joined from the ensiform cartilage to the umbilicus. One child lived two and a half days, the other three days. (*Lancet*, 1887, II. p. 1271 ; also another, 1887, II. p. 1044.) The Carolina sisters appear to have had only one part in common, the anus. They had each her own rectum. A similar duplex fœtus more blended is described in the *Lancet* (1887, II. p. 755.) Another case, united along the line of the sternum and abdominal wall. (*Lancet*, 1886, I. p. 19.)

Third class. In this, while the possession of the two heads and brains sustains the two distinct personal ego's, the organic parts of the two are so blended that though marking any combination of the parts of two or more organisms, the several members, as in the case of the Siphonophors, are all united into one co-ordination by the action of the common energy, with the same distinct power of individuism as is presented in the right and left members of normal organisms. In these cases the fusion may take place anywhere below the head, and occur on the same plane or at various angles. The four upper and four lower extremities may be developed more or less perfect, or one or more may have been absorbed, all having two heads, manifest two individualities if they live. Owing to the difficulties attending the delivery of such complex forms, many perish at birth.

In the Warren Anatomical Museum is preserved a double fœtus fused side by side through the whole length of the trunks, the external limbs on each side normal, but from the median line of the double back at the upper part projects outward a third arm, and at the lower part a third leg, forming a true tripod; the extra arm and leg were normal in the limb portions, but the hand and foot were the fusions of the two distinct hands and feet, the hand having no palm, but consisting of two backs of hands, each having the proper finger nails ; the foot had fused on the other plane, with two groups of three toes, one on each side; in the centre was a single toe with, as with the fused hands, a nail on each side. (*Descrip. Cat.* p. 120.)

In the *British Medical Journal* (1889, III. p. 33) is the case of a child born with two heads, one body, three arms, two legs, club feet, and caudal appendage; the third arm was between the two shoulders, the fingers discordinate. It had two spinal columns. To the lumbar region below it was one normal child ; it lived twenty-four days.

A duplex organism, having two heads, four upper extremities blending into one body, one vertebral column ending in the abdomen, below which all the parts would appear to have been absorbed; the other column carried normal limbs. These were face to face, and the ribs continuous from column to column. (*Lancet*, 1872, I. p. 563.) In another duplex fœtus, two heads were present on one pair of shoulders, all the other parts being single. (*Ibid.* 1872, I. p. 538.)

Fourth class. In this the double individuality is reduced to its lowest element, and had such not had an actual existence, it would have seemed the height of absurdity to suppose a personality restricted to the head only ; and yet we have cases recorded of men having survived for some time when from some contingency the spinal cord has been disconnected from the brain without the vascular functions being disintegrated.

An instance in which a second combined personality was reduced to the head alone is recorded by Sir E. Home in the *Philosophical Transactions* (LXXX. p. 296). A normally developed Hindoo child had a second living head growing reversed on the top of its own head, the faces not on the same plane but rather sideways; this duplex head without accessory parts ending in a soft round tumour. This second head is described as possessed of powers of action; it had a good sensibility, since violence to the skin produced the distortive expression of crying, and thrusting the finger in the mouth made it show strong marks of pain. When the mother's nipple was applied to the mouth the lips attempted to suck, implying the mental existence of that instinctive impulse, but its failing to be effective from the absence of all digestive power. The eyelids of this head were never completely shut, and the eyeballs moved at random. When the child was roused the eyes of both heads moved at the same time, but those of the superior head did not appear to be directed to the same object, but wandered in different directions. The tears flowed from the superior head almost constantly but never from the eyes of the other head, except when crying. The superior head seemed to sympathise with the child in most of its natural actions; when the child cried the features of this head were affected in a like manner, and when it sucked the mother, satisfaction was expressed by the mouth of the superior head, and the saliva flowed more copiously than at any other time, implying the existence of the mental concept of the purpose of food though the physical faculty had no existence.

In a later account (*Ibid.* LXXXIX. p. 28) it is said that "when the child cried the features of the superior head were not always affected, and when it smiled the features of the superior head did not sympathise in that action." The two brains were separate and distinct, having a complete partition between them formed by the union of the dura maters; a number of large arteries and veins made a free communication between the blood vessels of the two brains.

This interesting double-headed organism—the upper head sustained by nutrition through the anastomosing vascular parts—was unfortunately never inspected by any scientist, or we might have possessed many judicious observations on the distinct nature of the two minds and the influence of the association on both, more especially in what the mental developments were diverse and the specialities that resulted from the superior head having no personal bodily organs, so little practical sense exposition, and from its always existing in a position the reverse of the natural. As it is reported, we are certain that its mental faculties were independent of the bodily functions and faculties. This compound organism lived to be four years of age, and was accidentally killed by the bite of a snake.

A case of an imperfect head on the top of the head of a child otherwise well-formed is reported in the *Boston Medical and Surgical Journal* (LVIII. p. 159).

Fifth class. Occasionally a second more or less aborted individuality may be attached to an otherwise normal person. One Collereda, a Genoese, figured as a child, and afterwards, when twenty-eight years of age, of the average stature, had adherent to the lower end of his breast-bone a tolerably well-formed child, wanting one leg. This dwarfed duplex organism breathed, slept at intervals, and moved its body, but it had no separate nutritive functions. As Elliotson says it was sensible to touch and had some independent volition. The same writer further says:— "Montaigne saw a boy, exactly fourteen years old, who had a headless brother fixed front to front, looking as if a small child was endeavouring to embrace a bigger." Another like imperfect personality was seen by Winslow attached to the body of a well-formed girl. (*Physiology*, p. 1087.) In these two cases there was no appearance of a second brain and a second personal consciousness. Nor was there in the parasite on Ake, the Chinese, as recorded by Geoffroy St. Hilaire. The common sensibility and the common functions were, as Dr. Elliotson says, all ruled by the one brain; in Ake it was the same; in a case of external parasitism, as described in the *Medico-Chirurgical Transactions of Edinburgh* (*Elliotson, Hum. Phy.* p. 1088); as also in that of a duplex preparation in the

Warren Anatomical Museum. (*Cat.* p. 135.) In the same catalogue is the case, however, of another duplex child, the head of which was buried in the right hypochondrium. It had one upper and two lower extremities. This, which lived four and three-quarters months, must have possessed independent brain-power, as the adventitious limbs had power of motion. (*Ibid.*) The portions of a second child parasitic on the cheek of the full twin, which had independent growth, though not independent consciousness. This expressed independent animal powers, and that these accessory parts had no necessary relation to the normal twin was shown when, by removing them, it continued well and hearty. (*Ibid.*)

In these cases the parasitic embryo was attached externally, and more or less blended and fused with its twin, but there are other cases in which the parasite is enclosed in the body of its twin companion. In these instances we can obtain no knowledge of a second personality, though the entombed fœtus may have a fair average brain. Dr. Elliotson records several cases in which the twin fœtus was enclosed in the abdomen of the more developed embryo. These have not only lived, but grown with their strange internal burdens. One, a girl of two-and-a-half years, had it removed as a tumour; another, a boy of fifteen, was found to bear in his abdomen a pretty large imperfect female fœtus. (*Hum. Phy.* 1089.) In the Teratological Museum of the Royal College of Surgeons, London, are the remains of a second fœtus growing from the median fissure of the palate of another fœtus. In another, in the abdomen of a child of nine months, is a parasitic fœtus without head, and the catalogue reports (p. 35) that when it was taken out of the cyst it appeared as rosy and healthy as if alive. In another, a boy of fifteen, perhaps the case referred to by Dr. Elliotson, many of the parts of the enclosed fœtus had been absorbed, but the vertebral column, the ill-proportioned limbs, and the generative organs had existed in the lad for more than fifteen years. (*Ibid.* p. 36.) In another instance a fœtus remains were taken from the nates of a child of fourteen months, which recovered. A girl of twelve years had a sacral tumour removed containing the rude parts of a pelvis and limb, the bony growth extended into the girl's pelvis, but, as the mass was congenital and not increasing with the girl's growth, the inner bone was not attempted to be removed. (*Lancet*, 1887, II. p. 1270.)

In several instances quoted there is partial atrophy of some parts of the second fœtus, or it may break up and parts waste away or be destroyed, others becoming attached to the living embryo. Thus, in a case reported in the *British Medical Journal* (1889, II. p. 310), an accessory limb with two fingers and rudimentary thumb was attached to the scapula at the back, its attempted removal ensued in death to the developed infant. Often partially formed parts pass away without living attachment, or masses of organized parts, as we have seen, become accidentally enclosed in the living body.

Previous to the closure in the middle line in the developing embryo, it is comparable with the Siphonophores, as are all correspondingly developed animal forms. The aggregation of extra members occurs only occasionally in the higher animals; with the Siphonophores it is the normal state. With the higher organized beings the oosphere has but few elements, with the invertebrata these are many. Among most of the lower class of organisms these develop into distinct individuals, either at once from the germinal cells or by an after process, as with the medusæ. The special character of the hydro-medusæ arises either from the aggregation of several special functions of various kinds in one organism, due to many germs breaking up into individual parts, or in the one developing germ there are attached varied numbers of associated sets of parts. The ontogeny of the whole is never aggregated by closure, and consequently the individuality of the parts continues more observant than in those human combinations we have referred to, which are usually more energetically associated by the wrapping around them of the common integument in the process of closure.

Sixth Class. These are cases in which no second personality is present. There is no second head or brain, and hence no second consciousness; the superior fœtus has absorbed those parts that give sensibility, and the remainder of the second fœtus are attached as grafted duplex members to its own organic parts, and only act or are acted upon by the one dominant personal consciousness.

Jean Battista, a native of Faro, Portugal, as described by Ernest Hart, of St. Mary's Hospital, is nineteen years of age, well nourished, and of general symmetrical form. But he possesses two complete and well-formed penes placed side by side, and a large central third leg and foot. When the bladder acts it expels its contents through both penes at the same time, both simultaneously erect, and other functions are performed by the two simultaneously, implying a single dominant will. The third limb at first sight seems to consist of a large thigh with an abortive leg dislocated and bent up in front, and a misshapen foot, also dislocated; the foot is really the coalescence of two feet, as the central toe is the consolidation of two big toes, and it has on each side four toes, and a bifid tibia joins the double set to the one leg. Sensation simply organic, as it is said that the terminal part of the foot is devoid of sensation, the skin of the leg is only partially sensitive, but a slight power of movement in the third leg, none at the insertion, though it can be freely moved by the hand. The extra leg is disposed of by strapping it with webbing; then he is active, runs swiftly, and is a good horseman (*Lancet*, 1865, II. p. 124.) Baron Lalley exhibited a boy having a rudimentary supernumerary leg on the right thigh, consisting of a thigh, leg, and foot, six toes, and the trace of a seventh. (*Lancet*, 1865, I. p. 501.)

An infant born in Tennessee had two distinct external female organs of generation, and two external openings of the double rectum. The genital organs were as distinct as if they belonged to two separate human beings, it had four legs. The fæces and urine were passed most generally simultaneously from both external urinary and intestinal openings. The head and trunk were those of a healthy, well-developed, active infant of about five weeks, the lower part divided into the members of two distinct individuals near the junction of the spinal column with the os sacrum. Two pelvic arches appeared to support the four limbs on the same plane. (*Lancet,* 1868, II. p. 303.)

A still more remarkable combination of the same character is described in a later number of the same journal (1868, II. p. 397), as also in the *British Medical Journal.* (1877, II. p. 934.) This was a girl fused in the median line with two pairs of lower limbs. The right leg of the right pelvis was perfectly developed, the left leg quite rudimentary, both the limbs of the left pelvis were fairly developed, though club-footed. There were double genitals, but only one anus, the child micturated through both urethras, and evacuated the bowels by the single anus. More, as intimating that a portion of the organs of a third individual were present, at the junction of the pelvis was a well-formed penis, and below this had been a scrotum, which was removed at Paris, where the case had been exhibited, and as showing that this part of a third individual was in co-ordinate association, it formerly micturated through the penis as well as the two female urethras.

A child born with three legs is described in the *Lancet* (1865, I. p. 505). The supernumerary limb hung between the two thighs, ending in a good-looking foot. It rose from the pelvic cavity, and did not seem endowed with motive powers, nor did it evince sensation on pricking; its temperature was the same as the other limbs. As it had no active connection with the brain it was deemed advisable to remove it; this was done, the wound healed perfectly, and the child was well and strong. At Paris an infant was exhibited with three legs, three cuissees, three hands and three feet. (*Bullet, Soc. de Chie. de Paris*, II. p. 55.)

In another instance the child had two supernumerary arms springing from the scapulæ, and two supernumerary legs from the ischia. These extra limbs moved with the normal. (*Lancet*, 1886, I. p. 189.) In the case of Corban, reported in the *Boston* (U.S.) *Medical and Surgical Journal* (1868, p. 414), there was one head and trunk, but the lower part of the body consisted of the members of two distinct individuals. There were two urethras and recti, the fæces and urine being expelled in general simultaneously, they were situated between the left and right pair of legs. There was a double pelvic arch, and four distinct pretty-well developed lower extremities, the outer legs on both sides being the most natural.

In the *Lancet* (1862, II. p. 685) is the case of a woman, thirty-eight years of age, who had on her left upper extremity a supernumerary hand, somewhat smaller than that which it accompanied, the thumbs only rudimentary. Sensation equally acute in both left hands, but in volition they were as one, always grasping together, implying their nervous union to the same set, and the co-ordination not being mental.

These cases are interesting as aiding us in considering the relation of the extra parts to the one personal consciousness. They never appear to express equal mental affinity with the normal parts, only connection with the ganglia, except when they represent the doubling by divarication of special nerves, then they, though double, are treated as a single member, as in the instance of the two hands grasping in concert. More often these additional parts are simple secondary adjuncts, and might be removed often with advantage to the normal members, as in the instance we quoted; they are simply parasitic, and it is a consideration whether they represent buds, that is, mere cell divisions, or portions of separate sexual ova. The potentiality is very distinct in each class. In one it represents only the duplication on the asexual range that is limited to binary section and restrained to the lower asexual forms. In the other, the potentiality is sexual, and carries with it, not only the capability of cell multiplication, but full reproduction numerically great. More, while the first-class carry in them the powers of vegetative life, the higher series not only reproduce many bodies, but equally many minds, according to the scale of their evolution.

The asexual origin of parts is seen in the many and varied instances in which the reproduction of lost members or parts accrue; more, it extends to the evolution of a low class of personalities expressed in parthenogenesis and alternate generations. All these, whether coming from cell divisions, buds or unfertilized ova, are only capable of evolving like parts or like organisms, and it is not until sexuality is manifest and conjunction ensues that the higher physical and mental powers become evolved.

There are three sources assumed to have given origin to these extra parts attached to organisms; we attach no importance to the theory of maternal impressions affecting the modification or addition of parts, though sympathetically they may affect the normal health of the embryo. Having no faith in abiogenesis, we cannot admit its action, even to forming new parts. Our knowledge now is so full, yet so limited, of the origin of organisms, that we are assured that not only has each organism arisen from a distinct germ, but that the result was dependent on the special character of the germ. Hence, firstly, we note that new and even extra parts may arise asexually by a process of budding genetically; this potentiality is continuous in an organism, and though it may have superadded to its energy the greater potentiality of sex, the primary power remains in it, though in a latent form, and circumstances favouring its re-manifestation, it may intervene in a series of sexual evolutions, as by parthenogenesis and alternate generations, or as mere budding adjuncts to an offspring. Secondly, cells or ova may blend or combine, and in the process parts may be lost, absorbed, or devoured, and thus two or even more cells or ova may blend into one living germ, the parts grafting by fusion, and, according to their location, accommodating themselves to one another. Thirdly, a cell or ova may from some external, or even internal force, break up, and more or less resolve into fragments, each of which fragments would continue to retain its simple germ-power, and, like a seed under favouring conditions, it would evolve. But any such fragment would want all the organic faculties not represented in its plasma, and to evolve at all it will be necessary for it to become parasitic on an organism having those qualities of which it is deficient.

The first form-development by segmentation is the only mode among the lower class organisms, and prevails to a large extent among all higher organisms; the renewal of all parts and tissues capable of renewal result through its working, even to the replacement not only of integuments, but limbs and more supplementary personalities, as the asexual individuals in Daphnia. Of the blending of cells and the combinations of fragments of devoured or wasted cells as tending to produce modified cell-multiples, we know but little, yet there must be many such irregular associations among unicellular organisms, but of these we need not at present enquire, and all the combinations of organic life we are now considering arise from other causes.

To our second division are due all the most startling forms of multiple organic vitality. In the evolution of the human embryo there may be present several organic germs, and so with animals; in some it is common to have many germs growing in the same period; sometimes superfœtation takes place. Even in human embryology two or more germs may commence to mature together. These existing in the same uterus are amenable not only to all the contingencies that may arise by external action or the mother's vital movements, but they may act and re-act on each other even before fertilization. Thus, as we have seen, one ova may feed on the store-yolk of another, even upon its plasma. A. C. Haddon says :—" When many ova are deposited in the same egg-capsule, the more advanced embryos may devour those that are imperfectly developed, so that a very limited number, sometimes only a single individual, escapes from the capsule." (*Embryol.* p. 6.) Even at an earlier period, he says, " it not unfrequently happens—many hydrozoa, insects (some vertebrates)—that certain of the primitive germ-cells feed upon neighbouring germ-cells " (*Ibid.*), and " as germ-cells which have lost the power of reproduction but retained that of forming yolk, either the ovum or embryo in due course feed upon this reserve of food."

Thus we have to look upon the ova as well as the embryo's manifesting low volitional as well as organic powers, and under such conditions we may well conceive that part of one ovum may be absorbed by another; or that by the blending of the plasma in two they may become grafted together, and if in the one there is only part of the being, that may become attached as a supplementary part to its compeer. In most cases of monsters by duplication, it will be noted that the combination of the two are more or less symmetrical, the two bodies combine either at the front or back. If there are two heads they are associated on the same plane, even when one ova is partly fused in the other the junction is somewhat symmetrical; it is rare that they become grouped head to head in one line, as in the Hindoo double-headed child; that was possibly an accidental combination, the others are due to symmetrical association, hence an extra arm is always found on the shoulders, an extra leg on the pelvis, or connected side by side with another leg. Even when there was only a double hand, that was in the same plane as the other. We shall find this same law apply to other parts, whether structural, vascular, or generative.

Now, when the ovum breaks up by disintegration, other consequences ensue; the fragments of it may become attached as superfluities to any part of a full ovum, and grow there under the most discordant associations. We read of a child having extra feet growing out of its nates; portions of a second fœtus, the nostril, tongue, and lips, growing from the median fissure of the palate. (*Cat. Roy. Col. Surg.* p. 32.) It often happens that the minute germs of the duplex organism continued attached to the generative parts of the new organism, and afterwards evolve therein, hence the origin of so many ovarian and uterine cysts containing unabsorbed fragments of another fœtus, in general the most enduring and easily grafted parts, as hairs, teeth, bones, &c. Thus in the catalogue of the Warren Anatomical Museum we read of ovarian cysts containing a bone and two teeth; another, a bone with the crowns of several molar teeth—two pieces of bone from an ovarian sac, with molars and incisors—teeth firmly implanted in bone; one had seventeen teeth, the other thirteen. Like cysts with fœtal remains have been taken from various members of the body, both external and internal.

When we read only of a supernumerary thumb, finger, a double foot or hoof, or even the doubling by divarication of a limb, we are apt to assume that this appropriately situated extra member, or even faculty, may be due not to a second fœtus, but to the active persistence of the power of budding that the cell had potentially in it; not only the faculty of cell segmentation, but the acquired energy of evolving a duplicate finger, toe, or other part. From the cases recorded, it is possible that some duplicate parts are due to budding and others to the breaking up of fœtal germs, but we require more observation regarding the possibility of duplicate toes, fingers, and hands, and feet being due to bud origin.

The whole of these observations tend to show how wide and varied are the secondary personalities that may co-ordinate to form a human personality. In Appendix B we further illustrate the breaking up of a fœtus and the re-co-ordination of parts of it in other organisms.

CHAPTER II.

Discordinations—Mental and Organic.

We have seen that many distinct forms of co-ordinate consciousness may exist without disrupturing the general harmony of the whole. Some faculties, for a time, may remain in abeyance, others become prominently manifest for a time, and then the plastic being assumes again its ordinary phase of multiple affinity. But outside these many more or less co-ordinate manifestations there are others, mental and organic, that arise through the numerous inter-actions of the various powers in the organism, inducing partial or general morbid derangements, which may be classed according to their natures under general heads.

Some of these morbid mental and bodily states showing discordant adjustments arise from depressed mental powers, some from degenerate organic faculties, others from degradations, both mental and physical, which induce reversion to lower evolved forms of being. These various abnormal forms are due to general loss of energy, from one or more of the mental powers being deranged, or from some one or more of the physical faculties becoming diseased. The weakened, deranged, and discordinate ego, as a necessary consequence from these fundamental variations, either manifests lower tension in its mental or

bodily qualities or the normal higher co-ordination gives
way, and the being assumes a lower reversionary state.
General degradation through loss of vital energy is manifest
in the various forms of melancholia, hypochondria, and
paralysis. It may affect one mental power or several, be
manifest in depressed sensation, the negation of emotional
activity, weakened judgment, the various forms of aphasia,
or in the reduction of physical power, an irresolute will,
and general depression. Under these varying depressing
influences all the conditions of life seem affected ; the very
pleasure of being is lost; man becomes a pessimist, the
jaundice enters his soul ; healthy bodily activity succumbs
to *ennui;* he becomes hypochondriac; the whole world is
out of place ; every phase of nature, every human activity
has a baneful influence, until the wretched self-doubting
being wills to end the discordinate association it has
failed to control.

A large class of morbid symptoms arise from certain
mental and bodily faculties, being rendered discordinate
by special and local excitation, as any increased stimulus
due to undue activity in any co-ordinate function deranges
the organic harmony. As the necessary results of such
conditioning, there follow irregularly excited volitions,
with increased local tension ; the sensations become
specially intensified, the equipoise of the mental faculties is
thrown out of gear, and according to the functions affected
the morbid illusions and hallucinations take the forms of
mania, epilepsy, fever, apoplexy, erotic excitations, and the
special derangements that result from alcohol, opiates, and
drugs.

The excitation, limited in its nature and special to certain
mental powers, may result in the exaltation of the special
faculties under its influence, until they manifest increased
tension without losing their due hold on the general
functions. While such expanded manifestations may ever
verge on the disruptive stage, and betimes become dis-

cordinate, the exaltation ending in illusion, yet, still, under the exalted state some of the greatest of human mental achievements have been produced. The greatest co-ordinate mind-powers ever verge on chaos.

Another most melancholy form of morbid discordination is present to us in the atrophy of both the mental and bodily powers, we may note its insidious workings in leprosy and physical atrophy, we may trace it in cretinism and in mental lethargy, but its full expression is manifest in idiocy and imbecility, in reduced energy, reduced mental and bodily powers, the waste of the system, a more rapid passage of the individual through the stages of growth and decay, and ultimately the loss of genetic power, ending in the failure of reproduction, and the annihilation of the race.

In the midst of these many discordinating powers which tend to bring about the negation of the being, there is ever present the influence of a co-ordinating energy ever at war with the detergent influences, ever working to re-establish the organic unity, and may be to raise it to a more perfectly homogeneous status. We mark its presence in the endeavour in each new vitality to cast off its hereditary degeneracies in the being, in every new growth integration working for a like cause. We see it in the many attempts in the organism to withstand its own constitutional failures by transferring the detergent influences to other of its mental or bodily powers, with a view to recoup the normal organism. Does not each new organism start into being with a reserved power of vitality that seems almost super-abundant, and much of which in profuse activity is wasted by the thoughtless generosity of the young organism which wits not of the time when failing energies and a powerless will would rejoice in a tithe of the common vigour thus played away.

The human organism, like a well-balanced machine, works in untroubled harmony when the many elements, bodily and mental, are in co-ordinate sympathy, but we may not unduly use or lightly shift the various parts without destroying that unity which is the perfection of its nature. So in the human system we may induce muscular and nervous deterioration from over-work or want of use, parts may fail on long-continued action in one direction, or one power may render other faculties dormant. So delicately adjusted is the human mind, we may stimulate it too much, we may not cause it to dwell on fixed ideas, or express strong emotional feeling without producing detergent results.

Dr. Gowers has shown us in how many ways the nerves may fail to co-ordinate. Defect of movement may be present in every degree from slight weakness to absolute loss, there may be modifications in tactility in one, a single touch is felt as two or three, in another an impression on one part may be referred to other parts, even to the opposite side of the body. Both tactile and painful impressions may produce sensations that are abnormal in character. There may be absolute inability to recognize heat or cold, as such or only slight degrees of heat may be unperceived. There may be a perverse sensation whereby hot objects feel cold and cold, hot; and so varied is the nature of the apparently homogeneous skin, that if very minute points are examined at some only heat, at others only cold is produced. Need we then wonder if such seeming aberrations exist in the normal state that the abnormal liabilities to derangement should be very general. In some morbid conditions the muscular sense is lost, and the patient cannot appreciate the difference between light and heavy objects, a poker and a feather seem of the same weight, he is also unable to recognize the posture in which his limbs are put by another person. (*Diseases of the Nervous System*, pp. 4-9.)

We quote these observations to show the delicate nature of organic deteriorations and the range of dissonance they may express to the mind, leading to mental images and illusions which may become fixed ideas, and by their persistency cast a shade over the active volition of the other mental powers.   Thus arise diseased perceptions and diseased abstract notions.

Failure of attention is often one of the first signs of mental derangement, the mind cannot be fixed on the idea or object desired, but becomes restless, and fails in continuity of purpose. Still more common as a source of mental deterioration is the persistency of fixed ideas, it is bad to fail in mental concentration; one so doing may waste his life in idle *ennui* or pointless reveries, and, may be, go no further; but when one sentiment, one idea, commands the intellect to the exclusion of all other thoughts and even perceptions, the mental and often the bodily collapse is rapid. Thought and feeling, affection and associations, lose their hold, the mind becomes possessed by the one fixed idea ; like the sun at noonday, it glows on the brain, blends with every perception, and commands the will.

The one dominant idea may arise in the pursuits, occupations, or amusements of an individual, it may be the result of habit, may be due to emotional impulse, may be the result of fear, yet sufficiently mentally demonstrative to break the continuity of any train of thought, any act ; as Hammond says, rushing persistently into the mind, however it may be pre-occupied. In one case he records, it was connected with fatal thirteen, and took the anomalous form of God thirteen.   In another instance it was, "I have lost my pocket book "; in a third, "I am covered with mud." (*Hammond on Insanity*, p. 388.) A similar case is given by Dr. Winslow of a successful speculator whose mind was unhinged by his success. His constant occupation unto the day of his death was playing with his fingers and continually repeating without intermission and with great animation and rapidity the words, "Sixty thousand, Sixty thousand." His mind was wholly absorbed in the one idea, and at this point the intelligence was arrested, and came to a full stop. (*Obscure Diseases*, p. 379.) Boismont gives the case of a man whose fixed idea was that he died at Austerlitz. In another case, a veteran felt himself every night nailed in his coffin and carried by a subterranean road to Vincennes, where the funeral service was chanted, then he was brought back to his bed. (*Hallucinations*, p. 93.)

Fixed ideas may arise from suggestions, in this case they are allied to **hypnotic suggestions**; one instance will suffice. Dr. Oppenheim, of Hamburg, dissecting a man who had committed suicide in a very bungling way, remarked in a jocular way to his attendant, if you have any idea of cutting your throat, do it here at the carotid artery; the suggestion took so strong a hold of the man's imagination that, though in comfortable circumstances, he shortly after attempted a like form of suicide. (*Hammond on Insanity*, p. 397.) Mental epidemics have their origin in such visual suggestions, and there are many morbid crimes that wholly arise from suggestions stimulating a morbid imitation in which the special form of the impulse becomes a commanding idea.

Often fixed ideas have their origin in dreams, and thus intimate the coming derangement, even if they do not produce it. Thus Hammond relates cases of epilepsy, preceded by dreams of decapitation, hanging, perforation of the head with an augur, &c. Insanity is frequently preceded by frightful dreams, as committing atrocious murders. One dreamt after killing an individual, she tried to divide the body, but could not separate the head; then she filled the nose, eyes, and mouth with gunpowder, and applied a match, but instead of exploding, smoke issued forth, which resolved itself into the form of a police officer. She was imprisoned, tried, and sentenced to be drowned in a lake of melted sulphur, and in the re-action she awoke. For several nights her dreams were of the same subject, more or less modified. On the sixth day, without any premonition, she attempted to kill herself by plunging a pair of scissors into her throat. After she continued insane to her death. (*Hammond on Insanity*, p. 244.)

Often the fixed idea arises in the mind of the patient, induced from his own bodily state, or from some misinterpreted phenomena or incident, a clot of blood on the brain, local inflammation, a morbid perception, fear in any form, emotional or other excess, want of sleep, mental or moral excess. They may have committed the unpardonable sin, be shut out from heaven, guilty of any kind of atrocity. Even the one idea takes the form of words, echoing in the ear kill, kill; it may urge to steal, to betray, to hate, often to commit suicide, and the wretched victim of his own mental and physical frailty may fight against the horrible present impression until the bewildered mind consummates the frenzied act. A case in point is given by Bucknill and Tuke :—"A labourer said he must destroy some one; he felt a strong desire to commit murder, which he struggled against and thought a temptation of the devil. Whilst engaged in spade husbandry, he one day came to the writer, and begged to be taken from the garden, as he had the strongest desire to kill some of the patients with his spade. Afterwards, to avoid the murderous assault to which he felt himself impelled, he often requested to be locked in his bedroom, but more frequently tied his own hands together with packthread, which he could have snapped with the greatest facility, but which he said enabled him to resist the temptation." (*Psych. Medi.* p. 788.)

Betimes the ever present impulse may be a tone of feeling, a general mode of expression ever inducing the same special feelings, the same desires, the same restless or perturbed mental state. It may express grief, anxiety, spiritual dependence, or any emotional state. A vivid picture of such prominent feelings is quoted by Dr. Clouston. The unhappy lady writes :—"I watch every action, word, and thought, constantly questioning them, accounting for them, excusing or deprecating them. I reason, resolve, and hope, but the greater the effort to be

free, the greater the struggle.   I have been so oppressed
with this unspeakable distress, that I feel as if I were two
persons, the one tyrannically demanding to be gratified, the
other protesting and pleading.   I am often in despair,
and feel my life a burden.   At night I am glad that the
day is done, in the morning I am in terror that the day will
be a repetition of the former.   The most trivial incident
will occupy my mind.   I discuss it in all its bearings, telling
myself all the time it is not worth my consideration.
Someone is speaking to me, someone is talking.   If the
former, I answer (often very abstractedly) with the feeling that there is something in my mind, then I return
to the triviality.   If I had forgotten it, I must remember
it, and then, with a distinct effort, put it away from my
mind.   It steals back.   I tell myself that I have already
discussed it, but I must repeat the whole matter to myself, and that with no ordinary process of thought.   I feel
a strange strain on my memory, and again I have to use an
effort to banish this nothing.   Again it will arise and be
dismissed, and I number the times as carefully as if much
depended on it.   The efforts to dismiss the subject cause
the blood to rush to my head, the perspiration to break, and
I often find my hands clenched in the struggle.   All
through this I bear a calm exterior, no one knowing how
I am tortured.   This fret goes on in every circumstance.
I try to divert myself, and go here and there, seek the conversation of someone, seek solitude, try the piano, then a
book, until I feel like a hunted creature.   This strain upon
my mind I cannot endure, I seem paralyzed, I cannot
perform anything I wish to do, I spend any amount of
energy in fretting." (*Clinical Lectures*, p. 42.)

The prevailing ideas and the illusions that, through
their persistence, take possession of the mind, are often
dependent on the previous habits and pursuits, more
especially any emotional shocks they may have received;
these give a tone and colouring to the ensuing delusions,

and according to their tension is the progress of the disintegrating forces. Boismont describes the old *noblesse* and
their families terrified at the sanguinary recollections of the
revolution of 1798, trembling for their safety and fortunes,
becoming a prey to hypochondria, with a tendency to
suicide.   They imagined themselves surrounded with
assassins and executioners, they heard the booming of
cannon, and uttered shrieks of terror.   The emotional
perturbations that attacked those under the new order
of things in France, though of the same nature, arising
from prevalent ideas, took a contrary character. They
heard voices which spoke agreeable words and made great
promises; they thought themselves representatives and
presidents of the republic. (*Hallucinations*, p. 292.)

The self-induced prominent idea may take any form
affecting its own organism or those about it. Crichton
described the case of a painter of reputation, who imagined
all his bones had become soft and pliant, and that he must
necessarily bend like wax if he attempted to walk. A
baker, of Ferrara, believed he was made of butter, and on
that account would not approach his oven. The wife of
Salomon Galmus imagined there was a living monster
within her, while Vicentius thought he was of such
enormous size that he could not go through the door of
his own apartment. (*Mental Derangement*, I. p. 210.) It
may arise from any emotion or incident. Thus Boismont
gives the case of a girl of five or six, the niece of Prince
de Radzwil, who always felt an indescribable terror at a
picture of the Cumean Sybil, in his palace. She would
never pass through that room because of the sentiment it
excited in her. That it was an ever present fear to her
mind was seen in after years, when she was married in
the same old chateau. She had to lead off the ball, and in
doing so, had to pass through the Sybil room, but her
old terror recurred as she entered; she paused as she saw
the picture, and would not go on, but, pressed on by others,

and to prevent her turning back, the door was rapidly shut, with the shaking vibration the picture fell, a portion of the huge broken frame fell on her, and it penetrated her skull, causing instantaneous death. (*Hallucinations*, p. 201.) The presentiment in this case was the natural dread in the mind of a nervous girl and woman of a huge, may be, tragic face. No doubt the fastenings were rotten, and the trampling of many feet, the sudden sharp closing of the door broke the attachments, and the tragedy naturally ensued.

Spiritual capital is often made out of trifling incidents, and the fixed idea occasionally, as in the case of Lady Lee, becomes a prediction, and a highly sensitive nervous organism paralyzing the will ensures its definite issue. Boismont cites a case in which opium for once was used to outwit the spirits, or at least the delusion, of a dominant idea. A student, in a state of mental alienation, came home and said he was to die in thirty-six hours. Opium was prescribed; he slept long beyond that time. When he came to and was informed thereof, he acknowledged that it was an hallucination. He said, in his walk that night he saw a death's head, and heard a voice saying, you will die in thirty-six hours. (*Ibid.* p. 475.)

CHAPTER III.

Discordinations by Depression.

Morbid degradation may arise from physical degeneracy. The cause may be in the individual himself, it may be self engendered, it may result from local deteriorating influences, it may be a hereditary defect, or due to accidental causes.

Physical degeneracy may be apparent even at birth. There are many children born devoid of the general vital energy. They may linger for a more or less extended period according to the nature or extent of the organic depreciation, then pass away. Others are born with defects in one or other of the faculties, any sense may be aberrant, any power of a vitiated character, and the defects in the organism may be so great as to imperil its vital integrity. Yet we may not ascribe the malformations to any inherited defect from its father or mother. We may find no apparent cause for its want of co-ordinate equilibrium with its brothers and sisters, all we know is that as there are congenital exaltations of power induced—here in size, there in muscular strength, betimes the commanding energy of a Napoleon, the might of mind-power as in Shakespere — so there is a corresponding mental and organic depreciation in a dwarf. An atrophied child may be born of parents of goodly proportions, a mere cretin in soul of those gifted with more than ordinary capacities. It may be that in the almost vegetative ovarian and early uterine condition it is possible for mental and physical influences to modify the organism to the extremes in which it is often presented to us. At birth, and even after birth, an apparently small accident may, by impinging a portion of the skull or spine, predispose the organism for an attenuated or mentally or morally aborted existence.

We may not fathom the causes that induce the primary variabilities in powers that beings of a like origin manifest, but we can register the range of distinguishing qualities, and, as under the head of exaltations, we shall have to consider not only congenital but temporary and accidental mental enlargements, so now we may point out the many degenerate formations that render the co-ordinate affinities unstable and of a degraded character.

The congenital failures, as we have shown, apply to every organic form and faculty, to every mental impulse and power. As Dr. Maudsley says:—"Mr. Paget has described an idiot's brain in which there had been a complete arrest of development at the fifth month of fœtal life. There were no posterior lobes, the cerebellum being only half covered by the cerebral hemispheres, as is the case normally in many of the lower animals. Dr. Shuttleworth found in the microcephalic brain of an imbecile that although the frontal and parietal lobes were small and deficient in front, and their convolutions and fissures incompletely marked, the occipital lobes were quite rudimentary, exhibiting no fissures and convolutions, so that the greater part of the cerebellum was uncovered. Gratiolet found in the brain of a microcephalic idiot, aged seven, the under surface of the anterior lobes much hollowed, with great convexity of the orbital arches, as is the rule in the monkey. Every element of the body shares usually in the defective vitality of idiocy. Idiots are found who without any particular deformity, without any observable disease or defective development; their size is small, their sexual development takes place late in life, or perhaps does not take place at all; their circulation is languid and their sensibilities are extremely dull, their movements are not brisk, but feeble, heavy, and sometimes partially paralyzed. Their skin gives off an offensive odour, their teeth are carious and soon drop out. In mental capacity they are in advance of true idiots, for they can learn a little, are capable of remembering, and perhaps imitate cleverly." (*Pathol. of Mind*, pp. 176-181.)

Besides the mental atrophies and degenerations, idiots are deficient in cutaneous sensibility; they are often indifferent alike to cold and heat. Often reflex movements can hardly be developed by irritating the surface of the skin. There may be perversions in the special senses, the colour and texture of objects cannot be distinguished by some, and taste and smell are often deficient or perverted. Special malformations are common, the integration of the frame may fail in parts, there often ensue from the failure of the organic energy malformations of various kinds, as short limbs, club feet, contracted or paralyzed muscles, want of co-ordinate actions in the movements in walking, in the muscular mobility of throat and fingers. Endless are the varieties of special habits of movements evolved in all parts.

More or less the organic conditions and functions, as well as the mental impulses, are degraded, the physical degradation is observable in stature and development, in want of symmetry in the parts, in malformation, atrophy, or incordination of form. The lips are thick and everted, the gums often swollen, the eyes squint, the ears are large and ill-formed, the limbs are frequently contracted or paralyzed, the fingers attenuated. The mind may be so debased as to be scarcely alive to external impressions, one or more of the senses may be debased or lost, the stare is often vacant, the gait staggering, the mouth slavers, the grasp of the hand is feeble, the articulation monosyllabic, may be reduced to animal cries. There is even in the less degraded mental

characteristics great confusion of thoughts, failure of
memory; they are dirty, listless, ever muttering or scraping
together little things, paper, straw, sticks, or stones.
(*Bucknill and Tuke, Psychol. Medicin.* p. 177, &c.)

Nor is it always that the degeneric symptoms are con-
genitally manifest. As individual evolution is the normal
characteristic of every organism, so may the series of the
mental and bodily faculties be stayed in any stage of growth,
or hastened to the final consummation. The vital energy
may be exhausted in the individual at any stage in its
evolution, or any one or more faculties held back in development. The symptoms of cretinism often do not occur for
several years after birth, and the bright, may be intelligent,
child gradually manifests the various forms of dementia,
loss of memory, decrease of powers and faculties, inertness
of body and mind, a weakening of the moral and emotional
principles, the expression remaining listless and childish,
and the form loses its symmetry.

Perhaps the degeneracy is induced later in life, it may be
due to some detergent influence in the primary nature of the
organism, or it may arise from the individual's own want of
moral prevision, or even be accidental. On this subject
Dr. Maudsley says:—" Many men break down after puberty
from the enervating effects of sexual excesses. In later
manhood rheumatism and gout, a decay of the powers of
assimilation and nutrition. Later on the energy of feeling
and desire abates, there is a tendency to gloomy feelings and
hypochondria, lastly the tissues degenerate, the cerebral
vessels give way, or the brain shrinks into senile dementia.
(*Pathol. of Mind*, 120.)

The failure may be special, not general—it may affect the
muscles and nerves alone, it may be a retrogression to a
more instinctive state, it may represent only moral reversion,
or simply a lower evolutionary stage. It may affect the
muscular and nervous systems only, as in the following
case by Lewes:—" The patient, a girl about twenty, well

nourished, with powerful muscles. She could bend or stretch arms, fingers, legs, and toes at will; and the power over her muscles was such that I could not, with my utmost force, bend or straighten a limb if she resisted me. But her co-ordination was so imperfect that she could not walk unless leaning on some one, and even threw out her legs in a spasmodic manner. Nor were her upper limbs more under control. If she attempted to reach an object or to clutch one presented to her, the movements were singularly incoherent and never succeeded until after many corrections of the effort. It took her several minutes to button her dress, and there was a great disturbance in the ordinary regulation of movements of limbs." (*Brain*, I. p. 27.)

The failure may be general to the organism, bodily and mental powers all passing into a state of abeyance, and only the vegetative and lower instinctive powers be manifest. A lady gradually passed into states of torpor more or less continuous, at last in one it was found impossible to arouse her for nearly two months. When food was presented to her lips with a spoon she readily took it into her mouth and swallowed it, when she had taken a sufficiency she closed her teeth as a sign she was satisfied, and if importuned turned away her mouth from the spoon. She sometimes judged by smelling, closing her mouth in a determined manner to medicines possessing a strong odour. On recovery from the torpor, she appeared to have forgotten nearly all her previous knowledge, everything seemed new to her, and she did not recognize a single individual, not even her nearest relatives. She was delighted with everything she saw and heard, and altogether resembled a child. (*Brain*, II. p. 6.)

The degradation may take the form of muscular atrophy. All reflex action may be abolished, and the muscles become flat and toneless. The loss of power comes on slowly and gradually, and the extreme emaciation of the most affected parts, shows that the adipose tissue wastes as well as the muscles. The atrophied limbs are usually cold, may be livid or pallid; sometimes the skin of the face becomes thin and smooth, so that the dark iris has been seen through the closed eyelids. Occasionally certain areas of muscles undergo wasting, while the rest remain normal. The failure usually begins in one arm, then extends to the other, months and sometimes years intervene during the wasting process. The hands first become useless, then the arms; it is most common in the arms and the upper part of the trunk, with simple weakness and spasms in the legs. Idiopathic muscular atrophy may be manifested at the close of infancy, the impairment often begins at four, five, or six years of age, though sometimes no symptoms intervene until the age of eighteen or twenty. The shortening and contraction of certain muscles lead to distortions in the position of the joints with curvature of the spine; in the end the power of standing is lost, and the patient, even if the mental powers continue, becomes absolutely helpless. (*Gower, Diseases of the Nervous System*, II. p. 394.)

More often the mental powers manifest the want of the due co-ordination more than do the organic, and these give rise to emotional excitability and insensibility, and the disturbed mind passes into a state of depressed apathy, forebodings of misery, as in the various forms of melancholy, or it wastes its feeble, fretful energies in hypochondriacal, morbid, bodily suspicions.

Of the deadness of the emotional sensibilities, Bratchet gives a graphic but sad picture in the narrative of one of his lady patients:—"I continue," she wrote, "to suffer constantly. I have not a moment of comfort and no human sensations. Surrounded by all that can render life happy and agreeable, still to me the faculty of enjoyment and of feeling is wanting —both have become physical impossibilities. In everything, even in the most tender caresses of my children, I find only bitterness. I cover them with kisses, but there is something between their lips and mine, and this horrid something is between me and all the enjoyment of life. My existence is incomplete. The functions and actions of ordinary life, it is true, remain to me, but in every one of them there is something wanting—to wit, the feeling that is proper to them and the pleasure which follows them. Each of my senses, each part of my proper self is, as it were, separated from me, and can no longer afford me any feeling; this impossibility seems to depend upon a void which I feel in the front of my head, and to be due to the diminution of the sensibility over the whole surface of my body, for it seems to me that I never actually reach the objects I touch. I feel well enough the change of temperature in my skin, but I no longer experience the internal feeling of the air when I breathe. All this would be small matter enough but for its frightful result, which is that of the impossibility of any other kind of feeling and of any sort of enjoyment, although I experience a need and desire for them that renders my life an incomprehensible torture. Every function, every action of my life remains, but deprived of the feeling that belongs to it, of the enjoyment that should follow it. My feet are cold, I warm them, but I gain no pleasure from the warmth. I recognize the taste of all I eat, without getting any pleasure from it. My children are growing handsome and healthy, and everyone tells me so. I see it myself, but the delight, the inward comfort I ought to feel, I fail to get. Music has lost all charm for me. I used to love it dearly. My daughter plays well; to me it is a mere noise. That lively feeling which a year ago made me hear a delicious concert in the smallest air their fingers played, that thrill, that general vibration, which made me shed such tender tears, all that exists no more." (*Mind*, IX. p. 200.) Other victims to a like deadness to sensibility describe themselves as closed in walls of ice, or covered with an indiarubber integument, through which no impression penetrates.

Still more general is the disintegrating form of hypochondriacal personal anxiety. Ever the morbid mind is always searching for indications of the ill-health it dreads. He scrutinizes his tongue before breakfast, and notes during the day the influence of each meal on his abdominal feelings, of each exertion on his pulse, and of mental work on his head. An unfortunate sufferer, in whose physical condition no flaw could be found, other than a trifling occasional indigestion, said: "I do not breathe free ; I do not breathe clear. After I did my work yesterday there was a pain in my head. There is a little pain in the heel when I press upon it. I have a sensation of tightness round the sides of the chest. I have also felt a slight tightness about the knees. The appetite is not the thing at all. There is a slight distension, I have not found it to-day, but I did yesterday. Last night I felt the food in my throat and a noise in the chest, such as you feel in the ear. My head is hot on the top now. Talking even for a minute seems to affect the eyes and an uncomfortable feeling comes in them. This morning, too, in the train, after it stopped I seemed to feel for a moment as if I was going backwards and forwards. My forehead gets hot when I talk. Some days ago I had an uncomfortable feeling in the loins and afterwards in the bowels, and a week ago I had some pain in the armpit." (*Gower's Diseases of the Nervous System*, II. p. 956.) Such inconsiderate trifles render the morbidly sensitive wretched, life becomes a torture, yet such conditions may exist for years without any other ulterior result, or they may mark the tendency to lower tones of moral and intellectual power, ending in one of the forms of melancholy and despair, which manifest themselves as the mental discordination extends or acts upon the physical energy.

The melancholy man exhibits most often the symptoms of apathy and listlessness, he shuns society and seeks solitude, prefers his bed to any other place, neglects his dress, disregards his food, is averse to exercise, unwilling to move from his seat, and, if he does, goes with a slow step. He sits for hours without motion, seldom speaking, and is regardless of everything but his own gloomy thoughts.

He exhibits a pallid and fixed countenance, a dull eye, his appetite is low, the circulation languid, and he takes long and deep inspirations. His sleep is short, and his general condition torpid. Betimes there ensue perpetual restless watchings, confusion of ideas, which are often intensified by indigestion following on an inactive life. As the symptoms increase the perturbed state of the stomach prevents sleep, or the repose is troubled with frightful dreams, groans and inarticulate sounds alone issue from the sufferer in his struggles. Then want of sleep still more disturbs the mind, he grows suspicious of his friends, exhibits needless alarm, and becomes surrounded with illusive horrors and dreary solitude. At length the oft-recurring delusion becomes fixed, the mind is impressed with a false idea of poisoning or evil spirits, life becomes irksome under the perpetual fear, and he meditates self-destruction to escape from his foes. In this state of depression he may fancy himself ruined, and be incited to acts morally depraved, and be suspicious that his imaginary, dishonourable actions are known to every passer-by.

In epilepsy the greater degenerations manifest themselves more often in bodily discordinations. The auræ or premonitory symptoms are often muscular failures, the thumb drags, the hand is convulsed, the muscles of the mouth twitch, there is a tingling at the tongue, an inability to speak accompanied with rotation of the eye-balls, while objects seem to recede. To break the feeling of discordination the individual rises, runs forward or backward, or turns round. Then coloured vision intervenes with hissing and ringing sounds, there occur metallic or other sensations of taste, unpleasant smells, sensations in the stomach and other parts of cold, burning, choking, palpitation, and mental sentiments of horror and alarm changing into dreamy, drowsy feelings. These are followed by the usual

epileptic seizures, the muscular spasm, the rotation of head
and eyes, chewing movements, rolling of the tongue,
rigidity, tremor, and shrieks, followed by loss of consciousness, convulsions, sudden falling with distorted jaws,
convulsed tongue, the trunk and limbs thrown about, and
the secretions evacuated.   The gradual return to consciousness brings on feelings of lassitude and stupor, the
temper is peevish and irritable, sometimes a maniacal disposition forms a feature.   Of the body wasting, the mind
discordances that after ensue, we need not speak; great
disintegrations, whether epileptic, melancholic, apoplectic,
or paralytic, however varied their attributes, all lead to the
same goal, and all manifest to the fact that the energy in
the being failing renewal it is cast off.

Special degeneracies sometimes illustrate abnormal manifestations in other mental forms.   The following case in
its nature is not only similar to the trance self-induced
in the case of Colonel Townshend, but it is similar in
many details with effects induced in the somnambulic,
the mesmeric, and hypnotist states, and to the sense-
manifestations common to various forms of degradation.
Dr. Strümpell relates in *Nature* (December, 1877), the case
of a youth at Leipzig, the whole of whose skin was insensible to every kind of sensation.   An electric current or
burning taper produced no sensation of pain or touch, all
those sensations classed under the name of muscular
sense were entirely absent.   The patient when his eyes
were closed could be carried round the room and his
limbs placed in the most inconvenient positions without
his being in any way conscious of it.   Even the feeling of
muscular exhaustion was lost.   There came also a complete
loss of taste and smell, amaurosis of the left eye, and
deafness of the right ear.   In short, his only connection
with the outer world was limited to his one eye and one
ear.   These could be easily closed, and it was possible then
of completely isolating the brain from all external sense-

stimulation. If the patient's seeing eye was bandaged and his hearing ear stopped, the respiration became quiet and regular, and the patient was sound asleep. This artificial sleep could be induced at any time simply by withholding from the brain all sense stimulation. He could be awakened by auditory stimulation, by visual stimulation, by allowing the stimulus of light to fall upon his seeing eye, but not by pushing or shaking.

There are social conditions which induce every phase of degeneracy, both bodily and mental; unhealthy occupations, close, constant work in damp, hot factories, in places where the atmosphere is impure, where unsanitary conditions prevail. The food may be bad, the habits bad, and the climatal conditions deleterious; some of these influences by inducing endemic diseases cause rapid decay and death; in others, the bodily depression acts on the mental status and stimulates to alcoholic and erotic excesses, or passively enduring cretinism prevails; the pellagra works its ravages, low fevers and debilitating effects reduce the stamina of mind and body, and the unhappy peasant seeks relief in hospital or asylum, or turns melancholy and commits suicide, or becomes wildly maniacal or drivels into imbecility. Thus every form of degeneracy may supervene from debasing conditions.

CHAPTER IV.

Discordinations by Excitation.

The discordinating influences under excitation are as equally baneful to the united harmonious action of the various functions as when they ensue through depressing causes. Body and mind waste away in inaction, in ever brooding over morbid ideas, and often morbid hallucinations accompany the depressing influences, but they are most prominent when the physical energy is in a highly excited state. Then a species of mental exaltation is evolved : every idea, thought, or perception becomes intensified, the muscular sense partakes of the excitement in the brain, and feats of strength, of tact, and endurance mark the highly abnormal status. The senses become, for a time, more acute, the volition rapidly expressive, every faculty is at high pressure, and the tension has to be supported by mental and physical stimulants until, the strain becoming too great, the morbid excitement breaks the co-ordinating influences, and wild mania ensues.

The same disintegrating element that we have seen enter so prominently into the depressing departures from normal co-ordination also marks the beginning of maniacal disturbances. The one prevailing idea commands the mental forces; it may be present in the business pursuits, in the prevailing habit, in literary, political, or social excitation; it may be induced by over-work, in artistic, mental, or monetary excitation, in the thousand schemes that prolific energy seeks to evolve in the whirl of civilized life.

We have been told that this form of aberration is unknown to the rude savage, and only characterizes the extremes that prevail in civilized life, as if running amuck, and the sleuth-hound ferocity of the blood-hunter were unknown incidents. No matter what the phase of life, when one idea becomes a predominating, morbidly exciting power, when it commands all the energies of the body, all the vigour of the mental will, it only needs time to debase the other mental powers and allow all the feelings and impulses to be concentrated on the prevailing activity, when the moral and intellectual degradation becomes manifest. The will then has no power to resist the mind force. Any feeling or thought for others is obliterated; moral principles and social considerations are lost; intensely, may be savagely, the mind works out, often with mad recklessness, its predominating will, heedless not only of others, but of all personal considerations. The brain has but one idea: controlling the will, and filling the vivid consciousness with the wildest selfish hallucinations.

Are not the incidents innumerable in which the blood-thirst has culminated in ferocious mania, and the wretched victim of a morbid appetite has perished, indiscriminately destroying old and young, and himself perishing in the tragic fray. How often, too, in the mad excitement of the racial wars, the maddened combatants, like savage beasts, rend and tear, and even devour, one another. A like deranged condition is often induced in the initiatory rites at puberty by the mental and bodily excesses endured. The Indian boy sent fasting into the forest solitude to seek his medicine, and exposed to all the fears and privations incident to the search, often ends the fearful contest by being a prey to the illusions the situation induces. A

like result often follows the fearful, disgusting, often
bloody rites through which the priestly character is
assumed; even the thrice holy anchoret becomes a besotted,
drivelling human monster, or when the fit is on him, a
furious beast. Shall we speak of the erotic madness of the
Bacchic feasts, the Soma festivals, the bloody sacrifices of
Mexico, the Meriah madness, in which the applauding
victim goes exultingly to the stake. There are societies
whose initial state, as that of the Assassins, is moral madness, and there are states in which the feast of blood is
common slaughter, as Coomassie. These fits of mania may
be temporary or permanent, they may be inoculated by
drugs, by the madness of passion, the fury of the drunkard.
In the common pollution of soul the hot bloods kill one
another till the most frenzied perish, and the excitement
passes away. There are the madnesses of days and hours,
epidemic manias, as those of witchcraft and the convulsionaires, and the sympathetic madness of wild hysteria.
In the presence of a predominating fear, the mind of a
whole people may for a time be disintegrated, as that of
the Jews during the siege of Jerusalem, France at the
period of the Revolution, and Paris in the days of the
Commune. Let us take individual cases, ever the pride
of self-will rising into autocratic dominancy overpowers the
moral equilibrium. The petty chief, in a negro kraal, in
this respect may be enveloped in uncontrollable mania the
same as a King of Uganda, a Roman Emperor, or our Henry
the Eighth. Mania is the product of all times and countries, and of all classes of men; it may be induced by an
accident, it may arise from mental and physical conditions, it may be the result of overwrought mental
excitation; ever it creates illusions, it builds up prescience,
it founds myths—there is but little of the spiritual that has
not its origin in the madness of its promulgators. Ever
the outpourings of local mania were special to the most
powerful incidents affecting the life of a people.

There are but few forms in the madness of the old world races. They might arise from the ferocity of war; the savagery of revenge, like that of Jason's daughter; from the memory of crime; or, Cassandra-like, from the ministry of the fates. An Apollo for the time might become demented; a Hercules, unsated with blood, destroy his nearest and dearest; but the many stimulating causes that now produce exciting manias of all kinds were then unknown. We shall find that the main feature of this lies in the great variety of human pursuits, the infinite forms of excitement ever present, and the consequent reduced power of tension. A century ago even the range of causes were more limited and less dominant. There were the ordinary excitations of town and country life, the gambling hell, the wine bout, and sensual excess; there was the more limited influence of the mart, and the more sober pursuit of commerce, fashion, and frivolity had their victims, and religious frenzy overworked the enraptured soul. But now the world and the world's mart—all places, all conditions of people—are open to act and react on each other; and the wild pursuit of gain, of place, of power, fills not only the city's area, but rouses the rustic mind. The millions are too few, and life is too short to satisfy the flood of maddened aspirants, whose cast off aberrant minds clog the wheels of time.

If we would depict the manifold forms of the exciting craze we might take any pursuit, any mode of modern life, and we should find victims to its delusions. Yet less than half a century ago Willis restricted his illustration to that of the discordinate fox-hunting squire. In the first stage of the degeneracy he describes the gentleman as full of vivacity and excited by a larger quantity of wine than usual; talking wildly, obscenely swearing, and sitting up to midnight, then sleeping but little, rising, and going out hunting; returning thence quickly, he sets his servants all to work in an excited manner, betraying a violent agitation of mind, at the same time he is full of vivacity and sallies of wit. Another, as Willis says, may be of a literary taste —would be excited on the condition of his library, bustling about and arranging them, which, as soon as accomplished, would fail to satisfy his mind and needs must be done again; or if a tradesman, he would be full of business, ordering goods recklessly and in quantities beyond his business requirements; he would be for ever settling his accounts and never finish them.

After a time these symptoms would be followed by worse. The perturbed state of mind would make conversation distressing and irritating; the ideas would become confused, those about him would appear wanting in duty, the emotions and affections would change, those most loved would be looked upon with aversion, and the derangement would stimulate bodily disease. Then delirium would ensue, the ravings would be wild and incoherent, rage and laughter alternately exciting the mind, until the disorganized mind becomes savage or contemptuous, spurns at all, destroys anything in reach, with loud discordant screams, until the physical energy falls prostrate. After a time, when the victim comes to, a spell of obstinate defiance, hatred or indifference possesses the mind; he will not speak, clenches his teeth, and then breaks out again into wild and extravagant language and actions. If coerced and seemingly subdued, it is only with a desperate cunning, that he may watch his opportunity to do his will; but the glistening appearance and rapid movement of his eyes intimate that the state of frenzy is not yet over.

During this mental phase the body is in a state of irritability; he cannot remain for one moment in the same posture, he turns from side to side, puts his hand on his head, picks his fingers, takes up any object, and as without purpose puts it down again. He resists all advice, the countenance becomes mottled and bloated, the upper eyelid is much elevated, the pupils dilate and are always in motion, sometimes the saliva is increased into such quantities that it runs from the mouth; the head is hot, the hands and feet cold, the skin harsh and dry, the respiration hurried, the breath hot, the stomach insensible to common emetics, the bowels fail to be influenced by purgatives, the skin is painless—in fact, all the physical organs partake in the mental disorganization.

On the many special forms and the various results of mania volumes might be written. We can but particularise the most prevailing instances, and mark some of the many changes which tend more immediately to intimate the leading phases of mental manifestation.

Emotional disorder comes on or is exhibited in adult life. Usually the change in the feelings and conduct of the patient is gradual. He becomes more absorbed and reserved, and on any provocation, however slight, is unreasonably irritated. He becomes suspicious, liable to impute false motives to his friends and others, and to cast ungenerous reflections upon his nearest relatives. He becomes morose, the clouds gather, and he is, somehow or other, an altered being. At last the storm bursts, and some act is committed of an outrageous character.

In other cases the individual has been subject to over-exertion of mind, his powers have been over-tasked, or his feelings put on the stretch. He finds himself susceptible to the slightest mental emotion, loses his sleep or rest, is conscious of uneasiness about the head, a sense of tension, a dull aching pain, he has palpitation of the heart, the digestive organs become disordered, the appetite uncertain, the secretions depraved. He has impulses and tendencies, repugnant to his reason and moral nature, often to do violence to himself and others. At this stage he may know and feel the change, but be conscious of his moral powerlessness and implore help from others.

The homicidal maniac may believe he is conferring a real

benefit on the person he kills, or he may do it from a pure love of destruction, a mere motiveless impulse.

Ever these changes of character arise from the continuous expression of the same feeling, the presence of like sensations. As Dr. Tuke says:—" Sensation and motion are not merely more readily reproduced by the original impressions being repeated, but may be reproduced without our having the slightest resource to them, so that we may breathe an atmosphere in which the body feels, the eye sees, the ear hears, the nose smells, and the palate tastes as accurately as if the material world excited these sensations, and may perform muscular actions without and even against the will and with or without consciousness, solely in respondence to ideas, whether recalled by the memory or created by the imagination—the common centre acted upon by objective impressions from without, and by subjective impressions from within, being the sensorium and the resulting sensations and motions being in many instances as powerful from the latter (the inner) source as from the former, and in some more so." (*Tuke, Influ. of Mind*, I. p. 80.)

Of the progress of these influences we cannot do better than show their nature through the growth of illusionary conceptions. Boismont tells us that Van Helmont spent much time in intense thought on the nature of his own soul, he had visions afterwards in his sleep, some merely heterogeneous, but he describes the tension on his mind as lasting for twenty-three years, when he had a vision in which, as he thought, his own soul was exhibited before him. This illusion which he recognized, he does not say how, as his own soul, was a perfectly homogeneous light, composed of a spiritual substance, crystalline and brilliant, it was shut up like a pea in its shell. (*Halluci.* p. 205.)

Of the highly excited mental condition when the fixed idea may be self-illusive, Hammond presents incidents. Thus in the case of one lady it was only necessary for her to think of some person, living or dead, when she immediately saw the image of the person thought of, who spoke to her, laughed, wept, walked about the room, or did whatever other thing she imagined. At first she religiously believed in the reality of her visions, and that she really saw the spirits of the various individuals of whom she happened to think. But as the hallucinations became more common she lost her faith, and ascribed them to their true cause, disease. (*Insanity*, p. 314.) Like impressions have been produced by pressure on the carotid arteries; in some cases they arise through lying in special recumbent positions, in these instances the derangement is accidental and ceases on the withdrawal of the cause. In mania, on the contrary, the induced physical derangement may arise from mental or bodily disorder. Of the above induced hallucinations Hammond gives cases :—In one, a gentleman always saw a figure when he was lying down, when he stood up it was gone. In another, a lady by wearing an elastic band heard sounds at first of a hissing nature, then they took the form of ribbald words; these always ceased when the band was removed. (*Ibid.* p. 316.)

Such hallucinations at first figures of the will, become at last morbid presentations, commanding the attention. A gentleman all his life affected by the appearance of spectral figures, had his mind at last become so incoherent that when he met a friend in the street he could not be sure whether he saw a real or imaginary person. He had also the power of calling up spectral figures at will by directing his attention steadily for some time to the conception of his own mind, and these either consisted of a figure or a scene he had witnessed, or a composition created by his imagination. Though he had the faculty of calling up an hallucination he had no power to lay it; the person or scene haunted him. (*Ibid.* p. 312.)

The statement by Blake, the artist, of the progress of his

hallucinations from mere excited intense images to morbid hallucinations, whose fixed unreality disturbed his moral co-ordination, is fully illustrative of the progress of the mania derangement. He says:—" When a sitter came I looked attentively on him for half an hour, sketching betimes on the canvas, then I removed the canvas and passed on to another person. When I wished to continue the first portrait I recalled the man to my mind. I placed him on the chair where I perceived him as distinctly as if he were really there. I looked from time to time at the imaginary figure, and went on painting. I always caught the resemblance. By degrees I began to lose all distinction between the imaginary and the real figure. I sometimes insisted on my sitters that they had sat the day before. Finally I was persuaded it was so; then all became confusion. I lost my reason, and remained for thirty years in an asylum."

Among the almost innumerable forms in which the deranged co-ordination is presented, those resulting from an irritating anxiety are the most prominent, and fear in its manifold natures harasses the troubled mind. Very commonly it is expressed in dread of those it most loves, in suspicion of poison, cunning artifices, secret conferences to cause ruin. He is being conspired against, being defrauded, every one seems to look at him askance, he is denounced from the pulpit, he is in want, ever he fancies the police are in search of him for some imaginary crime, he seeks and yet dreads death. Perhaps the mania becomes a religious fear, the devils have possession of them, ever they seem to speak to him and to rejoice over him, he feels that his soul is lost, that he has committed the unpardonable sin, that he is equally unfit to live as to die. May be the fear takes the form of some secret and mysterious disease, or the body has been transformed into some other nature, is possessed by devils, it may be enlarged or shrunk to an atomy. If a woman, she is pregnant by some monster, covered with vermin, perhaps the climax is reached, and she is already dead.

Morel tells of a patient, the youngest of five brothers who had all been insane. He was a prey to the most intense apprehensions of future punishment for imaginary crimes, all his limbs trembled, while he implored the assistance of heaven and his friends. Soon after he rejected any attempts to console him, and all his thoughts became concentrated on one idea. He thought he was a wolf. See this mouth, he exclaimed, separating his lips with his fingers, this is the mouth of a wolf, these are the teeth of a wolf, I have cloven feet. See the long hairs which cover my body; let me run into the woods and you shall fire at me with a gun. He refused to eat his food, and said, Give me some raw meat, I am a wolf. His wish was complied with, and his mode of eating was altogether like an animal. He died the victim of his strange and terrible conception. There are other cases of monks believing they were cats, of a Convulsionaire barking like a dog, of a patient believing himself a horse, pawing with his feet on the ground, and prancing; of a young woman who believed she was turned into a dog; she said she smelt like one. (*Bucknill, Psych. Medic.* p. 203.)

Speaking of like cases Dr. Clouston says :—In some I am reminded of the resistance of a wild animal, or the behaviour of certain savages, when first caught. Fear, the instinct of self-preservation, unreason, suspicion, and the instinct of freedom, are all mixed up in some cases. (*Clinical Lectures,* p. 99.)

Vampyrism, lycanthropy, men tigers, and lamias, are special forms in which, in various countries, the morbid fancies are manifested. Have not the wild delusions of witchcraft taken the form of animal fears, and in the nature of cats, bats, dogs, or half bestial devils, the self-deluded wretches supposed they fulfilled the nature of their hallucinations? In Scotland we read of them in these deluding fears, becoming crows, hares, foxes, and other animals. In the *Journal of Mental Science*, one patient said a wild beast was in his body, burning his stomach, and biting his back, while a ball pressed upon his head. Another said the birds sang in his ear. Another, that a demon mocked him; he heard reproaches; he saw his dead parents; he was transformed into a monster. The pillow rose up at night before him; that the voices compelled him for three quarters of an hour to distort his mouth, while faces were peeping at him through crevices of the wall. (XXIX. p. 282.)

Even under this overbearing sense of oppression and fear all the social and preservative instincts are in abeyance. Ideas suggesting the destruction of property or life are ever present to the thought. A voice or presence is ever urging them to tear, break, and destroy, to murder, to commit suicide, to fire everything about them. In the wildness of the frenzy the earth itself seems a blaze, forms rise and glare and rush past them, and the wretched being dashes into the mental *mêlée* with furious savage energy. In milder attacks it impels to tear books, break crockery, overturn furniture, break windows, or throw water about with reckless profusion. Betimes a man will hack himself with knives, inflict extensive mutilations on himself, even plunge his head in a fire and exhibit expressions of satisfaction while doing so. A lady, in acute mania, cut off both nipples with a piece of glass procured by breaking a lamp shade. She said the operation was pleasant, and had she not been prevented she would have cut off her breasts. (*Hammond, Insanity*, p. 540.)

Another large class of mania deteriorations arise from over-weening self-conceit, personal arrogance and emotional pride; ever the notion of self comes to the fore and leads to the wildest delusions of individuality, in estates, wealth, and position. There is scarcely a madhouse without self-created potentates, princes, queens, ladies of honour, and men of the highest station. Here one esteems himself as a Pope;

another, who dabbled in politics, is an ambassador, a minister of state, or is the secret agent in mysterious political transactions. One speaks volubly of his immense wealth, his enormous strength or height. Another is going to cut out his intestines, and he will then be able to live without eating, he will get a boa constrictor to put in his inside, then he will grow to twelve feet in height. Another says he can fly, and has ten millions of money. Later on he writes cheques for millions, is going to marry two pretty women, then he talks of cutting off his head and having a new one. Another decorates himself with pieces of coloured worsted or anything of a tawdry colour, bits of metal and glass, and deems himself magnificent. (*Sankey, Lectures on Mental Disease*, p. 325.)

Hammond gives the case of a lady not previously noted for neatness either in person or attire, under the influence of mania, having that faculty specially excited. She became suddenly scrupulous in her dress, would spend hours in the arrangement of her hair, the care of her finger nails, the tyeing of ribbons, and the fastening of brooches. Then she began to talk about her beauty and attractions, the looks of admiration cast upon her. One gentleman, she declared, had followed her home. She was then sent into the country; on this she began to write letters three or four times a week to the gentleman she had referred to, in which she lauded him to the skies. So strong was the impulse in her that early one morning she made her escape, caught a milk train, and went to the gentleman's residence; from that she was sent to an asylum. (*Hammond, Insanity*, p. 404.)

Betimes pride and erotic feelings become, for a time, co-ordinate, as in the last instance. The same writer gives another painful incident of the same class of hallucinations. A lady had a delusion that her hand had been asked in marriage by a distinguished statesman. After she had the hallucination that he had passed the night with her in a hotel in Jersey city, and talked freely of it; so that troubles

would have been caused had not the gentleman been able
to show that he was in California for several weeks before
and after the imaginary seduction. (*Ibid.* p. 334.)

There have occasionally been instances in which the
personal vanity has induced the hallucination of change of
sex. A young man had obtained the idea that he had
become a woman from seeing, as he imagined, his own
image looking like a woman in female dress. He put on
woman's apparel, and remained all day in his room ad-
miring himself in the glass, and aping the movements and
attitudes of women. So satisfied was he that his sex was
changed, that he even went to a physician to be examined
in proof thereof. He congratulated himself that being a
woman, his emotional nature which, as he said, had up to
that time been very coarse and undeveloped, would now be
delicate and refined. Another case of an actor who believed
himself a woman. At all times, though he died in an alms-
house, he believed himself to be a dashing beauty, at whose
feet scores of ardent admirers knelt. He affected a feminine
voice in conversation, and acted in all respects as a female.
(*Ibid.* p. 336.)

Even religious pride may be associated with erotic sentiments. Johanna Southcott was the bride of the Lamb, she
had visions that Christ had slept with her. In another case
the woman fancied she was pregnant by the Holy Ghost,
and said that she was to give birth to the second Christ; she
also said the child left her womb every night and conversed
on the wonderful things he was going to do after his uterine
life. (*Ibid.* p. 332.)

There are few fixed ideas that exert a more deteriorating
influence than those of a religious origin. They may arise
in the individual from the long persistence on one sentiment of faith, or they may be due to sympathetic influence
through the emotions. Tertullian speaks of a sister who was
favoured with the gift of revelation. She received them in
the church, during the celebration of the mysteries, when

wrapt in ecstasy, conversing with the angels and sometimes with the Lord Jesus Christ. In her raptures she hears and sees the secrets of heaven, knows what is concealed in the hearts of several persons, and points out salutary remedies to those who have need of them. (*De Anima*, c. 26.)

St. Cyprian also describes a woman who fell into fits of ecstasy and announced herself as a prophetess. She did wonderful things, and performed real miracles. She even boasted of being able at her will to excite an earthquake. By her boastings and falsehoods she had contrived to subjugate all the spirits to such a degree that they obeyed her in all things. The evil spirit who possessed her made her walk during the most rigorous winter with bare feet in the midst of ice and snow unhurt. She seduced one of the priests called Rusticus, and a deacon. This woman was so audacious that she had no fear in profaning the sacraments in a strange manner by saying mass herself and administering baptism. (*Epistle*, p. 75.)

St. Francois d'Assise was an example of the religious ascetic emotionalists. He retired to a mountain called Alverne, between the Arno and the Tiber, and there gave himself up to the rigours of the most severe asceticism. His abstinences succeeded each other without relaxation. During one supererogatory fast, he thought that God commanded him to open the Bible, and there read what would be most acceptable to his Creator. Three times was the proof made, and each time the book opened at the Passion. From that moment he had but one thought, that of evoking in himself the affecting picture of the Saviour's passion on the cross. On the day of the exaltation of the cross he saw an angel, with six burning wings, approach him, bearing between them a figure nailed to the cross. While beholding it, it vanished, leaving painful sensations on the feet and hands of the anchorite, which were soon followed by ulcerations, the stigmas of the passion of Christ.

When the one religious idea, by long excitation, becomes intensified in the minds of many, the sympathetic emotional influence becomes almost unbounded. Then men and women will do to themselves and others actions of the most remarkable character. Such sympathetic emotional religious manias have been recorded in ancient and modern times. We read of them in Catlin's account of the fearful self-tortures at the sacred festivals of the Mandans; many writers have recorded the same conditions at various Hindoo rites; many monkish legends relate similar hysterical and epileptic manias. We have the same recorded of the Camisards in the Cevennes in the seventeenth century; and since, in various parts of Scotland, England, and America. John Wesley relates numerous instances in his journal, of men and women dropping to the ground as if struck by lightning, and the same results are ascribed to the preaching of Whitfield. Long, continuous religious exercises, sometimes accompanied with fastings and fearful wakeful nights of religious despondency or strained excitement, ever resulted in the nervous systems losing their co-ordinate action. Hence ensued weeping, prostration, screams for Divine mercy, hysterical cries, until the physical tension became overpowering, and the victims of fanaticism fell as if struck to the earth, sometimes in a state of catalepsy, at others rolling and dashing about as epileptics. The religious epidemic in Kentucky in 1800 may be quoted as showing that the same symptoms are induced in religious frenzy as accompany manias from other causes.

" Families came in waggons forty to one hundred miles to attend the meetings, and camps were established which continued four days, sometimes a week, and the fervour of religious feeling was kept up. At one the assemblage was computed at twenty thousand, and at night the glare of the camp fires falling on a dense assemblage of heads simultaneously bowed in prayer, with hundreds of candles and lamps suspended among the trees, while numerous torches flashed with an uncertain light, accompanied with the solemn chanting of hymns mixed with impassioned exhortations, earnest prayers, sobs, shrieks, or shouts bursting from persons under intense agitation of mind, then sudden spasms would seize on many and dash them to the ground.

"Some of the actors in these scenes have left their written records. One relates that, while under conviction, he went about the woods for two years, through rain and snow, roaring, howling, praying night and day. Hope at last broke on his mind, and he said, 'I made the mountains, woods, and cane-brakes ring louder with my shouts and praises than I once did with my howling cries. Sometimes I shouted two or three hours and fainted under the hands of the Lord. The brightness of heaven rested continually on my soul, so that I was often prevented from sleeping, eating, reading, writing, or preaching. I have spent nine nights out of ten with the slain of the Lord.'

"Not only nervous women, but robust young men were overpowered. Some fell as if struck by lightning, others were seized with a general tremor before they fell shrieking. Others felt a numbness of the body, and lost all volitional control of their muscles. Some of the subjects were cataleptic, lasting generally from a few minutes to two or three hours; in a few it continued many days. Others were convulsed, as in hysteria or epilepsy, in fitful nervous agonies, the eyes rolling wildly. Most were speechless, and the sensibility was annulled. Many fell at Cabin Creek Camp, and to prevent their being trodden upon, they were laid out in order on two squares of the meeting house, covering the floor like so many corpses. At Point Creek Sacrament two hundred were estimated to have fallen, at Pleasant Point three hundred were prostrated, while at Canebreak the number who fell is believed to have reached three thousand.

"Sometimes the nervous disorder took other forms. Laughter was only occasional at first, but it grew, until in 1803 the holy laugh was introduced as part of the religious worship. Sometimes half the congregation were to be heard laughing aloud in the midst of a lively sermon, as the excitement grew the infatuated subjects took to dancing, and at last to barking like dogs. Some assumed the posture of dogs moving about on all fours, growling, snapping the teeth and barking." (*Brain*, IV. pp. 339-348.)

To particularise all the drugs, drinks, and vaporous inhalations that have been used with the express purpose of inducing intense excitation, and thus at least temporarily bringing about a frenzied, more or less maniacal, demonstration were to enter into a large chapter of religious and social rites and mysterious manifestations; it will suffice to specify some of these personally or religiously induced symptoms to show their affinity with the morbid conditions they resemble.

The influence of opium in producing wild ecstatic hallucinations, has been made familiar to all by the *Confessions of an Opium Eater*, that we may all see the affinity of its action on the brain with those produced in highly excited dreams and special exaltations in mania. Most often the scenes and incidents presented to the mind are agreeable, wondrous, grand, or mysterious. Love, personal pride, admiration, and grandeur, all are highly intensified, and the physical world amplifies and exalts any person or object recalled by memory. Time and space are boundless, volition is universal, and forms evolve in accord with the aspirations of the dreamer. Ever the personality is exalted, the man has become an Indian prince, a chief, or a god. Nothing is beyond his capacity, and the most *outre* thoughts and ambitions are realized as soon as conceived. He ever inhabits palaces and vast camps, wanders in the dreamless abodes of enchantment, floating in the air, gliding over silver streams, over which are hanging luscious fruits, his ear delighted with the flowing cadences of sweet tones, the perfumed air soothing the enraptured soul. Fear, hope, and love, are alternately excited, and the wildest visions of glory and grandeur seem the mere ordinary incidents of life. That under such mental conditions the brain should be excited to descriptive composition, or burst forth into living poetry, is not only evident, when the like visions have a drugless origin, as with ordinary maniacs in asylums who in this state compose discourses, **write poems, and give** forth wild enchantment-like imaginings, as also in the products of opium-eaters **as** recorded by De Quincey, Coleridge, and **in the** writings **of Dr.** Abercrombie.

The general results of the action of opium have been **summed up by** De Quincey as follows :—" Whatsoever things capable of being visually represented I did but think of in the darkness immediately shaped themselves into phantoms of the eyes, and when traced in faint and visionary colours, they were drawn out by **the** fierce chemistry of my dreams into insufferable splendour **that** fretted my heart.   This was accompanied by deep-seated anxiety and gloomy melancholy, wholly incommunicable by words; I seemed every night to descend, not metamorphically, but literally into chasms and sunless abysses, from which it seemed hopeless I could ever re-ascend. **The** sense of space and the sense of time were both powerfully affected.   Buildings and landscapes were exhibited in such vast proportions as the bodily eye is not fitted **to receive.** Space swelled and was amplified to unutterable **infinity.   I** seemed to have lived seventy or **one hundred years in one night, and** had feelings as of a millenium passed in that time.   The minutest incidents of childhood **or** forgotten **scenes of late years** were often revived like intuitions and clothed in all their evanescent circumstances of feeling." (*Conf. Opi. Eat.* pp. 139-142.)

Of the nature of the hallucinations resulting from **hashcesh, M.** Moreau says :—" On one occasion, having **taken an overdose he thought** himself poisoned.   This gave way to the idea that he was dead and buried ; he believed only his body was defunct, his soul having quitted it."

Dr. Laycock on one occasion took a drop **of** tincture of

aconite and slept. About midnight he became sensible of
a novel state of perception, obscure at first but shaped at
last into strains of grand aerial music, now dying away
round mountains in infinite perspective, now pealing along
ocean valleys. (*Laycock, Mind and Brain*, I. p. 422.)

Hasheesh produces the sense of a double nature—a sort
of ecstasy, a sense of intense happiness, a dream-like state,
with a loss of all time and space. A French doctor under
the influence of hasheesh says :—" I saw the hasheesh I had
eaten distinctly within me under the form of an emerald,
from which thousands of little sparks were emitted. My
eyelashes lengthened indefinitely, twisting themselves like
golden threads around little ivory wheels, which whirled
about with inconceivable rapidity. Around were figures
and scrolls, arabesque flowery forms—half men, half plants,
and wearing a strange appearance. In this world of
enchantment, it seemed to him that he passed several
hundred years." (*Boismont, Halluc.* p. 340.)

Some drugs, like lachesis, produce a sense of depression,
a looking to the dark side of everything : fear of disease,
death, robbers, poison, a general sense of distrust and
peevish irritability, or the subject is rendered quarrelsome
—he finds fault, is loquacious. Nux vomica renders the
individual who has taken it obstinate, cross, irritable,
quarrelsome, violent on contradiction, anxious, restless,
over sensitive to noise, music, or singing and talking.
Stramonium induces delusions of men, ghosts, dogs, cats,
rabbits, flies or other living forms; in some, hallucinations
of being roasted and eaten, in others a sense of being
tall, or large, or small, with the general hallucinations
of hearing music, dances, voices, screaming, laughing,
crying. Some become outrageous under its influence;
they bite, strike, and injure others, or cry out in despair
from fear of death, from the feeling of being damned, or
going into a state of stupor, and are unable to recognize
their friends. (*Worcester on Insanity*, pp. 160-164.)

There is possibly no morbid or erratic state of mind, no form of hallucination but may be produced by drugs, vapours, and infusions. We have seen in the above few instances how numerous are the forms produced, simulating the various classes of dreams and mental aberrations. They have been used to second the priest in inducing mysterious mental conditions of holy madness, in which the half articulate ejaculations of the medium have been translated into denunciations, heavenly responses, or mysterious presentiments or warnings. Sometimes the influence has been produced through infusions, alcoholic, or deranging the faculties, as in the ancient homa and soma festivals; in vinous and fermented drinks of all kinds, in kava and pulque, and the black draughts of the North American Indians. Vapours produced the mysterious state of excitement in the ancient mysteries, as has laughing-gas in modern scientific amusements. Of all the forms of self-induced mania like mental aberrations, the one most prevalent and general is that produced by alcohol in various forms. Unfortunately not only in our large cities and at festal times, but in the domestic privacy, in the homes often of the intellectual and the socially advanced classes we meet with innumerable instances of the mental and moral prostration, resulting from its excessive use. Here one may be met with puling and maudling for emotional pity, there another sobs and frets, or bursts into hysterical laughter. Another may be drunk, paralyzed in speech, ideas, and volition, or variously excited, passing from irregular, noisy declamation to the wildest fury, or reduced to the stertorean state of insensible epilepsy. Some may give still more aggravated symptoms days after a wild drinking bout, passing into *delirium tremens*, or manifest the symptoms of delusive insanity, or from long, continuous drinking habits lapse into dementia, into utter obliteration of memory and mental power, and into premature old age, from which he will never emerge.

Of the mental and physical phenomena of alcoholism, Dr. Blandford says :—" In intoxication there is a disordered cerebral circulation seen in the flushing of the face, and excitement in talking and manner. Very soon the movements of the tongue and the lips is affected, there is loss of control. The words are clipped, and are not enunciated in a measured and even manner. The mental symptoms correspond to the motor. There is at first a want of co-ordination of thought, an inability to recall just what is wanted at the moment. *Delirium tremens* is but little removed from the acute delirium of the insane. In this there is a disturbance of the brain to such an extent that unless it subsides the patient is liable to die from exhaustion of his nervous power. There is an incessant discharge and emission, and the renewal of the exhausted force is prevented by the absence of sleep." (*Insanity*, p. 66.)

" After years of habitual drinking,—drinking which may scarcely have amounted to intoxication, far less to *delirium tremens,*—we may perceive the mind weakening, memory failing, and the dotage of premature old age coming on ; and not unfrequently with this decrepitude of mental power we notice some amount of bodily paralysis, which slowly advances at the same time. Then quite suddenly, without illness, sleeplessness, or excitement, memory gives way. The patient talks quite rationally and calmly, but does not distinguish yesterday from last week, thinks friends long dead are alive, and when set right makes the same mistake five minutes after." (*Ibid.* p. 68.)

Other effects of alcoholism are spoken of by Dr. Carpenter, all equally illustrating its affinity with the other forms of co-ordinate aberration. " Under this influence many men are more generous and conceding than in their perfectly sober condition, and grant favours and make agreements that their better judgment disapproves. Others are subject to an exaltation of the lower animal propensities, their power of self-control is weakened, and they become the slaves of any brutal passion that the slightest provocation may arouse." (*Carpenter's Mental Physiol.* p. 649.)

Among minor self-induced causes of both mental and physical degeneration, the longing for chloral has been instanced. Dr. Savage says it may set up a craving for its use much like that for drink or opium, and may give rise to simple moral perversion. It may produce very great emotional disturbance and irritability, passing into deep melancholia with suicidal tendencies. The terrible feeling of depression described by several patients who have been regular chloral takers was most marked on awaking in the morning, when the person felt as if he must precipitate himself out of the window. (*On Insanity,* p. 429.)

The same writer also observes that morphia injection has become so common that the Germans speak of morphismus as well as alcoholismus. In this state there is the same tremor, the same want of appetite, the same refusal of food, the same ideas of poison, the same hallucinations as in alcoholismus. There were in Bethlem patients suffering from both causes, they were equally suspicious, pestered by friends and enemies, and told to do all sorts of things. Both were much shocked on account of the ill-conduct of their friends, and both had feelings as of galvanic shocks. (*Ibid.* p. 430.)

It will thus be seen that there are drugs which produce all the varying symptoms of mania, and that so remarkably akin thereto as to suggest the possibility that in the chemistry of the vital organism its own organic parts produce the same changes on the secretions as the drugs we have specified do. The doctrine of transmutation by transference has yet to be expounded.

END OF VOLUME I.